Jeremy's Version

Also by James Purdy

63 Dream Palace and Other Stories

Malcolm

The Nephew

Children Is All

Cabot Wright Begins

Eustace Chisholm and the Works

I Am Elijah Thrush

The House of the Solitary Maggot

In a Shallow Grave

Narrow Rooms

Mourners Below

On Glory's Course

In the Hollow of His Hand

The Candles of Your Eyes

Garments the Living Wear

Out with the Stars

Gertrude of Stony Island Avenue

Moe's Villa and Other Stories

Jeremy's Version

James Purdy

CARROLL & GRAF PUBLISHERS
NEW YORK

Jeremy's Version

Carroll & Graf Publishers
An Imprint of Avalon Publishing Group Inc.
245 West 17th Street
11th Floor
New York, NY 10011

AVALON
publishing group incorporated

Copyright © 1970 by James Purdy

First Carroll & Graf edition 2006

Library of Congress Cataloging-in-Publication Data is available.

ISBN-10: 0-7867-1670-3
ISBN-13: 978-0-78671-670-8

Interior design by Maria Elias
Printed in the United States of America
Distributed by Publishers Group West

For William, Cora, and Richard

Jeremy's Version

No one hated more dearly my home town of Boutflour, planked down far south in this "Yankee state," than my Uncle Matt Lacey. I say uncle, though he was neither kith nor kin of mine, and as my half sister Della Gassman, with whom I lived, explained it, he was uncle to nobody of flesh and blood. Though I knew him by sight from his frequent comings and goings in and out of the court house, public library, newspaper office, and saloon, I would never have made his actual acquaintance had I not decided against my better judgment to take the "worst" paper route in town, number 9, which circulated down by the riverside, where houses and customers were few, and those few oftener than not dead-beats and quitters, but I was a "starter" as the woman at the head of the paper office emphasized, and could not be choosy, and it was the river route where all the boys began. Uncle Matt's house lay situated blocks apart from other houses, and was the last one on this route; beyond it was the city limits and the river itself.

One sleety December night, then, Uncle Matt, who had been waiting behind the stained-glass windows for the arrival of the Bee with its late dispatches, seeing me come up the long flight of steps, opened the door, and said, a bit sarcastically, "Come in out of the wet, if you know how, starter!" While I stomped off the slush from my moccasins, I told him my name was Jeremy Cready, and then after hesitating a moment or so, for he had left the front door wide open, I followed him into his big carpeted hall.

"Well, then, Jeremy," he turned to study me briefly in the light, "rest your wraps over here," he motioned to a hall tree, but I barely heard him, my mouth open wide to what came to view beyond, a reception room crowded to the rafters with chandeliers and shimmering mirrors as in an auction parlor, ancient furniture from a period before anybody of us now alive, sumptuous chairs and grandfather clocks, at least five of the latter, statues of wooden Indians and naked marble gods—who wouldn't have gaped, a "starter" or a "finisher."

Once my wraps were hanging from the hand-carved hall tree and I was seated in the crackling leather of an armchair in the parlor, Uncle Matt began almost at once on his picking at Boutflour (he found the name as dreadful as he did the place), asking how anybody could possibly stand to live in it, etc., and all the while I was remembering that he had had a career as an actor in New York, that was some years past of course, and had, they said, gone briefly to the top, but drinking and other things related to it had spoiled his success, and he had had to come "home" and now here he was living out the rest of his life in his Grandpa's house in the riverbend section which before the Civil War had a name which I suppose he would have abhorred even more, but which I like, Frog Hollow.

I began halfheartedly to defend the old town a little, pointing out that it did have fine trees and gardens, and palatial old Greek revival houses, some of which were put up before the Civil War, and once too, I went on, in some growing concern at the scowling dark lines of his brow and mouth, Boutflour had been a railroad center and a boom town in oil and gas. Now of course, I finished, in some genuine alarm over his moody expression, it's only a ghost town, and I felt like adding, it's got Uncle Matt as the leading ghost, which is how the local wiseacres described him.

Whether it was Uncle Matt's scowl, the drafty atmosphere of the parlor together with the cold and slush of outside, or what, I began to shiver suddenly, and my teeth, to my own surprise, gave a chatter or two that was quite audible. Wheeling about at once, he produced from a cherry cabinet under the shadow of the biggest of the chandeliers, a glass of something amber, and fairly pushed it straight into my teeth. Inhaling its heady fumes, hesitating to swallow it, though I wasn't exactly a stranger to drink, I told him I was only fifteen years of age, and that I was repeating the eighth grade that year for the second time.

Uncle Matt's face became even more like a thundercloud at my short speech, and so there was nothing to do but down the whole glass, which scalded my palate, and though I tried to control the urge to cough, finally I gasped so that he handed me a tumbler of warm-as-ditch tap water, and I tried studiously drinking this rather than look again at his angry mouth and eyes.

"I wonder if I may have made a mistake in you," he reflected after a silence of a minute or so. "At least, let me say, I had hoped more from a 'starter.' Still, what are we to expect, you were born and bred in Boutflour, an undoubted clodhopper with the cow-shit still hanging from your instep. Yes, I might have known!" He rose, the long tassels of his dressing robe rustling, and as he turned quickly he upset a large pile of foolscap stacked on a little tiger-maple stand by his chair, and it was the cascade of falling sheets of paper which perhaps made him sit down abruptly as if a party still more authoritative and uncontradictable had corrected him.

"What has your being fifteen years of age," he proceeded while trying to recover himself, "what has, in sum, any age got to do with your reluctance to accept my brandy, when it is offered you . . . You entered my home on invitation, why should

you balk at a drink on a wet and stormy night, be you fifteen, five, or a hundred and five?"

He rose now, and began picking up the scattered papers, and I hurried and bent down to help him.

"Sturdy enough to pass papers," he continued to jaw, "sturdy enough to take a sip of brandy on a wretched raw evening, if for no other reason than it's simple good manners."

When all the foolscap papers had been collected and put in some order, he went on studying the size of the pile now held a bit shakily in white hands which showed by their structure they had once been strong and probably steady, and then looking now at me, now at the papers, after some tussle with himself, he gave up his "secret" finally, "These are the Ferguses and the Summerlads."

I waited for him to say more, but when nothing broke his silence, I managed to get out, "Would you be mad all over again, Uncle Matt, if I was to ask you who the Ferguses and the Summerlads are?"

He put his hand up so like an arresting officer, I stopped. It seemed he was completely unprepared for what I had just said, for to be ignorant of the identity of the two families I had mentioned was to him, I gathered, like never having heard of Plymouth Rock or Gettysburg.

No sooner were the words out of my mouth than I did recollect Sister Della's speaking of the Ferguses (the Summerlads were more or less contained in the first family, as you will see later on), but always with contemptuous disapproval on her part.

While Uncle Matt, then, walked around the room cogitating I suppose on my terrible ignorance, the brandy was beginning to tell on me, and before I hardly knew what I was doing, I went up to him, tears in my eyes, put my hand on the worn lapel of his dressing gown, and said, "I want to hear every word *about the Ferguses from you, I want to know them and love them as you do!"*

"Jeremy, if I thought you were speaking from the heart, and not from the soles of your shoes!" he exclaimed, and he took my hand from his lapel and held it tight, "well, I would make you one of us here and now! Not a particle of a doubt about it!"

"Try me, Uncle Matt," I replied, and again I was as astonished at the words which came out of me, as if I heard them coming from the brandy bottle.

"Sit down, then, improbable visitor," he commanded a bit wearily, and yet with great relief.

He placed an index finger on his left temple, and then began in a soft but intense baritone voice first to excuse my unspeakable ignorance, and then to begin on what was to be a long winter-spring of uninterrupted narrative on his part on the only subject which kept him from the cold clay of the grave, the Ferguses.

Suddenly he stopped speaking and stared at me with fixed attention.

"But can it be?" he said softly. He rose and came closer to my armchair. He held his hand up over one eye and studied me, a thing I had never had anybody do before. "God in heaven!" he cried, "it can't be, yet it is. You are the very spit of Jethro! Jethro Fergus," he said irritably at a sign of incomprehension from me. "I knew, of course I knew," he went on. "Something clicked from the first sight of you. When you came up the front steps I had a strange premonition."

He almost sang now as he spoke, for Uncle Matt had one of the most remarkable voices I have ever heard, resonant, capable of wonderful octaves of rising and falling, deeply melodic, at turns sad and angry, humorous and chiding, kind and cruel. It was his voice which, in the opinion of Sister Della, put me under his "spell" more than what he told me about the Ferguses. But after a piece, the voice was taken for granted, and it was the Ferguses which drew me into my strange and awful relationship with him.

"You're not him, of course," he had taken hold of my hands in his and now he let them go. "No, you only resemble Jethro."

Turning his back on me, he talked into the great mirror above the mantelpiece. "I believe in destiny, Jeremy Cready. You did not come here tonight as a 'starter' without destiny having a hand in it. No, sirree. Perhaps they sent you, how do we know (he meant the Ferguses), but whatever it was, you were meant to enter this house and my life, and I was meant to come to know you. For I need someone like you," he veered about now and looked at me with his deep-set flashing eyes, "don't you see, somebody to tell *to, hear me? Somebody who will be all ears, and absorbed attention, who'll drink it up, and let them come out of here," and though he smote only the foolscap, I was beside myself with fear, and somehow expected to see at that moment a rush of ghosts from the great glass mirror, and feel their cold hands on my arm.*

My recollection of the last few hours at Uncle Malt's was cloudy, but before I left he must have put the foolscap papers into my empty paper sack, for the next morning they rested at the foot of my bed, where, I guess, I had dropped them, too lightheaded to put them on the top of the bureau. Picking them up now in my bedroom I noticed they gave out a faint perfume, which I later was to discover was patchouli, and I remembered then Matt's words to me as he had opened the hall door to let me out, "Get them by heart, and then between you and me we'll put them all in apple-pie order."

I carried the papers down with me to the breakfast table

where a somber-faced Della gave me a crabby talk on bad company as she fried the eggs and mush, but I believe she was more annoyed at my poring over Uncle Matt's papers, "lost to the world," than my having made the awful mistake of going into his house and drinking with him. Ignoring Della, who jawed on and on about how she would have to put me out one fine day, or send me to live with Cousin Garth, I read the account Matt had written about the families of Fergus and Summerlad, a kind of opera, all speeches or arias, which took my interest immediately, partly because it was all about Boutflour, though of a vanished age, but mostly because the Ferguses and the Summerlads struck fire to my imagination. They were on the surface "small potatoes" in Della's words, and perhaps disreputable, though coming from "somebody," that is "good stock," but as I read on through the speeches Matt had assigned to them, and their letters, which he claimed they had written, they got larger than life-size, so that I was finally under the impression I was reading about giants, rather than folks in my home town.

For some days after our evening together, Uncle Matt's house looked more shut up and deserted than usual, the big oak storm door remained closed and locked, the shutters were yanked tight against the windows, and only one light, in the front hall, could be seen burning. The paper, however, was taken in nightly, so I assumed he was at home, and alive, and it wouldn't do, I felt, for me to rap on his door and make myself easy with him again, for perhaps by now he had changed his mind, and was sorry he had made a guest of a newsboy.

Meanwhile a strange change was coming over me, for having met Uncle Matt, I began in a kind of dreamland to plan my life around him and the old mansion, and all the time I daydreamed I was sure my fancies were crazy and without foundation, sure to come to nought, but there was nobody at all

*in my life except Della, who could hardly wait until I was old
enough to leave her, and my meeting with Matt had suddenly
shown me, as in a summer lightning flash, how bare and plain
my daily fare had been. Had Matt been painted even worse
than he was, I believe I would have felt the same, ready to take
the risk of "going" with him. And besides had he not given me a
good excuse for expecting something of him? the excuse of
"arranging his papers," which on the surface would have
seemed to anybody in Boutflour as idiotic, for all knew how I
had failed in school, and being without a father or family was
hardly fit for society; but what nobody knew, with the possible
exception of inattentive Della, was that I was an incessant
reader of out-of-fashion fiction. I say out-of-fashion because
our public library, poorly endowed by a millionaire patron, has
not purchased a novel since the day of Blasco-Ibáñez. Perhaps
Uncle Matt had recognized at once I was this "reader" as he
handed me the brandy, for he was, or claimed to be, I knew, in
addition to a ventriloquist, "psychic," and could, so they said,
read people's minds. Why else would he have given me the
papers—merely because I resembled Jethro Fergus?*

*Finally, after a week of not seeing him, my suspense, or
curiosity, got too much for me, and I knocked resolutely on the
front door. Waiting a moment, and getting no answer, I noticed
the door had come open from my rapping, so I stepped into the
big hall, where I could hear voices coming from the parlor, and
more distantly, waltz music. Before I knew what I was doing,
I had advanced into the parlor, wishing I guess only to catch a
glimpse of the party Uncle Matt was giving, and then be off.
But the sight that met me in the parlor—nothing had prepared
me of course for that. There was no party, no guests, only him,
standing in front of the huge altar of the mantelpiece, a wine
cup in his hand, staring at some large photographs, and from*

time to time "throwing his voice" so that now he was one personage, now another, and each voice so different from the other that who would not have been deceived. A low cry coming from me warned him of an intruder, and before I knew what had happened, he had wheeled upon me, a second cry of intense pain and rage coming this time from his throat, and picking up a large Oriental paper knife, he rushed at me, stabbing me painfully in the chest. I fell down on the carpet, and lay there, thinking of my coming death.

"Good God, Jeremy, had I known it was only you!" I heard his voice vaguely, and smelled his breath strong with drink as he bent over me. He pulled off my jacket, my vest, shirt, undershirt, and then seeing still more protective clothing cursed the "sad bitch" of a Della for putting so many "damned duds" on me. But at length he got my chest bare, and hurriedly seizing a magnifying glass from the mantel, he studied my wound.

He left me lying there then and strode out to the back of the house. I raised my head and lowered my chin to examine where the knife had struck, which was a bit below and to the right of my left nipple. It was bleeding thickly, but laying my finger in the wound it seemed it might not amount to much. Still I felt somewhat giddy.

The medicine chest must have been a city block away, for he was gone a long time; he returned with a silver basin, some towels, a bottle of carbolic acid, and to my irritation, a newly opened bottle of brandy, which he immediately stuck in my mouth before I could object, and made me take a hefty swallow. He then cleansed this wound, which I saw was bigger than I had first thought, for his sterilizing the gash opened its true girth, and then he told me to put on my clothes and be seated in the same old easy chair I had occupied on the first night.

"I hope you realize the mistake you made coming in unannounced," he said after minutes of shocked silence had passed between us both. "It might have cost you more dearly," he spoke now without looking at me, and I had avoided glancing at him from his first word of apology. "You caught me, dear young fool, you see, in my ministrations," and out of the corner of my eye I saw him look over to the mantel with the photos of the Ferguses and Summerlads.

A few days after my "stabbing" Della came unannounced into the cubicle where I was sitting looking over the foolscap papers instead of buckling down to my homework. She held a yellow envelope in her oustretched hands. "It's a telegram for you, Jeremy," she said in a shaking voice, and I saw she was white as a linen tablecloth. Nobody sent telegrams in Boutflour except on the occasion of catastrophe or death, and nobody had ever been known to send one to a boy.

"I thought at first I would open it to prepare you for the shock, Jeremy, but I swear I was too scared to do so. I hope to God it ain't anything horrible."

I had not gone quite so white as she, but only because I had a kind of idea who it was from.

"It ain't bad news then?" she studied my face as I scanned the message.

"Not a bit of it," I handed her the message from Uncle Matt, which was a very long one for a telegram, and related in a very untelegram style something about how he had been talking to one of my teachers who had told him that I could take short-hand and type and that I had read "in advance of my years" in fiction, and so on, and acting on this, he had decided to offer me the job of helping him with writing down the story of the Fergus family. "Name your own price," the telegram concluded.

"You'll have to give in of course," Della said, and there she *was changing her whole attitude toward Uncle Matt in that split second, and beginning to change, I felt sure, her opinion of me. "After all," she handed back the telegram and was on her way to the kitchen, "money is money, Jeremy, and there's never enough of it."*

Still she could not help grumbling and whining to herself out there over the dish-pan from time to time. "Offering a job like that to a kid not much beyond his childhood, and his paperboy at that," she said. Sometimes she laughed when she thought of it, and I couldn't help joining in from where I pretended to study. But I never thought once of refusing the job from the start, or ever quitting after I began on it, and though my "brush with death" did come to mind more than once, in school, in bed, on the paper route, in fact all the time, I was so unhappy a boy then, as I look back on it now from a much older age, that I don't think I would have cared too much had Matt up and finished the job.

I am afraid Uncle Matt was at his best when he was drunk. When sober, which to give the devil his due was a great deal of the time, he was crabby, picky to the point of finding fault with everything, especially me. "Stand up straight, Jeremy, throw out your chest, look the world in the eye. What have you got to slink around for," he would take on, and I was astonished enough at his description of me that I would look up into the big mantelpiece mirror, for nobody had ever cared enough about me before to describe me. "Fear nothing," he admonished, "scare the world to its knees."

But when he was in his cups, though sometimes maudlin, and as I have shown, dangerous, then and only then did he come alive, and out of his throat came the "voices" of all the living make-believe of characters who alone were real for him.

Slowly one by one, each entered the parlor and was introduced to me, and so lifelike was their "appearance" that later at Della's I was all but sure that I had met them in the flesh, and that they did exist, living in rooms above where we sat, and congregating from time to time in some spacious upper ballroom from whence, summoned, they came down to visit us.

He let his "favorites" come down first, rather than introduce me to them all in order, Rick Fergus, first of all, for he had loved him as a brother, a tall, pale young man with ash blond hair, and the piercing blue eyes that I was later to recognize as a trait of the Fergus tribe, his mother, Elvira Summerlad, a woman of striking good looks and physical magnetism, and after her a gaunt, strong fierce-looking woman, with thick braids of gray hair, and a large assertive nose and passionate mouth, Winifred Fergus, aunt to Rick, and "immortal" enemy, in Matt's phrase, of Elvira.

"Aunt Winifred!" he paused, and he made a kind of clicking sound as if he had turned off the magic lantern. "Here, dear Jeremy," he took me into his closest confidence, "you must be very clear about my meaning, for though Winifred is one of my favorites, I am getting on marshy ground with her, so to speak, the river water of Boutflour is coming through my story, and yet isn't she the grandest of them all perhaps! And Wilders," he went on to the next figure, "the deposed head of the Fergus clan," and he drew my attention to a very tall handsome man with a shock of black hair going gray and startled hurt blue eyes.

And then taking the parts of all the many characters, each in succession, in his ventriloquist voice, he made them come to such lifelike exactness that the flesh of my scalp crawled under my hair, as it had on that first evening when entering the parlor I had been stabbed for not having announced myself.

At last coming out of my reverie, I heard him say in his natural voice, "So, Jeremy, I will give you their own speech and their own story, while you will supply the hand and the pen to write it all down into permanent form," and even as he said that I felt the pen move a bit under my nervous fingers as if it were guided by something beyond my strength or knowledge.

Sometimes, however, as he talked and I wrote, I could not tell whether the story being put down was about the Ferguses or the provincial town of Boutflour, which he hated unto the death. He wanted, in his own admission, to destroy it so that not one stone would remain standing. Once his scorn and venom reached such a pitch that again he moved me to a fit of weeping, for after all it was the only home town I would ever have, and to hear it abused and cursed so bitterly made me feel also under sentence of damnation. After my outburst, he was somewhat more temperate in his denunciation, but the meanness and unworthiness of Boutflour was always coming and going in his narration, like a chorus, and even had his wish been realized and the entire town been destroyed, he would have gone on, I'm sure, blackening its memory, and defiling its resting place.

His general argument against the town went something like this, it was, as far back as the Indians, wanting in and bereft of all virtues, either natural or historic. The town had been settled in the first place, he emphasized, by an insane ex-major from the war of 1812, who had turned freebooter and began the century and more of pillaging and exploiting of the region's few natural resources; he in turn was followed by other desperadoes and quick-rich pillagers of newly discovered gas and oil deposits, and they had been succeeded at last by the O'Toole family, who, three generations ago, had driven out all other contenders and now as billionaire magnates ruled supreme in the town. No words were terrible enough for the O'Tooles, but for the rest of the town's population he had, if anything, even more scorn, dismissing them as toadies and slaves, sycophants and crawling timeservers to the magnates who ran the town as their personal estate. Even the visiting farmers, whom I liked chatting with when they came in Saturdays to shop or loaf about the court house steps, and in addition to talk of crops and mortgages, told many wonderful stories about young girls got into trouble, ministers of the gospel surprised in adultery, hired hands who had committed awesome crimes, these plain folks he dismissed also as brainless, tobacco-chewing yokels who ignorantly served the interests of the O'Tooles and deserved no better. No! he cried, the only talented and original people the town ever had were driven out, ridden on a rail, tarred and feathered. When I went on in dogged defense, mentioning the town's Victorian mansions, pictures of which appeared in books on American architecture, he derided these huge homes with their cupolas, turrets, scrolls and scallops as having been built by the architects as jokes on the tasteless and provincial millionaires who had paid quintuple the real cost that they might be housed like princes.

Even Boutflour's natural beauty did not merit any praise or escape his contempt, such as Sunshine River, which passed old mills and gently rolling valleys, or Ojibway Creek winding through the little farms and fields filled with their pretty patches of trees, and the Indian cemetery, called Devil's Spine, owing to its geological formation, where as a small boy I used to pick up arrowheads and other relics, or even the town's altitude of seven hundred and seventy some feet, often praised as the cause of the good air; all these he dismissed as "short of memorable," and under sentence of his displeasure.

Once after an especially bitter tirade against everything Boutflourian (I could see, I imagine, even then what his intent was, Boutflour must be blackened past scouring white again so that the Ferguses and the role he played in their lives might shine larger than life in this setting), in a kind of desperation at such unfairness and downright malicious cruelty, I tired, as a way of changing the subject, to tell him how "interesting" the other customers on my riverside paper route were, and I had already somehow been able to describe to him the Cree Indian barber with his pierced ears, the six-foot-six Swede who ran the Walk-in-the-Water chili parlor, the old lady and her daughter who sang duets in their ice cream and candy kitchen, when a look of such thundercloud disapproval came over his face, that the words I had ready to describe other characters froze in my throat. From then on, I realized, I was to listen and use my pen, while he was to "ventriloquize" and tell the story that was the master passion of his life, of what life remained to him. After all, too, I told myself, I was a "paid" hearer and "paid" writer, though what he didn't know was that I was nearly as far gone even then as him, and would have undertaken my duties gratis. So I shut up, except for a few exasperated outbursts now and again, which he was generous enough to ignore.

"Your Uncle Matt, instead of falling in love with a local girl, fell in love with a whole family."

Those were Sister Della's words at two o'clock in the morning. I had just got home from the "manse" (so people in Boutflour called his house, though so far as any of us knew no preacher or his family had ever lived there), and was so tired out that I did not act surprised to see her waiting up, drinking some hot milk and chewing on a gingersnap.

I sat down across from her and pinched the bridge of my nose, closing my eyes.

"When there was trains to listen to in the dead of night,"

Della was saying, "insomnia was a lot easier to put up with, I can tell you. You know, Jeremy, though perhaps you don't, since I'm so much older, but I was a kind of train-watcher as a child, always down to the old West Main Cross depot, seeing which one comes in, which pulled out, and loved to listen to the old steam whistle. Now when I have to count sheep," she looked at me accusingly as the cause of her wakefulness, "what am I left to hear? Nothing but the produce trucks, which would jar the dead awake, and if I'm still open-eyed at dawn, the milk man and his wagon . . . Yes, since you become his 'amanuensis,'" and here she used Matt's own word for the job, and we both grinned, "I am the poorest sleeper in town."

Nodding, I heard her go on. "You know what Matthew is planning of course," she was a bit formal suddenly. "Oh you must, hasn't he had the grace to tell you?" she pretended astonishment. "I mean with all that stuff you two are collecting now for over a month together and you writing it down in earnest!"

When I still looked blank she gave me one of her pitying smiles, and then let me wait another long stretch before she handed out the information:

"He's going to give a whole evening to the Fergus family at the Grand Opera House," she announced with significance.

I was too bowled over to reply for a bit, then got out, "That big old empty barn of a place?"

"Empty barn or not," she studied my discomfiture, "it was pretty grand once, don't you forget it," she spoke with her secret knowledge again, "and what's more may be so again, for all I know."

Then while she went on about all the great people and events the Opera House had witnessed from politicians like William Jennings Bryan and the first Roosevelt to great actors like Sarah Bernhardt and Ellen Terry, not to mention the silent and the talking film stars who had appeared on the "silver screen," all I could think of was that I was being made party without my consent or knowledge to some future public event, and, who knows, would perhaps be exposed to the scrutiny of all Boutflour, if I continued with Matt in this unusual job.

"Well, a penny for your thoughts," she cried at last at my growing thoughtfulness and inattention to her reminiscences.

"I don't think I like the prospect," I said finally.

She rose on this and inevitably of course folded her arms across her thin breasts.

"Afraid it's a bit late for you to back out," she gave her opinion. "And besides you're only his note-taker. You won't be put up on the stage, don't worry," she comforted me, as she passed out of the kitchen into her own part of the house.

As I rode my wheel to the manse the next meeting night, I had made up my mind to speak my piece to him, letting Matthew know I didn't want any part in his public ceremony. The very thought that I, who had failed in all my school work, might have to appear on the stage of the Grand Opera House, reading the notes I had taken down from his dictating, made me as weak as a new-born babe, and also sick and cold.

He noted my sulkiness and pouting, and finally pounded with a baton he sometimes held as he dictated (other times it was a gavel, the kind used in auctions), and said, "See here now, Jeremy, we'll have no fits of temperament or vapors, no little-lady coaxing of me to inquire what is ailing you. I hired you because you were of the male sex. Women have to be petted or made love to in order to get a day's work out of them. I thought better of you. If you wish to give up your job, tell me, and this will be our last reunion."

At the thought I might lose the only good job I ever had, and along with it all the "life" that was now being offered me, I *came to my senses quick, and begged him to overlook my bad behavior.*

He was not so easily appeased.

"Then what in blue hell were you sulking about over there?" he said in his most cutting tones.

"Only the thought that all our work is to end up in public at the Grand Opera House."

He laughed, and said, "You've been putting your head together with that old hop-toad Della."

He pondered for a while, then said, in softer tones, "The Grand Opera House is a long way off. We could both be in our graves by the time we're ready for that," and with a gesture he dismissed the whole idea.

But he was still lingering, so it seemed to me, on the subject, for he was silent for some few minutes with his customary placing of his finger to his temple, when, with a sudden shout: "Let the Opera House wait till hell freezes over. The sorrow of the moment is, am I capable of starting at the very beginning of my story, however far back it may be, or must I crawl here with you on all fours till I find the particular strand belonging to the one yarn I am seeking, and to no other?"

I knew by now when Matthew was talking to himself and when he was "dictating," but sometimes the distinction was not always perfectly clear, as now, and then I figured it was best to write down everything, regardless.

"Yet," I heard him going on, "even I am not old enough to go back to the very beginning of it all." He turned and looked at the largest of the grandfather clocks. "I can hardly keep track of how old I am, or what year we are in now . . . But I'm sure at least Hittisleigh comes into our story no earlier than the opening of the twentieth century, a sleepy village in contrast to our gingerbready county seat of a town, for Hittisleigh was

entirely rural, rich in farmland and hardwood forest, and not entirely forgetful of Indian battles and skirmishes and the War of 1812, with flowering forests and hills, and valleys favored by yellow moonlight. This was where Wilders Fergus met and won the hand of Elvira. Summerlad, against the wishes of his sister Winifred, and probably against the better judgment of Elvira's womenfolks, so that everything was sure to begin wrong from the start."

"But will you allow me to ask you, my dear Jeremy, what is the meaning of the smirking smile you've been wearing on your face all the time I've been speaking?"

Matthew's voice was so charged with irritability and cutting contempt for me that I could not help recall my "knifing."

"As a matter of fact, Matt," I replied in a voice that was too loud and too shaky, "I wasn't smiling at you or anything you said, but was recollecting speaking with old Mr. Ed Mulhare (he was the retired editor of the Bee*) who somewhat contradicts you about your own poor powers of memory. He claims for instance you know more details about Boutftour than any other man who ever lived here—details—"*

"Stop where you are," he began to rise, but I went on, "—details like Shawnee Indian massacres, names of mayors past, and present, constables, dogcatchers, foot doctors, those who had to leave town, if not on a rail, at the town's request, and those too who had had to leave but later came back—"

"Damn your soul, Jeremy," he fell back in his chair with a laugh, "will you stop it!" Then collecting himself, he said almost penitently, "Say then that old Mulhare's half right. But he's talking about only one side of me. He's talking about people. I remember everything about people. It's my cross, I expect, and it comes without effort. But time is another matter. I never had much truck with it from boyhood. I abhor dates, especially

where those I love are concerned. And besides time has come to a full stop for me. I'm back, and don't you forget it, with Elvira and Rick, who don't exist in man-made time, and that's where I'll stay."

I think I had known it would happen from the first, but when I finally caught Sister Della red-handed sitting at her spinet desk reading all the notes I had put together for the past few weeks concerning the "lost" village of Hittisleigh and Elvira Summerlad, I felt more relief perhaps than anger, for I had wanted to share what I had found out with somebody, and who was after all better for it than Della, for there was a lot, as I was to hear straightway, that she had to tell.

"We've nothing then to hide from one another, Jerry," she handed back my notes in a lofty manner like somebody making me a gift of her own possession, "and it's time you included me in it all anyhow, for in many ways, I know more about the whole 'romance' than Matthew Lacey. He was head over heels in love with Elvira of course, though she was old enough to be his mother, when he come out of his service in the U. S. Navy . . . So Matthew knew Elvira late, when she was no longer the village queen and lily maid of Hittisleigh, but the proprietor of a boarding house."

Della waited for me to take all this in, and then went on very sure of herself and my attention:

"I knew Hittisleigh, for I used to visit my Uncle Otis Keith there, when I was a small girl, and when Elvira was a young woman. I also knew Wilders Fergus, who was wooing Miss Summerlad at that time. They both come out of a world, Jeremy, that is not only vanished but further off than the Covered Wagon or the Gold Rush. It's not just that it was all gas lights, silent movies, picture hats high collars, church picnics and the like. People were romantic then, and the whole world

was young. I doubt it will ever be so again. That must have been about before the beginning of the First World War," she thought back, and then suddenly I realized how much older than me Della was, old enough almost to be my grandmother.

"Matthew," she rambled on, "only knew Elvira 'dethroned,' for she had lived a wonderful life in her village before she made her cardinal mistake of marriage with Wilders Fergus, of Paulding Meadows. He could no more know, Matt, that is, what her life was before he met her in the boarding house here in Boutflour than you can. Elvira not only lived grand, her ancestry is grand, going back to before the Revolution, a D.A.R., and Eastern Star, and all that which it's important to know in light of the terrible reputation she finally acquired here in town, and her father, very elderly when Elvira was born out of his second marriage, was a young boy like you when he run off to the Civil War to fight with the Yankees under General Rosecrans and was badly wounded, then come back to Hittisleigh and made one fortune after another. But the best I can think of is a queen dethroned when I think of Elvira. She had never wanted to be what she became. Had dreams as a young girl of going on the stage, but her father, a dour sour Presbyterian, vetoed that, though her grandmother and mother wanted it for her. Then Wilders appeared, a rising young financier for those days, and as a matter of fact, more than that, with his first million in his pocket from a very daring scheme in Chicago. He was the tall lean appealing kind with a shock of black hair and blue eyes, but Elvira's father, I always thought, was more taken with him than Elvira, and Wilders would be a way of keeping her from the stage. But she fell in love, I suppose, and they had a fine wedding, but the ink was hardly dry on the marriage certificate before Wilders had lost his principal fortune. He gained back some of it in another

questionable deal, and to keep on his feet he persuaded Elvira's dad to go shares with him in some new enterprise, which the old man did, and they all lost everything. In just a year and a day, Elvira and her people were penniless, and she was married to the completest ne'er-do-well God ever thought up, and she was pregnant in the bargain . . . They lived in a kind of respectable disgrace for a while, and having lost their home, they moved in with her parents where they stayed till she gave birth to Jethro, and then for some reason or other, they chose to move here to Boutflour for their new abode, God knows why. I guess some speculation deal attracted poor Wilders.

"But there's the branch of the family for you, which you'll have to bring into your yarn, if you want the whole picture, Wilders's people, over at Paulding Meadows." Della was omniscient. "Nearly as sleepy a village as Hittisleigh. That's Winifred territory," and Della paused on the name. "Winifred Fergus. She was a match for anybody, believe you me, and Elvira and Winifred were a match for one another. That's where the real story is, if you ask me, the struggle between those two strong women. I could never figure out which one won. Maybe they both did. But it was a tussle that went on for more than a lifetime, and don't you dare to leave it out, Jeremy. Ask your Uncle Matt if he's up on that Paulding Meadows story the next time you go for your visit."

And having said this, and brought up Winifred, and Paulding Meadows, and the "real story," Della went off into her own part of the house, leaving me with the thought that it should be Della and Matt who ought to put their heads together, and collect their own notes, and leave me just to sit in the corner and listen to them do it.

While Matt and Della's voices rose loud as cross fire in my ears, one holding to one opinion as to what the main story of the Ferguses had been about, the other to another opinion, it seemed to me at any rate that I was beginning to come to some sort of notion all my own as to what was behind all the notes I had taken down. To Matt of course the story was about Elvira, Rick, Jethro and himself, and their love for one another; while to Della, who did not know the Ferguses so intimately, the whole thing centered around the titanic struggle of two larger-than-life women, Winifred Fergus and Elvira Summerlad, both of whom she confessed at last she admired more than any other women she had ever known.

Even Della and Matthew, however, when pressed, admitted there was more in the story than what they saw in it, that there were subplots, and other characters who came and went, and of course other points of view about the whole thing, but each stuck to his own idea of what was central, what was peripheral. (Under Uncle Matt's tutelage, I was beginning to be proficient in the use of difficult terms and phrases.)

But more persistent, if not louder, than the voices of my living commentators, were the continuous sounds I heard coming now, it seemed to me, not from a ventriloquist or a sister as old as a grandmother, but from the actual "sleepers" themselves, Elvira, and Winifred, Wilders, Rick, and Jethro whispering to me. And while I was listening to the sleepers who had been resting so long in the cemeteries kissed by moonlight, my own work both as a newsboy and a pupil came to an abrupt end. I lost my job as a paperboy for tardiness, and the same week I was permanently expelled from school for habitual truancy and failure in all my academic subjects.

Thus, there was only left to me my job with Matthew, and having lost pretty much contact with my own world, I settled down to that of the sleepers.

"One must go back, way back beyond the marriage of Wilders

Fergus to Elvira Summerlad in the white-frame Presbyterian church in Hittisleigh, to Winifred, Wilders's sister, and her terrible imprecation and curse against the marriage even before the two young people had become engaged."

I heard Della's voice coming from her bedroom down the hall from me. We were both sleepless now, for I lay all night awake thinking how I was a permanent truant and with no brighter future than being a secretary to the dead, while Della explained her situation as a good deal worse than mine since she had nothing to look forward to except the next world. But as I heard her run on, I could feel she was glad enough she had found such a good inexhaustible subject to occupy herself with in her insomnia, and since my hours and employment were irregular now, I guess she felt she could talk to me all night through if she felt like it, and I wouldn't have any real excuse for shutting her up. Indeed I heard almost as much from her that year I was "secretary," come to think of it, than from Matt himself, and I begun to wonder if there was to be an "event" at the Grand Opera House, which God forbid, based on my notes, would it be all Della and no Matt, or mostly Della and a bit of Matt.

"What an imposing woman Winifred Fergus was," Della's voice was full of admiration, almost awe, and I did not even need to say now "Is that so?" or "I see" or "Ahem" as I did when I talked to her in the kitchen, and somehow in bed I never once missed a word she said or thought of going to sleep while she talked, while downstairs I often never heard a single syllable she uttered.

" 'Hard-favored' was what they called Winifred, but that doesn't begin to describe her, any more than 'raw-boned,' 'hatchet-faced,' or 'she-devil,' all favorite terms with Elvira, and which she tossed at Winifred behind her back and to her

face time and again. Winifred's plainness couldn't all be laid at the door of a broken nose sustained in girlhood from a fall off a horse (she was a superb equestrian just the same, don't you forget it), no, it was something, if you ask me, deep down in her innards, Jeremy, for she was a warrior inside and out, oh, so fierce, and with too much mettle maybe to be the marrying kind; still, I've always thought for my own part she found her own four brothers so close to her heart, looked up to them so much, though you'd never have known it from the hateful way she treated them most of the time, those boys were, I say, so close to her no other man could ever hold a candle to them in her esteem. She was fondest of Wilders, as everybody knew, maybe because she and Wilders being the two youngest were the closest, and Winifred was the youngest of them all, and the only girl of course. Imagine being the only girl in a family of four strapping six-foot-four big boys over you, and every one a roughneck, except maybe Wilders who had been spoiled by his ma, but even he, compared to the men today, was no softie, God knows, and several times licked his weight in wildcats. Winifred was all wrapped up then in her brothers, and no other fellow she met ever seemed to come up to toe the mark. Everything with her was always family, family, so it was no surprise maybe to any-body, and certainly not to old Mother Fergus, that when the boys got to be of marrying age, Winifred would raise a fuss about the girls they were courting. As a matter of fact she broke up the engagement of the oldest and roughest of the boys, Garret Fergus, when he was going with Linnet Varnam, by insulting the poor girl till she nearly died of heart failure, and Garret ran off out West, lived with Indians, prospected for gold, and finally—I gather—got too wild and rough ever to think of marriage or settling down. As a result of what Winifred had done to Garret, Mother Fergus knew she had her hands full to keep her daughter from going over to Hittisleigh and breaking up Wilders's engagement with Elvira Summerlad.

"But go she knew Winifred would, and she knew she could not stop her were she to throw herself bodily across her path, and she was shamed to think that perhaps she didn't have it in her to stop her as much as she told herself she should.

"Then that morning before sunup the old woman heard the front door open and close softly, and she gave out a thin moan, for she knew that Winifred had gone out to catch the 5:30 A.M. train to Hittisleigh, leaving her to wait and fret till her return at some ungodly hour in the night.

"Under her hand-stitched coverlet old Mother Fergus shivered at the thought of Winifred's confrontation with the Summerlad women, and her daughter's cussedness to interfere with a marriage so soon to take place."

Whether it was Della's lullaby kind of voice or her story-tale way of telling it, I don't know, but I fell sound asleep as she spoke, persuaded I could see the village of Paulding Meadows stretching clean and green down to a muddy purling stream, and a half mile from it, out of a clearing in a sizable tract of oak forest Mother Fergus's solitary white-pillared house, dating well back before the Civil War, its alabaster white and sturdy lines of a timelessness like that of some ghostly temple.

The date on the calendar said April 2, 1908, but had a stranger like myself entered the huge front hallway and, while wiping his feet, as he looked about he might have thought himself back forty years earlier. There was a large picture of Abraham Lincoln in a far corner of the parlor, a small silk American national flag, and on each and every wall scores of photographs of Mother Fergus's dead husband, her four sons, and her only daughter, Winifred, who now, as nearly always, was speaking sharply to her mother, in a "duologue" which had been going on, in fact, with few interruptions for almost all their life together.

* * *

Winifred's relationship with her mother had changed outwardly considerable in the last two years, for in that short space of time old Father Fergus had died, her four sons had one by one left home, and Winifred had inherited a more than modest fortune from a great-aunt.

Winifred's "arguments" with her mother were long-standing and deep-rooted, and were based, the old woman confided to a few close friends, on the daughter's having a resentment of being the only girl among so many boys, and feeling, without having justice on her side, the mother insisted, that the greater part of Mrs. Fergus's pride and affection was centered in the boys, and only what love was left over had ever been bestowed on her.

"In God's name, how could you have done such a thing!" Mother Fergus looked at Winifred full in the face with flashing indignation. Not since she had been the head of the household twenty years before had the old woman spoken with such vigorous authority, such angry command. The purple marker fell from the book she was reading, and then the book followed, thumping to the floor. Nobody made a motion to pick it up.

"Why should I not have attempted to stop Wilders marrying that goose-brained fool Elvira!" Winifred shot back at her mother.

"I can see, though, by your face, and thank providence for it, that you have failed, Winifred," Mother Fergus said in less imperious tones. She sank again into herself, and then bent laboriously down to pick up marker and book, and as she did so gave her daughter a look of something like pity, a look Winifred did not fail to note, and was stung all over again with impotent fury.

Like all of Winifred's "defeats," her visit to Elvira on almost the eve of Wilders's marriage, had had much of the quality of a "victory," for she had been able to declare her enmity to the Summerlads.

Elvira's mother, Mrs. Summerfad, had been in the midst of putting the last touches on her daughter's wedding dress, and was kneeling, her mouth full of pins, while Elvira stood above her, ivory shoulders bare, her rich yellow hair down, her eyes fixed in space, when the heavy door to their room had opened without the warning of a knock, and there stood Winifred Fergus looking more galvanized than exhausted from her journey on the steam train. Mrs. Summerlad and Elvira were too dumbfounded by such an appearance even to speak to their visitor, let alone invite her to sit down, and Winifred had no wish, in any case, to sit.

"I'd like a word with Elvira alone, if you please," was the first thing she uttered, closing the door behind her, and speaking direct to Mrs. Summerlad.

"Anything you have to say to Elvira you can say to me also," Melissa Summerlad's voice rose quiet but with incipient belligerence.

During the pause that followed, the sliding gold-colored door behind the strange assembled group opened, and Elvira's grandmother Annette entered. Even Winifred seemed taken down a peg by the appearance of this dark-eyed majestical woman who came forward with the air of a priestess whose ceremony and meditations were disturbed.

The grandmother and the mother stood by Elvira, who breathing heavily had never taken her eyes off Winifred.

"I must ask Elvira then not to marry my brother, Wilders. It can never be a happy match, nor a durable union!"

This terrible sentence was what Matt had meant by the "curse," and Elvira, Annette, and Melissa took the words to be precisely that, a malediction.

But even fierce Winifred could do no more. Suddenly she tottered slightly, as if to fall, and the grandmother pushed a chair toward her, which Winifred had to take.

"I see my embassy has been in vain—today at any rate," she muttered, and she lifted her eyes to Elvira, who had never taken her eyes off Winifred, and the two women exchanged glances which said better than speech that they would be enemies for life, that neither would surrender until she had vanquished the other, and that not even death would end their rivalry.

*   *   *

Matt had come to the boarding house in Boutflour that May afternoon alone, whereas before he had always arrived in the company of one of Elvira's sons, usually Rick or Jethro. He came boldly into the garden, and stopped at the border of the rock garden, where spring flowers were giving way to summer ones. Elvira was drying her long yellow gold hair in the sunshine, having shampooed it a few minutes earlier, and was not at first conscious of his presence. When she did look up she did not know him for a startled second or two, then, with her long ivory comb, beckoned to him.

"You're so commanding in your uniform, Matt darling!" she explained away her failure to recognize him, and then looking closer at him, she put her hand to her throat in a gesture of dismay, for he was become a grown man since she had seen him last, though only a year or so older than her eldest son, Rick.

Then her embarrassment passed to a kind of pleased uneasiness as Matt threw himself down beside her on the soft pink Indian blanket she had spread for herself on the grass. He touched her hair briefly. Its long shimmering strands made his heart beat thickly, and he held painfully to her hand which he had taken in his.

There were two people, Elvira had always said, who pronounced her name with a deep tenderness and concern she could not resist, her mother, and Matthew Lacey. Everybody else pronounced it summarily, even when with affection or respect. Now Matthew said *Elvira* and then slowly, taking her other hand, he kissed her twice on the mouth.

Inside in the mammoth kitchen, she made him some strong coffee, and brought out of the buttery a fresh uncut cake.

As she watched him eat down to the last crumbs, she tried to stop the tears from filling her eyes, but looking up he saw them, and put down his fork with a sharp plunk on the thin hand-painted china plate.

"Can't you tell me, Elvira?" he came over and put his arms around her.

She waited a while, hesitating whether she should say it. But it came soon enough. "I suppose you've heard I may have to divorce Mr. Fergus," she said in plain loud tones.

"Is that all, Elvira?" he wondered. "All!" She flashed a look of impatience at him.

But then Matthew knew Wilders Fergus only as a vague continuously coming and going stranger, who was more often leaving than arriving, a very tall man with worried eyes, who, when Matt was a young boy and had played in the Fergus backyard, made him think of a highly placed messenger hired to fetch Elvira's special information.

"Let me make up for him," he spoke awkwardly, loud.

He held Elvira to him then and covered her with soft kisses.

All the way on the train back to the Great Lakes Draining Station, in Chicago, Matt sat lost in the thought he was in love with a woman old enough to be his mother. Of course he was almost equally fond of Elvira's oldest son, Rick, and he had always been a frequent visitor to the Ferguses. But now everything had changed, there did not seem to be any Rick, as if the son was to be divorced and put away along with Mr. Fergus.

He wished at times that he had not come back home, or if he had that he had made special sure Rick had accompanied him to the boarding house.

Elvira wrote to him regularly, and in all the letters poured out her heart as one would to a contemporary, or an elder, telling him of her long years of humiliation and suffering with Wilders, and of Wilders's family, beginning with Sister Winifred's "curse" on her marriage, her memories of her girlhood home in Hittisleigh, her "lost" village. Such eloquence, such narrative powers all poured out for a young sailor who had not had a mother or sister, proved for him irresistible. He was not sure which overpowered him more, her physical presence, or her epistles.

When his chance for re-enlistment came up, he turned it down, to the astonishment and hurt of his commanding officer, who had seen a fine navy career ahead for him.

"If you love me, hear me out."

Those words had begun Elvira's long correspondence to Matt while he was still in the navy. Her communications came almost daily, and sometimes two arrived the same day, to the amusement or amazement of the other sailors and the petty officer who handed out the letters at mail call. Sometimes she was careless enough to write on a Government card, and then Matt was sure all who had the chance had read what she wrote him. He devoured every line, reread each letter countless times, and kept them all tied up with expensive ribbon in a locked box among his other few possessions. After lights went out, he used a tiny pencil flashlight to illuminate certain sentences which had struck him as "very Elvira-like." Sometimes he kissed a favorite phrase.

He relived with her those girlhood days in Hittisleigh, and wished he had been born at the same time as Elvira, that they had been childhood sweethearts near the creeks and woods and valleys. The regret that he had not been thus so fortunate was so painful that he began to drink heavily in the evenings in bars on State Street and West Madison, and when drunk enough he felt that he had been her own childhood sweetheart, and that through some ununderstood chain of events had lost her to another.

Sometimes when he wrote to her, for he was not in ignorance that she had a lover now, George Gubell, oh such an ordinary man, and perhaps she had others, who knows, he would demand that she tell him if he was not first in her heart, but her reply to this was evasive, though she ended her note with effusive declarations of love.

Once he had served his last day in the navy, he felt he dared not go back to Boutflour just yet. He got a cheap room on South State Street, and one night while drunk allowed himself to be generously tattooed. This accident delayed his return home a couple of weeks more, for he was afraid that Elvira, a fastidious woman, might feel repulsion for his being marked up with tattoos, and he remembered ruefully that one day some years back when he had been helping Rick move some heavy furniture, she had called attention both to the strength of his arms and chest, and his "peaches and cream complexion."

In his cupboard-like room, waiting, he remembered everything about Elvira, and the more he remembered her life, and reread her letters, the more, oddly enough, he postponed going back to Boutflour, for it was then as always a place he loathed and hated. When he had got drunk enough times he knew he would return.

If he exulted in her descriptions of her idyllic girlhood in the enchanted village of Hittisleigh, where she was both respected and idealized by the inhabitants and lived like a princess in a thirty-room house, he was, if anything, even more moved by her having been plunged as a young married woman into a life of extreme poverty and need, by being translated to hideous Boutflour and there "abandoned" by Wilders, or at least she termed his absences, with her turn for exaggeration, abandonment, and her long years of suffering and humiliation in a strange town which knew nothing of her girlhood grandeur, but saw her only as a wretched woman with three sons to feed and clothe.

Landlords, sheriffs, creditors, bill collectors, process servers (Wilders was still in debt, and was hounded from almost every post office in the nation by his creditors), all the motley array of those who carry out the collection of money from the poor, a breed of men undreamed of by Elvira in her Hittisleigh days, now became part and parcel of her daily existence. In her kitchen, trembling lest the doorbell ring and some common plug-tobacco-chewing representative of the law serve her with papers and rate her for Wilders's forgeries and past-due notes, or weeping as she did the ironing or scrubbed the floor, always without fail she thought back to her village when she had known less about life than many children. Neither her mother nor her grandmother Annette had told her anything about the body, married love, the wedding night, babies, all that had been ignored in dreamy girlhood. Wilders had not been gentle on that first night of their being together and he had been, oh much too large for her. She cried still sometimes at the thought of it, and small Jethro, her second boy, hearing his mother weep came out of the nursery room, and tugged at her skirts. "It's nothing, Jethro, dearest," she comforted him. "Mama's lonesome, she guesses, for the good old days. They won't return, precious, for all the tears we shed."

Matt thought with sudden almost ferocious bitterness of the many lovers Elvira must have had since the disaster of her wedding night, when her husband had proved both too impatient and too inept, and he feared he might stay on here in Chicago forever, sinking lower and lower, longing for a woman he had never had, and would never gain.

Then he thought it would be as well to go back and go

down the drain with Elvira than sit here alone and ruin himself with strangers.

He might have nonetheless, he always afterwards thought, remained in Chicago, had she not suddenly sent him a telegram, in response to a discouraged letter he had written her. *Come home if you're that unhappy. Love, Elvira.*

It was the *come home* he could not resist. Even if she would never give him her love, it wouldn't greatly matter, he was her son by adoption, her husband by some unspoken consent. He would go at once.

It was difficult for Matt to see Elvira as any other than the golden-haired young-looking woman who had kissed him that afternoon in the garden. It seemed always to slip his mind that she was another man's wife, the mother of one grown boy, Rick, and two other younger boys, Jethro and Rory, and, as Boutflour gossip harped on it, a woman who had had many love affairs with other men during her ten years as proprietor of a boarding house.

At first, after his return he feared she had summoned him back with her telegram only because she felt sorry for him, or wished to be kind to him, and because, if anything, she would be even happier to have a fourth, if only "adopted," son sitting at her table. But he still flattered himself, though she did nothing now to kindle his hopes, that she loved him in some special unique and passionate way, and in any case he knew he was more than welcome.

But something in the atmosphere pointed to a "crisis," and it was clear she was deeply troubled. His being "summoned" must be, then, connected with this as much as being welcomed "home" for his own sake.

It was June, and the long line of catalpas which shaded the old sprawling boarding house brought one the feeling that an entire forest was spreading its branches within the house itself.

One morning, after a long-drawn-out breakfast, Matt found himself walking about the back yard alongside of Rick as companion, who next to Elvira was closest to him. If Elvira had not changed over the years, Rick, on the other hand, had changed greatly, especially during the time Matt had been in the navy. From being a slight, frail, almost spindly boy he had grown into a tall energetic wiry fellow who carried his head high and looked defiantly about him.

Indeed Matt had spent most of his time since returning studying Rick's metamorphosis, for Elvira's son had changed so much that he doubted now he would have recognized him had he passed him on Boutflour's main street.

"Well, Matt, I presume the old town seems mighty prosy after you've been round the world in a sailor suit," Rick spoke in an impatient, even angry voice.

Matt had been struck by two things about Rick, since his coming home, he had gotten handsome in his eighteen years, and he had also obviously been taking speech or dramatic lessons (he remembered now hearing this from Elvira in one of her letters), for Rick no longer spoke in the Midwest accent he remembered him employing just a few years past.

"Aren't you going to tell me about your *vicissitudes?*" Rick inquired when there was no further word from Matt.

"Seems to me I've had fewer of those than you," Matt spoke with a kind of offended dryness.

"Well, I'm surprised you came back to this mud puddle of a town, especially after you've been where you've been," Rick told him.

"I didn't come back for Boutflour, you can rest assured," Matt began uneasily.

"I hope *you* know then why you did come back," Rick pushed the issue a little further.

Elvira served such strong coffee that Matt always felt a little lightheaded after drinking one cup, and this morning at breakfast he had had three. They stopped walking at Mart's suggestion. A bed of peonies was nearby, surrounded by some blossoming chestnut trees and a great lilac bush, but the soft eddies of perfume from the flowering world about him only made him feel a bit more giddy.

"You don't know then why you've been summoned?" Rick took hold of his friend's sleeve. "Then let me tell you. She's caught you in her mesh too, Matt, as she has all of us. Aunt Winifred had the right idea about Elvira long ago before the wedding," Rick now brought out. "My mother's perdition itself, don't you forget it, and all of us fall who are connected with her." He laughed.

This speech was so unlike the old Rick he had known as a boy that Matt studied him now in openmouthed astonishment.

"All hell is breaking loose here," Rick went on, growing more cynical. "You see, her long-lost husband Wilders," and Rick stopped on the name as if he had mentioned a total stranger to both of them, "Wilders, it seems, is coming back home for good after being away traveling for ten years or so, living down South, you see, but you know all that better than I do myself, being as close as you are to Elvira," and he looked at Matt narrowly.

"So your father *is* coming back after all this stretch of time."

"It's made Elvira absolutely unshakable in her wish to divorce him, and that in turn has brought down on her and us the wrath and fulminations of Aunt Winifred, who threatens almost daily to come here and have Elvira committed to a lunatic asylum unless she gives up her idea of a separation. Divorce is unthinkable to Aunt Winifred. Well, to anybody in this backwoods.

"Don't tell me you're shocked too," Rick scolded.

Matt stood silent a moment.

"What is your feeling toward it, Rick?" Matt looked into the younger man's eyes.

"My opinion," Rick dug his pointed shoes into the grass, "why should my opinion matter? I hardly know the man."

Matt whistled in amused derision.

But something in Rick's voice and eye suddenly betrayed his cynical offhand manner. Perhaps he too thought of the age long gone by in Hittisleigh when Wilders had never been absent, and when indeed they lived at home as a family and not in a boarding house.

"When is he coming, Rick?"

"That's a very good question. He keeps saying he is coming, but then something always comes up to prevent it, as you'd expect, knowing Wilders. Now it's spring when he'll come home, then it's late summer, then Christmas. But I guess this time he's really coming." He sighed. "His birthday is in June, so maybe he'll be here to celebrate that." He gave his cold short laugh again.

Rick studied Matt closely, and then somewhat spitefully perhaps said, "So you see, that's why she's laid an extra place at dinner, she needs all of us she can get who love her to back her up against Wilders. She's counting on you, Matt, don't you forget it."

When Matt looked up then, Rick saw his eyes had filled with tears.

After the boarders had dined, Elvira cleared the table, took out two or three leaves from it, spread a fresh handsome Irish linen tablecloth over the worn white ash wood, turned off the bright center lights, and brought in a candelabrum of huge dimension with flickering beeswax candles. This was the "second" table already much commented upon by Boutflour, to which were invited only "special" friends, sometimes a star boarder or two, or Elvira's "beau" of the hour, and always at which sat in a kind of regal formality, as now, Elvira and her three sons, Rick, Jethro, and Rory, and frequently, as tonight, Elvira's confidante, a very young woman named Vickie Bowcher, initiated, and well seasoned in all the secrets of the establishment. Matt had now joined the second table as a permanent addition, to the general satisfaction and enthusiasm of all present.

Just as Elvira always changed tablecloths for the late sitting at dinner, substituting a fine one for a common worn mended thing, she also invariably changed and put on a fashion-plate dress in lieu of an uninspired muslin, a gown of timeless elegance, made over by her mother from one of her grandmother's, and she clasped round her white neck a necklace of purple stones.

Elvira sat at the head of the table, and tonight as Matt studied her he felt he understood once and for all why she did not wish Wilders to return. She was complete here without him, and his coming back could only diminish her. Not an eye at table tonight did not reveal love, admiration, reliance, even awe for her. No, he could see, there was no room, no place, no reason for Wilders's return.

What had he come back to, come "home" to, then, in the ironic phrase all used to describe Matt's "return?" Of course he had no home, as all knew, and their kindness in calling this "home" was now, he suddenly felt, almost cruel, as any pretense can be when carried on too long and too carefully. And what was the home he had returned to? A sporting house, Boutflour claimed. Yet Matt knew it was somehow more insidious a thing than that, and he stared at the boys briefly, especially the younger ones, Jethro and Rory. The year was 1929, prohibition, yet wine and beer flowed like water here, however covertly or carefully dispensed. As he sat there with the flickering candles hurting his eyes, dizzying his brain, he felt a little crazed, and he also felt that at any moment he would raise the subject of Wilders, and question the justice of Elvira's plan to divorce him, would even defend the absent husband-father, and mutter a "Poor Wilders." Yet he knew that if he had raised his voice in defense of the "wandering" man who had married her so long ago, she was capable of plunging a bread-knife into his heart. Wilders was "exiled" and must remain "exiled." There was only one person in charge here, only one rightful parent and protector of her sons, only Elvira. Matt felt then suddenly he was lost, more lost than Wilders, more "away" even than he. He would never leave the "second" table, he saw, never leave Elvira, never leave Boutflour. He had turned down a promising career in the navy for permanent resident in a house, call it "sporting," "ill-famed," "disorderly" (it was more dangerous he saw at once than all those pale pejoratives), and to cap it all (the scales fell from his eyes) he would never be allowed to do more than chastely kiss and embrace this woman who had summoned him to return for her love, for she reserved her serious favors for her "beaux," and Matt was to be her fourth son, a higher favor or position of course than she could bestow on any one of her transient lovers. But it would after all be only "tokens" in Matt's case, never the fulfillment and completion her eyes seemed to promise him that afternoon in the garden.

"Matt, my dear boy," he suddenly heard Elvira's voice, "you are white as a linen sheet."

He hurried to drink some wine, and tried to smile.

"I'm perfectly all—" he had begun, then stopped, his head spinning.

Rising precipitously he felt Elvira and Rick take hold of him and lead him into the adjoining room, which was Rick's own quarters, the "red parlor."

Lying down on a blue velvet-covered sofa, Matt looked about him, and it flashed through his mind for a minute that he was delirious or that he was imagining the splendor and elegance which now surrounded him. When Matt had left Boutflour these same rooms had been sparely furnished, though even then they bore the stamp of Rick's exuberant personality, and now, only a few years later, everything that met the eye was sumptuous, even if perhaps in dubious taste, as if some seasoned aesthete and collector dwelt here. A heavy gold curtain shut out the sight and sound of Boutflour while overhead an antique chandelier hovered radiant over thick carpets and a mammoth custom-made bookcase of choice walnut which carried behind its red glass casing limited editions of certain French and Greek classics, books which only a short time before would have been unthinkable in the hands of a Rick Fergus.

"You've prospered," Matt said weakly, and he looked at Rick and Elvira with a long questioning unquiet stare.

"The poor boy has done it all on his own," Elvira spoke as if in Rick's defense. "I'm afraid he's put too much of his hard-earned money into all this. But since he works so hard," she went on, "I feel he should spend his money as he pleases and on what he pleases."

Rick bit his lip and looked away.

"I wasn't prepared for its being so beautiful," Matt spoke almost in a whisper.

Elvira now glanced from one of the young men to the other, then she took up the thread of her interminable discourse, as if still seated at the "second table."

"I don't worry about Rick," Elvira said, "and even if he should leave me, which I know one day he will," and here she stopped to take her breath, "I know he will always be successful. It's Jethro I worry about," she confided. "He missed out on so much that Rick here had given him."

"Oh, Elvira, must you tell it all again," Rick had said in a low voice, but she had already begun.

"Perhaps Matt doesn't feel up to hearing all about our troubles!" he now cried, but Elvira had begun, the doors between the dining room and the three seated here were closed, and nobody could overhear.

* * *

While Rick had been born in golden sunshine, in Hittisleigh, little Jethro came into the world in a sunless hour, when one couldn't tell if it was dawn or midnight, albeit they were in midsummer, but the sun hid its face as at winter solstice. Yes, Jethro had been born under an "evil star," one might say, for all influences in nature and man were unfavorable that year. While Rick remembered the pastoral timeless happiness of Hittisleigh, when Wilders and Elvira had had means and position, property and even elegance, Jethro remembered only need and want, worry and confusion. Elvira had been "carrying" him at the very time Wilders "crashed," losing his entire fortune and finally that of Elvira and her family. All the time she had been pregnant with Jethro, indeed, there had been trouble of every kind, creditors swarmed the house, the sheriff opened the door without so much as a rap, her beautiful home and that of her mother were sold almost before they could move out, the very dress on her back was mortgaged. Whereas Rick could remember real happiness, what had Jethro to recall but want? And whereas Rick had known, she had to emphasize again, Hittisleigh, Jethro knew only Boutflour, and Elvira's smoldering hatred of the town had passed on to her middle boy, who, she feared, hated it more passionately and openly than she ever had.

"But you must have observed how Jeth favors his neck, letting his head hang down now and again, though straight as a stick otherwise, and for his frame, strong . . ."

Elvira touched gingerly her amethyst necklace before she went on.

About the time he was six, an event occurred which separated Jethro in some unfathomable way from all the life about him, though a right cord still held him somehow to life itself. Indeed had he died, he might not have been more completely separated from the ordinary traffic of life, even in a way from Elvira and Rick, for after this event, he seemed to be to them a transient, or visitor. He was already painfully separated, Elvira knew, from Wilders, who some thousand miles distant failed to give the boy some of the strength and growth he had partly bestowed on his eldest son Rick.

Ever a climber in old orchards, Jethro could not be restrained from shinning up all the tall trees in their own yard and in that of adjoining properties. Emma Causey, their landlady at that time, had warned the boy to come down out of the tall elm tree he was climbing at that moment, and when he had promised to do so, she went back into her ramshackle stucco house, and then, having put on her spectacles to look at a religious calendar her minister had sent her, she heard a scream so earsplitting, so scarcely human, she had to summon all her courage to go out.

Jethro had fallen from the tree, and had landed on the sharp iron spikes of the fence, which had perforated the base of his skull. Emma was unable to extricate the boy, and besides, as she stared at the little fellow below her, a mask of gore over his white features, she was certain he was dead. In a small town with one poorly equipped hospital, it took an age for an ambulance to arrive. There were still some feeble signs of life in the boy, as he was extricated after hideous delay, and carried off.

Jethro lay in his cramped tiny hospital cot, eyes open for the most part in a penumbra that was neither life nor death. Blundering flies lit on his eyeballs and mouth as on a wax figure.

Even Wilders returned from his interminable jaunts in the South, and Elvira and the boy's father sat at his bedside together, but there was no closeness to their reunion, no rekindling of the marital bond. They sat as at the deathbed of childhood itself. There was no hope in their faces, and no wish for it, no expectation of his recovery. When Jethro occasionally moved his eyes, there was no recognition or trust in them, no gladness still to be breathing, no forward look to life ahead.

Wilders tried to reassure the boy with phrases he had heard long ago, and Elvira wept perfunctorily.

Unable to afford a "specialist," which their general practitioner strongly urged, they finally took the boy home when he had regained consciousness. The doctor, drawing them aside in the long gray-green hall with its stench of chloroform and carbolic acid, told them the boy would probably never be "right" physically or mentally. The miracle was, he said, that he had lived at all. And smiling wryly the doctor added Jethro must have a constitution of steel, and he glanced quickly at both parents. What kept him alive?

Jethro's accident ended forever Elvira's youth and hope.

He was put on a cot nearby his little "den" off the large dining room and kitchen, separated by a sliding door from the rest of the family.

Then Wilders returned to the South, promising he had high hopes down there of making a "pile of money," and Rick and Elvira with the new baby Rory took turns sitting near Jethro, waiting for his death.

In late August, he stirred more and more, and one day Elvira discovered to her surprise and horror that he had walked out to where she was peeling potatoes in the kitchen. Her knife upraised, she waited speechless as she would for a ghost to make its bidding known.

"I thirst for a cool glass of water, Elvira," Jethro said. She walked over to the faucet and drew the water and held the cup for him. Having drunk, without a word he walked back to his cot. Elvira knew then that he would live.

While he slept sometimes, she turned his little head gently around and studied the fang-like wounds from the iron spikes. Her tears fell like a scattered June shower, but did not awake him. She sat on by his bedside weeping like a mother who had lost a whole family of sons. She could see no future for any of them. The disappointment of life bore down on her, as if she too had fallen from a height onto spikes.

He had lain like one without pulse or will for months, stirring to attention only when he saw the moon wandering over the darkening sky, or listened attentively to a few sparrows in the spirea bush. Then he had got up like one who had decided to go on with life for no particular reason. But from then on for some time he treated both Elvira and Rick as strangers, or more exactly, he was like a stranger who had been summoned by an unknown power to return to terrestrial existence.

Jethro was the stranger in their midst. He continued in his little den with drawing pictures of Jesus Christ and his disciples, birds, and floating angels. He spoke little and gazed often at both Rick and Elvira with inscrutable, seemingly disapproving eyes.

"We have a wanderer sitting beside us," Elvira wrote to Melissa, her mother, "a brief-time visitor as from another shore."

* * *

One early May morning Wilders returned to his small dingy hotel room in Norfolk, Virginia, and to his unprepared eyes and astonishment there appeared the familiar tweed suit, the iron-gray hair, and the long-familiar angular features of Sister Winifred. She was seated at his desk and engaged in reading a letter which Elvira had written to her brother a few days earlier. Her large but beautifully molded mouth opened and closed when she was surprised in the acting of reading his mail, but Wilders was too surprised himself hardly to be aware of her breach of etiquette.

"Where in the name of thunder did you come from?" he hollered.

"Shut the door, if you please. I don't want anyone to overhear what we say," she advised him. She coolly put Elvira's letter back in its envelope, and then swung her chair around in the manner of an employer about to interview an applicant. One would never have guessed that brother and sister were seeing one another after a separation of many years, and Winifred's whole manner at least was that of business as usual, and cold formality mixed with grave and somewhat irritable concern.

Wilders stood for a few seconds more as if he wanted to be sure she was not a projection of his own imagination as a result of the slight fever he had been running the past few days resulting from a bad cold, but Winifred was too real ever to be anybody's imagining.

"You don't answer my or Mother's letters, and from this wild complaint your wife has written you (she tapped Elvira's letter with her forefinger), I gather you don't reply to her either."

Wilders sat down.

"I'm here, I might say for only one reason," she began again. "But as I can see from your face, you don't know what that is, I suppose I will have to tell you myself . . ."

"Have your say then and get it over with, why don't you?" he threw down his straw hat on the flabby mattress of the bed.

Winifred's voice had been gelid and collected up to now,

but it trembled slightly as she began again, indicating that for all her "warrior" qualities her effrontery did not come quite so easily to her as people claimed, and that her long unannounced trip from Paulding Meadows to Norfolk had not been easy on her. Nevertheless she was ready to deliver her ultimatum.

"I've come here to take you back to your family," she raised her voice until even the shut door would not prevent its carrying.

Wilders made a whistling sound, and a kind of grin spread over his mouth, but then the outrageous statement hit home, and he began on her.

"Ever since you tried to stop Elvira from marrying me by all but breaking down the door at Mrs. Summerlad's the day they were fitting Elvira for her wedding dress, then practically stopping the wedding ceremony with your edicts and pronouncements, you've been meddling in my family affairs . . . Well, damn it to hell, you can just pick up your valise and take the next train back to Paulding Meadows."

Winifred smiled briefly, feeling perhaps his outburst had if anything helped her cause and strengthened her position.

"That's of course about the kind of welcome I expected from you, Wilders," she straightened the brooch on her dress. "But I didn't come all this trip to be welcomed, thanked, or cooed over. I'm old enough and I've seen enough to know that anything reasonable is impossible to expect from you in any case. Always was, always will be. But I did come here to tell you one thing, that you and yours are in a desperate state, and if you don't come home at once, well, tomorrow will be too late . . ."

"Tomorrow will be, huh?" he now rose, and looked out the small window which faced a block of dilapidated red brick homes around which straggling hollyhocks were growing.

"I don't know what in precious rot you are talking about, and what's more I don't think you do. As usual you're entering areas beyond your experience or stock of information, and also as usual you're meddling in affairs that are private, between man and wife, and don't pertain to you, and even if they did you're constitutionally incapable of handling them . . ."

Winifred swallowed, let her strong white hands relax on her lap, and then with an intake of breath came back at him.

"Yes, you can talk of what's my business and what's yours! You who've ruined the fortunes and lives of a dozen persons. The errors of a fool become the business of those who are still responsible! Had I not intervened years ago, tell me where you would be today?"

"The penitentiary, according to you," Wilders shot back with such frank incision, she was left speechless. He sank back into a low chair, and as they both saw they were in for a long session, they became less excited.

Winifred began again but in a calm almost pleasant tone:

"I suppose you know that Elvira threatens to divorce you," she took up this point first, since it shifted the subject slightly away from their own enmity and disagreement to his wife's enmity and plan of attack, and she believed it was after all the best "threat" to get Wilders to come back home.

"So I have heard," he was lofty.

"You've been gone from them, let me call to mind, your

wife and boys, for nearly ten years, and in all that long lapse of time you've only been home for very short visits."

"I've been gone for the sole and fundamental reason that I'm working hard down here trying to support them."

"That may be the case," she was half-conciliatory for a moment, "but the fact is that trying to work hard for them down here is not quite the same as being a father and provider for them there where they need you, is it?"

He stared at her in a kind of helpless horror and rage.

"And as a result, good intentions or not, your house is falling to pieces, and your family along with it."

"You sound as melodramatic as Elvira," Wilders rose again and began pacing over the threadbare rose carpet. He paused by the lavatory, took up a small cracked glass, filled it with tap water, and drank a swallow or two, dashing the rest down the drain.

"You can't be ignorant that your wife has been running a boarding house for at least the past five years, during which time you've never darkened the door of that place or scarcely inquired how indeed they were getting their bread. I've sent them money from time to time, and of course Elvira's mother has had to do so too . . . But a boarding house! Wilders, by all any of us stand for!"

"What in blazes are you driving at?" he cried, for all this time somehow he had but half-known or not known at all how indeed Elvira made ends meet, and he thought she merely lived in the kind of large house she had always inhabited, but hardly operated an inn for the public.

Even Winifred now hesitated to go on, but hearing him shout at her to continue, she got out:

"I'm afraid, to put it baldly, Elvira herself has gone wrong."

"What in blazes do you have reference to," he took on a deadly pale hue.

"I'm not going to explain it further than that," Winifred retreated now in great trepidation, for the gossip about Elvira Summerlad which had reached Paulding Meadows from time to time had, she knew, not been substantiated.

But Wilders suddenly towering over her, with all his six feet four height, and his shock of black thick hair beginning to go gray, made her cough up a few charges. "She serves liquor against the law, I'm told on good authority, lets in any riffraff who asks for a bed for the night, and just the other day that young Matt Lacey left the navy to be her inseparable companion. She has other suitors, I'm told . . ."

He turned away from her, and she spoke in a kinder almost feminine tone to his back: "Is there anything more important than for you to come home now with me and put your house in order, Wilders!"

He pulled on his blue suspenders under his jacket, keeping his back to her. "I don't believe a blasted word you say, Winifred. Ever since you were a girl you've exaggerated, our own Mother can vouch for that, and why you've spent the time and money and left Mother alone to come traipsing over the country to tell me a cock-and-bull story like the one you've just concocted, well, you can search me . . ." he broke off.

"Mother herself felt it was my duty to come here, since you accuse me of neglecting her," Winifred invented this on the spot. "She knows you've been shirking your duty more than anyone else, and I'll give you just ten minutes to pack and come home with me on the next train."

"Who in damnation do you think you are, ordering me

about like your hired man? I'll not pack, I'll not come back with you, and I'll do my duty as I see it. I'm about to make a fortune here in real estate, for your information, and were I to go back with you now I'd very likely lose the chance of a lifetime."

"Where and when have I heard that before!" she suddenly raised her voice and looked fierce enough for him to quail a little. "I've been listening to your wildest schemes, your improbable dreams all my life. And I've paid for some of them with my own money! Instead of buckling down and getting a steady job with a steady income you're always in search of some soap-bubble get-rich scheme, and the rest of us, including the Summerlad tribe even, have had to bear the burden of your imprudence and folly, of your very expensive continuous daydreams, chasing after the rainbow in other people's lives and investments . . . I'm telling you for the last time, you'll pack and come home with me. I won't take no for an answer, and I won't listen to one word more of your subterfuges and excuses . . ."

Having shouted themselves hoarse and worn themselves out by going back, as Wilders called it, into ancient history for proof of his misdeeds, they both then sat back for a while in total exhaustion and silence.

Wilders in a customary mannerism held his hand as an eyeshade over his brow, and Winifred folded her arms like one who is trying to overhear a faraway bar of music.

But it was only a calm and respite before greater storms and tirades.

"You are no longer the father of small boys," she began again. "Your sons are growing into manhood. They need a man at the head of the household, not a silly goose-brained girl-wife who spends most of her day primping in front of the hall mirror." She stared now at Wilders with almost murderous intensity. "You are already as a matter of fact too late," she now spoke as one in possession of secret information withheld up to now. "But you can at least come before the entire house falls about their ears. Or perhaps *you* want a divorce?" she lashed him, seeing that nothing she had said had made him really budge.

The word *divorce*, she saw, did strike home, had struck home earlier when Elvira had threatened it in one of her wild letters to him. For whatever was left to him of reality or self-respect, and there was a substantial amount, was his family. He had "deserted" them in Elvira's bitter phrase, but he had also been faithful to them every hour he had been gone, which Elvira either would not or could not understand. He lived only for his family. Even his "soap-bubble" schemes were dreamed up for them to win back his fortune for *them*, to return to the golden days of Hittisleigh when they had had their own home, own people, own way of life, and when the very thought of separation or "boarding house" would have struck them as insane mischance and impossible consequence.

Then as in some disturbed dream in which he had thrown off all the bedclothes and awakened with his teeth chattering, his toes frozen, he seemed to awaken at last from Sister Winifred and her visit, and to find she had departed.

Even her termagant and harsh upbraiding of him, he found, was better than the strangeness and melancholy of the South. Her tongue-lashing had made him homesick for his own people and for his own roof, for both Paulding Meadows and for Boutflour, and for his lost world of Hittisleigh, where he had been a successful young financier, proud and full of promise, and that period had never left his consciousness for a day, any more than it had left Elvira and Rick's.

Up to now he had construed Elvira's request for a divorce as an empty threat, but with Winifred's visit he could no longer do so.

He sat down now and wrote Elvira a letter in which he told her that he would be home and assume all responsibility, and that when they met she would see divorce was out of the question. He loved her and his boys, he protested, and he would be home to mend fences and set all past mistakes right.

Then he bade his new "schemes" to make a fortune farewell and prepared to close the books on his Virginia adventure.

* * *

Once Winifred had left Norfolk and was en route to the Yankee State by slow stages of trains, buses, and interurbans, her rage and ill temper abated bit by bit, and only her deep-seated affection and concern for Wilders remained. He was, she mused, half-asleep from all he had gone through, still a handsome man, though worry and disappointment had put deep marks on his face, slightly bent his sinewy build and put out the light in his blue eyes. Had she been one endowed with the facile release of tears, she would have cried doubtless all the way back to Paulding Meadows. But tears came to her about as frequently as to rock. She broke her trip in Cincinnati, from there telephoned her mother, found that everything was all right, and then instead of taking the direct route back to her home, which her ticket indicated she should, she did an extravagant and wasteful thing, she destroyed her ticket, and took instead the long bus route to Elvira's town, a good fifty miles out of her way. Immediately she had taken her seat in the bus, she realized what a foolhardy and unwise course she had taken, but by then it was too late, she opined, and she bit her lip over throwing good money out the window, and bit her lip again when she thought what she would say to Wilders's wife when she did get there. She and Mother Fergus had long since quit paying visits to the "Summerlad woman" years before, and they had never once considered going there after Wilders's home had been changed into a public boarding house.

She found Boutflour in a state of almost total disorganization owing to two concomitant events, both of which she found distasteful, a Ringling Brothers three-ring Circus, ads for which were plastered over every billboard leading into town, and an American Legion convention. In order to reach that part of the city where Elvira's house was situated, she had to hire a taxi at an outrageous cost for the driver was obliged to take her through the backways in order to avoid the main street choked with onlookers eager for a glimpse of the circus parade, and cordoned off from traffic. When she reached Elvira's, she saw at once that nobody was at home. Bidding the driver wait, nonetheless, she walked boldly up the long front steps of the pillared porch, and stood then gazing in the huge front windows. There was a look inside of inexplicable and factitious prosperity, almost elegance, which sickened her. There was nothing about the huge sprawling place that spoke of a "home" or domestic life, as had been the case earlier in Elvira's marriage. The sight before her made her think of a dance hall or a sumptuous old-fashioned skating rink, and she almost fancied she heard a golden band organ blaring. All was rife with irregularity, silent confusion, frivolity, and, she was sure, suffering. It was the sight of this house more than anything else which warned her that divorce might be inevitable, ruin might be inevitable, and that Wilders might never return here again, unless she took at once extraordinary measures and precautions.

With bowed head she got back into the taxi, and told the chauffeur to take her to the Chesapeake and Ohio station.

"You've got a four-hour wait for the next train north, ma'am," he cautioned her.

Her only response to the driver was to jam her hatpin more securely into her hat.

She would return, she comforted herself, yes, one day when Elvira and her brood were not out frolicking, and then they would hear her out or she'd know the reason why.

From a distant point she heard the circus calliope's throaty brazen scream as if it came from Elvira herself taunting her with failure.

* * *

Once years before Matt had come to live with them and when her sons had been still very young boys and not the young men they were growing into now, Elvira had announced one evening at supper when they were alone in the house and no roomers were part of their life, "What I've got to get me, children, is a divorce from that no-account man who may have given you his name, but stopped with that for his favors."

When Elvira had spoken both Rick and Jethro had looked at one another in astonishment if not horror. Outside a robin redbreast was giving his mellifluous evensong, and the city sprinkling machine was going down the paved section of the neighborhood cooling it off from the heat of day.

The word "divorce" was vague to them, but it somehow hit at them that something as terrible as murder, arson, upsetting tombstones in Oak Bend cemetery had been invoked. The word stuck in the air like smoke from a bonfire, as if their mother was no longer "Elvira," and as if indeed Wilders had not been, after all, their father. The brothers gave one another a yearning exchange of soulful looks, looking up from their plates from time to time, for though "daily enemies," in the end they were united by their own blood. This tie now came into being.

"You don't mean what you say, Elvira," Rick, the eldest, spoke in a hushed voice of correction. They were having potato soup and home-baked bread, nothing more, for the "wealthy fare" of the boarding house was yet in the future for them.

"Don't I!" Elvira sprang on him. "Don't you dare say *don't* to me, young man." She turned hotly on both the brothers, sensing a kind of conspiracy between them which had never existed before. "What has that fellow down there in the South ever done for you? Kept a roof over your head? Fed you? Taught you? Comforted you? What has he bestowed on you?" she cried seeing a movement of eyelids on Rick's part. "Was he here when you suffered your crucifixion, Rick?" Elvira turned her fury full on her eldest son. Rick turned away and, bowing his head, dropped his spoon and hid his eyes under his palms.

What Elvira had referred to was Rick's terrible early

disgrace in Boutflour, when fresh from the country town of Hittisleigh, he had been unmercifully hazed and mistreated by the boys in his new school, beaten up regularly by bullies, sent home in tatters with bloody nose and black eye.

"Where was your father when those spoiled snots of crooked millionaires attacked you? Who went to the principal and the superintendent, and watched over you? Who changed your Christian name from Percy to Rick so they wouldn't tease and torment you to death?"

Leaving the room then, Elvira went out into the kitchen, sat down at the great walnut table there, put her head down and burst into passionate sobs.

Not tasting their food any longer, first Rick, then Jethro tiptoed out to the kitchen and one after the other threw their arms around their mother, Jethro having to push Rick to get room for his own embraces.

"You are our dearest and *only* treasure," Rick told her, echoing Elvira herself.

"You are our own Elvira," Jethro cried in his own choice of words, less flowery than Rick's but perhaps more passionate. "Never give us up!"

"Who spoke of giving you up," she raised her wet face. Then she kissed first Jethro, then Rick. "I'd die before I left my handsome boys. Wild horses couldn't drag me from you two, or from little Rory. Nothing will ever part us, and should I die, even then I will be with you just the same, never leaving you, never forsaking you."

They all drew closer to one another in the little kitchen, and then Elvira went into the nursery and brought out the baby, Rory, and they all stood about him and admired him.

Her wrath and disappointment directed toward Wilders

having been voiced, and the father dismissed, all her passionate hopes and expectations were then focused on her three sons.

"Never you mind, boys, we *will* win out," she comforted them. "Our best days are ahead . . ."

Then like a storyteller who can never part from one favorite spine-chilling tale, Elvira went back to her first days of "exile" in Boutflour. All alone, without a man's hand behind her, she had kept the family together, had cleared up most of Wilders's debts in the town, the grocer, the butcher, etc., she had had to borrow money of course, of her mother, her brother, even stern Winifred, to keep a roof over their heads. It had taken all her strength, cunning, imagination, elbow grease. And in the process she had seen herself sink to the level of working class women, washerwomen, scrub-ladies. Only remnants of her own and her grandmother's beautiful china, hand-carved furniture, her own jewels and silk and satin dresses now sadly out of style (women smiled sometimes when Elvira appeared on Main Street in an elegant but oh so out-of-date gown, but smiled with tenderness) remained testifying to her of her past glory.

"If it hadn't been for Dr. Stoke," Elvira always came back to this, while both Rick and Jethro stirred uneasily in their chairs, "what do you suppose would have become of us?"

No one, Rick, Jethro, or Elvira's mother had ever understood how she came by the boarding house, that sprawling mansion of—was it thirty or forty rooms?

The boarding house had come to her when all money from Wilders, from her mother Melissa and her brother

Llewellyn had stopped. There was not a cent in her purse, and nothing to eat in the house but some sprouted potatoes and a pound of lard. She had no one to turn to that chill October day. She owed back rent for months. The gas was turned off, the lights were to be turned off next. Then shutting herself up in Jethro's play room, she had got down on her knees and prayed. After an hour of silent appeals to heaven, she got up a little calmer, and could go on absent-mindedly with her housework . . . Then the front door bell had rung imperiously, and she knew somehow it was the answer to her desperate supplication. At the door stood an old friend of her girlhood, Dr. Sherman Stoke. She burst into tears at the sight of a fatherly familiar face, one who had known her family and her from earliest days. He walked with her into the front room, as if they were leading a procession, but she could not restrain her weeping. Suddenly she had told him all the sorrows, disappointments, pains, the humiliations of her married life, even the nightmare of her wedding and honeymoon . . . Dr. Stoke, with his kindly elderly calm, his old-fashioned chivalry and attentiveness, had evoked everything from Elvira all that quiet afternoon, and she had lain in his arms and gone to sleep.

Before he left Dr. Stoke promised her future help and wrote her out meanwhile a check for a substantial amount of money. But as he was waiting for the ink to dry, he suddenly thought of something which made his old eyes light up.

"What if I were to deed to you outright the old Barstow property down by the river, give it into your hands as your own?" he began. "What do I need the property for, Elvira. There it sits, sometimes rented, sometimes not. Too big a barn for most folks to want, but in good repair, ever' inch of it. Tell me you'll accept it . . . I've known you all my life, and you've known nobody longer than you have me." He had kissed her and held her to him again. He had loved her as long as her own mother had, he emphasized, or her grandmother. With Dr. Stoke a page of her girlhood opened to her again, and a rush of her old happiness came back.

And so the day came when the Ferguses moved into the old Barstow mansion remodeled slightly to fit the needs of a boarding house at the outskirts of town, near Sunshine River, and the Turpin lot, where they held circuses and revival meetings and chautauquas, where in summer one could smell the grass crushed by multitudes of feet, and during circus time the stench of horse urine and wild beasts.

So ended for Jethro, Rick, and Rory the old intimate kind of ordinary family life together, and so the next time Elvira spoke meaningfully of divorce, years after her first threat of such action, the boys, much older, received the news with a kind of numbed listless acceptance.

* * *

Time, which had become blurred for Wilders since his great bankruptcy and failure of some twelve, fourteen years before—it had ended his youth and had early ushered in middle age, almost senectitude—now time suddenly began to swim into focus, and he realized he was the father of three sons, one approaching manhood. He studied himself in the mirror. His face under the thick hair was not heavily lined but it had a kind of thin mask over it now which was not youth's. It did not bother him too much, his change in appearance, for what he wanted, what he had always wished for was to become very rich. The desire had not waned, no matter how grandiose his failures, how crushing his defeats, despite the sickening realization that everybody who knew him well had lost faith in him *except*, and he groaned as he thought, except his hellcat of a sister, Winifred. And after her visit to him in his hotel room in Norfolk she had continued to write to him almost daily.

"Damned female," he muttered, "a rip on a broomstick. Hellish temper, mean to our mother, and mad, I guess, that she wasn't born a man."

He sat by the spittoon and the potted palms in the lobby and, in desperation to do something, spat into the shining gold receptacle, spat with his own spit, for he did not chew tobacco, did not smoke, did not drink, did not play poker. A crony of his had explained his failure in business as connected with his not having the manly vices, but he might have listed one, a hopeless unavailing weakness for women. He was crazy about them, but here again he had had no luck. A "fine-looker" was what he called women he felt drawn to. Suddenly he felt hungry, insanely desirous for Elvira, and her small compact body and white beautifully modeled arms, once thrown about him when life had shown nothing but promise. What in damnation had he stayed in the South so long for, he woke as if from a ten years' slumber. He must go home, no, not to follow or obey Winifred's imperious commands, he must go home to pick up the remnants of his life. If he didn't go now, he never would. But did he dare go back?

The phrase kept running through his mind like the bars of a popular song, *Elvira has been operating a boarding house*. Something direful, deep had been occurring, then, over the years of his incorrigible absence from her and the boys, his worst fears had whispered to him now and again, but he had not counted on a thing like the keeping of a public inn. Something had changed, he knew in his bones, and especially something to the simple little country girl he had married in long-ago Hittisleigh.

Could she refuse him access to his home, and boys? The question flashed at him as from a secret well of prophecy. A terrible unhinging fear seized him: had he a home, a wife, sons, or had his absence killed all his rights?

Then Wilders thought again as if inspired by thoughts coming to him from "telepathy" of the boys' music teacher, Agnes Coles. Why should he think of her, he wondered, but all at once he felt the attraction of this woman clear down here to Norfolk. It seemed that Agnes Coles more than Elvira was calling him back.

"A crazy world. It don't make any sense," Wilders sang out, his head lowered over the gold spittoon, and then he spat again into its shimmering inside.

Having failed, having lost his niche as the great young banker and small financier, the darling of a small financial set, he now lapsed back into the careless grammar and expressions of his dad, a horse trader, and railroad man. "Since it don't make any sense, the damned world," he went on, aloud, "I'll be damned if I don't go back home. Don't belong in the South nohow. Never did, and haven't made a damned penny from my whole sojourn down here. Don't understand the people and never will. Understand the damned niggers better. Have to pull in my horns and go home. Lower my sights and admit I'm licked . . . But I'll make it again back home. I'll clinch a deal someday . . ." He sat at his writing desk now upstairs, penning a letter to

Winifred . . . "By Christ," he wrote her, "one day you'll all be coming around me again, wanting this, wanting that, as you did when I was minting the money, saying Wilders this, Wilders that. By God, I'll make it all back, you'll live to see the day . . ."

Rereading this letter moments later, he tore it to fine bits, and let them fall into the wastebasket.

* * *

Jethro, who was now about fourteen, could dimly remember the far-off day when his father had finally "run off" for good, and that other distant time when Elvira had with a kind of desperate optimism begun her career as operator of a boarding house, and now when the hint came, as from a short-wave radio transmission, that Wilders might return, Jethro walked slowly as in a daze to the F. W. Woolworth store, purchased their cheapest school notebook, and from then on, almost daily, began writing down in his unformed shaky script all the goings-on of the house about him.

Before the boarding house, when they had been poor, with the gas shut off frequently so that they had to prepare their meals on a wood-burning cast-iron stove, read the daily paper by candlelight, and go to bed with the chickens if they wished to keep warm, their house, with its many vacant rooms and lonesome hallways and rattling window-panes, had at least belonged only to themselves. But when the boarders and roomers arrived, everything changed, and the family changed along with it. There was more food to eat, of greater variety and quality, and they had better clothes so that Grandma Summerlad no longer had to help out by making the boys' suits and shirts. But their old happiness and closeness in common sorrow was nearing its end, and without at first their hardly realizing it, Elvira and her boys began to go their separate ways.

The roomers were to Jethro like an invasion of Mongolian warriors, or a plague of locusts. Coarse, common limited men, for the most part traveling salesmen, they took over the spacious front sitting room and parlor, and Elvira and her sons moved into the back recesses of the house, the second dining room, the kitchen, and the still untouched red parlor. Owing to Jethro's horror of the strangers, Elvira fixed up for him a little "den" of his own in the vacant attic.

Though Elvira did not know that Jethro was keeping a "log" of all the activities of her house, the boy's sullenness, anger, and pouting disenchantment with her and everything that transpired under her roof conveyed itself to her as graphically as if she had crept up the stairs to his attic room and read from beginning to end what he scribbled down there. And if Elvira thought Jethro looked at her with critical jaundiced eyes now, Jethro in turn thought his mother no longer loved or cared about him. He spent more and more of his time alone in the attic over his notebook.

But his thoughts became so terrible that they filled even him with consternation, but the disease and its cure were the same, recording everything he could think of, everything he could observe, and always at the head of nearly every sentence which came out from his clenched right hand was one name that towered above all the other cast of characters, *Elvira.*

Jethro now came to the bitter conclusion that Rick and Elvira, the "lovers," had always been in cahoots against him. They, after all, had been "together" long before he was born or thought of, their knowledge of one another preceded him and their thoughts could always go back to a happiness he had known only snatches and samples of, in Hittisleigh. And time and again he would recall that goose-pimpling midnight conversation of some years back between these two when they had discussed Jethro's "case," for according to what they had said, Jethro's death was even then long past due. The injuries to his neck, and undoubtedly his brain, Elvira had whispered, could only mean he would never grow up. "Yet," Elvira had finished, in tears, while Rick, he supposed, held her hand covered with Annette's old rings, "the poor tyke lives on."

In the days when Jethro kept his notebook-journal, no decent woman in Boutflour, and perhaps America, smoked, and so he took special pains to describe how his mother indulged in the clandestine practice, how she picked from a red box on whose cover appeared the dancing harlot of the Bible, Salome, a gold-tipped perfumed small cigarette, and placed it carefully in her graceful lips.

As the boarding house prospered, Elvira took to going out frequently with strangers, men from nearby towns and cities. In the back of the big house inherited from Dr. Stoke was a small summer cottage where in June an assorted array of tea roses drenched the air with their perfume, together with morning glories, hollyhocks, and sunflowers whose petaled height shut the windows from close inspection. Here, after a movie or a drive around the river, Elvira and one of her male "acquaintances" would come for a "rendezvous." Jethro could look down from his attic aerie and see the lights go on as the "couple" arrived, then summarily off.

The thought that he was "scheduled" to die and that his mother was a whore became two principal emotions with him which like two unknown poisons, one alone of which would have meted out death to him, but being united with each other, they somehow allowed him to go on living. He would fill his notebook then with the chronicle of his mother's whoredom and deceit. At the same time he felt Rick was little better than she, selling his personality and his new "photogenic" appearance to all who were idle enough to watch him. When Rick had been a boy, Jethro remembered, he had danced naked in front of the big window of their old South Main Street property, kicking up his cock for all who passed to see. Now grown up, Rick sang and acted in public for money, but Jethro saw in it all the same exhibitionism which his brother had so scandalously been adept in as a boy.

It was difficult for Jethro to believe that his father was still alive. Somehow Elvira's decade of belittling and denigrating the absent Wilders had destroyed him more completely than if he were actually resting in Oak Grove Cemetery. Only sometimes of a soft late-spring afternoon like today, Jethro would remember the Wilders of far-off Hittisleigh. But that had been another life, another world, a far-off curling-under sunclouds town. Could this Jethro, for instance, with the broken neck and damaged head be the same handsome young boy in the starched sailor suit and broad-brimmed hat everybody had loved back "there," this Jethro who crouched in an attic and wrote down stories of a painted Jezebel, who was in that same long-ago the "real" Elvira, the favorite of Great-grandmother Annette, who had walked through church aisles and pine-tree cemeteries, praying and faithful . . . No, Jethro had died, he felt, and perhaps gone to hell and Rick and Elvira were angels of the damned legion who were assigned to torture him, while above on earth, in Hittisleigh, lived the true Elvira and Wilders who mourned their lost son.

Then the special-delivery letter arrived, the contents and purport of which, unknown to them had been dictated by Aunt Winifred's visit to Norfolk, and in which Wilders informed them that he was coming home for good.

Jethro studied his mother's face as she read the letter. She had taken special pains with his breakfast that morning, serving him a muskmelon with flowers and leaves of nasturtiums placed around the globe of fruit set on the hand-painted china plate, and an omelet with cream. He knew she had spent the night in the little summer house with one of her new lovers. The makeup from the evening's revelry was still on her mouth, but her face showed a new sorrow.

"Your father is coming back, Jethro."

She burst into tears, and put her head down on the laundry-fresh tablecloth, sobbing.

"When we no longer need him," she was nearly inaudible.

This time Jethro did not comfort her.

"Did you hear what I said?" she looked up from her weeping after a while. Jethro stared at her, immovable.

Musing, Jethro opined that at that moment he could remember nothing about his father except his "crimes." Wilders's perspiration was odorless, his hands manicured, he sat around on his "hind end" most of the time dreaming, or reading James Fenimore Cooper's Leather-stocking tales, talked of when he had been a hunter in Canada, stalking caribou, recalled his wanderings in the

Southwest and Mexico (once he had sent Jethro a pure silk handkerchief from Old Mexico and the boy had worn it round his neck until it fell from him in rags), but let no one be deceived (Elvira's voice), *there was blood on Wilders's hands.*

"He's shed blood," his mother had told him day after day, evening supper after evening supper, over the ten years past.

Jethro thought it was literal, but he could not understand then why his father's perspiration was odorless, his shirts always freshly laundered, and why he looked like some of the statues he had seen in a Roman Catholic cathedral, the church he was forbidden ever to enter by Grandma Fergus because the celebrants inside were, she said, idol-worshippers.

No one wanted Wilders to come home, all felt he should stay in the "stinking" South.

"But if he comes," Elvira's voice came to him as he stood in the latticed back porch, his hand motionless on the screen door knob, "if he comes there will be a showdown, believe you me . . . Oh, yes, I'm not going to support him and you children in the bargain. Let him go to his mother's, and Sister Winifred. They got money stashed away somewhere. Let him go over there and do his dreaming. He mined my family, Jethro. I had the most beautiful home, do you remember it? No, I suspect you don't. You were only three or four, back in Hittisleigh. No wonder you are bashful and timid, scared as a bunny. When I carried you I was running from the sheriff. They took all our beautiful household goods, the heirlooms, the Circassian walnut bedroom suite, all the priceless things Annette, your great-grandmother, had given us for a wedding gift. Annette too had been a wealthy woman, but she lost everything through your father. Where is the girl I was then, I sometimes ask myself, when I drudge for the roomers, worrying about their dry-cleaning and laundry, inspecting sheets, mending linens, a glorified washer-woman, and my own mother no better, niggering for my brother over there in the hospital he runs. We're ruined, do you hear, Jethro, and by your father's hands. That's why I say his hands are bloodstained . . ."

Jethro turned to face her, smoking a small cigar before her face. She ignored it. When he had been eleven he had stolen her cigarettes and smoked them. She had ignored that. She knew he was ruined the most of them all. He had already lived more years than any doctor had given him allowance for.

But hate Elvira as much as he did at that moment for all her "rottenness" in the summer house, he suddenly felt even sicker with hatred for his father.

"If the poor little fellow gets comfort out of tobacco," he heard Elvira's voice speaking to Rick, who had just come in and pointed out Jethro's bad continuing habit, "why, let him . . ."

Jethro thought of all the terrible things that had happened to him in his father's absence, while the two turtledoves, his lover-enemies, Rick and Elvira, stood by, and allowed it all to happen. One cold January school day, he recalled, his infirmity had suddenly attracted more widespread scorn and loathing for him on the part of some of the boys than usual, and at recess they stopped him to demand he show them his disfigurement. When he refused, and they pressed him, he had spat in their faces, and one of the leaders of the gang then decided to freeze his tongue to the metal fence which separated the

Woodrow School from the highway. They pushed his tongue on the metal bar and froze it there so firmly he could not remove it. An older boy from the eighth grade had run up, saw what was happening, beat off the gang, and then slowly, methodically removed Jethro's tongue, but injured it badly.

Then all the taunts and derision that had come to him over the years from the Boutflourians came back to him, like a chorus of wild cicadas singing all together: "Oh yes, the little crippled fellow with the busted noodle . . . Father a crook, mother a . . ."

Like Jeremy who so much later was to listen to his story, Jethro took to peddling papers in the "business" district over the river, where the Negro barbershop was his first customer, the Coney Island hot dog stand his second, the Greek candy kitchen next, etc. He had walked on in Wilders's absence, peddling and smoking strong tobacco, chewing wet snuff. A "to-pieces" wanderer from the unknown kingdom of all men's childhood. His hands got calloused, he looked manly holding his head painfully high over the place where the iron teeth of the fence had tried to sever the artery and spill his brains on the zinnias and lilies-of-the-valley . . .

Setting aside his "revenge" against Rick and Elvira for the moment, he planned to do something against his "absent" father, whose hands, odorless, manicured, still streamed with blood. He would make his father pay for all he had suffered. Then, afterwards, he would make the whole world pay for his having been born . . .

But then later that day while the robins sang their good-night song before settling into silence in the fruit tree boughs, a sudden flashing recollection had come to him and taken him back to the Hittisleigh he was always telling Elvira he could not remember, when Wilders had brought him "down town," the gas lights had popped on, and the posters on the brick buildings informed them that an acrobat from Ringling Brothers Circus would leap from a pole from atop the highest building in town. He would thrill everybody to death, and Jethro the most. That night suddenly now came back, and he felt, in memory, to his incredible disbelief Wilders place a firm hand in his small untried one . . .

* * *

Distracted by her worry over Jethro and almost beside herself that Wilders was returning, Elvira scarcely heard her eldest son Rick come into the kitchen and stand near her where she was washing in suds a cut-glass bowl. He had to call out "Elvira!" several times before she looked up from her task. Her eyes were immediately fixed on a long rather thick legal document which he held in his hands.

"Don't tell me you're in trouble too, for pity's sake, Rick," she looked away from him and the document. "That's all I need . . ."

"Why, it's good news for a change, Mother . . . So good I have been making Matt pinch me and tell me I'm not dreaming . . . It's . . ."

But Elvira had begun on the subject of Jethro. He seemed, she went over it all, to be practicing to make himself as wild and crazy as possible for his father's homecoming. He had been smoking cigars again, and hanging around the Starlite Stables, riding the mare there without permission, loitering around the Green Gables Dance Hall, and the Mexican shanty town.

"Forget Jethro, will you, for a moment, Elvira," Rick's voice was raised and peremptory. "I've got a very important piece of news . . . I've come into quite a fortune from Aunt Libby's estate! It's from the lawyer," he pushed the document toward her, but because her hands were covered with suds, she refrained from examining it for the while.

"To think we didn't even go to her funeral, either," Rick glanced at the document quickly again now, and read some lines here and there.

"It's quite a sum, Mother . . . six thousand dollars."

"Rick, you must be mistaken," she said in a whisper, drying her hands on a towel. "Please look again."

He walked over to her, and showed her the line of the document with the bequest clearly indicated.

Then in what was almost a wail, she said, "Why, Rick, it's all your dreams come true . . . You're free, just think of it, and of course now you'll go away . . ." She began to cry.

"Matt and I thought we might go to New York," he studied his mother's face carefully. "That is, we both want to go on the stage, you know . . ."

"But you won't go at once," she pleaded, ignoring Matt's part in all this, which angered her.

"We thought we would, yes," he said softly.

"But, Rick, with your father coming home, and Jethro driving me crazy with his pranks and irresponsibility."

"Oh, damn Jethro," Rick let his anger come out now against his brother.

"Surely, Rick, you can't be callous enough to leave me just now. Wait a bit, until things take care of themselves. And think everything over carefully before you take a major step like going into the theater . . . Do you hear me, Rick . . . Look at me, please."

"Damn it, Mother, why can't I go now, will you tell me!" his anger now began to get the better of him, and he flung the "will" down on the kitchen table, that table around which the family had given voice to so many sorrows and some joys.

She touched the papers with the hand on which her wedding band still shone dully.

"Will you tell me why I can't go now and make something of myself before it's too late? Or must I stay tied to your apron strings forever in this cabbage patch on the river!"

Stung more than he realized by his words, Elvira turned from him and gazed through the latticed partitions of the back porch into the thick grass of the yard which wanted cutting.

"I can't blame you a bit for feeling the way you do," Elvira spoke with unusual control and moderation, he noted, and he was immediately sorry he had spoken as he had. "But aren't you mindful of any happiness at all you've shared here with me?" she wondered in a soft whisper so unlike her usual speaking voice that he might have thought it was a voice he was hearing in deep slumber.

He didn't answer.

"Well, go, then, Rick," Elvira said. "I won't be the one to hold you back from your career. Somehow I'll keep the place going without you, how I don't know, for you're the only one I can depend on, but I will . . ."

"But I'll help you from New York," Rick started to move closer to his mother, but she put distance between her and him by going hurriedly to the big kitchen table on which rested the document of Aunt Libby's will.

"Of course you will," she spoke, distracted. She sat down, but did not pick up the papers before her.

"But I do want more than anything in the world, Elvira, to go," he spoke with a sudden passion. "My whole being cries out for me to leave, can't you get that through your head! Haven't I been the head of the house these last years? Do you expect me to stay with you forever?"

"When have I ever asked such a thing as that of you!" she spoke with the heat of real anger. "Will you tell me, Rick?"

"Elvira, Elvira," he replied bitterly, near tears.

"All I ask of you, Rick," she spoke now with full control, almost sweetness, "is that you see me through until Wilders has come and gone from here. I can't face that man alone after the terrible things he has done to all of us. Can you expect me to, answer me!"

"All right, all right," Rick's anger came back now again, directed this time against his father's shortcomings, "he has done nothing right by any of us!"

Then brushing way the hot tears of anger, he surprised her with his next statement: "As a matter of fact I don't see why you feel you have to divorce Wilders . . . Why can't you just separate, after all you've lived apart for most of your married life together . . . Why is a divorce, a public divorce, necessary, can you tell me?"

She looked at him with openmouthed astonishment, but immediately replied: "Because I want my freedom too, Rick, as much as you want yours!"

She rose and went over to the sunny side of the room on the pretext of examining a pot of geraniums which grew there. She plucked off some of the dead leaves, and lifted one of the drooping flowers so that it was full in the direction of the sunlight. "After all," she went on, "you're a rich man now, you can go scot-free . . . I'm the one that's stuck, as usual, as I've always been, I'm the one who'll have to raise Jethro and little Rory. No one else steps in, you can bet your bottom dollar, when the chips are down . . . And once, Rick, long before you were born, I wanted to go on the stage too. My father forbade it, and like a fool I married Wilders Fergus . . ."

"Oh, Judas priest," Rick muttered, inaudible.

"And the stage, of all professions," she spoke now as she sometimes did when alone by herself, "it's as risky and uncertain as all those speculative schemes and 'deals' Wilders has been chasing after for all his life!"

Rick sat down. He looked utterly crushed.

"And I don't thank Matt Lacey for coming here under pretext of paying court to me, so to speak, and then working behind my back to spirit you away from here," her full fury now fell on the absent sailor. "He can pack and get out . . ."

"I don't need Matt Lacey to let me know that I want to leave Boutflour," Rick retorted.

"Oh, Rick!" she could barely control a sob.

"Besides, it seems to me it's you he's so soft on, not me . . . And besides I don't see how you'll be lonely here with all the people who are always coming to see you," he referred now to her life in the summer cottage.

Without answering him back on this, Elvira turned from her flower pots, and sat down across from Rick, picked up the legal document and began studying it carefully.

"Aunt Libby was always fondest of you from the day you were born, Rick," Elvira reminisced calmly about the past now so that one would have scarcely realized passionate and bitter words had been exchanged. "She was your great-aunt, Annette's sister . . . I'm glad of course she remembered you . . . But what a great sum for a young boy like you to handle and be responsible for!"

"All right, then, Mother," Rick spoke at last after a struggle, in which cruel and bitter words came almost to be spoken, and then were at last swallowed, for he had come to a sudden but irrevocable decision. "I won't let it be said that I ran off on you the first chance I got. No, I'll stay for a bit of a while longer . . .

"Do you hear what I said?" he cried at her, his face gone the color of ashes.

Elvira raised her eyes at that moment from the papers, but dared not look her son full in the face, and waited without daring to breathe for whatever words might come next from his distorted features.

"Yes, I'll stay with you, Elvira. But only, mark you, until Wilders has come and *gone*. Not one minute longer! Does that satisfy you?"

He rose then and gave her a look of such passionate, flashing violent condemnation of her that she covered her eyes with her right hand, and shook with silent weeping.

"God bless you, then, Rick," she got out, hearing him leaving the room. "I won't require more of you, you can take that as a solemn promise, my son . . ."

* * *

"Where are you off to?" Jethro inquired, looking into Matt's room, and seeing that the sailor was busy packing.

Jeth had just come down from his attic room, by the back stairs, and Matt's door being partly ajar, he had pushed it open all the way and peeked in. Matt's eyes fell on the dime-store notebook Jethro carried tightly under his arm.

"I'll tell you where I'm going if you'll show me that notebook you've got there."

Jeth laughed, sat down on the floor and crossed his legs.

"They're just jottings," he pressed the notebook to his chest.

"And every jot a stick of T.N.T.," Matt said, imitating the "changing" voice of the boy.

Matt bent over Jethro and made a feint of taking the notebook out of the boy's grasp.

"Don't tell me Elvira has kicked you out," Jethro removed the book from Matt's grasp.

Matt walked back to the bed where his clothes lay ready for his bag and valise. "Let's say, Jeth, I'm leaving before she decides to tell me to go . . . No, I'm going to move in my grandpa's old vacant place down on the other side of the river. Going to fix it up and try to make something of it. Have my own boarding house," he snickered.

"I didn't know you had a grandpa, or family, Matt."

"Oh, didn't you now," Matt flushed under the remark, for the fact he did not know who his parents were still rankled in him, but he had had a maternal grandfather, or an old man who called himself so, and he had left in Matt's name the rundown old property on the opposite side of the river from Elvira's house.

"And when I get the place all fixed up, Jeth," he folded

the last of his suits and placed it in the valise, "I'll expect you to pay me a visit and talk over your writing there . . . Will you come?" Matt looked over at the boy.

"Why should I," Jeth spoke huskily.

"Why because the old place is wild and deserted, was the scene of battles and massacres and the like. Would appeal I think to an Indian like you."

Jethro laughed with some appreciation of the "dig" which Matthew now gave back to him with regard to his family, for despite his blond hair and blue eyes, Jethro's great-grandmother Annette had had, according to Elvira's often repeated statement, Indian ancestry.

"Why are you leaving anyhow, Matt?" Jeth wanted to know.

"Oh, 'twould take too long to tell . . ."

"Is it because the loverbirds are quarreling now?" Jeth wondered, meaning of course Elvira and Rick.

Matt glanced off into the rolling hills visible outside his window.

"Let's say I don't want to stay and see a son pitted against his father, no matter who the father is," Matt spoke in a solemn manner Jeth had never heard him employ before.

"I don't like to see people I care for . . . hurt one another," he finished lamely. He closed his valise.

"But I hope I'm leaving in friendship with each and all," Matt strode over to Jeth, and pulled his nose.

"If you ever want me for anything," Matt said with some awkwardness, "come over on your wheel and get me . / ."

"By the way," Jeth rose now and looked Matt direct in the eye, "who ever told you that I write things down?" he inquired, tapping his notebook.

"Nobody had to tell me," Matt replied. "I saw you."

At that moment, Rick, disheveled from his session with his mother, stood in the open door, his eyes focused seemingly on nothing. Gradually his glance fell on Matt, and he spoke in a voice nearly unrecognizable as his own.

"What are you packing for, Matt?" he gasped.

Matt's mouth worked, but he said nothing in reply.

"Are you going to New York without me?" Rick's voice rose in anger.

"No, Rick," Matt replied, shamefaced but still looking Rick in the eye. "Not till you go, anyhow. But," he went on, less sure of himself, "when you came into your inheritance just now, I remembered that all this time, after all, I've had one of my own, my grandpa's property over west of the river. I've been over there several times lately, and I liked what I saw . . . I've decided to fix it up, and meanwhile I'll be staying at a tourist lodge nearby so I can tend to things right away . . ."

"Did we drive you out, Matt?" Rick spoke in accusatory tone.

"I wouldn't say that at all." Matt picked up his duffel bag, as if to test its weight.

"Then why are you going in such haste? Elvira will be hurt . . ."

"I don't think so, Rick. I've explained it all to her."

"I somehow knew, Matt, you wouldn't have the raw nerve to go with me to New York . . ."

Both Rick and Matt started now as they heard the door slam on them in the room. It was Jethro departing.

At the same moment, Rick lost control of his feelings, and began to sob convulsively, which he immediately controlled.

Matt slowly put down his luggage, and cautiously approached Rick, and put his arm about his shoulder.

"Don't," Matt said, "you'll break my heart too to hear you go on like this. Rick, I can't tell you how it hurts me so to see you like this . . . New York will keep, don't you understand that . . ."

"No, it won't," Rick cried, a kind of ferocity coming over his features. "I'll never leave this hole-in-the-mud now . . . I know that. Never." He dried his eyes on his hands, then looking at the closed door, went on, "I suppose that little crippled snot is listening to all we say, his eye at the keyhole . . ."

"Oh don't be so hard on the little fellow." Matt withdrew now from Rick.

"You sound like Elvira," Rick stormed. "The boy's a monster and you know it."

Then folding his arms, Rick intoned in his actor's voice: "Now tell me why you're really leaving, Matt."

"Well, I've told Elvira and I've told Jethro why, and I could tell you the same story. Only I won't. It's true I want to fix up my alleged grandpa's old property of course . . . But I can't stay here, Rick, and watch you turn on your own father. Whatever your father has done, he's still yours, remember that . . . I wish I had a father, Rick, any father, I believe, would do, and your father is better than a lot of the others. Remember that sometime in the future . . ."

Matt picked up all his belongings then and walked out the door.

"Well, let me at least help you down the stairs with all your things," Rick called after him, in a mixture of sarcasm and concern.

"Suit yourself, Rick . . . I'll be more than happy if you do . . ."

But Elvira was waiting for them at the bottom of the stairwell, her face showed red and swollen from weeping, but in some way it only emphasized her good looks, and she went up to Matt with her old winning smile, and said, "You can't just skip out like this so abruptly as if there were hard feelings, dear boy. It's suppertime," she took him by the arm, "and your place is laid at the second table, come join us one last time before you go away, Matt, darling. I won't have it otherwise, and then you can go your way . . ."

Matt and Rick exchanged looks.

A few minutes later, the "second" table was in full swing. Voices were raised, the tinkle of glasses, Elvira's "carrying" voice relating an anecdote, during which one could hear the mingled laughter of Matt, Rick, Jethro, and little Rory, clear to the street, and one passing by there would have thought it was the reunion of a family which had never known a care or disagreement. And when Matt did leave later that evening for the tourist's lodge next to his grandpa's old mansion, it was only after he had given his solemn promise that he would come join the second table frequently, for in Elvira's words he was more than one of the family, he was her fourth, and carefully adopted son . . .

* * *

All upon a sudden, Elvira found her situation markedly changed. From being undisputed head of her family, with Rick in a strong, but yet always subordinate role to her own, as helpmeet, and Jethro as her faithful "side-kick," she felt almost without hint of a warning stripped of authority over her sons, deprived of all power, even her former dignity and winning ways. She was no longer directing their course, but was a passive supernumerary in the wings, whose humdrum task was to wait until called. Rick had revolted, and was besides "rich." Jethro was unmanageable and wickedly recalcitrant to her, the keeper of some dreadful book of evidence compiled against her. Even little Rory had a wondering look of doubt and uncertainty as she bathed and cared for him. "Cousin" Matt, without a word of warning, had decamped. And the comble of it all was Wilders's imminent return. Any one of these changes would have unnerved her, but coming as they did all together, she felt at times a kind of mania assailing her. And the thought never left her now that a great grand period of her life was drawing to a quickening conclusion, years which despite the suffering and anguish they had bestowed were, she was sure, the most soul-satisfying, if costly and harrowing, she would ever win for herself again.

Today she held in her hand Wilders's "last" letter, a scrawled note on hotel stationery telling her that he would be "home" within the week.

Had the letter come a few weeks earlier, it would have roused her to instant fury, and belligerent preparation, and she would have been able, beyond the question of a doubt, to marshal all her boys around her in opposition to him. She could scarcely understand her own feelings, therefore, now, of being, if not glad or relieved that he was coming, calm and deliberative with regard to his re-entry into their lives. It would create, at any rate, a problem which both she and Rick would have to deal with together, for she could not believe that Rick meant to leave her now, especially with Matt's having backed out, and without the sailor she felt he lacked the courage to depart on his own.

She heard Rick "vocalizing" in the red parlor. Looking in on him, she saw he was gazing at himself in the huge ceiling-high gilt-framed mirror, more intent on the image he saw there than in his progress as a singer.

She stood on the threshold with Wilders's letter in one hand, a cigarette curling smoke from her mouth, a humble supplicating bend to her body. At last her own meekness and servile attitude frayed her nerves, for she spoke up sharply:

"He's coming back the middle of next week."

"Who, pray tell?" Rick stopped his singing only long enough to get out these words.

"Who else but your father, Wilders!" she cried in a voice which had enough of its old ringing command to chasten him.

"So let him come home, Mother," he turned and looked at her full in the face.

"What are we to do about him?" she spoke with the same lash of authority. "After all he's *your* father."

"I have no father," Rick snapped at her. "You've made me see that very clear over the years."

Caught in her own idea, so to speak, Elvira could only lower the hand which held the letter, as if its weight were insupportable.

"I wish too that you would give up smoking," Rick scolded. "Or if you must employ the stuff, learn to take the cigarette out of your mouth like a lady, when speaking . . . You look appalling, Elvira."

Perhaps Rick spoke so cuttingly to her at that moment because Elvira looked so fetching, cigarette or no cigarette, and in spite of all her years of trouble, in the soft light of the parlor, she might have been taken for a young woman not much older than that of the shimmering reflection of her son in the antique pier glass mirror.

"You want to be free of me, Rick, you've made that abundantly clear."

"I want to leave Boutflour," his voice rose to a kind of wail.

"And you're doing so well here now," she shook her head. "We would never have dreamed a few years ago how well you'd do . . ."

"Whatever we dreamed or didn't dream, Elvira, this isn't the place for my talent and career. It's a country town, and I have more in me than to waste it on what's here. I've got to leave eventually, why not now . . ."

She recognized in this speech both the phrasing and reasoning of some of his "new" friends, who had filled his head with flattery and lavish promises.

Feeling a bit faint, she sat down.

"What is it now, Mother?" he spoke, if anything, still more sharply.

"I felt a bit giddy," she said, very pale.

"Oh, darling," he still spoke in the manner of his new friends of the theater, "you're always ailing, it seems to me. Don't your admirers perk you up enough?" he referred to the men who took her out of an evening.

But after a minute or two of pacing, Rick too sat down, in a reverie of such deep absentmindedness he forgot his mother was present with him in the room. What was slowly unfolding in his mind was as a matter of fact her "news," which at last came home to him, that is Wilders's imminent return. He too now turned pale. After all, his thoughts ran back, he did have a father, no matter how he and Elvira had pretended over the last years that he had none. And he was coming back now, perhaps for good.

Rick felt on a sudden he had been handed a revised and corrected communiqué in which was underscored new information to the effect that somebody long considered dead or unaccounted for was alive and ready to make his appearance, one who long ago had been dismissed as not connected in any real way with one's own life or being, whom one had given up forever, this someone was coming back, and would expect to be received as his father, be welcomed, embraced, and then join the family which had put him out of mind so long ago. It was no wonder Elvira was giddy, and Rick looked up, about to say something conciliating to his mother, but without his having been aware, she had left the room.

* * *

"You boys are changing into young men I do not know," Elvira spoke to Jethro and little Rory in the great shining kitchen of the boarding house, a day or so after her "scene" with Rick, and the departure of Matt Lacey, but both boys knew that she was referring principally to Rick, who had now gone off without telling anybody where or for how long. Prior to leaving, he had grudgingly driven Elvira to the Barstow and Kling truck farm where Elvira had picked out several bushels of tomatoes, peppers, onions and spices for her yearly making of chili sauce.

She had asked Jethro and Rory to help her with the cooking and canning of the "secret" recipe of the sauce, the making of which was a kind of ritual with her each year, carried on from the tradition of her grandmother Annette. Each year, too, as she stirred the red thick bubbling mash of ripe fruit over the mammoth iron-cast stove in the basement of the house, where the final cooking was done, it brought back peaceful and idyllic memories of her girlhood and Hittisleigh. But this season, as she stirred, assisted by her two younger sons, her thoughts remained heavy in the ominous insecure present.

In a kind of spoken abridgement of her deepest thoughts she reviewed within the hearing of Jethro and Rory, Rick's Boutflour career, as if the boys did not know their own brother's accomplishments, while she supervised their stirring, and tasted the progress of the cooking by sampling its rich red liquid with a huge wooden spoon, adding a pinch of seasoning every once in a while.

"Rick was ten when he came to Boutflour right from our little one-horse country town, as he calls it with disdain now," she rambled on, "but you couldn't have found a more unhappy or unpopular boy than Rick was at that period.

"For instance," Elvira went on, retelling now one of her favorite stories about Rick for the hundredth time, "shortly after we came to Boutflour, and Rick was put in Bess Buersill's class of fourth-graders, there was to be some kind of a St. Valentine program or party in the room, and each child was asked to bring a valentine remembrance to as many of his classmates as he wanted to remember. Rick and I stayed up half the night making valentines for the entire class out of some of Annette's beautiful gold and red wrapping paper, little stars and Cupid's bows, and lace-paper hearts, and when we were done we couldn't help congratulating ourselves on what stunning valentines we had turned out, each one different, and each one a beauty. When Bess Buersill, the teacher, handed out the greetings, all were of course astounded at the exceptional workmanship and unusual imagination of Rick's valentines, and there were plenty of oh's and ah's from girls and boys alike coming from all over the classroom, and Bess Buersill herself, as she later told me, said she had never seen their like, but as she handed out the last of the remembrances, it began to dawn on her that of all the children sitting there it was Rick and Rick alone who had not received a single valentine from anybody at all, and there he sat emptyhanded in the back row, biting his lip and clawing his hands to keep from sobbing. Bess Buersill walked back to her desk, almost as upset as Rick, and quickly rummaging through her drawer found an old valentine from several years back, and quickly putting it in an envelope that didn't fit, lamely presented it to Rick as coming from the entire class. But one of the meanest boys, that bully Jeff Bushwick, rose up at this, and tore up the valentine Rick had given him, throwing the pieces in the poor kid's face, and was about to beat him in the bargain when Bess Buersill dragged the nasty little scamp to the cloak room and thrashed him, but nothing could undo Rick's shame and humiliation.

"And that was only the beginning of his troubles as a new pupil, for the same kind of cowardly bullies that later was to pick on you, Jethro, made his life still more miserable. He begged me to let him change his Christian name Percy to an abbreviation of his middle name, and became Rick, so they wouldn't tease him about having a sissy's name, but then they picked on his having curls; off went the curls, and they beat him up for something else . . . But he fought his enemies and made them his friends, he fought the fact we were 'nobodies' in this town, though we had been everything back home, and now he's made Boutflour like and accept him . . ." And Elvira went on with her review of Rick's life, though the boys were weary with having heard it before. Unlike Jethro, Elvira now pointed out, who is moody and unsocial, Rick had through industry and ambition made himself "somebody" among the snobs and the four hundred of the town, partly owing to his fine singing voice, but more especially to his winning personality. He had secured a job in the offices of the great petroleum company which cast its shadow and influence over the entire town, and he had been as successful in its sober precincts as he was in the church choir and in amateur theatricals . . . But it had turned his head, she pointed out, with a kind of dark vehemence in her face and voice, and she looked with a warning supplicating expression at her two "remaining" boys. Rick was stage-struck, and what with his inheritance, she was afraid he would throw to the winds all the fine preparation he had made for a safe and lasting career in Boutflour, and go off, half-cocked and unprepared (for he was at bottom still a country boy), to New York City, where, God knows, many a high hope had come to nothing countless times before.

Jethro now exchanged a significant look with little Rory, and had his mother not been present, he might have expatiated on the theme that while Rick's star may have soared here in Boutflour, Elvira's had waned, if not set. She had never been accepted in society, indeed she had made no attempt to get in, while Rick, with a closet full of fine clothes and a tuxedo or two, went everywhere: the temples of middle-class worship, the Elks, the Country Club, the Thursday Club, the different churches in whose choirs he sang, all opened wide their doors to him, and at least the elite among those organizations welcomed him with real enthusiasm. The rank and file of the town, however, never accepted Rick, and never would, partly owing to Elvira's being proprietor of a boarding house, and the absence of any Mr. Fergus, which led many Boutflourians to suspect the Fergus boys were all bastards, each one sired by a different father, but also owing to the overrefined appearance and manner of Rick, perhaps to a certain slight delicate something that piqued and even frightened the average citizen. Some thought Rick was too "aristocratic" in bearing, others decided he was too clever, too talented, and far too theatrical—his speech had changed almost completely since he took dramatic lessons of the notorious old retired actress Adah Bayley, who lived in dubious circumstances with the Methodist minister. And Rick often complained bitterly to his mother that he was not typical "main street," that in order to be a success in Boutflour or America one must be "common" in every fiber of his being. Both talent and too much handsomeness of person were suspect.

As Rick had flourished, he became more and more critical of Elvira, and their quarrels and spats became not only more frequent, but increased in their bitterness. There were now quarrels about Elvira's not taking advantage of her changed, very favorable economic situation. "You no longer have to drudge like a charwoman, or some nigger beset by a Legree," Rick pointed out to her. "Why don't you get the proper hired help, instead of doing everything yourself? But no, you wish to be in charge of all and everything. You've always wanted to control all who came within your orbit!"

As his words and criticism of her became sharper, he remained away from home more and more, spending the night she knew not where, so that often she did not sleep a wink, wondering in whose bed he now lay, indifferent to her, forgetful of all they had been through together.

All this she now passed on to Jethro and Rory, who stirred away over the mammoth tub of sauce, as if out of their patient labors some resolution and remedy of her sorrow would be effected.

"You always told me I had no father," Elvira quoted Rick as he had spoken his last words against her, "and now when it suits your purpose, you are suddenly ready to tell me I am to welcome him home, and remain by your side to protect you from his return!"

Here Elvira paused, and kept back his last taunts and charges against her to herself—Rick's accusation of his mother of being little less than a common whore, who slept with whatever traveling salesman had the polish and the nerve to ask her to bed.

Then slowly Elvira had come from her long monologue back to the faces of Rory and Jethro, where her eye stopped. In the unspoken utterances and sorrowful faces of the two young boys she seemed to see some weighty and deep-seated criticism, at last dissatisfaction with her, perhaps more weighty than that of Rick. Their faces accused her, she felt, of having failed them.

Contrary to everything she had lived and hoped for up to now, she became desperate enough to wish Wilders home. Her own sons were turning against her, and so, she meditated, perhaps it was time the real "failure" returned for them to turn all their disappointed hopes and fury against him.

And so, when Rick had begun to act so inimical to her, proud and vainglorious with his inheritance, whipping her with his terrible tongue, absent, the "darling" of his own circle of friends, it was Elvira herself who had summoned Wilders home . . . The night the news of Rick's inheritance had come, trembling, half-unaware of what she was doing, she had put on her best velvet suit, the hat with the feather, and, barely able to restrain her tears, walked all the way to the Western Union (in that far-off era only desperate or wealthy people availed themselves of its service), and there she wrote with a stubby yellow pencil the direful message to be sent to Norfolk, Virginia, "Come at once, your sons need you."

* * *

For Elvira the one person who filled part of the void created by the death of her grandmother Annette, and the absence of her mother, Melissa, was her bosom friend, Agnes Coles, teacher of pianoforte in Boutflour, who with her strawberry blond hair and good figure might almost have been mistaken for Elvira herself. Since the Fergus family's early days in Boutflour, Agnes had been a constant visitor to Elvira's house, first as a teacher of piano to Rick, and then as close friend and confidante. Like Elvira, Agnes had come from a farming community and had aspirations for the theater, but unlike Rick's mother, she had taken the plunge and been briefly on the stage, but after two or three years of hard knocks and going without, she had had to give goodbye to all her young dreams and make the grim decision to go back to the old home town, and once returned, content herself with teaching beginning piano to the millionaires' children. Though Agnes might have married, in Elvira's exaggerated phrase, "any man she shook a stick at," some certain stubborn individuality and critical independence made her turn down always in the end every proposal, and now she seemed to have resigned herself, once she had passed thirty, to life in her studio on South Main Street, where from morning to night one heard scales from Czerny and fumbling renderings of "To a Wild Rose" and "Träumerei."

For the past ten years hardly a day passed without Agnes calling Elvira on the telephone or Elvira stopping by the studio for a half hour of exchanged confidence, while Agnes, on her part, always took the greatest delight in coming to the boarding house to taste home-cooked food, and share in the clannish closeness of the "second table."

After sending the fateful telegram, Elvira felt she could not go home immediately, and the only person whom she dared see in the state in which she found herself was Agnes. At the same time she did not wish to go to the music teacher's studio, which, by reason of its dark interior, cavernous without curtains or carpets or any domestic touch, redolent of cheap incense, always depressed her, for the darkness of her own life only made her long the more for sunlight and bright color. Stopping in the old run-down but still elegant hotel called the Swilly House, Elvira went to one of the curtain-hung private telephone booths and rang Agnes, begging her to come to the ladies' sitting room, off the main lobby, for an important "matter." Astonished and frightened at such an unusual request, fearing it might mean some tragedy in the family, Agnes could only reply she would be over directly.

Many a time in the past, when desperate with trouble, Elvira had gone to Agnes, they had secreted themselves together, wept, confided, confessed "all" to one another, and bewailed their lot as women in a town which offered them chiefly criticism and ostracism. And Agnes would always conclude their "talk-fest" with one of her ever-recurring epigrams: "Women are fools and men are devils, we can't live without them, but oh God how they treat us."

There was today, however, something about Elvira's peremptory plea for Agnes's help and sympathy which hardened the music teacher's attitude a bit toward her friend. As she often compared Elvira's situation with her own, she could not help feeling that Elvira's "troubles" were all in all lighter than her own, and though Elvira poured out all her own sorrows, somehow Agnes, in turn, never told her quite everything about herself. What Agnes did not perhaps completely realize was that Elvira did not tell her everything in return either.

Nonetheless Agnes knew nearly all the "everything" about Elvira, her girlhood in Hittisleigh, her dream of the stage, thwarted by her pious Presbyterian father, her marriage to a "prince charming" at the age of seventeen, the ashes of disillusionment of the wedding night, and the long grim years of penury and heartache that followed in its wake in Boutflour.

Elvira's confession of having sent the telegram—she blurted the whole thing out almost before Agnes could sit down as if it were a death notice—did not improve Agnes's disposition, strained on having been summoned away from her studio on such short notice. But the lines of worry and self-accusation on Elvira's pretty face had soon won the music teacher back to her old feeling of blind affection, admiration, and trust.

"You did right of course to call Wilders home, Elvira," she said after uttering worried phrases of "I see" and "What else could you do?"

After another thoughtful pause Agnes spoke with firm conviction: "Don't you see, there's got to be a showdown and now this will be it."

Elvira pondered Agnes's dictum a moment. Had she not sent the telegram, she reflected, perhaps he would have dilly-dallied more weeks and months in Virginia or, who knows, perhaps never have come home.

"What in God's name will I do, Agnes, when he's actually back?" she voiced her own fears now in clearest simplicity, and she took Agnes's hand in hers and held it hard. "I can't be a wife to him ever again, and he was never a father to my sons . . ."

Agnes now fell into a state of anxious absentmindedness, for she could not somehow bring herself to speak what was weighing on her heart, at least not while Elvira was in such a state of anxiety. She wished now she had come more out in the open with Rick's mother years ago. It had always seemed to Agnes, admirer of Elvira that she was, that she had never wanted Wilders to be a father to her boys, and that she had her own jealous passion of possessiveness for them which must have resisted from the beginning any encroachment by anybody on her unique role and position of importance in her sons' lives. They were *her* sons, nobody else's. They had no father, no family other than herself, Wilders's unimportant act with her in her bed did not constitute authority, ownership, custody or rights. She alone had been mother and father to her boys in the long lonesome painful Boutflour years.

"Sometimes as tonight, Agnes dear, I feel so desperate, I could go over to the deep part of the river, over old North Bridge, and let the waters close over me without a pang of regret."

"Elvira," her friend could only say in response, and touch her hand. Perhaps, Agnes thought, it was because she knew too much about Elvira, was too close to her, and loved her too deeply to be a proper adviser to her in a crisis like the present. Sometimes Agnes felt she loved this young woman more than she had her own mother, and for this very reason it was difficult for her to count all the mistakes Elvira had made over the years as wife and mother—her overpossessiveness, her "worship" of Rick, her "religious" carrying of all burdens alone, without wishing to ask others who might care also to help. Then there was the matter of Elvira's "lovers" or "fellows" as the town called them, a growing source of scandal and gossip. She had once broached this subject with Elvira, only to be told that it was all malicious talk, and that the "gentlemen" in question were casual friends, nothing more.

But there was one subject, delicate as it was, on which Agnes now decided to speak out, however upsetting it might be—the bad company that Rick Fergus had recently sought out.

She heard her own question come out so loud and clear in the hush of the small secluded room of the hotel that it made her jump as if another person had called: "Do you know who Rick is seeing these days, Elvira?"

Elvira's gaze of wide-eyed surprise answered her own question for her—the mother knew nothing about Rick's whereabouts when he was away from home.

"Well, I for one am worried about Rick," Agnes felt her way.

Elvira looked at her friend with a kind of mild misgiving. She was aware of course that Agnes knew everybody in town, was in the best homes, and over the years had come to be the confidante of many troubled persons, men and women, without ever being considered a gossip or betrayer of confidence in return. But though Agnes was circumspect, she did know "everything" and when she "told" she divulged her information only to another person as close-mouthed as herself. And so Agnes's secrets were carefully kept until everybody knew them and could gossip about them openly.

Speaking almost as if to a young girl, Agnes explained to her listener, who at every word grew more apprehensive, that all small towns and hamlets had their fast circles and Boutflour was no exception. Its wild set centered around the unmarried Dr. Gray who lived in a huge chateau-like house atop a hill, miles from any community of the smallest size. Toward his establishment all the disappointed and the ambitious youth for counties around somehow found their way, and spent weekends or entire weeks surrounded by every luxury and the entertainment and diversion of the doctor's unusual and brilliant friends.

But as Agnes went on speaking. Elvira's initial apprehensiveness relaxed, changing to a kind of amused condescension on her part toward her good friend.

"But I know Dr. Gray, sweetheart," Elvira remonstrated, straightening the hem of her skirt. "He's also a very close friend of Dr. Stoke . . . Of course he doesn't live exactly like the Presbyterian minister, but he's hardly an evil influence."

Elvira was aware of the white lie she was telling, if such a distortion of fact could be described so mildly, and she was aware that Agnes knew she was lying, but her worry was elsewhere now, far from the subject of moral influences on young men.

"Oh, well, I'm sorry I spoke so," she heard Agnes's somewhat tart tone of reply.

Then like one speaking for her own benefit, Elvira brought out her one real worry and the real reason she had sought out Agnes tonight:

"What I do fear, don't you see, is that Rick will leave me forever." Her voice shook. "And once gone, he'll not come back. I know that. Why should I fear Dr. Gray," she almost scolded Agnes now, "or any of his friends when I'm up against losing Rick forever . . . I'm afraid that's the reason after all why I sent the telegram to his father . . ."

Outside the hotel a sudden thick rain of confetti was falling, coming, as Agnes remarked acidly, from the Moose Lodge across the street. In a short while they heard loud shouts from the men who were celebrating.

"Don't drunk fools like that make you tired?" Agnes rose and shut the door which had come partly ajar.

As always in their relationship, the limits of the "confidential" had been reached, and a kind of painful quiet followed, after which they made a stab at conversation, speaking of things far from their heart, a political contest in the town, a recent marriage, a bridge which had collapsed and killed an entire family. Elvira found herself, while talking, pondering the future, Rick's and her own. She knew then as she had before she had spoken with Agnes that she must drive Wilders from her, if necessary by force. Perhaps that was the real meaning of her having summoned him now, so that once and for all she could drive him out forever.

Agnes too sat immured in thought. Her friendship with Elvira had always been circumscribed by their own tacit agreement as to how far they could speak in confidence. As Elvira's "lovers" and her inordinate possessiveness of Rick were subjects which could bear only the lightest pressure, so Agnes's son in New York, whose father was unknown and whom she had given away to be adopted, was almost never touched upon, scarcely mentioned.

Looking away from Elvira, Agnes thought of the irony of a mother who did not fear bad company so much as she did losing her son entirely. In the music teacher's own mind she did not see how young Rick could have found a worse influence than he had, if not in Dr. Gray himself, then in his friends. Was there any vice, she pondered, that they did not practice—and she remembered the gossip she had heard over the years—or any pleasure that they said no to?

Agnes woke from her reverie to feel Elvira's light kiss upon her forehead, a word of thank you, and the explanation that she must go home to see that everything was well with Jethro and Rory and with the house.

* * *

Elvira returned home to her boarding house with something like the happiness of relief after her depressing meeting with Agnes. There had been some unspoken criticism on the part of the music teacher toward her, Rick's mother felt, and then too the thought of how Agnes lived, celibate, lonesome, neglected, with only the four walls of her studio to go home to, and the eternal daily cacophony of the piano's being banged away. How does the poor thing stand to go on, Elvira pondered.

A letter was waiting for her, postmarked Hittisleigh, and Elvira opened this with the same desperate eagerness as one who has not been allowed to taste liquid for days takes up at last a tumbler of cold mountain spring water. It was from one of her oldest friends, Mrs. Hugh Bainbridge, who, well over ninety and partially blind, had never ceased to communicate with Elvira over the years. For Mrs. Bainbridge, Elvira was still the slender pretty-as-a-picture young girl of long ago. Inside the letter, with that carelessness of certain wealthy persons who seldom or never go over their accounts, was tucked away a hundred-dollar bill. Elvira kissed both the money and the letter, but the lengthy message of the letter was more welcome to her at that moment than ten hundred-dollar bills, especially after the inconclusive "interview" in the faded elegance of the now lugubrious Swilly House.

Despite Mrs. Bainbridge's advanced age, the ancient friend of Elvira's family still drove about the village in her electric car, surveying "changes," and wondering where change itself would stop, and although she was active in her church and lodge, and was not above an occasional "picture show," she could not help sitting alone in her mammoth house hour after hour once the servants went to bed, looking backwards. Out of these reveries Mrs. Bainbridge penned now not so much a letter as a shortened chronicle of her own family and that of the Summerlads of Hittisleigh, so that after reading this letter within a letter, and comparing the present condition she found herself in, Elvira experienced all over again her loss, her comedown, her exile to such an extent that she felt she might now slip senseless to the faded Brussels carpet under her feet.

But she went on reading: "I can never resign myself, dear child, when I pass your old home to see the uses the purchasers have put it to!" (She referred to Elvira's home's having been converted into a funeral parlor.) And the writer went on to bewail the fact that in the Hittisleigh newspaper, the *Clarion,* all the names which appeared there were as strange to her as if she had picked up a paper from some other continent, although she had seen a few weeks ago a mention of Annette in a little column called "Genealogical Lore."

Then the old woman took up in a kind of reluctant but exalted strain, like some bard of old, the "fall" of the Summerlads. (The fall of Wilders she had regarded as dreadful, but then after all he had been an outsider.) But most terrible of all, she could not help thinking, was the fact that so beautiful and talented a person as Elvira should be reduced to manageress of a boarding house. And worse fate than that, was it not, that Elvira's own mother, Melissa, should have to stoop to be matron of her own sons' hospital.

The letter concluded with a wish on the part of Mrs. Bainbridge (which somehow softened the sorrow Elvira had felt on reading the middle portions of the communication):

"Should fate prove even harsher to you, dear girl, come home, and live with me. We would be as happy together as two singing birds freed from their cage . . . The door is always open . . ."

Elvira sat there for a lengthy time, the epistle in her open palms, fluttering faintly in the evening breeze. She was almost sorry she could not walk out of the house and go toward that "open door," and never return here, where only her failures were remembered and served up to her daily, and where thanklessness and discord were her fare.

* * *

Wilders had been described by Elvira in so many conflicting ways and Jethro remembered his dad in most of his
waking hours like someone he had read of in a child's
storybook, so that when the man himself appeared out of
nowhere that soft cloudless summer day, at first the boy
could see only a lean greyhound kind of stranger, bronzed
by sun, with strong but (as Elvira never tired of pointing
out) manicured hands (manicured, however, by himself,
and with a jackknife). He seemed, if anything, taller than
when he had left (he was six feet four inches in his
stocking feet), and his eyes which Jethro remembered
earlier as having always been smiling now bore no hint
that they had ever smiled at anybody.

Wilders returned in a blue-black touring car of a kind
seldom seen in these parts, and the back seat was dripping
wet with fresh-caught black bass, though nobody knew
him to be much of a fisherman.

The sight of so many fish to be cleaned gave Elvira
pause. She was no longer in such straitened circumstances
that she took easily now to such menial tasks, and his gypsy
kind of return with "provisions" annoyed her. Wilders had
first bent down to kiss her, after having kissed Jethro and
little Rory, but she moved away from him before his lips
could touch hers. She did not speak at all to him.

The shock of such a "welcome home" was a bit too
much even for a man who had stood the unnumbered
disappointments he had, and what he did not understand
and was never to learn was that her lack of even casual
civility to him had been owing to her actually not having
recognized him when he came in the door petting her sons
(his friendliness provoked her, for she did not like
strangers to touch her boys).

So the week and day of his return, circled on the calendar with heavy pencil, had come, and if terrible, it was terrible without outward flurry, fuss or confusion, though nonetheless dreadful for all alike.

Wilders's clothes were thin in places, if not threadbare, he was the picture of defeat, if not down-and-out, and yet, to Elvira's sense of outrage, he looked handsomer and, in some ways, younger than ever, tougher certainly. His straw hat, too, was new, and expensive, so that he felt called upon to explain it before her questioning eyes, pointing to it, as he removed it from his head, as "a present from one of the real-estate boys" (meaning, Elvira muttered to herself, some blamed crook).

Musing still, Jethro studied the "broker" in their midst, which is the word his mother always put down on his school report card after the inquiry *father's occupation,* and which Jethro, the first time he had seen it written down in his mother's hand, had hesitated to return signed to his teacher since he thought that "broker" meant a man who was both out of work and crooked.

A phrase of Elvira's uttered a few months earlier as she rose from the supper table after a prolonged discussion of his father came back to Jethro, "Well, he was somebody once!" and this cry now almost formed itself on his nervous lips as he watched his dad anxiously. "Somebody once!" His greyhound father, at any rate, had come home, he thought, and he started as he caught sight of Wilders's wedding ring flashing on his finger, as if that round piece of metal at least proved his right to be among them, and the boy thought of that long-ago event when his parents had stood and made their vows to one another, when he was yet unthought of and unknown to them both.

The icy coldness of Elvira's reception was only one of a score of things which floored the returning husband. Nothing, for example, had prepared him for the size, the immensity of the boarding house, and how many rooms did it contain, he wondered, thirty, forty, more, and how in the name of conscience had she come by such a property? He also felt a twinge of the blues to see how Elvira's good looks were going, though she was still in anybody's book a very attractive woman, but with her new air of managerial poise, cold efficiency and easy authority, she was a far cry from the untried young woman he had left so many years before. He would never have recognized either of his two smaller boys, but when Rick walked in as tall almost as himself, with a kind of arrogant condescending irritability putting his white hand stiffly and briefly into his father's, he felt as he had ages ago when, a truant, he had had to come back to a birching in the one-room brick schoolhouse, anecdotes and reminiscences about which he bored people with from time to time. ("Well, I was born in the backwoods and never denied it," he would assume a self-deprecatory air when the anecdote failed to win his auditors.)

Elvira took her anger out on the fish, disemboweling and scaling them with unnatural efficiency and speed and ferocious skill. To Wilders's query, "Why can't I do that for you?" she shot back with the ready retort of one who has been quarreling with him daily for years in succession, "Because I'm more than halfway through."

"Suit yourself," he muttered, and picked up Rory and put him on his lap. Rory seemed to take to him, and pressed against his father's mended striped shirt, and touched briefly his stiff high collar with the gold collar-button. Wilders began giving the boy a short description of Virginia.

Elvira had finished cleaning the black bass over the huge "baby's bathtub" which swam with bloody water and entrails, and then without warning, a surprise to herself indeed, she burst into convulsive sobs and crying. All in the room advanced toward her, but all she wanted was to gain control over herself, and she moved away from her sons and husband, and stood with her face pressed against the back door.

"It's all right now, just leave me be," she spoke to Jethro who had taken her hand in his, and her mouth moved in a kind of grim smile.

She dried her hands slowly on the heavy cotton apron she wore, and patting the boy on the shoulder, said, "Best show your father now his own room, Jethro."

Elvira's mentioning *his own room* made the father's face go into sudden dark eclipse, and he bowed his head briefly, then rose and stood looking vacantly ahead. Rick picked up his battered valise for him, and put it in his hands, but he did not follow his father, who left the room like a man who is to enter hospital. Jethro led the way up the back stairs which led to the guest room where he was to sleep alone, on the floor above Elvira and the boys' quarters. (Elvira had rehearsed her instructions with her sons in thorough detail before Wilders's arrival, designating the sleeping room where they were to put him all by himself.)

"Did you miss your daddy?" Wilders said, in a voice so shaky with emotion it seemed threatening. He was unpacking just a few things from his valise, and he had deposited his straight razor and strop on the bureau, while Jethro stared at them, then handled the razor briefly (Rick used only a "safety" and hardly needed that very often as yet). Jethro studied his father's heavy beard, which Elvira had neglected to mention, though she had dwelt often on his father's "beautiful complexion," which she said was wasted on a man.

"Say, where the heck's the toilet, Jeth?" Wilders wanted to know after a sheepish look about. "Need to take a leak after catching all those fish, you know . . ."

Jethro pointed to a glass-enclosed door, saw his father go in, and began to follow him, but Wilders partly closed the door, and Jethro waited patiently on the threshold like a black servant who will give the person relieving himself a napkin to dry his hands on afterwards.

"I brought you a little something," the father said, going through his valise with one hand, while combing his hair with a broken pocket comb in the other.

He found something in the bottom of the bag, and handed the boy an object wrapped in tin foil.

Opening it, Jethro cried out in pleasure and amazement. It was a beautiful jackknife with a beast's tooth attached to it.

Wilders was engaged in showing him how to open and close it when he just caught sight of the boy's neck, the large jagged scar of broken flesh showing pink and white. Paling a bit, he could not resist touching Jethro gently on the place.

"Do you have to touch it?" the boy said in a cross tone. He moved away.

"Does it ever bother you now?" Wilders wondered looking out the window which looked down on the line of flowering catalpas.

Some fat angry white tears slid down Jethro's cheek, which he hastened to brush away with his fist.

"I been gone a long spell," Wilders mumbled, still at the window.

"You know something, Daddy?" Jethro piped up now, going over to his father and taking him by the hand. "You should give me a penny straightway."

"On account of I gave you something sharp for a present?" Wilders chuckled and his whole face now broke into a wide grin.

Jethro nodded, laughing softly.

Sitting down in a cane rocker, Wilders motioned for the boy to draw near, and his face grew all upon a sudden very serious and old-looking in contrast to the way it had looked when he laughed, and he put his arm around the boy's shoulder.

"Don't breathe this to a soul, Jeth, but your daddy is completely broke." His voice got lower and lower. "I don't know how it happened. You know before you were born, your daddy was quite a fellow."

When Jethro lowered his head, looking down at the fine old ingrain carpet on which their feet rested, Wilders seemed to catch himself and patted the boy on the back, saying, "But it's only temporary, you see, and I'll be back on my feet and make you proud of me . . ."

"Daddy, let me go downstairs and get a penny from Rory and I'll give it to you and then you give it back to me. That will prevent the knife from separating us from one another . . ."

Wilders stared at his boy gravely, then grinned and nodded his approval. Jethro hurried down the backstairs to get the penny.

At supper, Wilders was seated at the head of the table, perhaps an ironic gesture on the part of Elvira, he supposed, or maybe only because she could not in the end think of any better place for him. During the blessing offered by Elvira, Jethro slipped from his seat and handed Rory's penny to his father, who pocketed it, smiling broadly, and not keeping his eyes closed during Elvira's prayer, which he found too sugary and in questionable taste, her words to him resembling a telephone conversation concerning an order of dry-goods. While she droned on about thanks for God's providing the necessities, he continued to glance about him. He recognized nothing, and he would have felt more comfortable, he mused, had his wife seated him next to Rory and Jethro, for he was disinclined after his welcome home to preside over the table at all, for he knew he had not the slightest authority over a single person who put his feet under its groaning board. It seemed at moments he must be still in Norfolk, sleeping late on a Sunday, and all about him was dismal and unreal. He had caught a glimpse, too, of the "first" table, and had been put out by its hilarity and vulgarity, for there sat people whom he would not have so much as spoken to on the street, in his best days, let alone shake their hands, and yet there they sat, under his wife's roof, guffawing, jawing, with all the unrestrained unconcerned freedom of fun-seekers at a county fair. And his own Elvira in charge of it all, and seeming to enjoy it, she who had come from a good family, from "good stock," as old Mr. Summerlad had boasted, tracing his own ancestors back to well before the Revolution, well, what would he think now seeing his daughter managing what could hardly be called better than a disorderly house.

Just as the "second" table was getting under way, after the saying of grace, Matt Lacey came boldly into the dining room, caught sight of Mr. Fergus and, nothing abashed, went up to take his hand. Elvira immediately invited him to sit down and dine with them. Matt's coming was welcomed by everybody, perhaps most of all by Wilders, who remembered him as a boy, and managed despite the general awkwardness of the situation, to ply him with a few questions about his navy career. Talk then drifted dispiritedly to other subjects, for Wilders's return had checked and dampered all the usual "fun" and gaiety of the table. Rick discussed some movies he had seen lately, a Broadway play, a new novel by a mad Southern writer, and then there was general gossip about Boutflour, but the people discussed were as unknown to Wilders as the names of the motion pictures, play, and book mentioned.

While the others ate heartily of the fish he had caught, and all complimented Elvira on her culinary art, he could barely bring himself to touch knife and fork to his plate. As a matter of fact Wilders disliked fish. Somehow it always reminded him of Lent or of Catholicism, which his Presbyterian upbringing had soured him against. At any rate it was not the kind of victuals which tempted him. Hardly tasting a mouthful he listened inattentively to the frivolous talk about him, feeling himself as much an intruder as if he was a tramp received by them from the back porch. And to his ever-growing amazement now, studying his oldest son's face, he saw there was almost nothing about Rick to remind him of the young tow-headed boy of ten years ago. Not only his face and gestures and general bearing had changed, but his speech also, which was now a mixture of British and dramatic school accent, occasionally lapsing into midwestern drawl.

Excusing himself finally, he rose and went out the back door and sat down on the steps beyond which the lattice-work of the porch was casting queer shadows on the freshly mowed grass. A robin sang in a throaty evensong. A horse-drawn vegetable truck labored over a hill leading out of town. Some cicadas gave a few last drones in a beech tree. He had about decided to get up and take a walk in the direction of the river when he felt a small hand on his shoulder. It was Rory and beside him was Jethro. They seemed curious about this stranger who was their father and also pleased to be in his company. The warmth and friendliness of the two little men, as he called them, came as a sudden comfort after the stupefying events of the day. He took Rory on his knee and soon they were all three chattering and laughing.

In the back kitchen, however, he at last became aware of the sound of dishes being scraped, preparatory for washing. He got up with alacrity, went to the screen door and inquired of Elvira if he could not help her. It had been one of the tasks he always volunteered for when they were first married, and later over the huge sink of many a rented house, while the landlord had threatened and bills collected in the parlor spinet desk, he and Elvira had talked over their prospects and their uncertain future, while she washed and he dried the dishes.

"Vickie always helps me now, Wilders, she's fast and thorough, and knows where all the plates and silverware go . . . Thank you just the same, though."

Hardly waiting for Elvira to finish speaking, he came back to the steps and resumed his horseplay with the little men. But soon, their unflagging vigor and shrill little voices fatigued him, and he irritably asked them to leave off. Frightened at his sudden gruffness, they wandered off into the silky summer darkness. The old elm near the woodshed moved in a fresh rising breeze. Wilders heard horse hooves again. Many of the citizenry of Boutflour were still too poor to own a car. Times were bad everywhere, he muttered aloud, a phrase which, like a prayer, comforted him as many times as he repeated it, and checked a mite his heartsick sense of failure. He looked at the people passing in a horse-drawn cart. They had never been anybody much, he supposed, and so they could take it. Me, I can't very well, he spoke still aloud to himself.

Then he heard a woman's high heels coming close to him. He thought it was Vickie, for he did not associate Elvira with high heels, but then his wife's voice came to him, clear, cold, and smarting as the blow from a knout: "I'm going up town, Wilders, and if you want anything, ask one of the boys to help you . . . Well, I hope you sleep well . . ."

She was gone. And this was a homecoming! Bending his head down until his thick hair fell below his knees, he felt hot tingling sensations under his eyes as if tears of lead were coursing down his cheeks.

Bringing his head up like a swimmer coming from a deep dive, he spoke again out loud to himself. When you come too late, everything's over and put away.

But some of his old fight came faintly back to him. He would lift himself by his bootstraps, he promised, anything to keep his boys. He had forgotten till tonight the feel of being the father of boys. He would not let Elvira have them, damn her.

Jethro had wandered back to his father's side, and Wilders grabbed him by the hand in mock ferocity, brought him up to his chest, petting him briefly, absent-mindedly, then asked, while his fingers studiously avoided touching the scar on his neck, "Where does your mother go, do you reckon, Jeth?"

"She has lots of places she goes," Jethro replied after a thoughtful pause, "but tonight I believe she goes to see our music teacher, Agnes Coles." He studied the changing expression on his father's face.

"Well, I know *her* of course," Wilders said, and Jethro giggled nervously. "Didn't know, however, that your mother palled around with her. Is that something new?"

"Not 'specially," Jethro replied, and he looked worried under these questionings.

Wilders withdrew again into his own thoughts. He had heard from as far back as their first days in Boutflour certain things about Agnes Coles. He had put down most of them to gossip and the fact that as an unmarried woman who had to give music lessons she was frequently on the street, in and out of many homes and public places, and an easy mark for talk. But there were other things not so easily dismissed, the rumor she had an illegitimate son in New York, and worse suspicion. Yes, whatever the truth about Agnes Coles, Elvira had sunk considerable. The boarding house, he now saw with sickening revulsion, must allow all kind of unpleasant if not disgraceful things to go on under its roof, and in any case it was not a fit environment for young boys. Yet what could he say in criticism? He had hardly sent them enough to keep the gas and lights on. And the thought briefly crossed his mind of the ruin he had brought on Elvira's people.

"Well, see who's here!" Wilders spoke up in sudden merry greeting as he saw little Rory approaching him. "Shall we go for a spin in the old jalopy?" he inquired of the small boy. Both Jethro and Rory danced for joy at the invitation. They hardly ever went driving, and they were more than ready.

Wilders put his straw hat down beside a bed of straggling buttercups and nasturtiums, and without rolling up his sleeves began cranking the car hard, which did not respond for some minutes. Finally the engine gave out quick great gasps, at irregular intervals, and while it was still doing so, he jumped into the front seat beside Rory and Jethro, and they were off, the two boys breaking into song. They crossed over the old Locust Street bridge at a wild pace, and were on their way toward open country when the car showed signs of trouble, making ominous sounds as if it were about to explode.

Wilders cursed, then letting up on the speed, said, "By God, boys, we're nearly out of gas, can you beat that?" He gave out a string of fancy swear words, then turning to Jethro said, "I left that brand-new hat of mine back there in the flower bed . . ."

"There's a gas station about a mile that way, Daddy," Jethro pointed to where the sky was still aflame with sunset. "Near Three Forks, you remember?"

"Don't know if I can make this tin contraption get us that far or not . . ."

Just as they squeaked into the gas station, Wilders said in the tones of a man condemned to death, "By God, I've come away without a damned red cent in my pants pocket."

Jethro put his hand in his knickers and then held out in the palm of his hand some nickels and dimes and pennies. "Will this buy anything, Daddy?"

"It might at that." Wilders counted the change now into his own hand.

Yelling at the station attendant, Wilders inquired, "Will you put in a gallon of gas there?"

The attendant looked into the interior of the car at the occupants, sniffed, grumbled something, and then with slow shuffling deliberateness went to the gas pump, mumbling all the while, hosed out the gallon, and then returning took from Wilders's palm the accumulation of Jethro's "chickenfeed," and counted it out with slow suspicious thoroughness.

"Now for a spin around old Sunshine River, fellows," Wilders raised his voice in mock cheerfulness, for to tell the truth, having got the gas, he did feel a bit more chipper, and he pretended not to notice the sorrowful glum silence his two boys had fallen into.

After a long cessation of talk between them, during which Wilders hummed some old ballad whose half-pronounced words escaped the boys, Rory spoke up with a chirping querulous "You just brought the fish, then, Daddy, nothing more?"

Wilders laughed uproariously, and nearly hit a tree as he turned a sharp bend. He slowed the car, then stopped to laugh some more, letting his head drop over on the steering wheel. In a little while the two little men chimed in. "Just brought the fish!" Wilders quoted Rory, guffawing. "I declare, you Irishman, you," Wilders slapped Rory gently on the back, and pressed him to him. "You take the cake."

The summer night came suddenly black and redolent of the smell of sweet clover, and a short distance beyond them from a clump of woods they could hear bullfrogs, and the rustle of some small animal in the brush, a cry from a nightjar. Wilders turned about in a small clearing beyond the trees, and headed back for Elvira's. He began now to drive at a snail's pace, fearful lest the car would drink up the last of their gas leaving them stranded, and he sank into silent heavy-weighted thought. He was aroused all upon a sudden by the loud cacophony of clattering, as the car began to show signs of trouble again, as if this time it would expire and come to pieces on the gravel road.

"Sounds like some damned corn-shredding machine," Wilders mumbled.

After countless halting and starting, all the while the old jalopy gave out great cries of ghastly resonance which awakened all the dogs for miles around, they arrived back at last. Wilders parked the car alongside some shiny new autos belonging to the boarders, the three alighted, and then stood huddling together for a moment in the dark, looking up at the boarding house whose every window was aglow. Some jazz music came dreamily from the red parlor.

"The old can didn't leave us in the woods, anyhow, boys," Wilders opined, but he did not advance with Rory and Jethro up the flagstones, as if he had second thoughts about going in.

Putting a hand on each of the kids at last, he followed them up to the kitchen door to say, "Well, anyhow tomorrow's another day."

Turning to face his father at the entrance, Jethro now spoke up.

"Rick's most a millionaire now, Daddy."

"Yes," little Rory corroborated Jethro's statement, "Aunt Libby left him a goodly amount of money."

"I'll be switched," Wilders whistled. "Aunt Libby, you say. When did she die?"

*   *   *

"What do you aim to do with your fortune?" Wilders at last put the question to Rick the day after his arrival from the South. The two were seated in Elvira's back yard which adjoined the estate of Rogers Thwaite, one of the richest men in that part of the country, whose seldom-used mansion and acres of rolling greensward stretched before them now so that even the size of the boarding house and its ample lawn and gardens resembled that of a cottage on a modest plot of ground.

Wilders studied his son's face in brief surreptitious glances trying to find in the youth's almost too handsome features something of the young boy he had known in Hittisleigh and in the early Boutflour years. Only the shock of corn-colored hair and the flashing blue eyes with the unnaturally large pupils were the same. Rick had apparently relined his eyebrows for "work in the theater," and his face had a tightened look as if he had used too often actor's makeup. His voice had become, if anything, even deeper than his father's, but unlike Wilders he pronounced his words in staccato fashion, lacking the drawl and cadence common to the Ferguses and to Elvira's people, and this mannerism also Wilders put down to the boy's stage training.

Wilders sighed when there was no answer forthcoming, and he lazily watched a yellowhammer exploring the bark of a maple tree.

"Ain't spent it already, have you?" Wilders pursued the topic.

"Well, hardly, Daddy, I own I'm not that big a fool," Rick smiled at what he considered his father's naïveté and his complete lack of knowledge of him, but all the same he had begun to melt appreciably from contact with Wilders.

Something of Rick's old cockiness was gone, his tyrannical stance with his younger brothers had softened a bit, and his onerous duty to Elvira as her mainstay and head of the house weighed a bit less on him.

"As a matter of fact, I thought to try to get into the movies," Rick felt his ground, his face flushed, his eyes on his rock garden, where purple trillium, rose mallow and yellow lady's-slipper were in flower.

"You don't say so!" Wilders got out, after a lengthy pause of pained incredulity.

Wilders Fergus had no religious beliefs of any kind, had never been a regular churchgoer, and did not share Grandma Fergus's Presbyterian horror of the stage and screen, but he had his own private abhorrence of the acting profession, especially for a son of his. But his long absence, his own "ruin," his having ruined others, all this had stripped him of even a shred of pretense at authority over anybody else. He could only half-hint now where before he had been able to thunder.

But he could not resist his old calling: "If you could loan me that money you've inherited for just a week or so. A month at the most," Wilders leaped in on the thing closest to his heart, speculation, a passion so strong in him that he could even overcome the humiliation of asking such a favor of his own boy. "If you could trust it to me, Rickie, I could make us all a tidy fortune again . . . We'd be on easy street, don't you see? . . . And it couldn't be safer than with your own dad . . ."

Rick withdrew into himself at hearing such a proposal, and a giddy sense of incalculable danger overtook him, as if he had wakened on shipboard, his head downhanging into the bottomless green of ocean.

"What do you say, Rick?" he put his arm around his son.

"Excuse me, but you were never very long on luck before, I'm afraid, Daddy," Rick finally blurted out.

Stung by this reproach, although it had been spoken almost tenderly, Wilders still found strength to go on. "That was then, Rickie, before you can remember well. This is a different set of circumstances, a different age, and your father's older," he chuckled, "and a damned sight smarter. I wouldn't make the same mistakes over again, believe you me, or the sky ain't up there over our heads. . . .

"Mother has told me something of how you took all of her mother's fortune, Daddy, and then lost it, and I'd hate to see mine go the same way."

"But you'd like to see it doubled, wouldn't you?" he pressed home.

Rick's hands dropped to his sides.

"You don't oppose my trying to go into the theater then?" he said, somewhat sourly.

"Did I say I did?" Wilders was honey-sweet, evasive.

"You looked it, Daddy," Rick retorted.

"Oh, well, hell, then I looked it," Wilders spat to one side. "Fact is, you have changed, though, Rick," he confided, gently, "from when you was little, you know . . . I don't hold you responsible for it, why should I? . . . But was I ever surprised to see how things are here," his voice shook, and he struggled to control himself. "The boarding house and all, Rick. Jesus Christ and John Jacob Astor! It's no place to bring up a family . . . God sakes, Rick, look at me, and say you agree!"

Somehow Rick's long-standing anger against his father, rekindled daily through the years by Elvira, had begun to dissipate in the presence of the man himself. The son felt almost a certain warm relaxation—that would have seemed almost sinful in Elvira's eyes—in his just sitting here with the one who was, after all, his father. He would never have another, he knew, and whatever Wilders may have done in the past, he had at long last come home to him.

"Why don't you change your mind and choose a different profession, Rick? Have heard all kinds of good things about you, son. You got talent, a wagonload of it. Stage or screen's no career for a fine clean-cut young fellow. Let the monkeys go into it. It won't do for you for the long haul."

"I love acting and singing, and all that goes with the stage," Rick spoke softly but with firm decisiveness. He had refrained from mentioning dancing lest it kindle his father's wrath.

"Well, I won't urge you to loan me the money you've inherited, Rick," Wilders came back to his son's coming into a fortune. "But if you are ever of a different mind, and wish to let me have it, remember 'twould help all of us toward a better future . . ."

At the mention of a future, Rick thought of Elvira's fixed and unshakable resolve to divorce Wilders. Elvira had come into Rick's room the night of Wilders's homecoming, and in her kid-curlers with smears of white vanishing cream about her face she had looked so fierce and implacable, he had the passing notion he did not know her. She had raised her voice again and again with the words: "I won't live with him, Rick darling. I don't love him anymore, can't stand him to touch me, and he hasn't supported us for over six years. In his few visits back over the last ten years, his only contribution was to get me in the family way, with Rory, and with the others who didn't live, thank God, to be born. . . . We don't need him now, Rick. I want my freedom, and I want you boys to be free of him."

But Rick had been cool to her about the divorce. Having seen his father, perhaps, he mused, for the first time in his life, for he had been a kind of shadow before, Rick was somehow, if not on his father's side, not on his mother's side wholeheartedly either. Elvira had seen this, and become strident. Rick had kissed her good night as a way of stopping further argument and strife, taking on some of her vanishing cream by accident and wiping it off immediately she was gone on his pajama sleeve. Suddenly he felt he had no parents. He must try to get into the movies, at least the stage. The men from the antique shop had promised to help him, and with his fortune to back him up he could leave Boutflour and its terrible memories of humiliation and ostracism, and make something of himself. The words of Bob O'Fallon, the young man who had been in the films, came to him now: "With your looks and talent, kid, you can write your own ticket, stage, screen, night clubs, whatever you want. And you are marble, living marble for good looks. They will be crying for you, Rick . . ."

Neither Wilders nor Elvira wanted him to go into the films, he knew. Without telling Elvira, he had gone to New York and had a screen test a short while ago, and had passed. When he had told Elvira, she had put her foot down.

The next afternoon after his talk with his father, Elvira had asked Rick to step into her sewing room. He had just shaved, and was doctoring his cuts, and his hair was recently marcelled, so that Elvira faintly gasped at the "beauty" of his "set," as she put it. But his jaw set as his mother talked. He knew her too well not to realize that she had summoned him to give him bad news.

Nonetheless, he was unprepared for her almost complete about-face, as he heard her say: "I've had a long talk with your father. He needs help of course, and I've had a long sleepless night thinking over all our situations . . . It seems to me it might make things easier for all of us if you lent him the money. Now don't jump down my throat, Rick, and mind you I'm not saying you have to give him the loan. He has a lot of prospects, he said. He sounded convincing, Rick. I don't know quite what to advise, to tell the truth . . ."

"Have you taken leave of your senses, Elvira?" Rick rose now, his anger making him turn a pallor which struck terror into his mother's heart. "Don't you remember your divorce which you've planned so long, and are you going to give my money to a man whom you are planning to drive from the house, drive from his sons!"

"Oh, you don't understand at all, and have only half-listened, Rick," she turned from him, fumbling now in her sewing machine drawer for anything which might come to her hand. "I never said I absolutely intended to divorce him, and as to the money of your inheritance being given to him, it was only a suggestion, nothing more . . . It would be our final way of letting him see if he could prove himself, get back his old position . . . Oh, you see, how persuasive he's been with me, I've been a fool . . ."

"I hope he hasn't persuaded you to go to bed with him, and give you another son to bring into this hell you call life!" he shouted at her.

Elvira's hand closed the little drawer of the sewing machine, and there was a silence between the two so awesome both wondered if they would ever be able to break it again, would ever be able to say one word to another as long as either of them lived.

"You can rest easy on that score," Elvira's voice was unrecognizable and as far away as the tomb, "for that is one divorce that is final now and will ever be, Rick . . ."

"Why should I give up my inheritance?" he began to thunder again, oblivious for the moment of how deeply he had wounded his mother. "Can you answer me that, or can't you? Why should I ruin myself for you two?"

"You want to go into the movies, or on the stage, I know," Elvira was somehow gaining control of herself, how she did not know. "But I feel you're too young, Rick . . . You're so inexperienced, hardly more than a child. You know so little of the world."

"So little of the world!" he shouted. Suddenly he began weeping, and then stepping into the side room, he found a druggist's bottle of witch hazel, and began patting some of this on his face, as if he wished to erase any traces of recent emotion.

"If you can give me one valid reason why I should give that deserter any part of my future, tell me, and I'll throw the whole inheritance at your feet."

Elvira walked over to her grandmother's white wicker rocking chair and sat, or rather, collapsed into it, and once seated did not move to rock it, but looked like she had been pinned to the delicate strands of wicker.

Rick paced up and down the room, drying and patting his face, and loudly, between a steady stream of profanity, shouting, "I won't give up my inheritance, you can all burn in hell before I do."

"You'd be loaning it, precious, not giving it away. He

claims he has a wonderful way of doubling or tripling it in a short time. You'd get it all back."

"When did you know Wilders Fergus to fulfill a promise?"

"After all," she said like a woman in a deep trance, "he is your father, isn't he?"

A cry of almost insane triumph broke from Rick's lips. "Oh, after all the years of never giving him the benefit of a single doubt, blackening his every fiber of being, belittling his every move and motive, you're for him! You've lost your wits, sweet old girl!"

"Oh, Rick, for God's sake, do you have to talk to me like this, when my heart is so overburdened, I wonder if my next breath will be my last. Don't you see I don't know what to do, that I've never known what to do, that I've stumbled and blundered from the first, but I've always tried to do only what's best for you, because you're my whole world."

"I'll be damned if I give away Aunt Libby's money to him," he went on in maniacal concentration on this issue. "What proof have I he'll repay even the interest on such a sum. You're both trying to stand in the way of my career, that's what. And what career have I got here, in this one-horse town, living in a cheap fun house with a person like you! Answer me that!"

Had he struck her, she would have felt it less, and when the last sounds of his voice died away, she fell back in the rocking chair and it rocked once with her. She rose then and walked to the door.

"Elvira," he called her.

"No, no, you're right, Rick," she told him, her back still to him, "you keep the money. Invest it in yourself, and make your way, make something of yourself. I know you're not happy here, and I know I've failed you. You'll have to forgive me . . . I don't know what got into me to think that I would ask you to give him your money." She turned and faced him now. She was not weeping, but the horror of seeing the look on her face struck him dumb. "And after all the damage Wilders Fergus has done me, how could I ask such a sacrifice of you. For had Wilders not come into *my* life, I'd be a wealthy woman today, and so would my mother."

She was too angry for tears, for reconciliation, for love. At that moment she only wanted to return to the Elvira Summerlad of Hittisleigh whom no man, no son had ever insulted.

Rick heard her steps going down the back stairs.

He felt desperately sick. His love for Elvira at that moment was so blinding in its intensity, he sat down in the same rocking chair she had vacated and burst into uncontrolled sobbing. He didn't know what he wanted to do. He wanted of course a career in the theater, but he felt so weak suddenly, so frightened of life, so unable to go on without Elvira . . .

Then without warning, as if a hand had written directions for him in the palm of his own hand, he knew what his terrible decision was. He would give his father the money. A hysterical urge rose up in him to give it away. What would Bob O'Fallon say when he drove into the city the next day, and he told him what he had done with his inheritance?

Still, he would think it over that night, sleep on it.

Everything around him was spinning.

When Jethro peeked in the room on him, all his fury came down on the boy's head.

"What in the God-damned world are you doing home?" he shouted. "You broken-headed little puke!"

"Why, hear the star of the silver screen talk, would you!" Jethro spat out the words, and made a face.

* * *

Jethro noted a "strange conspiracy" now in his journal, the sudden whisperings, meetings, and exchanged confidence of the two mortal enemies, Wilders and Elvira, though perhaps Wilders did not know he was the mortal enemy of his wife. Elvira knew it, however, and her sudden intimacy was, whether she clearly understood it or not, only her desperate wish to let Wilders, let anybody save Rick for her. No, intimacy with Wilders would not include this time inviting him to her bed, that was forever over, both in view of her indifference to his body now, though that body was in many ways, she saw dimly, more appetizing than before, and to her almost demented fear of giving him yet another son, for no matter what method or trick was used as he lay astride her, always always he gave her another baby, and she vowed now even as she talked with him he would never give her another son and then decamp, better let all of them perish than have another mouth to feed, another ruined son brought into the world.

In July the foliage had reached perfection, trees, flowers were giving out a heady fragrance, even in such a town and such a vicinity as Boutflour, nature herself was lavish. They walked beside the peony beds, still in late flowering, passed by the four-o'clocks, the nasturtiums, summer roses in profusion, tiger lilies, and wall after wall of morning glories. They walked up and down like statesmen deciding the destiny of whole peoples. Elvira did most of the talking, and Wilders so much taller than she (occasionally she looked up at him as if to memorize again his extreme height), Wilders bowed his head, listening incredulous. How little he knew of human nature, she reflected. And perhaps, who knows, he knew as little of banking or anything else. He knew certainly so little of human motives, for he didn't know men, and hadn't a ghost of a notion what a woman was—like most men. He only knew where to put his peter, she reflected, everything else about her had escaped him. He was a stranger picked out of a whole county of strangers, for her.

Jethro went on listening to them behind the summer house.

"Something terrible has happened to Rick," the wind carried her soft voice to the son. "He's found the wrong kind of companion, to put it simply, and with all his promise, Wilders, his head is turned to spoil that promise. His good looks and his obvious talent . . ."

She had turned her face away so that the next words escaped Jethro, but it did not matter, he knew her whole speech by heart. He grinned, for he knew more than Elvira, for how many times he had crept into the "red parlor," that sanctuary of forbidden dreams, and forgotten sins, where behind the red beveled glass of the immense oak bookcase lay the packet of letters from Rick's various lovers, men and women, and on that heady fare Jethro had feasted for some years. The letters were sometimes too much for him, for even though he was more advanced perhaps (Elvira's version of it all here) than other boys, and though his body, actually robust, could take much punishment, he did not have robust nerves. What he had seen of life had been, he wrote in his journal, too strong for him to absorb, it haunted him by day and night, and the night and day were indistinguishable so far as his memory went, and the visions were continuous by daylight or dark.

"Something terrible has happened to him," he heard Elvira's voice coming to him over a box hedge.

He would have corrected her statement to this: not something terrible had happened to Rick, something terrible was inside Rick. Rick made everything happen, Jethro felt.

And now, he smiled, the two arch-enemies, Wilders and Elvira, were laying their heads together.

He heard more.

"If you can promise us, Wilders, you will make this money 'do' this time," the mother's voice came more distant now, as if she and his father were floating in the clouds rising from the summer horizon, "really, you understand, make it do . . . It would be a crime if you robbed the boy of his inheritance."

Lying back in the sweet fresh grass, sticking a piece of a daisy in his mouth, Jethro mimicked his mother, then added in his own wickedest tones, "Old Rick had that robbed a long time ago of him."

He hated Rick, he thought. Rick had always pushed him out of the way, tormented, teased him, made him conscious of his physical deformity, his short time in life, had made him feel he had been born with the scars from the iron teeth of the fence.

"You'll die young," Rick had once told Jethro when he came upon a poem which Jethro had written and had admired the verse before he knew it was Jethro's, then having learned its authorship, had dismissed it as shit.

"Let us strike a bargain," Elvira's voice came now very close, so that Jethro crawled quickly over the grass to behind an elm tree.

A full pink moon was rising now over the lilac bushes, and lest he be discovered Jethro scurried through the bushes toward the back porch, bound for his room.

"I thought I heard footsteps," Wilders's voice came to him, and he smiled. He could not hear Elvira's reply, but he assumed she had, as usual, told him some lie, that he had only heard a chimney swift brushing its wings against the eaves.

Passing by the red parlor, which was now deserted, Jethro deftly opened a little cupboard beneath the red beveled glass with a key he had had made from the original, and snatched up a packet of letters addressed to Rick.

Safe in his room, he untied the bundle of letters, and then opened his own journal which he kept in a more secure hiding place than Rick kept his letters. In this journal, instead of recording merely what happened to him, his exacerbations, humiliation, the biting pain of his injuries, his headaches, he recorded also nearly everything that happened to Rick and Elvira, the "lovers," as he called them, "all wrapped up in themselves, plotting against the rest of the world," which included him.

Elvira for all her possessiveness of Rick had never thought to look behind the expensive glass of the bookcase, custom-made, with secret shelves, secret partitions, and open one of the messages lying locked within, penned on thick rich linen paper, drenched with patchouli. Elvira didn't know her own son, Jethro smiled beatifically, no, amend that to her own sons. No, sirree. Jethro laughed then his wild chilling Indian way, and wrote down a paragraph or so in his journal. Then rising hurriedly he went to the high-domed window and looking down he saw Elvira and Wilders parting company, like two people who barely knew one another, conspirators of brief almost nonexistent previous acquaintance, who had met at a lonesome tree to plot their next move as their part in a secret organization. Jethro laughed.

Turning to Rick's correspondence now, he reviewed Rick's own secret life which only the packet of letters behind the beautiful red glass of the bookcase revealed. The "little society" had taken Rick up scarcely two years before, and was composed of brilliant failed "artists," antique owners, an heir or heiress or two, all refugees or exiles from New York or Paris, where they had met failure in different ways, or disillusionment, or shame, and had come "home," beaten, to bewail for the rest of their life their loss and exile, and whine and chide over the meanness of small-town life, express their horror of the "natives," indeed of America, and under great chandeliers and velvet ceilings hold readings of classic plays, or turn on the Victrola for the hearing of some rare recording. Sometimes a renowned pianist or harpsichordist was persuaded to come and give a special concert. The leader of the group in exile was Dr. Gray, a benevolent and successful physician, who had buried himself in a nearby hamlet, for obscure reasons, and who, it was said, had "starved" himself going through Harvard medical school, and for years supported an arthritic mother, who had lingered on until he himself was entering old age. He remained on in the hamlet where he was the only physician, to the puzzlement of his colleagues and his close friends. All of the "little society" had some connection, often quite respectable, with the outside world of commerce and householders, but they only came to life and self-realization when in the midst of their own group. Rick was now the idol and the hope of all these disappointed exiles. He was to be sent to New York at their behest, he was to become a great actor, he was to fulfill all their hopes.

The queen of the group was an elderly woman with alabaster skin, blind in one eye, but strangely beautiful despite or because of this impairment, with a pile of wonderful white hair which looked like a wreath placed on her by an eminent authority, exquisite hands which were free of rings or bracelets, but whose eloquent movements seemed to chronicle forever the "mistake" of her own life which had given her existence meaning, her affair with a married man of national renown. What had become of her child, reputed to be a son, nobody knew, but although her "mistake" had occurred at the end of the nineteenth century, she somehow continued to live in it and through it, without ever quite mentioning it to her closest friend. She was the scarlet woman of Boutflour, and its only woman intellectual. Some thirty years after the event, one saw in her gestures and in her brilliant "good" eye, in her mobile lips the ceaseless re-enactment of the only time life had touched her with implacable, furious force. She suffered more today, one suspected, than when she was a social outcast. Nearly everybody had died who knew her as a sinner, and the age in which she now found herself scarcely recognized sin, unless it was homosexuality, and since she was forever attracted to the forbidden or perhaps because this was all that was left for her, she was a constant companion to Dr. Gray and his "little society," Dr. Gray who, surrounded by youth (his great home resembled, his neighbors felt, a young men's academy), chose her as his sole confidante, with the curious concomitant phenomenon that neither he nor she ever divulged to the other any secrets. Their secrets were divined, and their confidence was silent. She loved Dr. Gray hopelessly, faithfully, and he required her company and her love which he could not return by so much as the pressure of a hand or a kiss on the brow. Dr. Gray, at the time Rick was coming into his own, had a slightly ambiguous, if not distasteful, reputation. The finest obstetrician for miles around, a wonderful "drug" man, meaning various things to various people, he was respected professionally, and loved by his patients, for the most part simple villagers and farmers, but the strangeness of his tastes, his passion for literature and the arts, and his being visited at all hours by young men in need of immediate medication, created a kind of distance between him and the village folk, a gulf which would have destroyed the practice and the reputation of a lesser man. He had served his patients so well and so long that though they grumbled more and more at his eccentricities, they resolved to bear with them, and even defended him against outsiders who came bearing tales. Dr. Gray had been a fellow classmate of Dr. Stoke, who had set Elvira up in the boarding house business (Jethro complained bitterly when he heard his mother use this detestable word).

Dr. Gray, though blinded by Rick's handsomeness and charm and flamboyant personality, felt, Jethro knew, that in the boy with the broken neck there lurked some strange disturbing and sure to flower talent, and once to the Doctor's astonishment he had shoved some pages of his journal under the elderly man's nose. He had read for a moment avidly, and then grasping Jethro's shoulder, had said, "Eveything wonderful is waiting here . . ."

Rick's visits to the Doctor in his palatial home in the country became more frequent, but were somehow at last accepted by Elvira as the price she must pay if she were to keep Rick with her at all. But she felt all the while, nonetheless, despite her own personal liking for Dr. Gray, that some strange kind of wickedness existed in "The Rookery," the name the Doctor gave to his estate, but she was powerless now to do anything about it.

"Except," as Jethro noted down in green ink, "give away her first-born's inheritance."

* * *

The next day a terrible conclave took place in the mammoth dining room, whose many doors were closed and locked against all but Elvira, Wilders, and Rick, who sat chairs apart, all white-lipped and drawn.

Before the final assent came, Elvira wandered briefly afield to take up the case of Jethro, who, she said, was going downhill, failing in all his academic subjects, reading unsavory French and Russian novels (she did not mention that he obtained these as gifts from Dr. Gray), smoking cigars, and perhaps worse, and frequenting the shanty town where Mexican beet-workers and migrant Negroes lived.

"You don't say," Wilders sighed, then returned to Rick's money.

Perhaps none of the three realized what it was each was doing.

"Where are you going, Wilders, when the money is given you?" Elvira's voice now rose mournful from the center of the table, so that one realized that all but the actual handing over to Wilders of the money was at an end.

He cleared his throat, and cocked his head to one side, the latter a mannerism which had always irritated her, even during their courtship.

He was going first to his mother's, he supposed, for the "deal" he had in mind, owing to the fact the financiers were in that vicinity.

"You mean to Winifred's," Elvira could not resist a gibe at his sister.

"Well, Winifred will probably be there, you know, as it's summer and her school in Boston is not in session . . ."

Suddenly Rick in a last hysterical attempt to assert himself, began to shout and yell, said he would not give up his money, but then sobbing and weeping, while Elvira patted his head which rested on the spotless thick tablecloth, said at last, "Take it, Daddy, it's yours, I don't want it, I never wanted it, but leave me in peace then both of you . . . Never question me, and never exert any rule over me. I've given you this, and let me be free . . ."

Reaching into his breast pocket, Rick produced a cashier's check which his mother had already helped him draw up in the bank. Then Rick rushed from the room, slamming the door behind him.

Meeting Jethro on the gravel path leading down to the river, Rick did a thing which he told Uncle Matt he regretted the rest of his life. He went up to Jethro and struck him full in the face.

"You've been reading my private correspondence, you dirty little sneak!"

The imprint of the older boy's hand lay across Jethro's face like a message he would bear on his features for life.

Then Rick disappeared for nearly a week, while Elvira wept as she did the dishes in the kitchen sink, or tidied the beds after the roomers, or sat alone in her drawing room, staring out the window into the flowering catalpas.

Happy as a prince, with some real money in his pocket, Wilders had gone home to his mother and sister, there to plan strategy to make them all a fortune, mend all fences, and become again head of his household, ruler of the roost, the old prosperous Wilders of Hittisleigh.

* * *

The rashness, the folly, the incomprehensibility of her act slowly struck home to Elvira. Only madness could explain it now, the madness she had accused herself of once before, when she had married him. But this new act of folly went against everything she believed and felt—to give away the inheritance of Rick to his father. It had been the boy's only chance in life.

She thought grimly of killing herself, but she could not fail her sons by such another act of irresponsibility, yet how kind and merciful death seemed at that moment.

But the complete realization of what she had done came, when after two, three weeks of nothing but silence, Wilders had telephoned her from Chicago. A long-distance call in that era, and especially for "ruined" persons like the Ferguses, could only mean unparalleled disaster. The moment Elvira heard the long-distance operator inquiring if she was Mrs. Fergus, she knew in the inmost reaches of her heart what the message which was coming would be, because not even for death would he have telephoned her, he would have written to inform her of death.

"I hope to recover a good deal of it nonetheless," he said in his idiotic cheerful tone, and she almost forgot what his first statement had been, the statement that all the money had been lost.

Indeed Elvira did not remember hanging up the receiver any more than a suicide recalls the sound of the gun that has killed him.

She went out into the summery back yard where she had been hanging up a heavy wash at the time of the phone's ringing, for Elvira insisted on doing most of her own laundry, the rest she sent to an old German woman with pierced ears who lived down the road. Today she welcomed the heavy task of taking in her sheets from the line, holding the clothespins in her mouth so that, she felt, she would not tear her own flesh with her teeth, but the intensity of her grief was so annihilating that she had to go back to the protection of the house itself, and sit on the steps by the latticed porch where, for a fact, Wilders had first begged her to get Rick to lend him the money.

"I've mortgaged the boy's future, and now I've ruined the one chance he may have had. How can I tell him?"

She was aware then of Jethro standing by the big elm tree, a blade of wire grass in his mouth, studying her with his terrible devouring eyes.

It was way past lunchtime, but he was not waiting for food, she knew.

She rose, took him by the hand, and led him into the kitchen where she cleaned off the knotty pine table, spread a pretty linen cloth, and from a huge kettle that had been Annette's mother's dipped him out a steaming bowl of dumpling soup. She sat on weeping a silent grief which had no tears in a corner of the kitchen as Jethro sipped indifferently on the rich soup.

"Any cheese in the house, Elvira?" he inquired.

She rose and took some longhorn out of the buttery, cut a generous portion, and then sliced some of her homemade nut bread and put this beside his bowl of dumpling soup.

"I bet I know why you're bawling, Elvira . . ."

She sobbed harder at this.

"Papa lost the money, ain't that it?" Jethro mumbled, perhaps too low for his mother to hear, as indeed her next statement confirmed, for she said, "Your father has gambled away all of Rick's inheritance . . . Oh, Jethro, Jethro, how can I face the boy?"

She embraced her son, and in so doing forgot how tender his neck was, and the boy suddenly cried out from her pressure. Recovering herself, she kissed the crown of his head.

"I'm 'fraid Rick will do something rash and terrible."

"No, he won't, Elvira."

"You're so calm and manly," she said, her own statement coming as a surprise to her.

Jethro studied his mother's face, his eyes, as she always noted, like clear water but without any bottom to their depth.

"Oh, God, how can I face him when he comes back to us!" she sought comfort from she knew not whom.

"Where is he?" Jethro inquired, at last, pushing back his empty bowl.

"He went out to see Dr. Gray, I suppose, and his crowd of scapegraces." But she spoke in a tone that was without criticism, as if she had said he had gone to choir practice.

"Maybe he'll stay out there."

"Oh, Jethro, he'll be so ugly to live with from now on, yes, maybe he should go and live with Dr. Gray . . . I've tried and tried to keep the home together, but whatever got into me do you suppose to suggest Wilders be given the money. Am I going crazy, Jethro? I must have been out of my mind."

She embraced Jethro, holding him to her again as if he were a young baby instead of the young man whose strong arms and back now writhed a bit under her smothering caresses.

Even Jethro was now afraid of such terrible grief, and though he did not like to kiss Elvira because her lips had belonged to strange men's and because she was a whore, he was touched to the quick, and being alone with her, her soft hair resting on his shoulder the memory of days he had completely forgotten came back to him when she had belonged, it had seemed, just to him, and he hugged her now against himself.

She broke away from Jethro's lovemaking, and they both returned as from a reverie of Hittisleigh to grim gray hellish Boutflour.

Pacing up and down, Elvira spoke on for her own distracted benefit. "How can I face Rick and tell him that it was me and me alone who ruined his life, destroyed his future, made him have to remain in a town he hates so passionately, when all the time he wanted to have a career in the theater, to escape this bilgewater, and escape me . . . Oh, don't I know how much he wants to leave me . . ."

"He can still do all that, Elvira . . . What's to stop him leaving and being an actor? Who said you have to have money to go to New York . . ."

"How can I win back his trust and love, Jethro?"

"But Papa took the money, not you."

"Don't talk like a little simpleton . . . I put the idea into Wilders's head, and your father need never have known Aunt Libby left Rick money . . . No, I've up and done it, Jethro. Rick will never forgive me, and perhaps now will leave us with such spite in his heart we may never hear from him again. He'll change his name, and never own us again as his flesh and blood. I couldn't blame him. That would be almost better than when I have to face him back here and tell him what's happened, and tell him the blood is on my hands . . ."

"When is Papa coming back?"

"How would I know," she said bitterly disconsolate. "And if that straight-nosed hellion has the gall to return, he'll find the door locked against him, do you hear?" she said savagely, as if to warn Jethro forever to leave all locked doors in her house locked. "I've got my cue this time for good. I'm going to divorce your father," she said in a whisper of ferocious bitterness, as if in her hands, already stained with blood, a fresh unused weapon now was held for Wilders.

It was then that Jethro broke down, and buried his face in his hands, he did not know why he was thus affected, for he had long told himself his father was dead, but Elvira, caught up in her own overwhelming passion, ignored him now, or was unaware even he was weeping, and went out into the back yard and began gathering up the sheets and pillowcases with frenzied efficiency, throwing clothespins with deadly aim into her huge wicker basket, and folding, folding the snowy white linen.

Elvira had found in hard physical work a panacea for her long steady succession of sorrows, disappointments, and final disillusionment in life and people. Her hands, which had once been the source of calm joy and admiration in her mother, Melissa, had lost most of their beauty, they were too strong for a woman's, too heavy veined, and the nails broken almost to the quick, the fingers and thumbs often discolored and hard. Sometimes in the evening hours, under an ancient floor lamp inherited from Annette, she would suddenly catch a glimpse of her own hands, suddenly as strangely unlike any part of her own body, as if the night breeze had swept into her lap some vision of ugliness, age and decay there to graft it forever upon her changed self . . . But the relief hard physical work gave her from her heartache was in the end more essential than the loss of her physical charm. And now, more than ever, hard work was needed, and as Jethro said, coming out on the back steps, "Elvira, you act as if Simon Legree stood over you with his whip."

When evening came and did not bring Rick, Elvira wondered if he had got word that she had given away his inheritance.

"And how oh how to explain that I gave it away to the very man who threw my mother's and my inheritance to the four winds," she mumbled to herself.

When one of her lovers called her on the telephone later in the evening she had Jethro lie for her and tell him *Elvira was out of town*, which Jethro did with grim satisfaction, grimacing at the insistent male voice on the other end of the wire, to his mother's amusement.

Days went past and still no Rick.

At last goaded by her son's disappearance, and her own folly in having thrown away his future, she removed her bracelets, and rings, and sat down deliberately at her spinet desk, took out a heavy heirloom pen, some equally ancient sealing wax, with its tiny candle, and then writing rapidly and wildly as if her hands held the bridle of a racing horse, she wrote Wilders:

> I have thought it all over for the last time, we cannot go on together as man and wife, no roof is high enough, no house big enough to hold two persons so separated by the terrible things which you and you alone have brought home to me. You not only ruined my own life and promise, but that of my people. We would be well-fixed, and probably happy had you never come on the scene. Now you have ruined my son Rick's future by squandering the last inheritance coming from my folk on another of your bubble schemes. I am writing this only to tell you that I am instituting divorce proceedings, and this house is closed to you.
>
> ## ELVIRA

Her "instituting divorce proceedings" was no vain rhetorical threat. She had already summoned a lawyer of her mother's, a fat somnolent man who conversed with her interminably now in his dusty, paper-cluttered office in the court house.

With Rick away, perhaps dead, so it sometimes seemed to her in her blackest hours, and her decision to divorce Wilders preying on her mind, and all the while mistress of a large castle-like house full of strangers and lovers, it was small wonder Elvira had not had a wink of sleep for four nights. Even her grueling physical labor did not appease the long accumulated sense of mistake which had begun with her wedding and had climaxed, so it seemed, in Rick's leaving her. Everything in her life had gone wrong. All she had done was wrong. She felt she was sinking under a salt sea of her own endless sorrow.

She conferred more and more with Agnes Coles, who ran the ouija board for her, and counseled caution, waiting, calm, patience. The two women went to a movie together, afterward stopping at Mike's Restaurant for a sandwich and some strong coffee. (Mike was a Greek, Agnes rambled on and on, who made coffee that would wake a year-old corpse, and why drinking his coffee night after night since she had returned from New York years ago had not killed her was an unsolved mystery, etc.)

As Agnes chattered on, filling Elvira in on the latest going-on in town, inattentive, Rick's mother looking at the murals on the restaurant wall of golden skies over green valleys felt the whole panorama of her life pass before her, her girlhood, as the "peony child" of Grandmother Annette, the streams, creeks, waving dandelion fields, golden-rod, flowers and foliage of her country town, its wild birds and small forest animals, sights, sounds, odors so long ago vanished, then the reality of a Greek restaurant at midnight, and the end of her marriage, her memory of Wilders who had been handsome as a prince of dreams, turned first into a gross farm animal, then an insipid wastrel, an aged and vacant nobody, and a thief. Her sons had disappointed her, her lovers disgusted her. Only Dr. Stoke heartened her, kept sending her checks, but he had warned her only a few days before at the height of her trouble that she must expect to hear bad news before too long because he was incurably ill . . .

"Elvira, dearest!" she heard Agnes's chiding worried cry. "You're a thousand miles away, dear heart. Are you all right?"

Then Rick returned.

She saw that something beyond his having heard the news of the loss of his inheritance had gone wrong with him. He was frighteningly pale and as thin as if he had suffered a wasting illness. But she laid it to the awful news of her "crime."

Yet when she began with her confession, "Rick, I have ruined your life, and you have every right to hate me for the rest of time," he only replied, "I knew all that years ago, precious."

She hardly heard this queer remark and went on with her eternal "I don't know what got in me to give your father your only hope for a future."

"Elvira, for God's sakes, will you listen to me for once in your life and quit prattling . . . I've been arrested," he said. "They let me out only because I'm under age . . . But we haven't heard the last of it yet, I fear . . ."

She forgot Wilders then and the rest.

It seemed, her dazed mind tried to take it in, that he had been arrested in a neighboring city, not too far from New York, and there was, it seemed, some suspicion he was the possessor of a drug which she supposed he had got from Dr. Gray, well, from somebody, what did it matter.

"Who arranged for your release, Rick?" she wondered, vacantly.

He told her some name.

She poured him a cup of chocolate, and they both sat down at the same time as at church, when the anthem has been sung, and the preacher will address the congregation.

Rick hardly seemed to care about his having lost his inheritance, and when she told him about her divorce proceedings he nodded, and said, "It had to come, Elvira, for you have set your heart on it, as we all know . . ."

"I'll handle Elvira, Wilders, you can rest assured on that score!" Winifred had cried at him at the height of the most vehement altercation between the two in all their long years of quarrels, strife, and recrimination, which had now gone on to nearly the space of forty years.

"You summon me in here," he had cried at her until she wondered whether he would burst a blood vessel, but even this did not stifle her supreme wrath, "summon me as if I were a dirty-mouthed snot who had broken your dormer window . . ." He looked about the giant room, packed with her heirlooms and possessions, her carpets and clocks and mirrors.

"Isn't that just about what you are, though since you are in long trousers and look the soul of respectability, your destructive, your annihilatory power is so much greater. All should tremble, Wilders, when you appear wherever money is the business of the day!"

"I've never seen such antagonism in a damned female," he roared at her. "Such spite, such a hellion's soul . . ." He thought of Mother Fergus's explanation of Winifred's soul, the stock pale dictum that her anger against life stemmed from her having to bear the cross of being the only girl in a household of so many big strapping boys, and he rejected it, as he might have an explanation of the power of the Devil. And in the end, carrying her "big cross," Winifred, he knew, had turned out to be stronger and more indestructible than any of Mother Fergus's sons, indeed in any of the tribe of Ferguses.

"If you'd learn to hold your horses," he began, struggling to control himself, "if you'd listen like a human being before you jump into any fray before your eyes, for fighting is all your joy, damn it . . ." He broke off in a kind of sob of fury.

Mother Fergus had come into the huge study at that moment, her purple Paisley shawl thrown hurriedly over her spare shoulders, for the angry voices tonight were angrier than ever she had remembered, even in those long years past when as head of the household she had tried to arbitrate in vain amongst so many passionate hearts, and when now as then her voice was ignored, her prayers greeted with stony silence, almost contempt, she had left them, closing door after door between her and the contending parties with all the strength her old bones could summon, slamming behind her the forever recurring past.

Too sickened even to weep by what had occurred, she sat down in her white cane rocker and thought of the new catastrophe. Actually both she and Winifred had been too horrified that Wilders had lost young Rick's inheritance even to speak of the subject for days.

Wilders had come home late to supper one evening, and kept his eyes on the china plate of Parker House rolls, and the serving dish of cold roast beef, as if now it was his turn to speak, to "confess," and that it was to these leavings of the repast he was to announce his having lost his boy's fortune.

"Yet again?" Mother Fergus had cried, when he had

repeated what he had done. She could not have said a more cutting thing to him, and she never said another sentence with reference to his deed.

Winifred had silenced her, though that was, the daughter knew, unneeded, and the one she really was silencing for the moment was herself, and the old lady had gone into her bedroom, without excusing herself, had taken out a clean linen handkerchief, daubed the corners of it in camphor and held it to her nose. Then letting out one hopeless moan, she had gone to sleep.

Winifred, after their mother had left the room, in one of the most frightening disguises of her temper to one who knew her as well as Wilders did, turned all of a sudden sweetly kind, and oh so deceptively asked the details of how he had lost the money, as though his losing it were indeed an event over which he had no control or volition, for which he was blameless, that it had been an errand he had had to perform, that he had been entrusted with such a sum of money, had been commanded to invest it by powers greater than himself, so that of course they would all become very wealthy, at least comfortable, and the money, quite understandably under such circumstances, had been lost, they were all poorer than ever before, and one young man, the splendid, energetic hopeful Rick Fergus was exactly as he was before, without a cent in his pants pocket for his future, and though having been an heir for a few charmed days, was, as before, a young pauper.

Was there, Winifred seemed to be saying with her eyes, her usually tense lips, now relaxed as if in silent laughter, was there anything unusual or even worthy of much comment over this insignificant event. She continued in a lackadaisical, somnolent fashion to worm out of her brother all the details, in order, it seemed, to make after-dinner conversation. Yes, the whole thing was both trivial, and if anything, unexciting, it had nothing, in fact, really and truly, to do with her, Wilders, Mother Fergus, Rick, the heir, or even his appalling mother Elvira Summerlad. They had merely read in fine print on the financial page of the newspaper that a small fortune had been lost, and in larger print one was informed that autumn was coming, and after it, winter was expected. One folded the paper, yawned, and prepared for slumber.

The "confession" done, Winifred, as sweet as the young girl who almost a half century before had bidden her father good night, now stole from the room, leaving Wilders both horrified and feeling slightly mad, for he knew her calm, her saccharine deception, was some hideous play-acting to make the coming storm more cyclonic and of the nature of a holocaust, and that this assumed sweetness was more ominous than had she thrown the heaviest of the ironstone platters straight at his head.

The next day, at a loss to whom to turn, when he had shown Winifred Elvira's letter informing him that divorce proceedings had been begun, his sister again showed a kind of benign and concerned calm, again mixed with sweetness.

Then as with the cyclone, it hit without warning.

A mad woman in the violent ward would have been calmer.

All his crimes were raked up anew, the ashes of disgraces everybody had forgotten but her, were fired into leaping flames. The dead were dug up, and their moldering flesh and rotten bones thrown at him. Monstrous crimes against them and the living, committed only by him, were listed, magnified, and explained in minute details, as in a learned legal treatise. Winifred was judge, jury, supreme court, she lectured, accused, gave what paltry defense could be picked out of such irresponsibility and monumental wickedness, and then in a ringing cry that seemed to come from some bird of prey from the skies, found him guilty on all counts. He was ordered to stand and say what shred of excuse, or reason, he might have, before he was to be shot dead at her feet.

The hidden fountains of her wrath now flowed beyond her own power to impede them.

"You have ruined us all with your blamed damnable meanderings in quest of riches. You should be locked up. You're not safe outside doors. Kinder for all if you were chained, or your hands hacked off so that you could never write another bad check, or appropriate another person's life savings. You've ruined and disgraced all of us! Brought us again and again to the edge of beggary! . . . And you can sit here calm, as always, for cold blood is your stock in trade . . . But as to Elvira," she now went to within an inch of his face, "Elvira, and a divorce," she began suddenly to be out of breath, indeed to look as if she had gone beyond her own strength, "I say," she got hold of herself, "no such final disgrace, especially one planned by that abandoned thing, will take place . . ."

"I'll take care of my own wife and family!" he raised his voice at last, and strode out of her proximity.

"You wandering eclipse of an idiot! Take care of them! What verbiage from the lunatic asylum you can talk. You dare seat yourself there and speak such stuff to your own sister, whom you ruined along with all the rest of your victims. Who indeed under the dome of heaven have you not ruined!" She looked out the dark heavy shutters of the room. "You've ruined all of us. You were born to ruin. And ruin you shall always and will never stop unless I take things in hand for once and all . . . You have no wife. What support you've given that bird-brained fool has been given to her by others. By men, principally. Yes, by men," she repeated when she saw the look of incredulity, succeeded by genuine sickness, come over his face.

"Damn such a blistering tongue in a human throat!" he got out, but the rain now beating against the shutter made them both look toward the window.

"You, to complain of a blistering tongue, tomfool of all tomfools," she went on, suddenly gaining her second wind, and ready, so it appeared, to spend the night in this rehearsal of mistakes her whole being had cried out for for so many years.

"You'll bow to my will this time, Wilders Fergus, or you'll not leave this room alive, do you hear me . . . I'm going to Elvira's . . . And you'll stay here with Mother until my mission is completed . . . And don't open your mouth again unless it is to proclaim your own guilt, your folly, your having again thrown us into an open pit. Do you hear what I intend to do?"

"With your voice, heaven and hell, and the continent thrown in, are informed," he scoffed.

Rising he was about to leave the room, when a sudden paroxysm shook him, and seizing a handsome ancient chair he broke it immediately to pieces . . . In times past she would have feared his physical strength but today seizing one of the broken legs of the chair, she brandished it over her brother, while she screamed, "Try to kill me if you like to, but I am taking the reins, do you hear, from the crossroads robber and swindler, who if I have one breath in my body, I'll prevent from any further of his adventures! Do you hear me, I'm taking the reins."

Cries from old Mother Fergus stopped them, perhaps even calmed them at that moment, as their mother entered the room, and perhaps prevented their attacking one another, but even as the old woman stood between them, turning now to one, now to another, Winifred, with the last word, had shouted:

"I'll see Elvira tomorrow, and you can be damned if you think of stopping me . . ."

She then hurried off to her own part of the house.

* * *

"Useless, useless to reason with her!" Mother Fergus sighed, the next day, after Winifred had left them and gone off to Boutflour, to see Elvira, and she was alone with her "boy," Wilders. A kind of heavy calm, a peace almost like that of happiness had descended upon the house once the daughter had departed, but as mother and son sat dawdling on at the breakfast table, looking up suddenly at a shaft of sunlight which fell directly on Wilders, she saw with unbelieving eyes that he looked at that moment as old and tired as if he had been a near-contemporary of hers, and oh so worn and haggard he had become, and so unlike her boy.

"Winifred should have been a man," Mother Fergus folded her napkin and placed it in the silver ring with her initials on it. He helped her now into the sitting room, where she sank down into her rocking chair. "A will of iron, a tongue like whips of barbed wire, a fierce glance like a wild cat . . . What did I do, Wilders, to make her turn out like that. She was always so angry she couldn't do as you boys did. Wanted something I didn't know what. Always a terrible ungovernable temper. And she did so many things better than you boys. She always rode a horse like some-body in a circus, I once told her, and she never forgave me. Well, I meant it as praise," and here Mother Fergus laughed softly in spite of herself, in spite of all the sad things which had happened recently and over the long age of her life. "What man could have tamed her, Wilders," she covered her shoulders with a new shawl Winifred had purchased for her only a couple of days before.

Wilders scarcely heard his mother. He was thinking that had he been a drinking man he would be lying in the gutter in the alley where Jim Barstow's saloon had been before prohibition. But so many of the manly pursuits had never been his, whiskey, horseracing, common gambling. Two sins he stood convicted of, however, philandering with women, and squandering other people's fortunes. He long ago ceased to wonder at these things in himself. His mother and Winifred only guessed at his philandering, but of course Elvira knew, and probably, for her tongue was as unbridled as Winifred's temper, she may have told her boys, which perhaps explained their odd reception of him, their shyness, and coolness toward him, who knows. Mother Fergus still called him her boy, while his own boys, God sakes, were already on the way to being men, except for little Rory, who in a way seemed closest to him. What had happened over the years, he half-mumbled aloud. He had been gone, it would seem, longer than Rip Van Winkle, and he found the world more changed than that old failure had. All was blurred, indistinct, wavy in outlines, a something hardly remembered, the road which was his life, Norfolk, Virginia, and the hundreds of little mean towns in the Midwest, and South, where he had been hunting for success after the earthquake and ruin at Hittisleigh.

"That will be a fracas, Wilders, in Boutflour," he heard his mother's voice now again. "I fear they'll come to hair-pulling," she droned on, half-amused. "But it won't help things . . . Do you think, Wilders, you can patch things up over there, with Elvira? A divorce is out of the question, you know." She sighed, and then, puzzled at her own remembrance, said, "It's so peculiar that the one who opposed your marriage the most is over there as a kind of sheriff to make Elvira keep her bargain . . . I'm afraid Winifred will have no more success this time than when she went to Pauling Meadows to have Mrs. Summerlad call off the marriage!"

"God in heaven, did that happen?" Wilders cried. He had not known about it till now. Had things been less jagged with menace and disaster he might have risen in anger, been incensed and driven to action, but he could only nod at his mother at this new bad news, which was so old.

"I've made a hash of everything, Mother," he began. "Yes, I have, don't contradict the truth," he protested at her prayerful excuses for him. "I've failed. Not only have I failed, I've ruined everyone else in my struggles to keep from going down . . . But I mean to make a start again . . . I know you've heard that before," he cut short her protests, her affirmation of belief in him . . . "I know more about banks and the banking business, finance and speculation, than any damned broker on Wall Street . . . But I've made a hash of things. I was too honest. Too damned reliable. My partners all took the bankrupt law and skidooed, leaving me holding the bag . . . Had I been crooked, we'd all be on easy street today, Mother. You know that, even your wildcat daughter knows it . . . But no, we won't have a divorce. By God, we won't have it. But damn Winifred for putting her two cents in over there, at a moment like this . . . She'll muddy the waters till they can never settle. Meddle, meddle, that's the damned old maid in her . . ."

Wilders cared nothing about the religious principles, the Presbyterian scruples which haunted Mother Fergus with regard to divorce. He scarcely ever thought of God, beyond a swear word. Obsessed with the late-nineteenth-century glorification of success and position, the Gilded Age's gods, divorce in his case was some personal impediment, incompatible with rising, with the possession of fortune and place. He had dreamed of making a fortune ever since he could remember, beyond boyhood, he must have dreamed of it in the crib, and he knew, if he knew anything, he would still be able to come through, he felt it in his bones . . . But he suddenly doubted he could stand a divorce. For one thing, should divorce come, and he eyed the room about him, he would have to come home here to his boyhood birthplace, the thought flashed by like the sight of one's own tombstone, already engraved with name and date of birth, and he would live with his mother and Winifred, and it seemed now worse than death, share Winifred's charity, eat her bread . . . A cell in the state pen might be more comforting. And how close a shave that had been, he thought back, going to the pen . . . Why he was not there, and he seldom could bear to think of it, was owed only to the ruin he had had to perpetrate on the fortunes and homes of his own people, and of Elvira's people . . . He had ruined those nearest to him. Yet had he gone to prison, who knows, he sighed, perhaps he'd have ruined them more. And it was ancient history like that appalling story he had just heard from Mother Fergus, that Winifred had tried to stop his wedding. Its outrageousness made him quickly smile.

Mother Fergus talked, and Wilders talked, they talked on all that day, and till midnight, until Mother Fergus, too exhausted even to rise from such a day and evening of out-pouring, outpourings such as one thinks of as coming at the Day of Judgment rather than in life, had to be helped to her bed, and tucked in by her son. How delicious at that moment it was to have him back. She grasped his hand, and Wilders, breaking down completely, laid his head on her wasted breast. Her boy had come home, and she was almost reconciled for a moment to the scandal and shame that permitted such a reunion.

"We do have a roof over our heads, Wilders," she had said, but her thankfulness to providence for this favor only stung him with horror.

"A roof like a coffin lid," he muttered.

* * *

For as long as she could remember, Winifred had planned her open confrontation with Elvira, and for many a sleepless night over the long years of Wilders's marriage, she had rehearsed the speeches, together with all the accusations she would level against her. Winifred was now as proud and exultant in the interurban electric train en route to Boutflour as any soldier going into combat. Her nostrils flared, her blue eyes danced as they never did at home or in her classroom, her rather heavy mouth moved, moist with the continuous pressure of her tongue as she phrased what she meant to say. She intended to bring Elvira to her knees today.

Winifred had telephoned Elvira that she was coming to have a talk with her. This announcement, like the palpable realization of a nightmare which had afflicted her for many years, struck Rick's mother for a few minutes into a kind of paralysis of speech or movement. A visit from Winifred was in a sense the thing she feared most from life, why she did not know, but she admitted to herself now in her terror it was so. Winifred was Elvira's primal enemy, a woman whose very presence in her home, even in halcyon days, brought out goose flesh on her body—she was coming to fight with her. Elvira would have preferred to fight with any cruel and heartless man who disdained women, she thought, rather than face this virgin Amazon, who had never known love or indeed pain.

"Can I bear it?" she cried out at last to her three sons, who were, unusual for them, all finishing breakfast at the same time. Rick, come off his pedestal by reason of his arrest and its ensuing disgrace, allowed his mother to speak without interruption. "Can I let her in, even?"

"Who on earth are you raving about now, Elvira?" Rick spoke at last.

"Who else would I be speaking of?" she spoke now more sharply than was her custom to Rick, for her first great sorrow over his loss of inheritance had begun to abate, and her firmness with him now reminded him of his own shaky position as a result of the "mistake" which had put him under arrest.

"I only hope she doesn't goad me into taking the butcher knife to her," Elvira said. She sat down. Her hand lifted a fragile hand-painted china cup, and she sipped a bit of tepid coffee. "That woman has always brought out the worst in me. There she stands over the rest of the human race, like some faultless Diana, above all our common failings and feelings . . . Ice water runs in her veins of course."

"Then why don't you lock the door against her or go to your mother's?" Rick said.

"Because," Elvira countered with more passion of anger than Rick could ever remember his mother having put into a speech directed to him, "I face my responsibilities, and besides have nothing to be ashamed of here, nothing fundamental at any rate," she cast her eyes down on the worn ingrain carpet beneath her house slippers. At the same moment, her hands trembled on the gold border of the little china cup.

"The whole world fears Aunt Winifred," Rick said, without his usual dramatic intonation.

His statement sent Elvira to reflection. Why indeed, she wondered, did the world fear this unremarkable-looking old maid, Winifred Agatha Fergus? It was a question, she was sure, which passed through the minds of the principal people in Winifred's life, Wilders, Mother Fergus, her brothers (but they had long ago left home, and did their level best to have nothing to do with her).

Nothing in Winifred's mere exterior prepared one for her when this same exterior was galvanized into action, into "battle" as Winifred herself described her performance, described it without humor. The "old maid" was about five feet nine inches high, but easily gave the impression that she was as tall as her six-foot-four brothers. Her nose, broken in early youth, robbed her face of the least feminine delineation. Her eyes were rather too far apart, and very large, and of a piercing blue Elvira found more blinding than a cloudless July sun. Her mouth was full and passionate, her chin granite, her arms sinewy. Elvira remembered Wilders having said outright that Winifred should have been a man, and that he was sorry she wasn't so that he might be able to knock her down every morn, and throw her out of the window every night. Another time she had heard Wilders say that Winifred should have been a sergeant in the army, or the matron of a reformatory. Her voice was of course, when raised, thunder. She loved nothing better than a "fight." Indeed her whole daily life was one skirmish after another, one prolonged never-ending war, chiefly with those closest and dearest to her, but the battle was easily extended to foreign territory. Everything was military strategy in her relationship with people, her mother, her brothers, and now her sister-in-law and her young nephews . . . Nobody was conducting his affairs properly, in Winifred's eyes, and it was her calling in life to set things straight. Therefore whenever she appeared, war clouds quickly gathered, and soon cries of the wounded and dying would rise above the flat plains of the Yankee State, and Winifred would appear in general's uniform on horse, shouting orders, threatening with execution those who disobeyed her . . . Then the battle sounds would die down, and whoever had won or lost mattered not, her side or the enemy's, she would walk off the field with a smile on her face, victory in her bearing. She lived and breathed battle, and was incapable of understanding defeat.

Elvira and her sons lapsed into silence now as they waited for the arrival of Wilders's sister, as a family will wait for the announced coming of a natural disaster for which no real preparation or protection is possible.

At last Elvira spoke up. "This time your Aunt Winifred is coming into my house, I'd have you know, boys. It's not your father's. He hasn't kept the roof over your heads, or filled your mouth with food in years. Everything you see around you, do you hear, is mine. You'd never have grown to man's estate if you'd waited for your father, and I hope you'll tell your aunt this if she attacks me, and tries to belittle what I've done here . . . Of course I've had some help from outside," she suddenly seemed to spring to her own defense. "But I did that for you boys, too. Everything, everything I've done for you, and I won't be criticized, I'll not allow any she-bitch to attack me in my own home, among my own possessions." Elvira now turned her full gaze on Rick, thinking he would show some criticism or defiance of her, but she saw with some relief, if not complete satisfaction, that he sat there wilted. His recent arrest, his having lost his inheritance, well, the whole accumulation, she supposed, of the sorrows of his young life had suddenly struck him dumb, without pulse or will. He sat there her obedient, reliant eldest son again, waiting her commands and direction.

"This house is mine, and nobody will invade it, and tell me what to do!" Elvira cried. Suddenly a sob escaped from her.

"I'll kill her if she tries to browbeat me!" Elvira warned.

Little Rory burst into troubled tears, but Elvira did not look in his direction, it was Jethro who comforted the "baby" of the family. In the old days when Rory had been an infant, Elvira had cautioned Jethro never to touch the top of his head where the fontanelle or soft spot was situated, where the bones of the skull had not yet closed, and where a blow might kill him, but the fontanelle had long since closed, and Jethro patted his brother on this place now, and hugged him, while their mother paced up and down, talking, defending herself, explaining the past to her sons, wondering at the future, and cursing destiny.

"She'll find one thing changed," the mother went on. "Yes, Winifred will see I'm not the sweet ingenuous little country choir singer whom she disapproved of so much as a bride for her brother! For her whole world centers around her brothers, and especially Wilders. And a poor world it is! She fought against all their marriages. Wanted to keep all her brothers at home with her. And not one of those boys amounts to a tinker's damn. They're all failures like your father. Except Uncle Garret who had sense enough to run out West, where, since you're nearly old enough to hear this, he led a very low-down life, was adopted finally, they say, by Indians, while prospecting for gold and precious ores . . . Well," she said, suddenly fearful of what she might say, "say, he led a very rough life and let it go at that," for she had decided to drop the subject, and she could not very well raise her eyes to heaven about scandal when there sat her own boy Rick. Perhaps Rick was taking after the Ferguses, after all, she decided.

"But Winifred," she proceeded, "no, Winifred never made a mistake in her whole life. She was born perfect, and has improved considerably since birth . . ."

Rick now laughed outright at his mother's statement, and despite the unpleasant prospect in store for her, Elvira finally joined in, with the two younger boys then following suit.

The tension somewhat broken, nonetheless Elvira could not stop her evocation of Aunt Winifred's character:

"Her own mother lives in mortal fear of Winifred. Trembles at the least movement her daughter makes in the room ... And Winifred, mind you, is the only one who has retained some of her fortune intact from Wilders's ruinous 'borrowings' from everybody else, and my own people in particular ... For she's still a wealthy woman today, though to hear her talk, you'd think she was planning to go on poor relief. Yes, she's rich and no more has to teach school in that Boston girls school than she has to swim the English Channel, which she's capable of doing, too . . . She must love the domineering that is parceled out to her over the young ladies in her charge, teaching them in her finishing school how to ride mares, dance on the green, and toss volley balls across a net. So long as she can command, she's Winifred."

And Elvira went on, despite the waning of attention of her sons, who had heard all this countless times, describing Aunt Winifred's calling, her teaching physical education to young women of wealthy families, as if such a vocation was a deliberate madness, not approved of by society and practiced against the law and public safety.

"But she'll meet her match today!" Elvira now rose, and folded her arms. And her sons could only begin to agree with her. Their mother stood there very warrior-like herself, and a match for anybody.

*   *   *

Winifred, traveling on the interurban electric train in a compartment deserted except for herself, was not quite the indomitable warrior Elvira pictured in her own insecure mind. Indeed the maiden aunt's courage had failed her once she saw the outskirts of the town of Boutflour, that hideous county seat with the monstrous court house whose green cracked dome was adorned with a patriot of the American Revolution, who looked down upon unpainted Civil War cannon in its square, ragged ruined farmers spitting tobacco juice around the edifice's marble pillars, a decayed boom town, with mortgaged farms and homes, and creeping paralysis seen in the grass growing on the big bridge which linked the town with rolling farm lands, and under which shaky structure, damaged again and again by the river, in which now shrunken by summer heat muskrats swam lazily blinking in the sun.

"And I must face that vain pretty little nincompoop today," Winifred spoke aloud, "no more worthy to have married into our family than . . ."

But her mind wandered. At the depot, Winifred had a good mind to return to Paulding Meadows, and wash her hands of Elvira, Wilders, everybody, and go back to Boston and shut herself up there until her whole family was dead.

It was mid July, baking hot, and no season for a fracas.

Elvira had heard Winifred compared to a sergeant in the army and a matron of a reformatory, but perhaps she was most like a horse trainer in the depths of her own consciousness. She had, as a matter of fact, broken in horses when her father had his farms, to the sullen approbation and grudging "hats off" of her glowering brothers.

And once inside Elvira's house today, in the catalpa-shaded dining room where they had all taken their seats as at a solemn conclave of their church, with the exception of Winifred herself, who stood, she felt very much in her old role, that of a woman about to break in not one horse, but four.

Elvira sat ashen pale, her fingers expanding and contracting like freshly severed tentacles, for she was desperate for a cigarette, but she knew that Winifred's fanatic mania against the use of tobacco would seize on her puffing at a cigarette as a perfect weapon to direct against her today, for to Winifred and Grandma Fergus a woman who smoked would do anything, of which prostitution was the inevitable consequence.

Rick, white as bread, stared into vacancy like a blindman and even the two younger boys, Jeth and Rory, seemed glassy-eyed with terror.

Winifred began her remarks with a kind of address to Rick, in which there were oblique and veiled references to his having lost his inheritance.

"I am more than willing to help tide you all over financially," she repeated this one statement again and again. "I will not let you go without," she spoke in a pious manner unlike herself.

"No sum of money you can dig out of your drawers will bribe me into living with your brother," Elvira said in calm collected tones, having purposely chosen the vulgarity of the word "drawers."

Elvira's voice, which was always strong, now carried louder than if she had placed a megaphone to her pretty lips, and her "pronouncement" had the effect of some great public bulletin coming over the radio to an assembled nation.

But after her first shocked disbelief, surprise, Winifred opened her mouth, grateful for the first shot's having been fired, with:

"Wilders Fergus is the father of your sons!" the aunt

cried. "Has that no meaning to you, Elvira Summerlad . . . These sons here, can you in any conscience divorce them from their father . . ."

"The simpleness of some people who pass for educated!" Elvira could not restrain a sneering laugh. "The whole world knows Wilders Fergus divorced himself from his boys and his wife years ago . . . In fact his only act as a father was to get me in the family way . . ."

"We'll have no more of your common coarseness, if you please, Elvira," Winifred smiled deprecatingly.

"No, what Mother says is the truth, Aunt Winifred," Rick suddenly stood up and faced their visitor. "Wilders has always been away . . ."

Winifred was too astonished at the oldest boy's statement to make a rejoinder, and Elvira and Jethro and Rory were alike astonished at Rick's changed demeanor, at his atypical and undramatic speech, which he now enlarged with another statement. "Besides he robbed me of my inheritance."

Having said this he sat down. Rick neither looked nor acted like the youth of a few days ago whose every word and gesture appeared to have been coached by his drama teacher. The thought must have struck him that he was suddenly thrown into a role in real life which he had played in an offering of the Little Thespian Society of Boutflour a year or so ago, a youth of divorced parents, and broken home. But what was happening here in the boarding house had none of the light chatter and crumbly drawing-room conventions of that play. Aunt Winifred's raw direct vividness did not fit into any play he had ever read. The whole scene that was unfolding here indeed was too "real" for the theater, too plainly terrible, and all of them present, including himself, seated in the big sprawling dining room at the table where the boarders would assemble in a few hours, had a flatness and monotonous ugliness which would have driven him to fury a few weeks ago before his own arrest. Yes, he thought, what was unfolding here would be called in the parlance of his dramatic coach very "rough," and of a gloomy, even grimy realism that was defeating to the purposes of real drama . . . And in a sudden blinding flash he saw his own life as it had unfolded as forever divorced from the glitter of the theater, he saw Elvira in her tacky little apron, her hair in kid-curlers, her face gray with age and worry, the two younger boys, his brothers, looking like none too bright waifs, and himself—for who had he been fooling?—hardly better or more grown-up-looking than they, not carefully shaven (the razor had shook in his hand that morning, and he had cut himself most unbecomingly in several places, and these nicks had not been missed by Winifred's merciless eye, who put his untidiness down to poor supervision by Elvira). Alas, he thought, one could not make a play or movie out of what was happening here. It was too small-town and shabby, Rick delivered himself over to despair, and he was, he saw, the most small-town of all perhaps, and his feeling of failure and hopelessness was so over-whelming that he could not restrain a few short sobs, which he stopped by digging his nails into his palms.

"Give up that sniffling, Rick, you're a young man now!" Aunt Winifred raised her voice to full volume.

"Don't shout in my house!" Elvira warned her. "And don't shout at the very son your brother has just robbed! He doesn't need any more punishment from the Ferguses!"

Pleased that the "civility" of the first minutes were

behind them, leaving her free to deal barehanded with the impossible Elvira Summerlad, Winifred now moved directly into the fray.

"You're not fit to raise boys, Elvira, and you yourself, I've always thought, have always realized it," Winifred spoke in calm hurtful emphasis.

"If you say another word of such reproach in my house, I warn you I won't be responsible for what may happen to you, Winifred!"

"I hope you boys have taken proper note of your mother's threatening me just now," Winifred turned to the three sons with all her consummate calm and poise.

"You see, my dear," she addressed Elvira, "your ungovernable temper is only underscoring my statement that you are not a fit mother to raise sons . . ."

"Yes, you dried-up old maids can ever sit in judgment of the rest of the human race," Elvira began in a voice which was strangely calm and under control, "but you've come to the wrong place this time to act like God Almighty, and you can't win these boys over to you and their no-account father's side of the house . . . whatever you say. And to come here, just at the time when he's proved his true character, not being satisfied with ruining my mother, my father, and my own fortune, to destroy before all our eyes, his first-born son's inheritance, gone up in smoke like all his other wild schemes."

"Whatever his faults, Elvira," the aunt said in a quieter less assured voice, for she had quailed before the mother's incontrovertible argument, "you have no right to threaten to turn him out of your house, no matter what he's done, for he's the father of your sons, and your promise to serve their father (here she looked direct at the three boys, one after one) with papers at the hands of the sheriff, no, Elvira, I will never allow you to do such a thing, do you hear. As long as there's breath in my own body, you shall not . . ."

"I should have turned Wilders Fergus out of the house before I married him, before he ruined my mother, my brother, and all who were snared in his net."

Jethro now rose, and looked apprehensively in his mother's direction, for she had turned so white and her hands and head shook so violently that the boy feared she might fall down dead before his eyes, and he stretched out his hand toward her, all his old love and affection returning in that gesture. Elvira did not miss his movements, and she took his hand, held it, and helped him sit down.

Winifred, though more shaken perhaps than she had expected to be, grew even sweeter and more reasonable in demeanor, as was her custom just before delivering a mortal blow to an enemy. Her voice, however, retained a certain warrior-like edge as she said:

"You have turned your home into nothing less than a roadhouse where every common creature and roustabout in the nation is welcome! Haven't I heard countless stories of the goings-on here!"

Elvira laughed in a manner so threatening that Aunt Winifred paused, and Rick, hearing such a laugh, remembered his own mother's aspirations to the stage, and he felt that she was, in any case, outshining all of them in her dramatic power.

"You, in whose mouth butter won't melt, can make mumbo-jumbo about moral character . . . How would you have supported three boys who looked at you with hungry stomachs, with the landlord pounding on the door, the unpaid bills of the grocer and shoemaker and the rest piling up . . . How would you have supported them, can you answer me that, when their own father's address was unknown to them?"

"You could always have called on me, Elvira . . . And please don't turn our meeting into a rehearsal for a melodrama. Placating will get you nowhere in any case, certainly not at your age . . ."

"Called on you . . . Oh, could I! . . . You who opposed my marriage to your brother in the first place, bursting into my mother's own home in the same wild-eyed preposterous way that you have come here today, unwanted, unbidden, superfluous . . . You outlandish thing! Who ever did *want* you anywhere! . . . And you come as a peacemaker when the mere sight of you brings thoughts of war to all nature! Yes, you'd have me live with a man whose very touch is ruin to protect the name of Fergus in the county! All for your brother, who is neither father, husband, nor indeed man . . . He's a milk sop tied to his mother's apron strings, and his sister's riding habit!"

"If I were you, boys, I'd never speak to this harridan who calls herself your mother again." Winifred was at last herself.

"Will you come home with me, boys, to your father, and leave this terrible creature here to rave out her life alone? Will you?"

"Will they?" Elvira cried. "I'll answer for them . . . They'd rather die than leave me and go back to that mausoleum you call home, you venomous-tongued, conspiring old rip!"

Going up to Winifred, as she finished these words, Elvira slapped her smartly across the face, and then pausing, in the quiet manner of a hairdresser who feels one added touch is needed to the appearance of her client, she hit her a resounding blow across the mouth, bringing blood.

When Winifred now attempted to restrain her, she found she was as powerless to do so as if she had grappled barehanded with a mountain cat. In the fray that followed, though Winifred attempted to hold Elvira's hands in a tight vise to prevent further harm to herself, the mother eluded her grasp and in a sudden freeing of her hands, caught hold of the aunt's dress, and in one wrench tore the garment entirely from Winifred's body. Both the mother and the aunt stopped, too surprised at what had happened to make any more show of force, and Elvira gazed bemused at Aunt Winifred's dress, or what was left of it, in her hands. It was torn too badly ever again to be a garment.

Winifred was the first to recover her power of speech:

"All the commonness of your ancestry comes out at last!" the aunt cried.

Stung again to belligerence, Elvira reached for Winifred's umbrella which she had laid across a chair, and began beating her with it now, and ordering her out the front door.

"Elvira Summerlad, there are laws!" Winifred cried, flinching under the blows.

The boys would have intervened perhaps, but somehow they could not recognize either their mother or their aunt. They felt they were having a prolonged nightmare, at any rate they could not credit their eyes. The vision of Aunt Winifred in her petticoats, her muscular thighs bare, her small but firm breasts nearly exposed, the veins in her throat standing out in huge green ribbons, and then their own gentle beautiful mother beating their aunt with an umbrella until the front door had opened and closed on her. It was fortunate for all that it was dark by now, Rick thought, but then he looked out and saw Aunt Winifred under the street lamp in just her underthings.

Elvira locked the front door.

Returning, she had such a tigerish look on her face that none of her boys dared say a word. Swearing like a man, using words that she would have punished her sons for by washing out their mouths with soap, she appeared oblivious to any other fact in the universe than her enmity to Winifred Fergus.

Beginning to come out of his own shocked disbelief at what had happened, Rick walked over to the dormer window out of which he saw his aunt, head held high, walk into the filling station on the corner and begin to talk with one of the gasoline attendants. Rick recognized him as Bud Cramer, whom he had gone to school with, and Bud did not seem so flabbergasted as Rick thought he might have been.

Later, even Elvira was to remark she had admired the way Winifred marched nearly naked, her hair down, scratches pouring forth blood on her cheeks, a swollen eye, to the filling station a half block away, had approached the young man who was getting ready to "close up" for the night, and cool as marble, as Rick's mother had expressed it, talked with Bud as if she were wearing a fine dress and big hat, and that the umbrella she carried in her right hand was not broken and coming to pieces but was a fine new parasol. She had explained then to Bud Cramer, who was speechless, that she wished to telephone Mrs. Fergus and instruct her that she must be provided with a coat, as there had been an accident. Bud telephoned, gave the message to Rick, and then he accompanied Winifred—at her request they had not gone to the front but the back door, where tramps knocked for handouts or the ice man and gas meter man paid calls.

Bud knocked, and Rick came out, his face swollen from weeping, and shame, and he handed Aunt Winifred his best trench coat, which fitted her, he saw, rather well, for she had put it on immediately.

"Such self-control and superhuman poise," Rick could not restrain himself from saying a few minutes later, still seated at the dining room table, and in Elvira's critical description "bawling his head off."

Elvira had taken herself to her sewing room, off the dining hall, and stitching away there on some curtains at her Singer sewing machine, she repeated one sentence from time to time, "Oh, she'll get over it. No bones broken." But the victory, as all realized, the boys and Elvira, was Aunt Winifred's. Aunt Winifred, defeated, scratched and nearly denuded, having to go to a gasoline attendant for assistance, had held her head high through all of it, and come out, well, some sort of great heroine.

"She looked just like the lady who rides in the lion cage in the circus parade," Jethro had wanted to write a long description of the scene in his "log," but he found he had mislaid it somewhere, hunt though he would. "And I know Aunt Winifred wouldn't like this comparison," he wrote now in his head, "because she doesn't approve of circuses or their parades, and has spoken slightingly of the ladies in the circus as 'beneath us, far beneath any of us or the townspeople . . . You must not admire circus people, Jethro, and the rumor that your great-grandmother had Indian blood is stuff and nonsense . . .' "

Mother Fergus had sat up past her bedtime with Wilders awaiting Winifred's return, the evening of the following day and evening passed into night and the old hall clock had struck eleven, and the old woman could barely keep her head from nodding into her lap when Winifred's step was heard on the front porch and her latch key turned, then the door opened. Mother Fergus and Wilders stirred at the sight of her, and in their amazed silence neither of them greeted her, and Wilders did not get out of his chair. It was not only the fact that she was wearing Rick's trench coat which had taken them unprepared at their first glimpse of her, her entire appearance shocked them. She had managed to put her hair in some order in her journey back on the interurban train, but the scratches, no matter how much she had worked on them, remained in all their red outlines, and were perhaps best described by Mother Fergus, who finally greeted her daughter with "Why, what on earth's happened to your face, Winifred?" Winifred came close to losing her temper at her mother's outburst, but held her tongue for once, put down her valise, and walked out into the kitchen where she prepared herself a late supper of buckwheat cakes and hot tea. She closed the door as an indication she did not wish them to join her at her repast, and once she had finished eating, she went up the back stairs, without bothering to say good night.

"What I have to report," Winifred said the next morning, entering the parlor where her mother and Wilders sat, patiently waiting for the meeting to come to order, and the sign of that had been given by Winifred's habitual rubbing of her hands together, and her blue eyes looking more martial than ever, her mouth set, "and what I'm glad to report," she smiled now at Wilders, "is that it's perfectly all right for you to go home to your family . . . I don't think Elvira will dream of going through with a divorce . . . I've settled everything on that score, I believe."

"I'll bet you have," Wilders said.

"I thank God if you've brought her to her senses," Mother Fergus opined with anxious hopefulness. "If you've been able to patch things up, I'm sure we'll all breathe a sigh of relief . . ."

Winifred's sense of assurance and confidence, however, seemed to depart suddenly, and as suddenly she sat down, and was silent. Though she had patched up the disfiguring marks of Elvira's nails very well with cosmetics, the vision of her humiliation, without warning now, struck home. Owing to the great heat of the evening before, all the neighbors had been sitting on the front porch when she had returned, and she had had to speak to at least fifteen or sixteen people, though she thanked fortune none of them inquired why she was wearing a heavy trench coat in such a hot spell.

"I think the best thing now, Wilders," Winifred spoke after a funereal silence, during which Mother Fergus had lost all hopes that a peace mission had been accomplished, "and the wisest course is for you simply to return to your wife and boys as if nothing had happened, as if there had been no plans for a divorce . . ."

Wilders rose at this, and strode out of the room without opening his mouth to say another word.

There was no indication in the days that followed, however, that Wilders intended to return to Boutflour, and

Winifred, unusual for her, did not force him to perform an action which she had decided was best for him and for his family.

But at last Winifred's patience was exhausted.

Coming into his bedroom one late afternoon, without so much as a rap on the door, all her old confidence and spleen returned, she interrupted him tying the laces of his high shoes (a style which, like his high collars, and elegant cufflinks, he had kept to long after everyone else in the nation had given it up).

"Wilders, your place is over there with your boys, and you've got to go to them without another hour of delay, do you hear me?"

"I'll bet you stirred up the hornets' nest over there good and proper," he spoke without even looking up at her. Spitting on his shoe, he rubbed off a spot on the leather with a kitchen rag.

"If you don't go now and take your place with your sons, it'll be once and for all too late," she spoke now with real conviction, and no trace of common anger.

Without warning, she forced four ten-dollar bills into his hand, and as she did so, his palm came open like that of a wax dummy, and the bills put into it fluttered briefly, then became still and unmoving as the hand into which they had been put. With a sudden and terrible movement, she closed his hand over the bills.

"You've got to go to them, there's not a minute to lose . . ."

But it was too late, he knew, every laggard mile back in his beaten-up Haines car. When he saw the outskirts of the "wrong end" of Boutflour, with the fumes from the cigar factory, and the rubber refining plant smarting his nostrils, he ground his teeth, swearing . . . "If there was any chance, that hellcat of a sister of mine has killed it, damn her hide . . ."

* * *

In the time that followed Winifred's return from her encounter with Elvira Summerlad, Mother Fergus found herself, for a few brief days, at least, again head of the household. Wilders had gone back to Boutflour, though how long he would remain there seemed to the old woman more than doubtful, and Winifred, since her return, dressed in Rick's trench coat, with her face clawed like that of a woman who has been training tigers, had remained closeted in her room, or when she came downstairs, she kept her head bowed over her breakfast bowl of fresh strawberries and cream, like a dutiful and pious daughter without a will of her own.

Winifred had not expected any real sympathy from her mother, for ever since the daughter could remember her mother's counsel had been always that of "Know your place as a girl, Winifred, yield to your brothers, and you'll not get yourself into all the trouble you're forever bringing down on yourself and others . . . Don't fight with people you can't beat, only to end up just making more enemies for yourself," and so on.

But after days of her not daring to ask her daughter questions about her trip to Boutflour, the old woman one early morning at table could not restrain saying, "What did happen to your face, Winifred? . . ."

"Supposing you tell me, Mother," Winifred shot back, and from then on their roles began to change back to what they had been before the "fracas," Winifred again taking the reins and being ruler of the roost and the sole support of Mother Fergus's invalid old age.

"I can't stand the thought of Elvira laying her hands on a child of mine!" Mother Fergus spoke with real indignation now at the thought that somebody had tried to harm one of her own.

"For heaven's sake, Mother! You can spare that kind of pity. She only succeeded in making a fool of herself, I thought you realized that!"

The old woman gazed into her daughter's eyes, and the daughter looked hurriedly away. Both women had admitted in their exchange of looks that Winifred's visit to Elvira had been a great failure, a hopelessly unwise step, and that she had only succeeded in making a fool of herself.

"Do you think there is any chance at all, Winifred, that Elvira can be persuaded to live with Wilders? For the boys, that is," she added quickly, seeing the cloud of anger and irritation coming over her daughter's face. The old woman was actually thinking at that moment of how all the neighbors around them must be talking, too, of the quarrel at Boutflour, and commenting on the sorry condition Winifred had been in when she returned to Paulding Meadows in her nephew's trench coat, with her face as torn as if she had fallen into a thorn tree.

"Well, you can't blame Elvira perhaps for not wanting to live with Wilders!" Winifred suddenly threw out this remark, for she was ever perverse in argument, and was angry that her mother had found out the failure of her mission, as well as the humiliating trouncing she had taken at the hands of Rick's mother. Indeed, this morning, Winifred was so angry with things in general, she did not know on whom to vent her anger the most, Elvira, Wilders, or helpless Mother Fergus.

"You seem to feel more concern for Elvira Summerlad than you do your own daughter! . . . Well, I realize I have always been a keen disappointment to you because I did not marry!"

"Have I ever so much as hinted at such a thing, Winifred?" The old lady's hands shook so that she dropped her napkin ring on the floor, and upset a tumbler of water. Neither of them moved to pick up the silver ring or wipe dry the pool of water on the linen tablecloth.

"Hinting wasn't even necessary, Mother. I could read your thoughts as if you'd conveyed them in thunder . . ."

Then bracing herself to say what she'd wanted to say all her life but which all her life she had dreaded she would say, Winifred cried in a voice that was a ragged whisper: "Of all your children I'm the one you've taken to the least!"

"You're the one I've spent the most time worrying my heart out about the most, if you only knew," Mother Fergus had recovered all her old grand calm and dignity, "but you never seemed to want me to give you any love, Winifred, from the time you were a little tiny girl, you spurned it . . . But I won't sit here day after day and put up with your scolding and your anger. I'll go to the poor farm rather than hear your blame and bear your rancor and ill temper, do you hear . . ."

Needing some sympathy and affection at that moment more than anything in the world, a sympathy and affection she was too stiff-necked to ask for, this sudden "revolt" of her mother, coming as it did on the heels of her disgrace and mistreatment at the hands of Elvira Summerlad, had an unforeseen reaction for both the women. The great horsewoman, disciplinarian and iron-willed mistress of herself, broke into short convulsive sobs, more painful for her to let out than it would have been for her to plunge the bread knife lying at her finger's tip into her own throat. Her mother stretched out her hand to her, but her daughter did not grasp it.

"All right, Mother, all right," Winifred was the first to speak. "Let me apologize for what I've said. I'm sorry if I've given the impression that caring for you was a burden, when it's the only thing in life that makes my life . . . I'm only sorry, however, that I wasn't born a man, and I think I'd been a better son to you than I am a daughter . . ."

"Oh, Winifred," the old lady spoke in a low voice, "I'm afraid you expect too much of life, too much of yourself, too much of others . . . I don't know how you can doubt that I care for you, and that I suffered more than you'll know at what happened at Elvira's."

"If you care for me, Mother," Winifred rose now, again in possession of her harsh schoolmistress poise and clear voice, "never mention that again to me and never threaten me again with so atrocious a thing as speaking of the poor farm! How dare you threaten me when you know what I've been through!" She threw down her silver napkin ring on the table . . .

"If you would only learn to tend to your own affairs, precious girl!"

"I have no affairs, Mother!" Winifred's voice rose, a voice that could now be heard throughout the entire neighborhood and was listened to, one may be certain, with rapt attention this morning. "My only affairs in life are you and my brothers," she seemed to confess now beyond the reach of any old shame. "And do you expect me to sit idle and let that common slut Elvira ruin Wilders and his sons?"

"I don't understand why you should refer to Elvira Summerlad in such language," the old woman was now deeply hurt and offended, for after all Elvira was her son's wife and the mother of her grandsons, whom she adored, and besides, as the old woman was about to tell her daughter, Elvira came from a very good family.

"If you tell me once again," Winifred intercepted the coming remark, "that the Summerlads took part in the American Revolution, I will leave this house and not return . . ."

"Well, Winifred, we can't very well deny history," the old woman had salvaged some of her sense of humor, and she began to mop up the spilled water with another napkin, and to take a quick sip of coffee. "But it comes as a very painful surprise to me to hear you describe Elvira in the way you just have. It doesn't become you to say such a thing, even if there's a grain of truth in it . . ."

"A grain of truth indeed. What that creature is doing over there is nothing more or less than running a disorderly house."

"I won't believe it," the old woman put down her coffee cup into the saucer with a resounding bang.

"Don't then. Defend her, Mother, and love her. I think you always have!"

"How could Elvira misbehave with her own sons right there before her, with Rick a young man by now, and Jethro not far behind him?"

"Oh, Elvira could deceive God with her charm!" Winifred shot back. "Could and does . . . You yourself have always been under her spell, always defending her from even before the wedding . . . I repeat, she is running a disorderly house . . . Can I be more explicit?"

Old Mother Fergus now rose, and took the empty heavy ironstone meat platter with her out into the kitchen, but Winifred, pursuing her mother's steps, cried out, "In any event, Mother, she's right on one score, Elvira is . . . Wilders has failed all of us! He's the source of all our disgrace, and he's the one you showered the most on of all of us . . . He wanted for nothing, Mother, when he was a boy, and see what he has brought home to all of us, wretched Elvira included . . ."

The old woman closed her eyes, and put down the heavy platter.

"Leave me to my own thoughts now, Winifred, if you please . . . You've given me enough to think about for many a year to come . . ."

"I can leave you the entire house, if you wish it, Mother," Winifred cried.

Old Mother Fergus muttered now alone in her kitchen, and having dried her eyes quickly of tears, plunged her bent fingers into the hot suds of the dishpan. "Children," she spoke aloud to herself, "seem to exist only to cut one to the quick."

* * *

As Wilders was packing to leave Paulding Meadows for Elvira's boarding house, he saw in the bottom of his valise an object which was unfamiliar to him, and which he now picked up to handle, and examine. It was Jethro's "log" or journals, which Wilders must have packed by mistake that day in Boutflour when Rick had finally given him the money of his inheritance, and when Wilders had had such haste to be gone in order to make back for all of them his lost fortune of years ago. He studied the firm handwriting of the log penned in green ink on ruled five-and-ten-cent store stationery, held together by a ring-clasp imitation leather cover, with the name *Jethro Summerlad* written over it. He stared with a kind of horror at the boy's using his mother's family name. Then he packed the notebook with his own things, muttering he would return the notebook to Jethro when he got back to Elvira's.

But on his way back to Boutflour "to reinstate himself" with his family, in Winifred's queer phrase, he began to lose any courage he might have had to face Rick, whom he had robbed, and Elvira, who, he was sure, meant to end their marriage. What neither Elvira nor Winifred probably knew was the horror which Wilders did feel in his having lost his son's fortune, a horror indeed so great that the father could scarcely feel it, like some fatal cancer which is queerly enough painless. He knew, too, how much both Elvira and Rick must have built their final hopes on what the money might do for them, and he had come again only to wreck all they had built their last dreams on.

Close to dusk, he stopped the old touring car, under an elm tree, and tried to get hold of himself. A half block away he spied a rundown tourist lodge, at which he decided he would spend the night. Wilders was now in that section of Boutflour which years before had been inhabited by those citizens who had made the town "great," the old original millionaires who had finally lost their all in the panic of the 1870s. Most of the fine old mansions were now tourist homes, cheap hotels, small business offices, and funeral parlors. He signed his name at the desk of the tourist lodge, and then watched with some apprehension the sallow-complexioned woman at the desk with white thin hair and stooped back study his signature carefully as if either the hand or the name stirred something in her mind. She insisted on accompanying him up the two flights of stairs, and even wished to carry his valise for him, though looking at her, he was certain she must be seventy-five years of age. Wilders put down his lean hand baggage and studied the yellow-stained wallpaper, and looked over in the corner at the wafer-thin mattress of the cot he was to sleep on. As the old crone lingered in the room, he offered her some small change for her trouble in having brought him upstairs, but she shook her head in refusal, and her eyes had that same expression of mental effort as they had when she had studied his signature. Finally she got out, "Ain't you Jesse Fergus's boy?" His face changed to a kind of series of smiles, each broader than the other, as if he himself had remembered who he was and where he had come from. "I am for a fact," Wilders said, laughing now. "Did you know my father?" She nodded, smiling, but then a bell sounding from downstairs, the smile faded from her face, and she was all preoccupation again, and in another second had left the room.

"Didn't know there was a soul living remembered him," Wilders took off his new straw hat and threw it sailing to the bed.

"Jesse Fergus's boy," he heard the old woman's words again. He only vaguely thought of his own father now, who had been a livestock dealer, breeder of horses, horse trader, he guessed he would be called, and then finally, in later years, in Mother Fergus's phrase, he had been with the railroad, a railroad man.

Wilders rummaged in his valise now for a face towel and his straight razor, and there again in with all his things, a bit wet from yesterday's face cloth, was the little black imitation leather notebook with the rings holding the papers together on which Jethro had written winding paragraph after paragraph in green ink.

He opened the notebook, then shrank back as if he had touched the nozzle of a cold revolver.

Elvira is sleeping with the roomers

was the first sentence his eye fell upon.

Every night she goes to the little house, and lies down with one of her new lovers. Her own wedding night, I've heard her say, was far from happiness.

Wilders closed the book, went into the lavatory, and bathed his eyes in the tepid water from the faucet. He tried the water from both taps, but both were the same, neither hot nor cold, neither comforting nor awakening.

"Jethro must be touched," Wilders spoke to himself aloud now. "From that accident of course," he thought, and he began leafing through the pages of his son's log again, his eye falling on one damning sentence after another. He was an indifferent reader of the Bible, since he never thought about God or religion, despite his strict Presbyterian upbringing at his mother's hands. And Jesse Fergus had pooh-poohed religion, too, though never in the presence of Wilders's mother, but now Jethro's strange short sentences written in the firm flowing handwriting reminded him of apocalyptical passages in the Good Book where cities and whole nations had been condemned in the space of one short verse.

Rick gives his naked body to men and women for
a shove upwards on the success ladder.

"Oh, Christ," Wilders said. "He is touched. Will have to be put away, I guess." At the same time Wilders found that he believed all the things written down against his wife and eldest son. And yes, Winifred, if he did not disremember, had hinted at terrible doings in the boarding house.

"Was she forced to it all, do you suppose?" he went on talking aloud to himself, and he meant of course Elvira.

He did not go out to eat. Looking out the window, he saw the rain beginning to fall through the heavy trunks and leaves of the Dutch elms onto the dirty windowpanes. As the rain came down harder it blurred all vision, leaving only a kind of green smear to look at, like scum on a pond.

As he had read on and on through the log, he faintly heard Jethro's tiny voice come to him, as if through the split in the boy's skull. After an hour or so of reading Wilders put his head down on the small mahogany table which stood unaccountable and meaningless in the very middle of the room. Like all rooms for transients the tables and chairs here appeared to be resting untouched and untouchable in their own eternity. Whoever stopped in such a room was meant to move on almost at once, a slap of the washrag to the face in lukewarm water, a few minutes or hours on a gutless mattress, a walk over thin shoe leather to the toilet, then close the valise, and go to the next lodging place in the next town, waiting for a deal to come through, a farm to be sold, a business block to be negotiated for, but never home.

Wilders is said to be the greatest swindler outside of bars in the nation.

He turned another page, and sank down into the green waving lines of ink, deeper than an ocean for him:

All who have had dealings with my Dad are ruined and Elvira is no better than a whore.

In this midst of these jottings was a kind of a poem-story about the town music teacher, Agnes Coles, and her visits to her illegitimate son in New York. Agnes, a beautiful woman, statuesque, with a crown of red hair that shone over her peaches-and-cream complexion—Wilders remembered his own description of her now as he had once daydreamed of her in his Norfolk, Virginia, hotel room—taller than Elvira, in a way more beautiful, more fetching, though she was a bit too tall for him—he liked shorter women. A sudden impetuous and irrational prompting swept over him that he should get up at once and go visit her . . . Wasn't Agnes Coles, after all, Elvira's closest friend in Boutflour, her only bosom friend, as his wife put it, and he smiled at the term. Wilders's virtues, which were not mentioned in his son's log, were that he neither drank nor smoked nor played poker, which had made him a rarity among his business partners, but they knew, and Jethro's journals had put down what Wilders knew was the truth, his failing had been that he was a ladies' man, and a mishandler of other people's money. A long career behind him of being a ladies' man, he repeated, to himself. Well, he said, why not? why shouldn't it be again?

He looked now at the wallpaper, which appeared to be temporarily pasted on, for pieces of it fell in ribbons to the floor every time you opened a drawer, or moved a piece of furniture.

Walking up and down in the room, listening to the drops of rain still falling from the elm leaves, he began to blame Agnes Coles for everything. It was the teacher of pianoforte, he was almost certain, who had led Elvira astray. Reading the wandering green penmanship he found, according to Jethro, that Agnes Coles, who had come from a farm background like himself, and yet had lived in New York for some time, and had had an illegitimate son, was certainly the inspiration and cause for all his present domestic distress and ruin. He suddenly almost felt she had caused his financial ruin likewise. He felt she had been at Hittisleigh, and presided over his ruin there. He was intoxicated all upon a sudden with his own blaming of Agnes Coles, drunk on accusing her as if he had consumed a fifth of Weller bourbon.

He would go to see her now, he thought, and have it out with her. He picked up his straw hat, and then turning he picked up the little ten-cent-store notebook, and in a sudden onrush of passion, crumpled it viciously, then holding it gently, he smoothed out the imitation leather which he had damaged. His own son had written it, he pondered, patting the terrible testimony, and then he remembered back to the boy's accident and the look on the doctor's face which had seemed to say that it was too bad Jeth had not died when he had fallen and cut through into his skull and brain, and Wilders let the boy's accident now explain away all that he had read put down in the log.

Agnes Coles's "studio" faced an alley and a brick wall, she had to go down the hall to the lavatory and toilet, and on the same floor with her was an old impecunious foot doctor, who long past retirement still kept office hours, but had few or no patients, and being deaf was the only one on Agnes's floor who was not bothered by the sound of the piano going from morning to night. The hall runner on her floor which led to her rooms was threadbare, and though the Mileson Building was still part of the business district of Boutflour, and one would have thought would be kept in repairs, the landlord, an elderly woman who lived on the ground floor, felt the least expense was unwarranted, and the walls had begun to show their laths, and the stairs crumbled under heavy footfalls.

But in the studio itself, one immediately smelled expensive incense, which Agnes brought back with her from a Chinese firm in New York, the walls were hung with framed photos of movie stars of the era when Agnes had been growing up, in the 1910s, and a grand piano, which must have cost a small fortune and was still in good condition, occupied the main part of the room. If now she lived in a "hole in the wall," her term for her living quarters, there was every suggestion all about that once fortune had smiled on her, and that somebody had been generous, or as Boutflour gossip put it, rich gentlemen admirers had "established" her as the town's foremost teacher of piano.

As Agnes neared middle age, her mistakes and the generosity of her gentlemen friends had become only a vague memory, but her influence was still considered suspect on the young, and because of her firsthand knowledge of New York, all the dream-sick youth of Boutflour flocked to her studio for "inspiration" and encouragement to leave the "backwater" for the thrilling risk of the big town.

Whatever exaggerations or outright lies there might be in Jethro's "description" of the life of Agnes Coles, there was one fact Wilders could not dispute, the music teacher's influence over his wife and his eldest son. Agnes's mission in life indeed seemed to be to fire Rick with a passion for the stage, and his wife with a passion for a life of wild freedom.

And so suddenly, Wilders put all the blame for Elvira's changed character, and the very existence of the boarding house, Rick's wildness and being stage-struck, even Jethro's writing a journal, all this was laid at the door of Agnes Coles, and as he began to walk down the stairs of the lodging house that night, he was prepared to accuse her outright of all the harm she had done him and his family.

* * *

Matthew Lacey stopped in the midst of his narration with the abruptness of a man who hears bullets whistling about his ears, and stared into the air. It was clear to me then, and later, that he was far from omniscient, though I believe he laid claim most of the time to being so. And when after a bit, when Matt did come out of his funk, and asked, "Where were we, Jeremy?" he proceeded for a time with marked uncertainty, stumbled, retraced his steps, and at last all but owned up to the fact that his "version" might have some holes in it, at least "hereabouts" (meaning the Wilders visit to Agnes Coles).

For one thing, it seemed doubtful to Matt that Wilders Fergus would ever have gone to Agnes's studio that night (though he may have promised himself he would go), had not the most unsettling thing in Wilders's very unsettling life taken place, for he was, without warning, served papers by the sheriff as he came down the steep rickety steps from his tourist lodge room.

Already a bit unsteady from his having perused Jethro's journal, he had just buttoned up his mackintosh against the downpour of rain, when Pete McLaren, the sheriff, who easily recognized him, stepped out of a car, and mumbled the apology, "Hate to be the one to hand you these papers, Fergus . . ."

Wilders had stretched out his hand to take the papers from the sheriff, but his fingers seemed for a moment to jam, and stuck out depending from his sleeves stiff and useless in the rain. More than the shock of the appearance of the deputy was his wonder at how Elvira could have known he was in town, and where he was—some local busybody must have spotted him, he decided, and as he thought this, his fingers snatched the papers, and anger and shame making his eyes swim unsteadily as he tried to run them over the contents of the document, which informed him that he was defendant in a divorce suit, charged by his wife with nonsupport, desertion, cruelty—and there he stopped reading, and he pushed the papers into his coat pocket.

Wilders had wandered about in the rain for an hour before he finally headed in the direction of Agnes Coles's studio, and he was going there, he felt, for the simple reason he could remember nobody else in town would open a door to him, let alone listen to a word he might say in his own behalf, and he must see somebody or go down to the river, and never come back.

*   *   *

What happened in Agnes Coles's studio was never clear to anybody, Elvira or her sons, the townspeople of Boutflour, and it may be it was never clear to Agnes or Wilders. Agnes had finally told Elvira what had happened, days later, in an anguished and often hysterical interview, which Jethro made a point of overhearing from the floor above; there placing his ear to an open hot-air register, one of those which has a black string attached to its lower metal aperture to signify whether air is going through it or not, he listened patiently for over an hour. After each paragraph of description, Agnes would repeat one sentence over and over again, like the first line of a refrain, "I felt I had to tell you, for there seemed no other way."

Wilders had come to see Agnes on the pretext that he wanted to know how he could patch things up with Elvira, and since Agnes was her best friend, perhaps she would have the best solution. However, he had come to her door at midnight, dripping wet from rain, and there was a sheaf of legal-looking papers half-coming out of his macintosh.

As they talked on, Agnes opened a fresh pack of her favorite perfumed cigarettes, Salome, gold-tipped, evil-looking. It was her principal mistake. To Wilders, despite his "education" hobnobbing with the New York and international bankers back in his glorious, short-lived heyday, a woman who smoked, in that remote epoch, would do anything, indeed, and to Wilders, the cigarette was lit not to be consumed or enjoyed but to inform the man sitting across from her that the lady was "available." He had taken hold of her hand then, and she had warned him with a severe frown—those frown marks on Agnes's brow were almost the only sign of age on her body, Boutflour gossip remarked, and they were arresting. Her frown came and went constantly, and gradually left a deep recess between her eyebrows, like the vestiges of a haphazard blow from a weapon. Had she not had this deep recess she would have passed perhaps for an unusually beautiful woman, but with the heavy furrow there she was both beautiful and forbidding, and it was perhaps because she looked forbidding he would not let go her hand. Whatever she might have said or done that night, she could not have stopped him. He had suffered too many humiliations in the past days, years, and letting go her hand for a moment, he drew the legal papers from his raincoat, and showed them to her. The sheriff, he went over the whole thing again, had been waiting for him at the bottom of the steps of the lodging house, and had served the papers on him, informing him that he was the defendant in a divorce suit. He was forbidden to enter his own home, that is to say (and he smiled wryly) the boarding house. But he had run through the streets after the sheriff had given him the papers all the way to Elvira's and pounded on the door, but there was no light and all was as quiet within as Oak Bend Cemetery.

Agnes had thought then for a moment that she was "safe," that the encounter with the sheriff and his being served with the papers had overwhelmed him, and she allowed him to ramble on, telling her of his surprise and wonder that Elvira Summerlad could have done such a thing to him. He told how again and again the sheriff had appeared from nowhere. Had it been a writ for his execution, he could not have been more surprised. For hours afterward he had walked around the streets and alleyways of Boutflour, past the old icehouse and quarry, Sunshine River, the old fairgrounds and the circus lot, the stretch of ground before Ojibway Creek, where he stopped, and threw stones into the water. He could not return to the lodging house. Then, he told Agnes, he had thought of her and her friendship for the family.

She had said something but he had not heard it. He told her how much she looked like Elvira, and indeed at that moment, when he began holding her close to him, she had looked like a woman men say they see in fever, and the right hand stretches out to her from shadows which threaten to hold one down in sleep forever.

"Think of your sons, if you won't think of anybody else," he had heard Agnes's voice, as he drew her down with him to the sofa. She did not really fight him at first, thinking she would be able to persuade him, and then somehow, all her hairpins had come down in a rush, as if drawn from her hair by magnets, and both Wilders and she listened to them fall like tiny hailstones, one after another, until after one last eloquent pause, the last hairpin fell to her worn carpetless floor. Several times, late as it was, they heard somebody at the door knocking, then slowly, suspiciously, the person rapping had gone unwillingly away.

* * *

Years later, in old age, Wilders put the whole thing just narrated down to a damned lie, and said he had never "touched" Agnes Coles against her will and still put her down as the architect of the ruin of his marriage, and blamed her for everything, including Rick's breaking into the movies. He could not read what he had done in Agnes's studio in Jethro's notebook—this crazy but not improbable possibility flashed through his mind many times afterward—only because Jethro's jottings had been composed before the "rape" had occurred. But if one accepted the verdict of Boutflour, and perhaps it was right, he had forced Agnes to give herself to him because there did not seem to be much else either of them could do under the circumstances, and he had lain on her all night, groaning and crying, cursing and reaching fulfillment, kissing and damning, inveighing against all and sleeping on her breast, and she was too terrified and confused and also too tired, tired from everything that had been her life, finally to do anything but let him.

* * *

The fine drizzle had stopped; everything in the countryside glistened with wet, the bark and leaves of trees went on dripping so that one felt a gentle rain still came down.

Wilders Fergus remembered less of what had happened to him since he had left Winifred and his mother's sprawling old mansion to return to his family than the habitual town drunkard might have been able to recall.

The chronology of the outrage of events was badly shaken, for now it seemed to him that he had been in bed with Agnes Coles before ever he was met by the sheriff holding the papers or before he had run all the way to Elvira's boarding house to demand explanations. He recalled later having talked with the state troopers for having violated a traffic regulation somewhere out in a no man's land of dirt roads, cow paths, creeks and forest damaged by a tornado of a few summers back. The tornado had chewed the woodland to within a few inches of the ground, leaving only jagged sharp prongs of what had been trees, so that one felt that a family of prehistoric animals had grazed here. He left his car after the state troopers had dismissed him, and began walking nowhere in particular, through fields of sweet clover and some other crops he was not sure of in the dark of evening, perhaps alfalfa, and then another acre or so ahead some breast-high stalks of corn, and then open land. Had he remembered to take his shotgun with him he might have shot himself along the ditch here.

Going back after a long time to his car, he had trouble starting her. Then he drove past Two Forks, a small crossroads, over to Bethridge, a hamlet of some twenty houses, then past flour-refining mills, one-room schoolhouses here and there, a deserted shoe factory, a brewery, silos, the green and red lights of a train junction, then more fields of corn and wheat, and cattle huddled under a cottonwood tree. In the immediate distance he heard music from a dance hall. He parked his car nearby, and saw he was in the vicinity of the fairgrounds. He slumped suddenly over the steering wheel, the bone-aching weariness from absence of sleep for countless past nights had overtaken him. A boy came by with a woman, and they looked in the car. "Out like a light," the boy said.

"The trouble with you is you don't have no good bad habits," he heard in slumber a man's voice talking to him back in Virginia. Then he winced as he heard Elvira's final accusation against him, "You've ruined the lives of every person you've touched, that's your only accomplishment in this world . . . Don't defend yourself," she leveled the words at him, "you're guilty as any man who ever walked on two feet . . . Where do you think my mother would be today had you not come into our home that evening, and my own father was fool enough to take to you. He should have married you. You deceived him, you deceived all . . . You . . ."

His eyes had opened, as if they had never closed. Was he looking at his own son Jethro coming down the dirt road? In this time of the consistently improbable, it was not too surprising if it was Jeth. He pulled himself away from the steering wheel, got out of the car stiffly, and walked in the direction of the boy. What was he doing out at an hour like this, the father wondered.

It was Jeth all right, smoking a cigar, which he tried haphazardly to hide. Wilders ignored his smoking, bent down and kissed him, and smelled the liquor on the boy's breath. Fourteen years old, it ran through Wilders's mind, smoking and drinking, and so on, but he could feel no concern, dismay, or wish to reproach. If the world was ending in fiery conflagration, you would not correct your son for minor bad habits. Still, he wondered, who had taught the boy . . .

"I work in the Green Gables Dance Hall," Jethro now answered a question from his father concerning his being about at this time of night.

"Want me to drive you home, Jeth?"

"If you've got enough gas," Jethro replied.

Wilders ignored the taunt, well, perhaps it was not a taunt, only the way the boy spoke what was the facts, after all when he had come home with the back seat full of a catch of fish, he had been strapped, flat broke.

"Heard the news, I suppose," Wilders kept both hands on the steering wheel like a man driving in a race.

For some strange reason which seemed to both of them now natural, Jethro climbed into the back seat, and Wilders did not ask him to move up in the front with him.

"Yes, Daddy," Jethro replied, "I heard." Wilders did not

like Jeth to call him Dad, Papa or Daddy, never Dad, when Dad would somehow have suited the boy better.

"Your mother turned me out," Wilders said, starting the car. "Might as well have shot me, too, while she was at it. Served papers by the sheriff like I was a housebreaker or escaped cutthroat . . . Don't yet know how she knew where to send him to serve the papers on me, either."

His last words were soft, feeble, with no querulousness, no conviction, hardly even spoken with any expression of hurt or regret.

"I suppose you do feel awful bad, Papa," Jethro spoke after a long silence.

"Am I such a no-good fellow, Jeth?" Wilders wondered, not looking in the mirror to see his son's face.

"Do you have to work in a dance hall, Jethro?" Wilders did not wait for the answer to his earlier question.

As there was no answer from the back seat, Wilders went on, beginning to drive faster. "What do they pay you?"

"Fifty cents, and sometimes a tip or two," Jeth spoke now with the first bit of animation in replying to his father.

"For how long?"

"All the evening through."

"Mm," Wilders said, but perhaps he had not heard Jethro's answer.

"Do you think you like it there?" Wilders went on doggedly, but Jethro did not reply.

"I'll drive you back to your mother then."

They didn't exchange any words on the way back, a stretch of about four, five miles. The old car rattled and stopped, choked and banged down the sleeping streets, and Jethro putting his head out the window caught a glimpse of the red taillight, the reddest taillight he had ever seen, or so it seemed at that time of night.

Wilders got out of the car when they had reached Elvira's boarding house, opened the back-seat door for the boy, who got out unsteadily.

Wilders could not help putting his hand on the place where Jethro had been injured. "Don't, Pa-pa, please . . ."

He bent down and kissed Jethro. "Tell me the truth, am I such a bad fellow?" Wilders inquired. He looked about him, at the black windows of the boarding house. From inside one dimly heard a radio beating out dancing music.

"See you soon, Jethro," Wilders spoke to the retreating boy, who waved holding his palm up, his face and shoulders melting into the shadows of the house.

Wilders stood there waiting by the spirea bushes and the honeysuckle until, he suddenly realized with a start, he was staring into a house barred to him by the sheriff.

"Jeth has held on somehow, after all," he muttered aloud, before getting into his car and driving off.

*　*　*

During his strange trance-like encounter with Jethro, Wilders never associated the journal (which he had picked up by mistake and then read and reread with amazed horror, disbelief, and belief) with the boy he had given a ride back to the boarding house, for such terrible jottings could scarcely be imagined, let alone put down, except by a divine maniac. On the other hand, it never occurred to Jethro that his father had found his journal, had read all of it twice over, and still could not think of him as the writer. As Wilders had read and reread, he had visions of some recording angel turned demon penning the lines.

Jethro had gone to the five-and-ten-cent store and bought a new notebook to replace the old one, but the thought that "someone" might have the old filled-up one made him hesitate now as he put down his words, as if he was writing for another eye to scan his words.

The horror of the journal had been erased from Wilders's mind for a while by the added horror of what had happened to him on his return to Boutflour . . . Had he "raped" Agnes Coles, for instance, had he in fact even called on the piano teacher? At any rate, he must have been in her studio, for his jacket pockets and pants cuffs still coughed up from time to time one or two of her hairpins. And before he had been with her, there could be even less doubt, the sheriff had served papers on him, for the papers were in his breast pocket, and he had reread what they charged as he had reread Jethro's journal, one document dovetailing the other, and both sets of "papers" charged him with the same thing, desertion, nonsupport, and some other claims of "crime" until his eyes had swum blurred, had not seen, his vision seemed to be failing him too. He still wore occasionally an old-fashioned green-goggles for "motoring" which dated even before his time, and which made him look still more out of fashion. However, he threw the goggles now out of the window. He wanted to see everything with his own eyes. Hell and salvation, he muttered, looking down at his high shoes, I am out of fashion, I'm out of the God-damned world, if you ask me . . .

He could not get over the sight of Jethro, with his infirmity, and the information that the boy was working in some cheap dance hall. Then, as he drove up to Winifred's big house, with the fine lawn, the acres of trees, the expanse of shrubbery and rolling greensward, so like another country, the remembrance of the journal came over him. He would have been incapable of writing those words when he had been Jethro's age, even had he known about such things. He could only conclude, feebly, that the boy had heard all this at his job at the Green Gables Dance Hall. Then, he recalled, there had been liquor on Jeth's breath, and he was smoking a cigar, but worst of all, was the expression in the boy's eyes, an expression not that of a boy but of a soul pained with a knowledge that should not even come to man's estate, let alone boyhood . . .

Wilders promised himself he would keep the journal under lock and key.

* * *

"You'll fight of course," Winifred told him, after she had closed several doors so that Mother Fergus would not hear Wilders and her. Winifred had read, and reread, underlined, and made marginal notes on the papers the sheriff had served Wilders with. A look of determined exultation was on her face, while her brother sat immobile, his lips occasionally forming the words of the one sentence that went through his brain constantly, *Turned out of a man's own house,* as if this was the disaster which had crowned all others.

Winifred stirred uneasily from time to time as she penciled out her "plans" on the legal papers, stirred at the spectacle of his capitulation, which she felt, nonetheless, would be temporary. And her anger, which she knew ought to be turned against Elvira, was turned more toward Wilders than the terrible Summerlad woman. Winifred grew angrier and more vociferous because so much of what the charges claimed in the papers the sheriff had handed him were almost the same accusations she had leveled against her brother. But the truth of these charges were, she knew, irrelevant to what must be done, and if they were true, they were irrelevant to the real truth. There could be to Winifred's way of thinking no such thing as a divorce where children were concerned, especially where those children were boys. Elvira was too incompetent, too harebrained and flighty to raise boys. On the other hand the evidence stared her in the face in the words of the legal papers before her, Elvira had raised the boys, for Wilders had not been home, had always been away, and a sudden disturbing admiration for the mother, and for her own sex, flitted across her mind, and in a flash of recognition she saw her own struggles in the world as not unlike those of Elvira Summerlad, for like Elvira, Winifred had had to fight her own way in a world where men ruled, but unlike Elvira she had not had the slightest wink of admiration or assistance from the opposite sex. Winifred had had to fight as a man in a man's world, and the strain, while it had hardened her, even calmed her, made her strong, stronger than Wilders, stronger in some ways than her mother, though the old woman *was* strength, had also deformed her, and had sharpened her tongue into a lethal weapon, as Elvira knew, and had turned her whole character into that of a fighter, unlovable, stern, invincible, firm, and all the while starved for the other side of her nature which she had destroyed.

"We'll fight," Winifred spoke on and on in words heard now only by herself. "Elvira can't win."

"The devil you say," Wilders heard the last sentence. "A lot you know about justice or courts," he warned her from his more liberal experience, and suddenly he thought of Jethro's journal and he turned a ghastly pale. Then collecting himself, he said, "Do you think a fellow like me can win against a pretty woman in her day in court?"

"Elvira's not so very pretty now," Winifred spoke less vehemently now than he had expected.

"How would you know?" he shot at her. She accepted his jibe at present, knowing she would get at him even more savagely in some thrust later on.

"Now all we need do is plan our campaign. Having said this, Winifred rose and looked out the great front window which opened on an expanse of thick growth to trees and bushes. Strange for her, she was wearing that morning over her light summer dress a string of amber beads, which she had purchased, on a whim, from an import store in Boston, and had never worn until today, for she almost never affected jewelry. She touched her beads now as if they were talismans.

"Elvira can't win," she spoke between a mumble and a whisper.

Winifred was nursing the wounds Elvira had inflicted on her, as Wilders was trying to digest the horror of the journal he had perused. He must see to it, he thought, that neither Winifred nor his mother found it, or any of the women who worked in the house. Perhaps he would burn the notebook some evening out behind the woodshed in the bonfire, when no one was watching. That seemed the only decent thing to do. Nobody would wonder too much at what he was doing, even if they followed him out into the back yard, where once a month there usually was a burning of papers in the old bonfire pit, where in happier times there had been wiener and marshmallow roasts for the children, and in still older days, barbecues. He would let each page be consumed carefully and completely, for if a gust of wind should pick one leaf only and carry it to a neighbor! Each leaf was almost a confession of murder, for nobody was spared in that childish handwriting.

"Jethro is crazy," he said, and to his mortification he realized he had spoken aloud.

"Well, who wouldn't be living with such a mother," he heard Winifred's tart reply, with something like relief. Winifred did not even show surprise at the non sequitur of his exclamation. "Who indeed," Winifred went on, seemingly grateful he had said at last something, "who could live with a mad woman without going mad? Jethro'll snap out of it, though. After all he's a Fergus."

As he let her ramble on, planning his life for him and that of his boys, the thought occurred to him that Winifred had always fought for men, for her brothers, that is, and that was her lifework, even though she complained constantly about being a woman in a man's world. The phrase *inheritance through the father* kept going around in his head. Even their own mother was cruelly treated by Winifred, perhaps because she was a woman, and women brought out the worst in Winifred.

"You were driven out, *you* complain," he heard her voice now, for she had never quit speaking since they had closeted themselves together, "but consider yourself lucky. I was horsewhipped out of her house. And think of yourself as treated like a fine gentleman for you had only the law to deal with and not the nails of that insane baggage who is your wife."

"Yet you want me to win the divorce suit, and to live with her!" he roared out his anger with her now.

"Who spoke of living with her! You have a duty to your sons," she roared back. "Once you've stopped her from having a divorce, things can be settled," she spoke softly, her imagination working as she spoke. "You can bring your sons here to live, after things are settled," she touched now on the thing closest to her heart. "They belong here," she almost whispered.

"You don't include Rick in that, do you?" Wilders said. "He's grown up and about to leave home."

"For where?" she wondered, for she had included Rick, quite definitely. She had included all the boys.

"He's stage-struck or movie-crazy," Wilders was meek. His own failure with his sons nagged at him now, and certain lines and pages of the accusatory journal of Jethro came to him now like white-hot irons on his eyeballs.

"We'll get the stage and the movies out of his head once he's out of her sphere of influence," Winifred dismissed Rick's ambitions. "Of course it's Elvira who has put such ideas into his head."

"You give Elvira superhuman powers, for Christ's sake," and he leveled a string of bad words at her. "She's only a little country-town girl, with no education and no guile, not the harpy you always try to make out she is. She has no control over any of her sons. And God damn it to hell, neither do I."

"That's why you have to fight for them, then, you simpleton. And fight hard. There's Rory, almost a baby. You've got to fight for him, and of course Jethro. We've got to bring them here!" She walked up and down the edge of the room facing the glassed-in bookcases, a kind of exultant, even ecstatic expression on her face, which he studied with a kind of alarm.

Turning to him, she said, with a kind of ferocious defiance, "I want them here, do you understand?"

He understood her plan, and winced at it. She would be the head of the family, she would have the boys, and him. The divorce would not be allowed to take place, because it offended her and her mother's principles, but the mother would be sent away just the same. He could think of no worse solution to the mess he was in than, well, nothing short of the penitentiary. How bleak the outlook was, he mused, whatever solution came, and he was positive he could not win the divorce suit. Nobody contested divorce suits, without some slim hope of victory. And Elvira, he felt sure, had everybody on her side. Nobody would believe him in or out of court. He had been gone too long. Nobody knew who he was. And as Jethro had written in his log, "Everybody supposes we boys are bastards, that our last name is Summerlad, not Fergus, and Elvira is a whore . . ." Well, didn't she run a whorehouse. He sat down under the weight of his own reflections. Then suddenly, as if she had entered the room, to assist Winifred in her prosecution of him, there was Agnes Coles, and what he had done there in her imitation New York studio . . . He got up from the cane-bottom chair into which he had collapsed, swearing a blue streak. His obscenity and profanity, he felt, kept him at that moment from going to the lunatic asylum, but he had forgotten his sister's presence, and now he looked at her.

She was not looking in his direction, and then quietly she had left the room, perhaps, he grinned, to get soap and water for washing out his mouth.

The chorus of Winifred's commands and exhortations kept ringing on in his ears as perhaps his obscene curses did in hers, as she walked down the long hall to her mother's room.

We will fight the case. Win or lose, no matter. I will pay for all the court costs, Wilders . . . We can't let that baggage have the boys. And when she's lost in court, we can begin anew here, where we've lived so long . . .

* * *

Both Winifred and Elvira were mistresses of great houses, as Jethro had pointed out so many times in his log. The great house of Winifred, however, was not the one where she lived with her mother, and now with Wilders, but a mansion of some thirty rooms situated about a half block from Mother Fergus's home. It had been willed to her by a maiden aunt, and though everybody had advised her to sell it, and give up the burden of looking after it, she refused to consider parting with it, and visited the property daily. In its old interior she did some of her "studying" (Mother Fergus's phrase), and often went there of an evening in addition to her daytime inspection, to think things over, varnish a chair, or study the chimney and flues. Mother Fergus was always afraid that a housebreaker might give Winifred an ugly surprise, and begged her daughter not to go over there alone. But once, after the old woman voiced her fears of such a thing, Wilders made the rejoinder that any housebreaker would more than meet his match in Winifred, at which remark Mother Fergus laughed heartily for the first time in many months.

"I'm afraid, however," the old lady remarked, "Winifred may have more than met her match in Elvira the other day . . ."

Blinking, Wilders prepared himself for hearing the story all over again, for it always seemed to the old lady that he had not got all the details of it from her.

"Of course the poor girl went over to see Elvira with the best intentions in the world," the old woman began, again on the encounter between the two women.

Down the street old man Cheyney who had been a captain in the Civil War, and who was nearing a hundred, crossed over the lawn, and then disappeared from view into the green of the adjoining clump of trees.

"Winifred would skin me, Wilders, if I told you all these details, for I could hardly get them out of her . . ."

Wilders muttered under his breath, and yet he listened on.

"Elvira tore her dress clear off her back," the old woman tried to speak in a matter-of-fact way, but her face was wreathed in smiles.

Suddenly Wilders himself came to attention, for he had not known that the two women had gone this far in their "encounter."

"Yes, yes," Mother Fergus told him, "Winifred had to go to a gasoline filling station, and call Rick to help her out. That's how Winifred came home in the trench coat. It was Rick's . . ."

Wilders wondered whether he had heard this part of the story, had forgotten it in all that had happened since, or whether he had paid no attention to these details the first time it was told to him.

"Rick has an extensive wardrobe, according to Winifred," he heard his mother's voice as she continued to talk on. "Where do you suppose he gets such a lot of clothes, Wilders? How can he afford them?"

"Oh, he has a job, Mother," he reminded the old lady.

"Winifred says he's a Beau Brummel . . ."

Wilders was not listening now, and his mother's long rambling retelling of the meeting between Elvira and Winifred caused him to recall certain pages in Jethro's journals. All of a sudden he started, as if a shot had been fired, but his mother rambled on. What had startled him was his remembering he had mislaid Jethro's jottings a day or so before. It worried him. What if the hired girl or one of the neighbors had picked the journals up by mistake. They would read them of course. And even if they didn't believe what they read, for how could anybody *believe* such outpourings, still it would make a terrible impression on any reader. For though what was written down was not credible, one would go on thinking about it, and remembering it, until, as in his case, it would seem true!

"I hardly know your boys now," he heard Mother Fergus's interminable gentle monotone . . . "Even little Rory is getting to be a stranger . . . It's sad how soon they're grown up, I always say . . ."

She now spoke only for herself, and her eyes rested on Wilders, who sat before her gray-headed and bowed, when it had only been yesterday afternoon you would think that he had been "little," and she had been a young woman who had come out here to the Middle West from the East, to this wilderness, which is what it was when she had arrived, with no more knowledge of what lay ahead of her than a fledgling robin . . . Now the wilderness was getting to be concrete highway, the forest land was going, the deer and other wild animals all but disappeared, and all people around her talked about was property and "deals" and divorce and getting the better of one another . . . The Civil

War had been real to her, her own brother, a boy of just fourteen, had run off to enlist, and had been killed.

"Served her right," Wilders referred to Winifred's disgracing herself at Elvira's, and succeeded in confusing the old woman, who had left that subject minutes before. But he jumped up before he could explain to his mother what he was referring to. For suddenly the thought came over him that it must be Winifred who had taken Jethro's notebook. She was nosy as all get-out, yes, stuck her snout into everybody's business but her own.

"You should bear with her," his mother suddenly realized he meant Winifred now, and had come back to this topic. "I have to keep telling myself that again and again . . . She has that deep resentment working away inside of her."

Mother Fergus's attention wandered again from the room with Wilders, and the problem with his wife, her failure with her daughter to a period, long ago, more congenial. She could remember back to nearly a century, and when she thought of such a stretch of time, a gentle fatigue came over her, so that she wondered now as she so often did when sitting here in her rocker, breathing so faintly, sometimes with such tiring effort, if the next breath would not come, and then slipping back into the satin cushions of the chair, she felt she might awaken to some fine days of long ago, hear the door opened by her own mother, and wake to home and Christmas gifts.

"Winifred is the damndest tomfool who ever drew the breath of life," Wilders raised his voice, and the old lady awoke. "Fighting my battles . . . engineering my divorce suit!"

The sordid wrangling of present reality brought the old woman back from reverie.

"You must fight it of course, Wilders," she spoke quite matter-of-fact, almost hard. "For the boys' sake . . . But maybe even if the worst comes to the worst, you'll get custody of the children. Oh, I do hope so," she brightened. "I want them here."

"Of course, I'll fight, Mother," Wilders said, but even as he made this affirmation for her, the memory of Agnes Coles came to him, like a visitation and a presentiment of inevitable failure. He gave a kind of snort which sounded like defiance, but which was more like that of a man who makes one last effort not to suffocate.

He could not believe, nonetheless, he told himself that Elvira had been running a whorehouse. Not knowingly, it was too much for him to swallow with all the rest. Yet what would have put such a notion into the mind of a boy of thirteen? He felt that Jethro must be ruined in some moral way even more than he had been marred by his physical disability.

"My boys have seen the seamy side of life, I'm 'fraid," he spoke aloud and immediately regretted having spoken.

His mother nodded, an expression of wise, deferred judgment in her eyes. She seemed to understand. Had *she* been reading Jethro's notebook!

"The boarding house atmosphere, you know," he amended his statement.

She nodded again. But the talking and joking and the laugh she had had, the gentle fun at Winifred's expense, and the thought of her own long life had had its effect. She asked Wilders to help her onto the divan near the rocking chair.

"I'm all right now, don't look so grave. Just tired. And I've laughed so hard," she smiled faintly.

* * *

Although Elvira Summerlad had been a member of one of the leading families in Hittisleigh, and she still kept her membership in the Daughters of the American Revolution "back home," and Wilders Fergus could trace his ancestry back to the Battle of Culloden, in Scotland, they were considered nearly nothing in the commercial success-mad atmosphere of a defunct oil and boom town, Boutflour.

The news therefore that Elvira Summerlad or Mrs. Fergus was suing her husband for divorce struck the townspeople as somewhat absurd, if not laughable. Indeed Wilders had been gone so long that many newcomers to the town had more than a faint suspicion that Elvira had never been married, and that her sons each had a different illegitimate father.

Divorce was still rare in small towns, and granted only for unusual or perhaps "terrible" reasons, and the rich always traveled to other cities to obtain their divorces or were agreeable to formal separations.

Elvira Summerlad's mother, Melissa, who had almost never been known to say no to any whim of her daughter, balked. Like Mother Fergus, she could not give up her old-fashioned ideas, she disapproved of Elvira's smoking, she had never liked the idea of the boarding house, though she understood it was a "dread necessity," and divorce brought up the subject of the boys, in whom her sun rose and set. "When there are children," she wrote her daughter, "the parents must try to settle their differences."

But Melissa also knew that Wilders had never supported Elvira, and her own puny fortune, salvaged from the wreck caused by her son-in-law, had had still more drains made on it by Elvira's incessant need of money.

Now a matron of her son's hospital, in reduced, almost disgraceful circumstances, as old Mrs. Bainbridge never wearied of pointing out in her letters, Melissa tried in one way or another to dissuade Elvira from going through with her plans for divorce.

But Melissa had always spoiled Elvira, the favorite of all her children, the joy of her life, and from earliest times, only Elvira's grandmother, Annette, had been able to say no to the girl. Melissa had never been able to refuse her anything.

Now Melissa's "little girl" had not only asked for a divorce, but a large sum of money to fight it, and Elvira would send on to her mother all of Wilders's recent letters, in which he informed her that he would fight the case all the way up to the highest court in the land before he would give up his sons.

Both women were struck with amazement at his sudden "character," his unsuspected doggedness, which they had either overlooked or forgotten he had possessed, and Melissa begged her daughter to think twice now about her plan to go through a "contested suit," for as the mother reminded her of instances in their own family, "When you enter a court room you cannot know who will win."

Now Wilders wrote letter after letter, his natural shyness seeming to have left him when he was alone with a piece of paper and his thoughts, but in these letters there were phrases and entire sentences, casts of expression, which she was sure came from the angry mouth of Winifred. Perhaps she dictated the letters. At any rate they were inspired by that harridan. And Melissa agreed with her daughter. They decided that all three of the Ferguses, the old lady, Winifred, and Wilders sat in the parlor phrasing and composing these epistolary warnings and threats.

Wilders's letters struck home. Losing her nerve for a time Elvira supposed it was madness to have a public trial, which is what it would amount to, in that forbidding crumbling six- or seven-story court house with its maze of stifling rooms dating back to before the Civil War, decades of stale cigar smoke, spittoons, dreary poorly illuminated marble halls, the hollow echoing voices of litigants, and the faint stench of urine from the comfort stations situated, it seemed, every few doors on each hall. Next to a hospital or morgue a county court house, Elvira had always felt, was the most depressing thing in the world, and here of course her trial would be held! She doubted for the moment she could stand up under it. Yet something drove her on. She had tasted freedom, such as it was, as much as she had known worry and despair over the years of Wilders's absence. She had become used to being her own boss. She had proved she could make her way and be free, or at least she thought so, for she did not think of her dependence on Rick, her "keeping him by her side." It would never have occurred to her to say that she was free only because Rick had taken Widers's place. She would have denied such an allegation hotly, would have insisted that it was she who had been father and mother both to her oldest son, to Jethro, to Rory and if she had sometimes failed them (she was sure any failure or omission was minor here, and that she held a place in the hearts of her boys which Wilders could never occupy) no one could be perfect, not in this life, and she and she alone, outside of perhaps Melissa, had stood by the boys in every trial and sorrow. "No matter if you travel the ends of the earth," she had once told them at a dark hour, "you'll never find a friend who loves you as deeply as Elvira Summerlad . . ."

Rick who had suddenly begun again on "hounding" her to let him leave and start a film career in New York was summoned one evening to Elvira's own private study, where she composed her letters, and went over her financial transactions.

Rick had seemed less than interested in her "divorce suit," and whenever the subject was broached, she was appalled at his withdrawn look, his glacial indifference, his evasions, his stony gazing at the carpet.

"You act as if you didn't want your mother to be free!" she had cried at last under his unyielding hostility toward her.

Then rallying to his old affection for her for the moment, Rick could only say, "Elvira, you know me better than that!" and drop his eyes again.

"I thought you would fight for me, Rick!"

He considered this a long time, then said, "Can't you just live away from one another until some time in the future when the thing can be settled quietly?"

"What time in the future? At my funeral?" she cried. "Do you want me to allow him to come back here, have him sit around on his behind and loaf, manicuring his nails while I support all of us, and do all the backbreaking work, as I've done for ten years? . . ."

Rick smiled bitterly, for he knew the money he had earned as a secretary paid many of the expenses, and without his financial support he had often wondered on sleepless nights what Elvira would ever have done.

"If the trial comes, for your father intends to contest the

suit, Rick, my lawyer feels you will be, well, the principal witness."

He stared at her with complete shock, disbelief, terror written across mouth and brow.

He stood up and made his way slowly to the window, pulled back the curtains and breathed in the cool air of evening, which conveyed at that moment the perfume of the four-o'clocks.

"Must you, Elvira?" he mumbled, and the thought of public obloquy struck him at that moment as more horrible even than his testifying against his own father.

"Don't tell me you'll refuse," she cried, and she followed him over to the window," and tried to take his hand in hers, but he pushed her away roughly.

"Listen to me, Elvira," he began, and he had turned so deathly white that his whiteness seemed almost phosphorescent. "I won't refuse you, if you ask me, but don't ever ask another thing of me then in this world, do you hear?"

"You have no heart, is that it, to set me free from that man?"

"I don't know what I have a heart for," he put his head against the brand-new blinds of the window. "I think my heart is dead."

He was about to leave the room, but seeing her in tears—she had returned to her spinet desk and had put her head down in what he felt was real, rather than counterfeited despair—he went up to her and said without emotion: "I'll testify for you, Elvira, I'll do that, but you've got to get one thing straight, I'm going away then, and this time nobody's to stop me . . . I've got to make a career for myself, and I can't stay home forever. And I won't stay home for you, do you understand? I have some right to freedom too as well as other people . . ."

Rick left her then without a comforting touch or a kiss, left her too shaken even for the relief of weeping. And ahead she saw yawning before her that massive stone court house with her public trial and contest facing her, and with the possibility of defeat and ruin.

*   *   *

While Elvira spent her days in consultation with a lawyer appointed for her by Melissa, and the two of them went over the trial that was to be, and the charges against Wilders of "gross neglect and nonsupport, desertion, and cruelty," her mind kept wandering from the "rehearsals" for the court room to thoughts of Agnes Coles. There had been no communication between the two women for several weeks, and finally when Elvira had telephoned the piano teacher, there was a coldness and paucity of words which could only mean some rupture of friendship, some radical change of feeling on the part of Agnes. At first Elvira had been too much engrossed in her own worries to try to determine what had happened to her friendship with Agnes. Finally when things quieted down a bit, she wrote Agnes a short note asking her to come to the house for dinner. There was no reply. After waiting a few days, past the proposed day of the invitation, Elvira telephoned her friend again, but Agnes was evasive, coughed, a stage-like affectation with her, and offered no comments or remarks to help along the conversation. Even when Elvira began to tell her about her preparations for a divorce suit, there was a more than distant demeanor on the part of the music teacher, a stream of "I see" and "I understand," and "But it was inevitable of course."

At last angered by this inexplicable conduct, Elvira while shopping one afternoon on South Main Street, in a sudden impulse, walked up the iron steps to Agnes Coles's studio, and hearing no sound of the piano inside, felt she might have come at a good and propitious moment for having things out.

Elvira rapped peremptorily. Inside there was a sudden flurry of movement of papers, a cigarette was stamped out (Agnes dared not let her pupils know she smoked), and after a long wait, the door was opened. Instead of the old effusive kiss and hug, Agnes merely stood there, scowling, as if in the presence of a total stranger.

Rick's mother pushed her way in, without invitation, and sat down on the old davenport, hard as a pile of rock.

"Will you tell me what I have done to deserve this kind of treatment from you, Agnes?" Elvira cried.

Elvira's almost belligerent directness, and a flash of her blue eyes made Agnes hesitate. She had never had a quarrel with Elvira, and she suddenly saw that this was exactly what was about to happen. She felt sick with apprehension, and the sight of Elvira told her how much she had missed her and her friendship.

"I'm waiting for an answer, Agnes, and I mean to have one . . ."

"I'm afraid it may be impossible for us to be friends anymore," Agnes began, every vestige of assurance or poise missing.

"But what on earth have I done to lose your friendship and love?" Elvira went on heatedly but in full control of herself. "Will you tell me?" The anger in Elvira's voice, for all its control, came too as a surprise to Agnes, for she did not know the passionate stubborn indomitable inner core of her friend. She knew her only as the put-upon little housewife who had suffered the wreck of fortune, and who cried and confided to her so often.

"I'm not leaving here, Agnes, until you've told me what you hold against me. You owe me this explanation and I'll not allow anybody, do you hear, to treat me as you are treating me . . ."

To Elvira's astonishment, and for the first time to her knowledge, Agnes Coles burst into sobs. Elvira was too taken aback for some time to say a word, let alone comfort her. For all these years of their "bosom friendship," Agnes had always stood for her as the all-knowing self-controlled self-sufficient "professional" woman, the most sophisticated person in Boutflour, who knew New York like the back of her hand, who was full of the latest ideas, and who, poor as she was, always dressed in the latest fashions, and could speak intelligently on any subject. As Agnes wept on, turning her face away from her friend, Elvira remembered the music teacher's own origins, which were even humbler than her own, for Agnes had been brought up on a farm, and had gone through every hardship to try to make something of herself. As she cried now, all the New York veneer and polish, so dearly paid for, came peeling off with her last night's makeup, and Elvira felt she saw an aged and broken woman like the ones she sometimes caught glimpses of on the back steps of some mortgaged farm property.

Elvira threw her arms around her friend.

"I can't tell you, darling, because it concerns you so directly, I guess."

"There, there now," Elvira calmed her, holding her close to her, and kissing her on the eyes, and so drying her tears, but even as Elvira comforted her, a growing sense of uneasiness came over her because of Agnes's words, so that she was almost sorry now she had come here today at all, and inquired so deeply into Agnes's silence. Elvira felt it must somehow concern Rick, yes, there was the secret, she felt sure, now about to be revealed, to add itself to all her other burdens and cares, and she went white as one of her own freshly laundered sheets, after a morning's sunning.

"I can bear it, Agnes," Elvira said, still thinking of Rick. "Tell me what he has done," she half-coaxed, half-demanded, and she stroked Agnes's hair gently.

"He was here, Elvira. I was never so surprised in my life. It was so late for one thing."

"I had no idea he had come to see you," Elvira left off her embraces, and stood up unsteadily, and then sat down in one of the straight-back chairs above which was a framed picture of a once famous silent screen star who looked out vacantly as if over the expanse of an ocean.

"He'd hardly tell you, Elvira, that he had been here," Agnes had gained control of herself, and sat with parched lips, dry eyes, her heavy frown rigidly held now between her eyes.

"But what happened, dearest?" Elvira pressed the clasp on her purse until it pained her finger, and she laid the object on the floor beside her, waiting for the blow of new anguish to come.

"He came here in great agitation," Agnes began now. "Before his visit, I had no idea he was interested in me at all, certainly not in the way he evidently is . . ."

"Agnes, for pity's sake, don't stall and shift. Bring it all out at once. Then I can go home and die."

Puzzled by such a violent reaction, Agnes was less ready than ever to tell her friend what had happened, but seeing that Elvira must know something of what had happened already, she brought out, "Very well, then, since you ask for it, he forced me to go to bed with him . . . I said forced, Elvira, so don't look so hurt and accusing!"

"He couldn't! He couldn't!" Elvira rose, and walked over to the windows which faced the alley. "And what do you mean, he forced you! He's only a boy, for God's sakes. Tell me," she turned suddenly on Agnes, "that it's not so. Tell me at least it didn't happen, even if it did! Lie to me, and send me home with lies, why can't you, if it's this kind of truth I've wormed out of you!"

"Who on earth do you think I am talking about, my poor darling?" Agnes cried in a voice loud with horror, and some anger.

Elvira waited, her mouth working, the pupils of her eyes so large they seemed about to burst.

"I'm not to blame, as God is my witness," Agnes stared at Elvira with growing apprehension, for she had never seen her, or anybody look so menacing, indeed so dangerous, for there was a wildness about her eyes and mouth which reminded her of some forest beast she had once seen, shot by hunters.

"Supposing, Agnes, you tell me in the name of God who you are talking about, or I'll surely do something we'll both regret . . ."

"I'm talking about your husband of course, Wilders," Agnes now screamed out. "Who in hell did you think I meant! Who, Elvira?" seeing that Elvira had misunderstood all she had been saying from the beginning.

"Oh, Wilders, is that all?" Elvira helped herself back to the straight chair, and put her hand over her eyes. "Wilders was it," she mumbled.

"And you thought I meant Rick," Agnes cried in whispered consternation, and Elvira nodded.

Agnes rose now, and the long gold chain she wore down almost to her knees made a kind of clanking sound, as she walked over to the Chinese lacquer box which contained a package of perfumed cigarettes. She gingerly offered one of these to Elvira, and the two women, perhaps more hostile now than before, sat smoking, and were comforted at that moment that they were able to do something so disapproved of by Boutflour society. Agnes blew great perfect rings with her mouth, an accomplishment which Elvira had praised her for many times in the past, but today her feat only made Rick's mother purse her mouth, and look over at the piano, where some sheet music of Ethelbert Nevin met the eye.

The door bell rang violently, but Agnes motioned to her friend to be quiet and remain seated.

"As long as they don't hear the piano," Agnes whispered, they won't think I'm home . . ."

After a while the two women heard retreating footsteps, and Agnes went on blowing smoke rings.

"The damned cur," Elvira almost whistled out the phrase, but there was more relief than anger in her words.

On the other hand Agnes felt a kind of disappointment and anger toward Elvira, which finally was expressed in her saying, "I don't know how in the Sam Hill you could have ever thought in your wildest dreams I would do such a thing with Rick! I'm damned provoked with you, and I may never get over it." She gave out a short sob, and quickly daubed her eyes, then puffed wildly on her cigarette stamped it out, and took another. The perfume of the Salome cigarette and the cloudy aroma from

Agnes's Buddha incense burner made Elvira breathe with difficulty.

"You'll have to overlook anything I may have said, thought, or felt, then, Agnes," Elvira strode over to the window and opened it, letting in some air, an action which somewhat irritated Agnes the more.

"If you don't believe me of course about Wilders, I won t try to convince you," the piano teacher scolded.

"How could I not believe you there," Elvira protested. "And as to my accusing you of doing anything of that kind with Rick, why can't you forget that, and forgive my saying anything I may have said to hurt you . . . I've been beside myself."

Talking on and on in this fashion, the two women finally took one another in their arms, and Agnes kissed away Elvira's tears, and held her to her as tightly as if she were her child. Then leaning back with her "burden," rocking in her chair, in slow monotonous tones, Agnes told Elvira how it had all happened, how Wilders had rocked and rocked in this same chair they were in now, making the chair go faster and faster until Agnes had been as if hypnotized by his rocking, finding no explanation in his doing so, until he had sprung at her . . .

But Elvira's tears were coming now, as Agnes understood, not at sorrow over what Wilders had done, or sympathy with Agnes for what she had suffered, but with relief that it had not been Rick who had come here and attacked the music teacher, happiness that Rick was cleared, was innocent. And from this relief came a gladness, even, a gladness that Wilders had committed so shameful an action, for what he had done in the piano teacher's studio had freed her from him forever, had dissolved any tie he may have had with her and her marriage. She could not feel now any grief at divorcing him, at robbing the boys of such a father. He had "raped" a good personal friend, what more could one ask for pretext for divorce . . . Of course, she would not use such a thing in court, it was not needed, and it was more than she needed. She could scarcely therefore believe her ears when she heard Agnes say:

"And if you should need me to testify, Elvira, I will . . . I want you to have your divorce at any cost . . ."

"Don't ever again so much as think of such a sacrifice, do you hear?" Elvira spoke now with her hand on the door, ready at last to go home. "It would ruin you, Agnes, and would not help me in the least . . ."

"But if you saw, say, that you could not win your case," Agnes insisted. "I want you to have your freedom more than anything in the world . . ."

"You must forgive me for thinking such a terrible thing of you and Rick," Elvira went back to this, and the two women embraced. They knew then they would be friends again, but at the same time their friendship had changed. It was deeper and it was older, it was very old. They were indeed more like sisters now than ever before in the past, almost like mother and daughter. What had happened to Agnes had made them this close.

But the important thing was not what Wilders had done, but that Rick was cleared in Elvira's mind.

Jethro was waiting for his mother on her return from her visit to Agnes Coles's studio. His face was angry, flushed and accusatory, but she scarcely saw his face let alone his expression. For a long time now he had ceased to be her "darling," and beginning to show down on his cheeks, growing taller by the day, stronger, haughtier, he took issue with all she did or stood for, and his critical eye spared her nothing.

"Elvira, have you taken my journal?"

"Your journal, Jethro? What ever are you talking about!"

"I bet you took it," he snapped. "It's like you to do so."

"What journal? Is it the name of a book you have in school, or what? Can't you see Mother is worn out?"

"Someone has taken my journal!" he cried, near hysteria.

"Let me tell you something, young man, that will give you an excuse to cry about," Elvira turned on him with real anger. She had never meant to tell Jethro about his father and Agnes, rehearsing with herself all the way home the necessity for secrecy on this one issue, for she was shamed many times over what she had told him against his father in the past. But now the boy was so nasty to her, so overbearing, almost like his Aunt Winifred, whose tongue he seemed to have inherited, she suddenly felt like telling him. Jethro hated her, Rick hated her, everybody hated her, it seemed at that moment.

Wishing to keep silence, she went out into the kitchen, and opening a cabinet drawer took out one of her perfumed cigarettes. She sat down at the white ash table that had been her grandmother's mother's. Elvira's hands in which the veins now swelled like those of a much older woman by reason of her hard work, stroked the white pliant wood, unfinished and carefully sanded and cleaned, with its mysterious pattern of grain.

Jethro had followed her out, however, still harping on his journal.

"Your father," she began against her will, then choked, stopping. She did not know why Agnes Coles's story had moved her so much. Actually she did not care what Wilders did, yet his having gone there, assaulted her, her closest friend in Boutflour, raped her, yes that was the word, why avoid it . . . He had done it, she seemed certain now, in order to sully her and not Agnes, to show her his loathing and contempt for her, and to get even with her for her coldness and her withholding of what he called "conjugal rights," for she had not been intimate with Wilders since after the birth of Rory. She had had no husband in all that time, no head of the family, and she took reckoning now of the fact she was more alone than ever I before, she was facing a frightening public divorce suit instead of the quiet "settlement" she had hoped for. Her sons hated her, at least were indifferent to her, and perhaps she deserved it all, for had she not been the cause of Rick's losing his inheritance, and had not this the most foolish action of her entire life been the real reason that Rick was planning to leave her?

"What's wrong, Mother?" Jethro spoke at last, moved in spite of his long-accumulated anger and resentment against Elvira, at the sight of her deep trouble. He bent down, as if in sleep, and kissed her white creamy neck. She took his hand in passionate and painful embrace.

"Your father forced Agnes Coles to go to bed with him, Jethro," she too spoke as if sleeping. "Isn't that a terrible thing to have done?"

Then to Elvira's and perhaps Jethro's horror, he laughed aloud. She looked up at him thunderstruck.

Words, perhaps of remonstrance, correction, formed on her lips, but did not come out.

"You understand, Jethro, what I'm talking about?" she said, as he went on laughing.

Jethro sat down on one of the ancient little chairs that had come down to the family from the possessions of the Summerlads, and which ordinarily nobody sat on.

"Jethro!" she admonished him as he laughed on and on in uproarious lack of control and almost delirious pleasure.

Rising, her cigarette between her lips with the smoke curling into her eyes, she tried to explain her statement, since she had given out the secret in spite of herself, how Wilders had entered the studio, had come under pretext of finding out about Rick's progress in the theater, etc., but Jethro only laughed on, until tears coursed down his cheeks.

Then Elvira laughed, horrified to do so, but as uncontrolled as her middle son.

They both were seated now in the kitchen in the midst of ancient furniture and heirlooms laughing until they cried.

Finally, ashamed or perhaps frightened, they both came to a simultaneous halt.

"My God, what came over us?" Elvira wiped her eyes, beginning to get control of herself. Walking over to the kitchen sink, she let a little cool water run over her hands, then put her hands on the nape of her neck.

Walking over to the window sill where she kept certain favorite plants, Elvira watered them from a cracked pitcher, the African violet, Wandering Jew, geranium, and an assortment of ferns.

Finished she turned to face the boy, who had sobered up considerably and had his usual expression of gloomy bemused doubt.

"Well, now you know who your father is at last, Jethro," Elvira sighed. "At last, at last," she turned from studying his features, for she saw nothing of the father in them, only her own people's cast of expression looking back at her, the Summerlads.

"And you don't know who took my journal, Elvira, dear," Jethro returned to this loss.

Something of the old affection between mother and son had returned. The ugly, improbable, and queer episode which she had just related concerning the returned husband somehow did not touch them deeply, or if it did, in some deep crevice of their being, they could not respond to it. Wilders had left them too far back, too long ago, his absence had impaired their memory of him, their feel for his reality, the meaning of fatherhood itself had got lost and mislaid forever. He had returned of course, with empty pockets, had been driven out from the house, humiliated, and been served papers by the sheriff, then had gone back to where he had come from in the first place, to the taunts of Sister Winifred, the sorrow of welcome and reception by Mother Fergus. His returning to Boutflour to rape Agnes Coles at last seemed to mother and son as only queer and irrelevant, meaningless and ridiculous, forgivable because it was beneath contempt or blame. And there was at the same time no real sympathy between them for Agnes. They both blamed her somehow, by what they failed to say concerning her, and by an avoidance of her name.

But finally Elvira did turn to Agnes and her proposed "sacrifice."

"If necessary," Elvira now came to this, "and should the suit begin to go against us," and here she stopped, as if her mind was suddenly assailed by conflicting possibilities and chances, all of them evil, "then Agnes will testify at the trial for me ..."

Had Jethro heard what his mother said now, he probably might have laughed again, but he did not appear to be listening. And even Elvira did not think about Agnes's "noble promise" after this, and she knew it would never be necessary.

And if Agnes had lied or imagined it? Elvira wondered, opening a cabinet which contained a bottle of painkiller. "Well, who cares, if she told the truth or not," she spoke to an empty room now, for Jethro had left. "It was past and done with, over and forgotten, water under the old town bridge . . ."

* * *

Winifred, like all the Ferguses, had a strong unsleeping conscience, although she seldom went to church, a dereliction which pained her mother, but Winifred's ethics were, if anything, more ironclad and inflexible than the old woman's, and her severity toward wrongdoing almost as fierce as that of a Jonathan Edwards. When on that pleasant summer morning she had set eyes on the journals of Jethro on coming into Wilders's room to tidy it up (it was the most beautiful of all the sleeping-rooms, large and airy and facing a honeysuckle bush and a great clump of ancient fine cottonwood trees), she had taken the notebook away with her without it ever occurring to her she was walking off with someone else's private property, or that she was about to enter a moral territory undreamed of by her in her worst imaginings. Indeed on recognizing Jethro's handwriting on the plain frayed imitation leather binding, she thought it must be some prize essay he had written in school—she was unaware how wretched his progress was in his education, and that most of his marks were failing, and though she was sharply aware that the boy had had no father to supervise his education all this time, and with only the harpy Elvira to monitor his training, she put such stock in the boy's being a Fergus, she felt assured of his normal growth, development and maturation by reason of blood alone. He could only make all of them proud.

Wilders missed the journal almost at once, and when he was sure it had been removed from his sleeping-room, he sat down, suddenly sick at his stomach, and plowed his hands through his hair. He knew at once that Winifred had taken them, as the old lady who took care of Mother Fergus never touched papers, and the hired girl could scarcely say her ABC's. Wilders belonged to that generation of Americans who felt that their mothers and sisters knew nothing about basic facts of life, but Jethro's notebooks, he now reflected with awe on their being in Winifred's hands, went far beyond the elements of sex and centered on depravity and unlimited license. The only explanation Wilders could offer himself for the phenomenon of a young boy's knowing such things was that he had an untrammeled imagination, perhaps fed on immoral books (he was an omniscient reader according to Elvira and Rick) and perhaps movies, but these feeble explanations, he realized, would not do, and he had no way of deciding on where the boy got his information except the sorry one that he had got it from life. Had his discovery of the boy's log come at a period of his life less involved and calamitous he would have turned his full attention, he supposed, to Jethro and what he had written, but now that he faced a lawsuit which it seemed doubtful he would win, now that he had lost his wife's love and respect, and the love and respect of Rick through his having thrown away the boy's inheritance, and now that he had made a fool of himself with his having slept with Agnes Coles, and had come home beaten to accept the charity of Mother Fergus and his sister, well, wasn't his having more or less thrown Jethro's journals into Winifred's lap only the inevitable crowning of all his shame and disasters, and so it would perhaps seem only natural in view of all the other disgraces and calamities. Once Wilders was certain the journal had been taken from his room, he went at once to his sister's room, which was, in that large and vast house, nearly a half mile away from his, it seemed. Winifred came to the door in her dressing gown, her long hair down in braids, and almost unrecognizable from the Winifred who presided at table, or over a game of chess in the parlor during her "public" appearance of the day. But if Wilders was embarrassed to see his sister in a state of undress, she did not appear to be.

"Did you pick up a notebook by accident?" he inquired without greeting her.

Caught as she was at that very moment in reading the journal, she pretended she did not understand what he meant.

"Jethro's notebook," Wilders went on, knowing full well she had it, and he tried to look into the room.

Closing the door on him now until she spoke only through a few inches of space, she gave him a warning scowl, and said, "I did pick it up by mistake, as I thought it must be his schoolwork."

"Would you return it, please, straightway."

She opened the door perhaps another inch, moistened her lips, and was suddenly speechless. He stared at her.

"I don't know just now where I can lay my hands on it, Wilders," and she winced at her own barefaced lie. It was clear that she was undressed and getting ready for bed, but her discomfiture he saw at once came from something else, from the notebook, and though it was unusual for any of the Ferguses to rap at the door of the other, after retiring, and only the most urgent emergency could excuse it (their deep pain at being seen undressed set them apart from most of their contemporaries even in that remote era), Winifred's strange behavior at this moment came from some powerful present emotion working on her like quicklime.

"I will return it to you in the morning, Wilders," she spoke now with some of her old command and haughty authority.

Wilders went on standing before the small opening of the door.

"Did you hear what I just said to you?" she raised her voice.

"I'd like it now, Winifred, and please hand it over."

"In the morning, Wilders, in the morning. Good night, now," and she closed the door on him. He remained standing for some time before the cream-colored heavy door. From within he thought he heard the stealthy arranging of paper. "Tomorrow it won't matter," he muttered to himself. He went on standing there a few seconds more, then he walked the long corridor back to his own chamber.

* * *

Wilders did not sleep that night. His sister was perhaps more of a mystery to him than he or his brothers had always been to her. Perhaps he hardly regarded her as a woman, she was just Sis Winnie of old, and now Winifred, hard-favored, plain, homely, whatever word you chose for an unattractive woman, too tall and athletic for the fair sex, a wonderful horseman, swimmer, runner, and so forth. She had put him to shame in many athletic feats. But he could not think of her as a woman. As the saying went, she had never been kissed. A kind of awe came over him as he thought of her untouched virginal starched and sour life. She had the energy of ten average men. She had acquired a fortune over and above the one he had wrested from her years ago. When she appeared, in the parlor or on the sloping greensward off the house, one felt a small army of men equipped with axes were come to chop down forests, clear the land. Yet he had stood so long as a suppliant at her door tonight because he knew one thing: Jethro's notebooks might fell *her*. Yes, he would have to say it over and again to himself, since there was no one else to whom he could speak, the journals were the most terrible "messages" he had ever read from one human being to another. He could not believe Jethro had written them, and yet who else could have put down such thoughts with pen and paper. No grown man or woman, short of perhaps a lunatic, would have spent even the time required to pen such monstrous reports on human life. Finally they reminded him of an autopsy he had read about many years ago where the entire skin of the victim had had to be removed, from head to toe, to determine the cause of death. Jethro's journals were the scalpel of the doctor of autopsy, stripping each piece of skin from all those who had so much as stepped in front of his gaze.

Several times he was on the point of going to Winifred's

room again and without bothering to rap, break open the door and take the papers from her hands. But he could not face her again, and besides she must have already wandered into the worst of the log by now.

After having slipped on his trousers over his night shirt, and thrown his bathrobe over him, he went down the back stairs into the kitchen, and from there out into the spacious sweet-smelling back yard, from which, looking up, he could see the lamp lit in Winifred's room, and thought he caught a glimpse of her shadowed form bent over her reading. The thought crossed his mind that in the morning they would find her dead, stretched out across her Navajo blanket, a page of the accusatory papers in her hand, for the descriptions of Elvira, though terrible, were not so terrible perhaps as the descriptions of the Ferguses, of himself and Rick, and then finally there was also a portrait of Winifred which, if pitiless, was not false.

Then the final thought came to him in complete clearness at last that everything that was put down in the young maniac's notebook, though exaggerated in some disquieting indefinable way, was also literally true, nothing put down there, that is, so far as he knew, was false, except possibly the bald statement that Elvira was a whore, and even it—

Toward morning he fell into a deep sleep, and it was Winifred who, ringing the breakfast bell directly outside his room, awakened him at last. She had not had recourse to the old bell for many years. It had been used in the days when they were children. Winifred rang the bell with more than her usual morning vigor, and the thought crossed his mind then that her reading of the journals instead of killing her must have given her greater strength and power than before, an alarming contingency. He dressed hurriedly, not bothering to shave, combed his hair with an ivory comb given him years before by an old lady down the street who had always "admired" him, and then walked down the long carpeted staircase to the breakfast table.

Though it was midsummer, Winifred ordered the cook to prepare a heavy breakfast of raised buckwheat cakes and farm-fresh sausages. As he ate he studied her face, but could gain no knowledge from it. Her features looked more settled in mean determined lines than ever. She asked him how many cakes he wanted in her old voice like that of a woman who inquires how many blows of a knife she will have to give to kill someone. "Oh, a couple," he mumbled his reply. Since he had come to live here he constantly pretended that he required very little food. Yet in the end, he ate more than when he was a boy, seated at the same table where he had sat then. So she had a good stack of cakes prepared for him, and she herself brought in the pure maple syrup and the freshly churned farm butter.

He ate silently, without precisely hurrying, then excused himself, after putting his napkin in the silver ring, and walked off in the direction of the front parlor. Whether Winifred had eaten anything earlier this morning or not, he did not know, but after a very short while, she followed him into the parlor and then closed the heavy mahogany sliding doors that separated this room from the rest of the downstairs.

"I'm very sorry you read it," he spoke at once, but without looking up from a book he pretended to read.

She was rubbing the traces of some kind of lotion into her large hands, for though they had a hired girl and a nurse for Mother Fergus, Winifred insisted on doing many tasks about the house, often washing the dishes and doing the cleaning, and her hands often became chafed and raw from such work. She wore no rings or adornments except a small very costly Swiss wrist watch which sparkled like a precious gem.

"Why should you be sorry about anything?" she said dryly, but there was no savagery in her voice, only a kind of tone of relief, almost sweetness.

"Well, damn it, then, did you enjoy what you were up all night reading?" he snapped.

She accepted this statement also with equanimity and a kind of amused joy.

"I don't think I skipped anything," she said with a sort of schoolgirl brightness.

He stared at her with an expression of mingled horror and appalled apprehension.

"Of course," she began sitting down in a rocking chair near the mammoth horsehair sofa which nearly everybody avoided sitting in, "it's all a child's imagination." She stopped like a person who hesitates to congratulate himself, yet expects perhaps applause. "Nothing in it," she went on, "is true. Elvira has given him or allowed him to read trash, dreadful books. Also bad companions, older than himself. That's obvious. But because he wrote this stuff and nonsense and has it out of his system, I think we can rest assured that's all that will ever come of it . . . I'll have a talk with Jethro of course the first time he comes over again, and then we can forget the whole shebang."

She rose, prepared to leave.

He studied her, thunderstruck. He understood her, he realized, and he guessed women, less and less, if one could consider Winifred a woman, or indeed human. Was she play-acting? Was this calm Olympian coolness some pose of hers before she tore off her mask and attacked him? Or had she perhaps not read what Jethro had put down in green ink on ruled paper. Or was she too virginal and untried in the world and nature to understand what she had read. Here she was, come down from a night's reading of a boy's dislodged hallucinations, in which he smirched and befouled his parents and all those who had surrounded him from infancy with all the minute and damning descriptions of sins and crimes one could hope to find, and she stood here as untouched and shining as the polished antique furniture and heirlooms which surrounded them, and as refreshed as the lilies he could see outside the windows, sparkling with summer dew. Winifred was, yes, it was the word, dewy with relaxed peace and content.

He rose then and stepped out ahead of her from the parlor, and then to cap it all, he heard behind him her merry peal of laughter.

* * *

Then there came the relapse, or in medical parlance, delayed reaction, in Winifred's case.

Wilders, though no student of the human psyche, had dimly foreseen it all. Winifred hated, he was aware, "nature," sweat, pain, sickness, madness, heavy breathing and tears, sorrow, and death—all the things that had to do with blood, and the journals of Jethro, though weird and exaggerated at times, underlined everybody's relationship to blood, and blood often gone berserk.

Winifred had told him one day after her reading of the

journals that they were all rubbish, nothing more, that Jethro had "copied" them down, and that the whole thing merely underscored what an unbalanced, giddy, wretched silly woman Elvira Summerlad was. The journal also pointed out of course, as everything pointed out, what Wilders had done wrong. And her own sermon began, her tongue loosened by her reading. She could have managed things much better, he half-heard her from across the living room, and he gathered, as he always did from her after-supper lectures, that she had more endowment as a man than he did. (She was steering clear of any precise mention of the subject matter dealt with by the young maniac.) Winifred had managed her life discreetly, she had not infringed on others' charity, or drawn in friends and relatives into wild-eyed financial schemes, while he had mismanaged everything, business, fortune, and above all marriage, and then having botched it all, had come home to eat humble pie with her and Mother Fergus. And the reason for all this debacle, what was it? He had gone against her instructions, advice, and wishes, had flouted her good counsel and patient instruction, had gone diametrically opposite to common sense and wisdom and had married his little country church choir singer, and had plunged all of them, the Ferguses, that is, in ruin. One would have thought hearing her talk, had one been a stranger listening at the window, that the entire Fergus clan lay now as their ancestors had at the Battle of Culloden, bleeding, dying, run through and disfigured, broken, their very name taken from them, their property and fortune gone up in smoke, all because the youngest son had left home to marry Miss Summerlad.

But her sermon was only the first symptom of the

breakdown. The reaction came, and Winifred, swept off her feet at last by a kind of aftertaste of the poison she had imbibed, became like the frightened little girl he had saved from a rattlesnake when they had got too deep into the woods so many years ago. She had surrendered to his presence and protection then, after he had beaten the snake to death, and now again, she gave up, and kept to her bed.

Mother Fergus called the doctor after talking with Winifred, and informed Wilders rather crustily that her daughter was feeling a bit under the weather.

"Since she's never been sick within either of our memories, what do you judge she has?" Wilders spoke up so sharply that his mother could scarcely restrain a wry smile.

"I can assure you, there's something rather serious the matter," the old woman looked worried.

Dr. Tweedy lived only "next door," though that was a good half mile away, and he came now as he had been coming for the past forty years, carrying his little black bag which he had in his possession since he began practicing medicine. Knowing how much Winifred disliked being examined from the time she was a small child, Dr. Tweedy was not looking forward to seeing his patient, but he was curious what could be wrong with a person who was never ill, and who, in his private opinion, did not seem heir to human sickness.

Winifred would not allow her mother to be in the room with her during the doctor's examination, but unlike her behavior in times past, she allowed Doctor to examine her with as much cooperation and good manners on her part as she was capable of. Her very compliance struck the old physician as peculiar, and he decided she was ill indeed. Mother Fergus met him outside the sick woman's door, and asked in whispers what he had found.

He was halfway down the long staircase before he replied to the old woman. "She's running a temperature with a trace of fever. Nothing to worry about."

Dr. Tweedy walked on and on through the endless succession of carpets and grandfather clocks and hanging tapestries, while Mother Fergus hobbled after him in her purple dress, the brooch on her breast gleaming in the amber light.

Wilders joined them, and to Doctor's amazement, acted concerned, and the old physician looked the younger man up and down for a moment, perhaps trying to remember him as he had looked as a boy.

Near the front door Doctor stopped, put down his black bag for a moment, while he wrote out a prescription, then almost snapped:

"What sad news has Winifred received lately, I wonder?" He stared obliquely in the direction of Wilders and the old woman.

"None that we know of," Mother Fergus looked anxiously at Wilders.

"Oh, she's worried about some investments, I guess," Wilders spoke up dispiritedly, after his mother had fixed him with her gaze again.

Dr. Tweedy shook his head. "I've never seen that girl so down," he looked at Wilders carefully now, and then turning away from him, handed the prescription to Mother Fergus rather than to her son.

"Don't let her exert herself, and if you can, try to make her lie down most of the time." Doctor chuckled now as he said this, as if to add, "Make an Amazon rest!"

*   *   *

"It's extremely queer she should closet herself in the first place with an injured child's imaginings, and then even queerer she should come down sick."

Wilders was speaking to his mother. He had told her about the journal, as much as he could, and the old lady sat there with this new knowledge a long time. To his surprise she seemed to have taken it all in, and even to have understood it all more than he and Winifred had. He watched his mother with a new kind of appreciation of her. In the end, he thought, she seemed to know more than he did, certainly more than Winifred, at least about things like children and illness, misfortune and bearing up.

He could seldom speak what was on his mind to his mother, but he began to feel, owing to her calm collected demeanor, that perhaps this was his fault. She seemed to have weathered all storms. She did not ask more about Jethro's journals, and to his relief she did not want to see them.

He supposed that from her point of view, too, it must take a lot of getting used to him all over again, having him back home, that is. It had been so many years since Wilders was home that it had taken her some time, he felt, for her to see him as her son, a mature man with early gray in his hair, a man who had once been so eminently successful that he had been discussed in the great New York financial publications. When he had been at the height of his good fortune, Mother Fergus used to sit for hours in the back yard near the summer garden and muse about it all. Then everything as in a tornado had bent and fallen, gone down, with nothing to be salvaged. And now he had come home when she had very little strength, no more than to prepare herself for death. Here he sat, a stranger, with no prospects, not a penny in his pants pockets, "ruined" was the word they used, and as the two of them sat here together now in the thickening twilight, mother and son, it was as if they had returned to a period thirty, thirty-five years ago; she was worrying about the illness of one of her children and the problems of another, her youngest boy.

He rose now and began walking around the room, trying to control his profanity, but letting some of it slip out from time to time. The old woman listened as he unburdened himself, accused himself, scolded, and ranted. He damned the bad luck that had made him bring home the boy's musings in his valise. He wondered to her if perhaps Jethro would have to be sent to an institution. The little fellow seemed bright enough, and what he had written, he explained to his mother, had perfect clarity, but it must be all a pack of lies, that is fancies. Or say nobody could lie that consistently without the help of an unusual imagination. But there must be something stimulating his fancies. What was it?

Damnation take everything, he said at last, and picked up his straw hat, and went down the street, having told his mother he would be back in a few minutes.

"Where are you going, Wilders?" she had opened the front screen on the large porch to inquire of him, just as she had done thirty or thirty-five years ago. He had stopped. Her calling him like this gave them both pause, as if time had been rolled back. He stood there grinning, looking vacantly about him, as if he neither knew who she was nor who the man who stood in his shoes was. He was a penniless cuss without family, job, or prospects, and had been asked a question by his ancient mother as to where he was going.

"Up the street to see a fellow on business," he told her.

He had prospects of an important business deal, he wanted her to understand.

Both she and her son understood there was no fellow waiting for him and certainly no business deal.

"Don't tarry too long if you can help it, then," Mother Fergus nodded her head in a kind of encouraging, comforting manner. But she also meant that she wished he would not leave her alone too long with sick Winifred.

"Will be back just as soon as ever I can," his voice drifted back to her from the gathering twilight.

* * *

As he walked aimlessly down the street, away from the center of town, toward the small Disciples of Christ college and a forest of oak, he had the strange feeling that Agnes Coles was with him, even that she was following him. He fancied he could still smell the incense from her studio on his clothing. She seemed to him, the more he thought about it, the very spirit of divorce, and more than that, the cause of his about to be divorced. And he had never been able to get over the fact of how much she resembled Elvira, as if Elvira had a second self. She was the Elvira who had not obeyed her old Presbyterian father and had gone to New York, even if she had not been on the stage or made a success of herself. He thought of how all three of them, Agnes, Elvira, and himself had the same background, they had all been "born on the farm," as the phrase went, and they had all aspired to great things, they had all been supremely ambitious, and all their hopes had come to nothing. Wilders's dream of becoming a financial magnate, Elvira's never-stifled ambition to be an actress, and Agnes's wish to become a great song-writer. Wilders felt himself smiling broadly as he considered the tricks life played on their kind. He stopped and looked about him. He had already left the city limits of Paulding Meadows and was walking down a country road, but for some reason, whether it was the sight of a solitary farmhouse, or what, he kept thinking of ambition, which was born, he felt, in just such a farm, and he came back to Agnes Coles, as if her life carried some kind of lesson or instruction for him, some meaning which if yielded would explain his predicament. Shortly before he and Elvira had moved to Boutflour, Agnes had had a modest success in having one of her songs published in New York, and sung for a few days by a popular singer of the day, but this early success and promise was not repeated, and though she had other songs published, they came stillborn from the New York publisher, were unremarked, no singer asked for them, and even she had forgotten them. Agnes had continued to go to New York, the Mecca for her of all glamour, life, reality. She waited with almost frantic anticipation for September to come round when she was off for the New York season, and would then return a month later, with eyes sparkling, her figure trimmer, and would be able to pour out to Elvira and her "better pupils" all the wonderful things that she had seen and experienced in Gotham . . . It was Agnes, the conviction grew on Wilders, who like a siren disguised as a good and trustworthy friend, had lured both Elvira and Rick to bad principles and frivolous ways. Agnes preached the freedoms of the time, whatever the current ones were, and her studio with its stale cigarette smoke which her Chinese incense tried to disguise, and its fashionable New York magazines, and walls covered with photos of movie and stage stars, the languorous expression in Agnes's eyes, all seemed to sing a silent hymn of praise to sex and success.

When Wilders had learned from Jethro's journals that "Agnes was the faithfullest best friend of Elvira," he could only come again to the conclusion that it was Agnes who was the architect of his own ruin, as well as his family, and the real cause of the coming divorce. And he was the one who was to be divorced, he felt, while Elvira was to be made free, to live as she wished with her sons. For her sons were her own, she had raised them, not he, and they were to be entirely hers.

How badly he had played his hand! He was positive that Agnes had already gone to Elvira and told her everything, and he based this certainty and conviction solely on his having read Jethro's journals, for this devilish composition seemed suddenly to explain everything.

And now his sister Winifred had read the damned thing, just when he needed her support for the coming divorce trial.

He felt at that moment he might break down completely. He had already, without consulting Winifred, gone to see an attorney about his defense, Seth Mayhew, and he had not been encouraging at all, claiming that women had come into their own now, and it would be one devil of a job to contest the suit of a woman like Elvira Summerlad, Seth Mayhew knew something of Wilders's own financial failures and ruin, his long years of wanderings to gain back his fortune, and sensing there might not be much hope of collecting his fee, he was not promising at all, and indeed did not say he would take the case. But at the last he had mentioned to Wilders a large sum of money he would have to have if he handled the thing for him.

Back in his bedroom, from his long walk through the countryside, Wilders went over his "chances." Now as always the two women who controlled his destiny, Winifred and Elvira, were planning the coming public confrontation in the court house more than he was. Of course he knew he would have contested the case, had Winifred not been on the scene, but could he have carried it through without his sister, not even taking into account her financial backing of him? He supposed not. And though Winifred wanted Wilders to be able to prevent the judge handing down a settlement of divorce or separation in any legal sense of the term, she did not, he was absolutely sure, wish him to go back and live with Elvira, an inconsistency and even madness, and a point of view which fitted in with Winifred's character, which he had had a whole lifetime to study. She wanted, in other words, for Wilders to contest the suit, and prevent Elvira from winning any settlement, and then have Elvira put away as a mad woman and creature of indeterminable immorality, though Wilders knew that like himself Winifred would find it hard to credit Jethro's allegations that his mother was running a bawdyhouse. Yes, Winifred had it all put down in apple-pie order: he was to win out over Elvira Summerlad in court by preventing a bill of divorce from being granted, that is to disprove in public that he was guilty of gross neglect, nonsupport, and the other points, and then having vindicated himself, he would put wild demented Elvira away, and as the crux of it all, fetch the boys to Paulding Meadows to live with *her*.

"This is the only conceivable and the only right place for

them!" Winifred had thundered in one of their consultations together. "Perhaps Rick will follow his mother," she was beset by this one dark doubt. "I don't know," she mused over Rick's folly of wanting to go on the stage. "But the other boys shall be brought here . . ."

Winifred acted "recovered" from her reading of the journal. In some ways even, whatever had been wrong with her—and her "illness" posed a peculiar question mark in the minds of all who knew her, since she had never been ill before, or kept to her room—now that she had fully recovered, she looked suddenly stronger, younger, more in the pink than anybody could ever remember seeing her. She was ready to work with her brother Wilders, she announced to him, on the court case (she avoided using the term bill of divorcement).

"Of course I will hire the attorney required," she spoke to him over the breakfast table.

"Why in hell don't you represent me while you're at it," he threw down his napkin, but though he pushed back his chair, he did not leave the room.

She accepted his little outburst with a grand good humor this morning, and her mouth turned down ever so slightly as if to say that one could afford to treat with indulgence those who are completely in one's power. And Wilders was in her power, with not a dime in his pocket, no roof over his head but hers, no wife, and with sons who were wild, if not mad, and beyond any control he might exert; even Mother Fergus sat, as if in a corner, dependent on Winifred for her bread, with little suggestion in her wasted appearance of having been the feared matriarch of years gone past . . . All this Winifred managed to convey to him in her terrible good humor of the breakfast table, her smile, her ever-nodding head.

"The attorney I have been thinking of is Ed Depew," she brought out, with a sudden crafty abruptness.

"That numbskull!" his hands sought to pick up something on the table, but found only his napkin ring.

"Ed Depew feels you can win without the shadow of a doubt," she smiled again.

"Well I'm glad he's so damned optimistic," Wilders shot back with splenetic lack of control, "for I don't think a man has a ghost of a chance in a case where the plaintiff is a good-looking woman with the whole town on her side to boot . . ."

"Elvira's good looks are largely in the minds of those who knew her when she was a girl," Winifred studied the grain of wood in the heirloom chair in which she was sitting. "The judge may not see her as a beautiful young woman at all."

"The judge perhaps will be you then," he said, but his irritability ended as he spoke. A gelid despair, now almost his constant companion, came over him. He felt suddenly he would have been more himself had he gone to the penitentiary with his other buddies, who had left him blameless of course, but had also given him the almost lifelong task of making up the financial losses his schemes had caused in the first place. The freedom he had today was worse than any bondage he had ever imagined. He saw vaguely then, while: his sister petted the grain in her ancient chair, that his life from now on would be spent in or near this ancestral Fergus home, and the thought depressed him like the whiff from a mausoleum in damp weather.

* * *

Winifred could hardly fail to reflect on her illness from time to time. After all it had been her only illness since she was a girl. The Ferguses prided themselves on their sturdy Scotch ancestry, and sickness was regarded by them as a kind of willful disobedience to God, a perversity, even a hostile act against the family and others. And people who were continuously ill were expected, it was implied to die. Of course Winifred's strange indisposition had not been of much duration, or seriousness, but it had been the more queer for that very reason, and for her it was most disquieting and ominous. The more she tried to dismiss the memory of it or pretend she had not been sick, the more the thought of it came back to her. Locked up in her beautiful sunny airy room with the ancient but very clean wallpaper with designs of shepherds and fleecy sheep, she had at last been brought face to face with the two things that ever stung her into madness, her own solitary virgin state, her being forever relegated to the tribe of sterile slaves in the world's scheme of things, and now the tormenting anguish of witnessing through little Jethro's journals of the animal and human freedom personified in that wretched and inferior woman, Elvira Summerlad. A rage against Elviras sexual being, an envy against her having experienced every satisfaction and fulfillment and fruition came near to dethroning her reason, and a kind of film of blood seemed to burst in her brain and cover her entire body with a stinging completeness as if she had been suddenly whipped with a garment of nettles or some pitiless hand had struck her with a bale of barbed wire. And for the first time she was able to admit to herself her

ferocious envy of Elvira's embodiment and epitome of sex
and womanhood, and more terrible yet, motherhood, and
her own cankering sterile virginity. She was able to admit
it indeed to such a degree that she sat down before some
pages of foolscap and for an hour or so wrote down all her
disturbing and cankering torments . . . Later, when her
sickness had passed, she took the pages and walked out to
the back of the Fergus lot, where there was a huge wire
container, in a pit, reserved for bonfires. She paused for a
moment before depositing the papers and setting fire to
them in the pit, remembering in times past the wiener
and marshmallow roasts she had had here in the company
of her nephews when they had been little, and she especially remembered now how little Jethro had been there to
assist her, his handsome face reflecting the glow from the
conflagration, and his eyes shining happily in consonance
with the light in her own. And so before she lit the match
to the papers of her "statement" and "confession" she
admitted in mumbling and soft tones her jealousy, envy,
her immense hatred of Elvira, her loathing of her own
withering virginity. As she set fire to the foolscap her
hatred for Jethro's mother swept over her as if it were
flame, naphtha, an engulfing sheet of burning water,
smothering and drowning her, for Winifred's disturbance
and sickness did not come, as Wilders had feared, from a
prude's recoil at Jethro's descriptions of animal lust in
Elvira's boarding house, but from her having to witness
Jethro's own overwhelming, unconscious love for his
mother, though this was expressed in rage and hatred, and
the equally passionate love for his mother which moti-
vated every one of Rick's extravagant actions. Elvira was
both a whore and mother, and as the flames rose from the

pit, Winifred could easily have plunged a knife in her rival's throat if she could usurp her place.

Walking back to the house after the papers were illegible ashes, calm and almost happy, Winifred reflected on her brother Wilders's myopic reading of what his middle son had written. Wilders saw in the journals only the outpouring of a distempered young brain, while she saw that the boy had put down the truth, distorted and childish though the cast of expression and the presentation were. She also saw with absolute surety that Jethro would be a man of talent, whether a writer or poet or what he might be, he was, she saw immediately, a child of remarkable gifts. Wilders either could not see this far or would not admit it even to himself, but Winifred knew it, and loved Jethro the more. Indeed when she had read the hideous revelations of the journals, she knew she loved Jethro with as strange and violent a love as she had felt for Garret, her oldest brother, and afterwards for the youngest son in her family, Wilders. All the years Garret had been gone, after he had run off from home, she had kept the one good picture her mother had of him, taken, or more plainly stolen, without her mother's ever having known what became of it, and kept in a locked keepsake album by her bedside. At night even now sometimes she would throw the bedclothes away from her, rise, and open the keepsake to look at the photo . . . All other men she had met, even had they been capable of loving a girl so plain as herself, would have seemed like yokels and clodhoppers compared with the handsome adventurous Garret who had run off to Colorado.

And now she knew she would keep the journals by her

and look into their printed depths. It must be Jethro's spirit she was in love with, she opined. And he was like her; under his timid and palpitatingly nervous exterior, the heart of a warrior was beating. How else could one hope to describe it. The journals were the work of a very brave boy. How she admired him, envied him also. And with even greater fiercer resentment she saw that this courage and frenetic frankness must come from the Summerlad side of the house, in whose veins she knew there was Indian blood. This blond boy with the broken neck was a savage. So that all this while when Mother Fergus and Wilders lamented Sister Winifred's exposure to the young boy's distempered marshaling before her of the rude facts of sex and degeneracy, wickedness and lewdness, all she had been concerned with and concerned to the point of their having made her sick were a regret and a distaste for her own withering purity, and an envy and a passionate jealousy of Elvira with her hold over Jethro and Rick and Rory, and that house of the many rooms and doors where unfettered love and ecstasy and every unrestraint had gone on so long without a husband and father to hold back the tide of it all.

*   *   *

Elvira Summerlad as she paced the floor in her Boutflour boarding house, looking nervously from time to time from behind her white muslin curtains onto her grape arbor, which was beginning to yield the grapes she always made into a special jelly, was, had the Ferguses only known it, even less confident of winning her case in court than Wilders was of preventing a bill of divorcement from being handed down, depriving him of his dignity and his boys.

Elvira had thought, you see, for one thing, that all those near and dear to her would back her to the hilt in her "crusade" to free herself from a ne'er-do-well like Wilders Fergus, but as real preparations for the trial began, and after long consultations with an attorney, Elvira found that her mother, her brother, and her sons, while giving lip service to her "case," had no stomach or enthusiasm for the contest at all. Indeed she discovered by accident that her own mother, Melissa, had written a letter to Wilders expressing her pain and disappointment that a separation was being contemplated, Melissa, who had been ruined by this man!

And then in today's mail a letter fell out from all the other mail, postmarked Paulding Meadows, in Winifred Fergus's hand, with her return address on the back of the envelope! Elvira turned ashen pale at the sight of it. A strong sense of guilt, of being "discovered" swept over her, for at this time her friendship with George Gubell was occupying an important part of her life. He was a man of unknown background and small formal education, short, hardly taller than Elvira, his face scarred in an industrial accident dating back to his early youth, but a hard-working sober man, who had a very well-paying job for those times, and was the owner of a brand-new Fierce-Arrow automobile. He had become not only Elvira's star boarder, but her "friend," which meant, as Jethro knew, that the little cottage behind the boarding house was visited almost nightly by the pair.

When Elvira saw the letter from Winifred Fergus the thought flashed through her mind that her affair with George Gubell had been discovered, and that this letter from her sister-in-law was the death knell to any hopes she had for her freedom from Wilders, and that contained in the letter itself, indeed, she would find an order by which she was to reinstate Wilders at the head of her household at once.

On finally opening the letter, however, Elvira found to her relief, if not her pleasure, that Winifred was only asking for permission to invite "little" Jethro over for a short visit of a week or so with his father and grandmother.

Yes, Elvira cried to herself, she would give the permission, for she wanted the boy out from under her feet, and away out of her sight with his accusing eyes and suspicion-ridden remarks to her. Indeed Jethro was almost her greatest problem, and when the boy said sullenly he guessed he would go, she packed his clothes, and walked him part way to the depot, as if she wanted to be sure he would actually get on the coach, and not return clandestinely.

* * *

Winifred was severe enough with strangers but she was truly terrible and even violent with those she loved. She respected neither Mother Fergus's advanced age nor Jethro's extreme youth. He was in years only a child, Mother Fergus kept repeating to Winifred, prior to the boy's coming visit. But it was his journal perhaps which had made Winifred regard him as "responsible as a grown-up," but then Winifred being Winifred, she probably would have been as cruel and searching into the boy as she was shortly to prove to be, as if he had done nothing, had never penned a line of his journal, had he, in short, done nothing but be the son of Elvira Summerlad, or correct that, rather, to that he bore the fault of being the son of her youngest brother Wilders. Winifred, someone had once accused her to her face, was "jealous of life," and this same person had said Winifred felt she could control everything, and when the day came that her brothers not only married but had children, she felt cheated of her authority and command. She should have chosen their wives, issued permission for procreation, and been in charge of the education and upbringing of the boys. Indeed, she secretly many times wished for the divorce, so that she could "interfere" directly into the family's affairs, but she could not approve of it because it was Elvira's desire, and because it was a thing which might besmirch the Fergus name. At any rate, the divorce was not her idea, and had to be scotched.

She had therefore summoned Jethro, one hot August day, and while he was riding in the coach of the Big Four railroad, wondering which was worse, life with Elvira or a visit to his aunt's, Winifred was sitting in the parlor, alone, with the journal he had written beside her on a tiny antique marble-topped stand. She was going to hand it back to him today.

She would not be parting with the journals entirely, however, she sat musing, a smile on her lips which would have made recoil anyone who had chanced to glance at her at that moment. For though Winifred knew she must return the journals, she had no intention of giving them up. And without Wilders's or her mother's knowledge, she had had a copy made. This had required some thought, however, for to whom, in that small community of pious and mean mentality with its zest for gossip, could she entrust the copying of such a pile of horrors? She thought well and carefully in one sleepless night after another, all the while Wilders was hounding her for the return of it. Finally she had remembered Doris Bayliss. Doris Bayliss some years ago had had to give birth to a child without being married, and instead of leaving the village, like a decent compromised woman, she had her baby in the local county infirmary hospital, and then, to the added indignity of the pious, had raised the boy in sight of everybody—he was now about Jethro's age; in addition to her own private scandal, Doris's brother had been convicted of some sex offense, which remained nameless, and which whenever Winifred had raised the topic, she had been thundered into silence by looks from her brothers. Doris Bayliss earned her livelihood by typing manuscripts for college professors and a few students who had the money for such things . . . Winifred had therefore approached Doris, paid her so extravagant a fee she was sure she would keep her mouth shut, and in a week or so had the manuscript back, beautifully typed smelling faintly, however, to Winifred's annoyance of coal oil.

* * *

On Jethro's arrival, after allowing him to speak briefly to his grandmother and his father, Winifred ushered him into the great parlor which always seemed to the boy to stretch out for acres on into the continuing swell of green lawns outside and to empty lot after empty lot which Winifred had somehow by her business acumen, even in bad times, and by "going without" herself acquired over the years. Some said she was rich, Jethro remembered. Certainly the parlor looked like riches, for it was crammed and stuffed with old furniture, horsehair sofas, ebony cabinets, an ancient wooden Indian, sea chests, a couple of gold umbrella stands, a rosewood piano, badly in need of repair, and ticking away facing them a great majestic grandfather clock, whose belabored rhythmic beat seemed the very voice of Time itself. As Jethro's eyes swept over each article of furniture, Winifred noted the boy's powers of observation, and this filled her with irritation anew for it pointed out to her his being perfectly capable of having written the journals. She knew of course he had written them, yet it was necessary to prove, she felt, for the sake of everybody's satisfaction, that he had not. Otherwise the universe was unsettling itself.

She now brought forward the original manuscript of the journals from the marble-topped table, and set them on her lap.

"How did you leave your brothers, in good health, I trust," she began with a kind of cool sullen formality, after having indicated he should sit on a horsehair chair, which was most uncomfortable owing to his wearing only short breeches and so his bare legs were exposed to the discomfort of the prickling horsehair.

Jethro replied perfunctorily to her question, and then added with a kind of devilish tone in his voice, "And Elvira is very well also."

Aunt Winifred's eyes took on a distant look, and she went on hurriedly with "Rick is quite a young man now."

Jethro nodded, but a tiny sigh escaped him, which she did not fail to observe, and since it was, it seemed, a token of weakness, she did not like it.

"Are you tired, Jethro, because I have a lot to ask you?"

Seeing he was "something," if not tired, she clapped her

hands for Mrs. Greenholm, the woman who cared for her mother, and asked her to fetch the pitcher of lemonade, already prepared and waiting in the kitchen.

When Mrs. Greenholm had set down the pitcher, Jethro indifferently sipped some lemonade, and immediately Winifred warmed to her subject.

"I am sorry to say I have read your winter diary," she began.

Puzzled at her term for it, and still more puzzled she had read anything he had written, he looked blank.

At this moment she raised from her lap the offending stack of papers, the journal, which he had, for all the powers of observation which she had given him credit for, failed to notice.

"Take it back, Jethro," Aunt Winifred commanded.

In his confusion he upset his glass of lemonade, which in other circumstances would have brought a reprimand. She helped him mop up the liquid, and then allowed him to settle back with his manuscript secure in his own lap now.

"Your father, you see, by a perfectly understandable mistake carried away your notebook."

She paused for a long while.

"Jethro," she cried, ire in her tone, "we have all read it, and skimble-skamble stuff it is!"

"By mistake?" Jethro echoed her ensuing explanation of how Wilders had come by possession of his work, and he leafed through what he had written now as if he were trying to ascertain how the words must have struck his father and aunt.

"Your father shared it with me in his concern over you," Winifred winced slightly at her own lie . . . "I am considerably surprised at what you have put down there!" a high tide of anger now broke out from her, perhaps at her having lied to him, perhaps for countless other reasons.

Jethro had always been very much afraid of his Aunt Winifred. He had inherited a great deal of his fear of her from Elvira's own fear and hatred of the aunt, but his fear was giving place very quickly to feelings which rose from his inmost being, and his inmost being had been what he had put down in the journals. She and his father, but especially she, had taken a peep into something they had no right to lift even the corner of for any spying within.

"You ought not to have dared," he lifted his eyes toward her.

By now her own fear and confusion made her sweep on with the words, "Where did you learn those terrible things you have written about everyone? Where did you learn to be so unsparing? You write like a man who has lived a long life but has learned no mercy," she was astonished at words she had never meant to say. "If I knew such things, I think it would put me in my grave!"

He put his papers down with a heavy bang on a taboret near his horsehair chair.

Aunt Winifred paused over her own weakness, and then she returned to herself, to her self-control, and her hardness and her astringent poise.

"I think, Jethro, what must be done, and the sooner the better, is see that you come here to live with your father, while there is yet time!"

"Oh, you do, do you?" he replied with no attempt to conceal his sarcasm, but he had never taken his eyes off his journals, looking at them as he might have at a close friend who had blabbed and betrayed him to enemies.

She controlled her temper, but also paused to look at him with some wonder.

"I think you should come here, and so does your father!"

"Well, Aunt Winifred," Jethro turned his eyes to her, "I don't think you've got it right at all, and I don't think I will!"

"I think you will if your father so decides you shall!"

She struggled with herself to do nothing now to let her mounting anger spoil her domination of the situation.

"Won't we have to wait for what I am to do or not do on the result of the divorce suit?" Jethro spoke with lofty knowledge and detachment.

"You don't think for a moment, do you, Jethro, that that wretched lost woman who is your mother can win a divorce? Look at me! Do you? Not in any honest court of law! She will be soundly trounced!"

"But Elvira will never live with Wilders no matter what the court says!" he cried.

She had always allowed him the disrespect of using an adult's first name when it touched his mother, but she winced when she heard him call her brother Wilders.

"A boy's place is with his father," she brought out with deadly emphasis.

"It's Elvira I've been used to," he spoke now in a voice which rang through the cluttered room, "and she's the one I'll be best satisfied with."

He cocked his head as if to hear the meaning of his own words, which had surprised him.

"You can say such a thing in her favor after what you've written!"

"Yes, I suppose so, why not," he spoke in a musing tone. "And I don't like you making me sit here, as if I was on trial, when you are in the wrong, you and Wilders, poking into my private affairs, reading a thing you've no business reading."

"You'll not call your father Wilders in my presence, if you please!" she cried more to have time to collect her thoughts than to reprimand him.

"As to your private affairs," she went on immediately, "your journal or whatever the wicked thing is called, it's been looked into, and that's all there is to it, so we shan't go into the right and wrong of our having peeked . . . I should think you might thank providence that nobody in an official capacity had found your scribblings and read them, or who knows, you might have been sent to a place of detention!" She had chosen this last phrase carefully but was immediately sorry she had said it, since her words contained a hint of a threat.

"I mean," Aunt Winifred appealed to him, "what would people think if they read what you've written, Jethro . . . You can thank fortune only your father and I know!"

"It was not written for anybody else to read," he raised his voice again, frightening her now. "It was for my own eyes, and instruction!"

"Instruction!" she cried, stung by such a word in this context. "You mean you or anybody could be instructed by reading such a revolting series of horrible and wicked fabrications!"

His eyes rolled on the last word, but it was not the word which made the whites of his eyes alone show, but his own horror at remembering one thing and one alone which of course Aunt Winifred would have read, there was no possibility of her having skipped it, for it formed a kind of chorus to his whole journals. There were many episodes which must have troubled her, he recalled them now, as if

looking into the opening of a huge illuminated kaleido-
scope, for instance the parts about Hardin Lincoln, the
wildest boy in Boutflour, who was captain of a small gang
into which Jethro had been impressed. The boys ran wild
around the dam of the river, and one evening Hardin had
enacted a gruesome ceremony, in which he had posed as
some kind of Indian, masturbating himself and the boys,
and forcing them to taste one another's semen, mixed with
blood and excrement, and later Hardin had made them
witness his mounting a young mare. There were other horrors, too, and now Jethro allowing his eyes to come back
into focus looked at his aunt carefully, remembering all the
talk he had ever heard about her from Elvira, from Rick,
from Wilders. Winifred was that strange being, according
to them, that awful mistake, a permanent virgin, who
knew nothing, so everybody had assured him, about the
human body, especially the male human body, and lived in
a kind of ignorance, renewed daily by her own will power,
of how babies came into the world. But Elvira, he reck-
oned now, did not know what she was talking about
maybe, for here facing him, angry of course, concerned of
course, was Aunt Winifred, composed and not bowled
over, and asking for answers ... But the answer he felt she
was seeking was the lines, like those from a chorus, he had
left after nearly every paragraph of the pages which he
now again held patiently on his lap.

Between the two of them, Mama and Aunt Winifred, the
words of the journal reverberated now in his mind, *they've
done a clean good thorough job of snipping off Wilders's balls.*

He had heard the journals drop to the floor, but even
before that Aunt Winifred's face had begun to blur and
swim before his face.

It had seemed to him, before he slumped to the floor with his journals, and the word *fabrication* reached him long after Winifred had spoken it, and he had smiled, because not a word of the journals was made up, nothing was made up in it, it seemed that he had again fallen from the elm tree onto the sharp teeth of the iron fence, and this time his brains, loosened at last from the round dome of his head which had kept stored up all the affliction and pain of his life, had spilled on the flowers and grass before his own eyes.

Then he had come back to himself, oh so unwillingly, from out of the dark swimming mass of things before birth, this time to look into not his mother's eyes, but Aunt Winifred's, observing him with awe and fear, and a kind of fierce tender calm hope.
"There's not a thing to be afraid of, Jethro. You're going to be all right," he heard her voice.

* * *

Whatever more Aunt Winifred may have hoped to sift out from his journals and from Jethro himself, and whatever knowledge and illumination she was expecting from such a heart-to-heart meeting, all such attempts now or in the future were out of the question, she had seen for once and all as she sat patiently beside Jethro as he lay stretched out, still only half-conscious on the rich fabric of her ingrain carpet. She would question, she would cross-examine no more, at least about the journals. She had already seen too much for her own comfort, even sanity, she had pressed too hard. She would leave, she told herself now, as she waited for Jethro to come to himself again, she would leave alone certain things which her own life had not taught her and allow them to remain undiscovered, certainly she would not try to wrest secrets about men and women from a boy who was still in years little less than a child.

Therefore after she had helped him up to a chair, and had given him some brandy to drink, she had gone on talking silently to herself, admonishing herself. Tomorrow, she promised herself, she would ask Jethro what he wanted to do, return to Elvira Summerlad, or stay here some few additional days or as long as he wished in the company and only in the company of his father, for she would absent herself from any long periods with him. She had hoped he would choose Wilders of course and not Elvira, since he was the lesser of the two evils, and as this thought crossed her mind, for a moment she felt shamed at thinking it, and then she told herself no, why should it be shame, since think it she had, and it had a truth for her.

Meanwhile permission had been granted by Elvira for Jethro to remain on for a "stay" at Paulding Meadows (Elvira had agreed only with the utmost reluctance and soul-searching, torn between her dislike of being constantly spied on by her middle son, and her simultaneous and conflicting feeling of wanting him ever within reach of her voice), and Aunt Winifred, in turn, true to the promise she had made to herself, put father and son together to be steadily in their own company, while she remained secluded in her parlor, surrounded, perhaps comforted by the generations of heirlooms, though tempted occasionally to peek into the copy Doris Bayliss had made of her nephew's notebooks.

Wilders, who in the first place had only glanced at the

journals, scanning a page here, a few lines there, had by now nearly forgotten them. His own troubles were so momentous, so larger than life—when had he not had troubles? he wondered to himself—his own ruin was so absorbing of his own thought and attention, that even had he devoted himself to all Jethro had penned with the attention and closer concentration of his sister, it is doubtful if he had been as affected as she had been and still was. He had long ago forgiven and nearly forgotten whatever the boy had put down, and now he welcomed him with alacrity to his lonesome poor company. Indeed it had seemed to Wilders suddenly, when Winifred released the boy to him, that Jethro was the only friend he had remaining in the universe, these late summer nights. And Winifred's remaining "scarce" and out of sight and sound, allowing the two of them to be together, was to the father a more remarkable phenomenon than Jethro's having written lengthy scandalous things with pen and ink. In any case, he was thankful for Jethro, and he was the last man on earth who would take the boy to task now for anything he had done.

After Wilders and Jethro had done the day's chores about Winifred's house and her adjoining properties (Wilders was scarcely more than his sister's hired hand, it pained Jethro to note, as he plodded along with his father helping him cut the grass, trim shrubs and bushes, paint outbuildings and clean cisterns), the evenings belonged free and entire to the father and the son.

Almost the first day of his arrival, Wilders had given Jethro an old star chart dating from his own boyhood, and using this as a kind of guide, the two would walk out into the night and down one of the many unfrequented dirt roads, and then at some favorable spot, where the lights from the town interfered with vision the least, they would gaze up into the pullulating profusion of sky luminaries. After a lengthy sojourn in one spot, they would walk on, still with their eyes on the sky, past breast-high fields of corn, beginning to turn brown and sere under the intense heat of August, past acre after acre of oak and pine trees, from whose midst came vibrating the calls of tree frogs and whippoorwills.

While Wilders gazed in a kind of rapt attention at Pegasus and Pisces, or turning his gaze southward studied Aquarius and Job's Coffin, Jethro was unable to devote his entire attention to his astronomy for the reason he was sure he heard footsteps following them at a discreet distance, stopping when they stopped, silent when they were silent, and shuffling forward again when they strode forward.

Once Jethro would have sworn he caught sight of a man, slightly younger than his father, who stood under the protection of a great oak tree, in the midst of a vacant field, looking toward them. When the boy brought this to his father's attention, Wilders pooh-poohed the whole suggestion, told him they were in friendly country, where the people were decent and kindly, for they were not, after all, living in Chicago, and not to take on like his mother or Rick, who were always seeing dread portents in things, and lived by their intuition and feelings. Nonetheless Wilders acted more cautious from then on, and he too noted the sound of light footfalls in the still-ness of the countryside now and again, as if somebody followed at a convenient distance. Sometimes also Wilders fancied he heard movements among the stalks of corn, or caught the sound in the road behind of a stone's being kicked up, cause for the crickets to stop chirping for a moment.

One night shortly after a full cerise moon was rising slowly over a gloomy stretch of oak and pine, a tall outlandish figure of a man emerged from a copse, with long black uncombed hair, and hollow agitated dark eyes, who coming close to Wilders as if to be sure of the identity of the man he was approaching, took him then securely by the lapel and held on.

"Remember Birch Barstow, do you, Fergus," the man spoke out of a mouth of broken teeth.

Wilders did not lift a hand to remove the heavy fingers from his clothing.

"Course I remember Birch Barstow, and you ain't him." Wilders spoke now with the same twang and slight drawl the stranger had used in addressing him, as if he remembered not only Birch Barstow but other things still farther back in time. "No, you ain't him," Wilders spoke again, this time with a kind of bravado Jethro had never heard him employ before. All the while the man had his hands on Wilders's lapel Jethro felt a sickening terror, and his father's passive refusal to take the man's hands off him, despite the note of confidence in his voice, frightened the boy even more.

"So it's you at last, Wilders Fergus," the broken teeth spit out, "the smart fellow that ruined my grandpa and dad, ruined all of us Barstows. And ain't I been layin' for you for a good long day, you damned dirty feist."

The words, more violent it seemed than many blows, echoed through the dark patch of oak trees, and though the words meant, Jethro was sure, murder, and struck terror to his heart, they were like so many sudden and violent things, slightly unreal, and with the indifferent moon lazily rising higher and higher above them, seemed perhaps destined to pass also into silence and disappear. And all the while Wilders merely stood, did not speak, did not defend himself.

Then suddenly, to the boy's inexpressible relief, his father took the man's hands swiftly off his lapel and threw them down as he would have a branch from a tree. The man immediately attempted to put his hands back to their position on Wilders's coat, and Wilders pushed him backwards. With a sudden onrush the stranger struck Wilders a blow with his fist, and Wilders fell to the dirt road.

"Get up now for some more," the broken-toothed man stuttered out the command, "for this is my lucky time after all, to have caught up with you, and in a place meant for what I've got for you."

Wilders had risen, with a quiet almost sleepy look on his face, and as quietly and sleepily had put up his fists, much to his son's consolation, but still the boy saw no conviction or stomach for fight in Wilders's mien or the stance he took.

Again there was the murderous sound of fists and knuckles and Wilders as before fell to the road. Jethro smelled even before he saw blood—great gouts of it flying from the fighters, as Wilders rose, and they began again. His father's hat lay in the nearby ditch, and the crickets and tree frogs had gone into a prolonged attentive silence. Felled again, Wilders again rose, and held his fist up in the sleepy bored manner of pugilists in old engraved prints. Then came the dull nauseous sound of bones and flesh being struck as if by iron. Down yet again and again his father went, and then rising, and again blood flying like rain so that Jethro's own shirt was spattered, and looking toward the assailants, the boy saw his father's coat and shirt were as torn as if razor blades had slashed at the fabric. Jethro seemed incapable of watching the other man, he could keep his eyes only on the injury and punishment visited upon his Dad.

Then, as if from a signal from an invisible referee, the fight changed almost completely. From the reluctant and passive refined gentleman who, in the words of Elvira Summerlad, smelled of lilac toilet water, with manicured hands, the Wilders of the disconsolate and bowed head of failure, another new man stood before Jethro. Indeed for a moment, Jethro felt that a "second" had come out of the silent cornfield, and taken Wilders's place, some moving shadow which had determined the once prosperous banker should not fail in at least one fight in his life. For some moments, indeed Jethro could not recognize Wilders despite the progressive illumination of the moon. A man nearly completely disrobed, panting heavily like some beast escaped from irons, with a smarting reek of blood and torn flesh, his hair turned coal black again and from the sweat of his scalp gone to tiny ringlets, and the pupils of his eyes so distended and full that they looked like small eggs about to fall from their place, eyes that in daylight had been blue as robin's eggs were now of a black like that over dying coals. His father, now the aggressor, he dimly saw was not so much fighting the man before him as the whole echelon of forces which had defeated and wronged him, humiliated and tried to unman him, bringing him at last to the state of the simple nonentity who cleaned Aunt Winifred's cisterns.

Though the assailant struck Wilders more viciously than before, and his father's face was unrecognizable for the mask of blood and gore, and bones and knuckles cracked more gruesomely than ever, Wilders seemed to stand as erect and unmoved as if all the while he had been girt in a coat of mail. Then Jethro's eyes fell full at last on the stranger, and a kind of gasp escaped from him, for he saw the man was nothing but a vessel of blood, like a giant communion tumbler. Suddenly both assailants fell locked in a common embrace to the ground, but Wilders extricating himself from his opponent's clasp, rose unsteadily, and pulled the man up with him, about to deliver him another blow, when Jethro cried in a voice which could barely have reached his father, "Don't finish him for pity's sake!" But whether Wilders heard him or not, he struck the man again, and the stranger fell and lay without moving.

The slaughterhouse stench, the monstrous sound of uncontrolled breathing, which had no resemblance to anything human he had ever heard, the ferocious and murderous language of the two men, which made his own journals seem like the pen of a tired old gentlewoman, this sudden unprepared-for picture of murderous hatred and animal ferocity, with the stinging nauseating stench of body sweat and gore, made Jethro turn to the ditch and vomit painfully into its slimy green waters. Then turning, he walked back to where the fight had taken place. His father leant gasping against a tree, watching his assailant out of the corner of one eye as the beaten one hobbled off toward a clearing, and then walked unsteadily, finally to slink off and disappear through the cornfield.

"That son of a bitch won't be back," Wilders said in a voice as unrecognizable as if the corn shucks had spoken.

But even more unrecognizable than his voice was Wilders's face, which resembled a visor of brains and gore, or his body, nearly naked, its veins and arteries seeming to have been opened to the air in some grim nighttime dissection. Still hanging from his body in ribbons which resembled pieces of bleeding flesh were his trousers and a section of his much-mended shirt.

When Wilders put his hand suddenly on Jethro, as if to stop the boy's convulsive trembling, Jethro only trembled the more under his father's pressure.

"Jethro," he spoke again, and this time his voice was more like his own, "you may have to help me home, and if I go down—are you paying heed?—you may have to go back to town for help . . . Now, we'll go the back way through this cornfield yonder, and let's hope nobody lays an eye on us till we get ourselves at home. Now, let's get," and groaning to himself he walked along beside his son.

They began that slow queer walk back through the whispering stalks of corn. As Wilders from time to time would rest his hand to steady himself on Jethro, a thrill of some indefinable, all-pervasive kind ran through the body of the boy, and even now when his father would stop from time to time to vomit out clots of gore that came, it seemed, from his inmost guts, the boy felt at last he could endure all this and more. He was walking with a man he had never before known, and someone who was clothed, it seemed, only in blood, and the stains from vegetation and earth, but at the same rime he felt the person beside him was someone he had always been meant to know, and who in turn knew him, and that they were meant to be with each other as they were now, and the very stench of the blood and the red drops which fell staining the ground as they walked confirmed the feeling.

* * *

Wakening in his room the next morning, the wind moving the green blinds, all Jethro could remember for a while was that during the fight with one of the members of the Birch Barstow clan while he had noted the cries of whippoorwills and peepers, in memory another sound now came back to him which he seemed to have been oblivious to at the time, but which must have been actually more noticeable than that from frogs or birds, the singing of the telephone wires, and now they continued to sing in his ears until he got up and put on his clothes, shivering a bit again in the cool hint of fall in the air.

But he found he had been allowed to oversleep, it was near noon, and Aunt Winifred had gone off bright and early to a neighboring village to investigate a farm up for sale, and as a result she had not laid eyes on Wilders or found out about the fight. Wilders (he found out later) had gone out the first thing in the morning and seen a doctor up the street, not their own family physician, Dr. Tweedy, but a "new" man, and now there his father sat, in his own words "patched up" a bit, in his accustomed chair in the living room, silently poring over some legal papers which Jethro supposed were connected with his mother's divorce trial. They spoke only briefly to one another, a kind of constraint between them now that was in forceful contrast to their closeness of the night before, and then Jethro walked out into the dining room and had some breakfast, and during his meal he heard his father leave the house.

Jethro walked, hardly knowing he was doing so, right

into Aunt Winifred's parlor, and avoiding this time the horsehair chair, he let himself down in Winifred's own seat in which she had conducted her "investigation" of him. Here Jethro passed an interminable period of time, lost in the astonishment and unbelief of what had occurred, puzzled though happy too to find his father looking so well and spry after his deathly, yes spectral appearance of the late night (Wilders had joked at the time that they both must look "tomahawked," for a good deal of blood had spattered over the boy's head and body). Jethro reviewed again and again for himself the joyous and incredible feat accomplished by his father, who had defended himself so doggedly against a younger man, and had won a fight for which he had so little stomach . . . Then suddenly it seemed to the boy that the old Wilders who Elvira had always dismissed as a failure, neither man nor father, was no more, disappeared from the place by the cornfield under the singing telephone wires and rising moon, and as first his hat and then every stitch of clothing had been torn from the old Wilders, it seemed a new father had appeared made only of blood and bone, a man Jethro had not only never met before, but had never heard anyone tell him existed . . .

Starting up from his dozing in Winifred's chair, Jethro realized then that he had slept hardly more than a few winks last night, and all the night, from time to time, he had gotten out of bed, and gone to his father's door in his bare feet and listened outside patiently until at last he could be sure he heard Wilders snoring, and that he did not lie dead within.

Jethro thought back then also to the long detour they had taken to come home, his father cut to ribbons, yet hardly having to lean on him once. Up until that walk back, Jethro had been ever horrified of blood, for when he had cut his foot on an open tin can as a child he had found it unendurable, and then during and after the fight seeing so much blood on his father, on himself, he had been cured of his horror. He felt almost that he liked it—certainly now when he thought of it he felt something almost like calm.

And suddenly the long tension he had felt living with Elvira in the boarding house snapped for a moment, and he felt almost free.

Once Aunt Winifred had returned from her visit to her farm properties, Jethro had half-expected her to summon Wilders immediately into the cool still parlor for *his* cross-examination and interrogation concerning his "fight"—the sparse information concerning which she had got bits and pieces of from Mother Fergus, who had obtained the little she knew from Jethro. And Jethro knowing how Aunt Winifred felt about life, that is, she disapproved of all of it that went on outside her own jurisdiction or that of those like her, Jethro, then, was sure that a series of rows would now take place between her and Wilders over his infraction of her rule.

But the direct opposite came to pass. And Winifred, like Mother Fergus, seemed to shrink into herself at the first sight of Wilders's battered face, and like her mother at that first breakfast when Wilders had shown up in the "ruddy shape" he was in, she never asked him how he had got into such a condition, and she wore the same expression that Mother Fergus had, one that showed she was appalled but proud and content, and if not exactly triumphant, satisfied.

After his savage mauling at the hands of the man from

the Birch Barstows, Wilders bore himself, at least for a few days, with a haughty withdrawn coolness the boy had not seen in him before, and which did recall to Jethro Elvira Summerlad's having more than once said that in "the old days" Wilders had been the most stuck-up of men, haughty, proud, aristocratic-acting, sneering, and contemptuous, and with the look on his face of knowing more than God Almighty. Well, something of this old Wilders, the Wilders before Jethro had been born, had returned now, though it would have a brief reign. With his slashed brow, black eyes, loosened teeth and cut jaw, he had returned in appearance to his youthful prime, and he acted, in every gesture and expression, the conqueror. Sitting at the head of the table that evening of his sister's return, Wilders's lofty self-assurance put both Winifred and Mother Fergus in their place, so to speak, and returned them to a period of many years earlier when Wilders had been head of the family, ruler of the roost, and favorite son, whose most foolish action had been "all right," and both Winifred and her mother conversed now in quiet tones over their supper, almost as if begging permission to speak at all, from the stranger at the head of the board, and Jethro could only stare openmouthed, beyond astonishment.

But heroism soon lost some of its force. Recovered from his mauling, more jaunty than ever, but still the Wilders without a red cent in his jeans, and with no prospects ahead and nothing to look forward to but the public divorce suit in a "county seat," he began to shrivel back into his early middle age of defeat and despair, gloom and self-doubt.

But Jethro would not forget the battle under the telephone wires, and it was this Wilders he patiently looked for under his father's tame old exterior of business suits and straw hats. Jethro would have given anything to have had his father take him out to the road by the cornfield every night without fail and re-enact the battle there, with real or imagined opponent, but Wilders seemed scarcely aware of his son's admiration. To him he was just a little boy he hardly knew what to do with, and who had written a terrible "document" which had put him in hot water with his sister and mother.

Speaking one day, however, of the "fight," after some prompting by his son, Wilders had said, briefly grinning, "Well, Jeth, at one time I was in pretty good trim, as you may have noted ..."

But Jethro saw with sorrow that Wilders was again looking backwards, and if there was any forwards he didn't know about it, and wasn't planning for it. The chill of old age and disappointment was in the house of Grandma Fergus again, and the mantle of warrior soon was to pass back to Aunt Winifred, who, it was clear, was likewise not afraid either of the taste or sight of blood.

Then all of a sudden, as if a signal had come from some unknown quarter, the plans for Jethro's staying on were abruptly changed, and Wilders told him during a last walk through the countryside that it was best he should go back to Elvira's. Then he added, lamely, "At least for the present."

In the face of the boy's stony silence, Wilders went on: "It don't look right, Jeth, for you to be here with us when this cursed divorce case is coming to trial. 'Twould seem as if we were holding you as some kind of hostage ..."

Jethro looked away, mumbling some reply, but thinking

all the while how suddenly old and defeated his father acted now in contrast to the way he had used his fists to such advantage on almost this very same spot.

There was no moon tonight—it rose late—and the landscape looked most dismal to both of them.

Back from their walk, Jethro sat, somewhat stunned, in a cushiony satin armchair. He had been asked, more or less, he could see, to leave. Sent back, one might say, to Elvira Summerlad! And all without the final show-down which he now found he had been expecting, after all. And to his own considerable surprise he found he was disappointed that Aunt Winifred would not now be summoning him for another interrogation. Instead of a new inquisition, she had instead packed his bags for him, leaving them still open for the putting in of any forgotten items. And so, after expecting she would demand of him not only more explanations on the sub-ject of his journals, but many details concerning Wilders's fight with the man from Birch Barstow's, he had the real letdown of seeing himself simply ignored and allowed to spend his time as he chose until train time, whilst Winifred and Wilders, closeted together in the parlor, were entirely taken up with going over papers and plans for the trial in Boutflour.

Without hint of a warning, a sickening thought came to the boy, as clearly spelled out as if he had seen it appear before him in cold print: Wilders would lose the lawsuit. Wasn't this suspicion of what was to happen in the very air everybody breathed, in the way each person looked at the other, in Winifred's overfierce confidence and bragging defiance, and in Wilders's solemn or hangdog, dispirited mien. And Jethro began to have the unsettling feeling that at the conclusion of the trial he would lose both his parents, and that he would be sent away to live by himself forever in some remote seldom-visited place. He felt, to his own puzzled astonishment, that he wished both Elvira and Wilders to win the case!

It was at this moment that rising in a kind of absent-mindedness like that of sleepwalking he brushed against the old cupboard, which opened at his pressure, revealing within in addition to some old pewter tankards and broken clocks and timepieces, a brace of pistols. He stretched out his hand and touched one of the pistols. The cold metal brought as much shivering to him as the day he had stepped by chance on a rattlesnake while out gathering buckeyes. But as if he could not let go of the thing, he took the one pistol up and held it to him, then looking about carefully to see if he was observed or not, he picked up a box of shells which lay beside the guns, and then swiftly ran up the backstairs to his room, where he packed the pistol and shells deep in his valise as one of those "last forgotten items" Aunt Winifred had promised him he would discover, and closed the grip securely.

With nobody to meet him at the depot, or help him with his valise and the many packages Aunt Winifred had insisted he lug home with him, and with all the collected heat of summer seeming to have settled about him from baked pavements, and a kind of Sunday night stillness over the town, Jethro lumbered on home, stopping to rest every two or three blocks.

Once arrived home, he tarried some moments in front of Elvira's boarding house, feeling something within was amiss. The main entrance was wide open, for one thing, and no lights on downstairs. Depositing his valise and the packages by the staircase in the big hall, he turned on all the lights, and walked through the house to the kitchen, where he found a note from Elvira, pinned on the lampshade, which explained

> Dearest Jeth, We have all had to go unexpectedly to Bethridge, to see your Grandmother Melissa—Rick, Rory, and me, for many things connected with this trial need straightening out, but you will find plenty to eat in the ice box, on the second shelf. Your clean clothes are hanging in your closet. We will be back tomorrow. Please lock all the doors when you go to bed. Ask Vickie for anything you need. Your loving Mother.

While he was reading the note, he heard sobs, muffled, but prolonged. He sat down at the old white ash table, listening carefully, wondering. It was a familiar voice, crying, Vickie's. In the lonesomeness of his homecoming her crying almost moved him to tears.

Then Garner, one of Elvira's favorite roomers, whom she always addressed, along with so many other young men, including her own boys, as "my old stand-by," came running downstairs and out into the kitchen.

"Jeth," he greeted Elvira's son, "am I ever glad to see you!"

Jethro looked up, but the smile beginning to form on his lips froze as his gaze settled upon the roomer. Wearing nothing but his shorts, and despite his pleasant face and physique made admirable by reason of his having been a lumberjack in Ironwood, Michigan, Garner's whole appearance now was grisly, throwing the boy back in memory to Wilders's fight, for the man's body was covered with lacerations, some still bleeding, and looking as if someone had whipped him with barbed wire.

"Jesus, Jeth, judging by the expression on your puss, I must look like the buzzards and crows were ready for me . . ."

Garner now sat down at the kitchen table. "When I get my breath," he went on, "I'll tell you how I got this way." Then grinning wryly after having looked quickly down at himself, he opened a fresh pack of Old Golds, and began smoking.

More as an excuse to occupy himself with something than because he was hungry, Jethro walked out into the buttery and opened the door to the ice box, and brought out a sandwich which Elvira had placed there for him, wrapped carefully in old Christmas paper, over which she had penciled small x's, meaning of course kisses.

Having removed the wrapping, however, he could not bring himself to take a bite out of the sandwich. Garner's "massacred" appearance brought back again and yet again the shuddering horror of his father's scrap in the dark, and he found that his immunity to the sight and smell of blood must have worn off, for he shook and looked peaked and pale.

"I think what I'll do, Jeth," Garner said after taking a slow careful look at the boy's expression, "is make us some strong black coffee."

He got up then and went over to the stove and put water on to boil, and then opening a small white cupboard, as he had seen Elvira do many times, he took out some roasted beans, and the grinder, and began grinding the coffee.

There were no more sounds from upstairs of sobbing, Garner and Jethro drank one cup of strong coffee, followed by a second, and then Garner, rubbing his eyes like a man wakened from a long nap, said, "That was Vickie bawling," and Garner's story began. As it unfolded, it seemed to Jethro like a narrative he himself had put down in his journals and then forgotten, and in the boy's somewhat dazed state he suddenly began to feel as Aunt Winifred and Wilders must have felt as they leafed through his notebooks, for something terrible was being told him, he recognized, but it was not this time his own kind of terrible thing, which familiarity and close knowledge had robbed of some of its sting, but somebody else's terror and shame.

It seems Garner had always been "soft" on Vickie from the first day he put his grips down in the boarding house, and he saw her standing over the dishpan, in her bare feet, the suds glistening on her hands, and a few bubbles of soap resting close to where one caught a glimpse of the curve of her breasts. She had seen his "look" and had given him as good as he gave, he thought, in return. But they had hardly ever met after that, just passed one another in the long dark halls of the boarding house. He had been too smitten with her then (he was to see and understand all this only much later) even so much as to think to speak to her. She brought him to a kind of stillness, wonder and confusion he had never felt with other girls. And yet each time they met, when he sat down at Elvira's "second" table, or when they sat not too far from one another sometimes with the other roomers in the sitting room, she had showed him with the expression in her eyes, and a kind of way she opened and closed her mouth that she favored him more than just a little. But something was always preventing their being alone together. Of course, too, he was on the road a good deal (he was a soap salesman), and in the evenings when he was in town, after he had had his supper at Elvira's, it seemed she always preferred to help his land-lady with the dishes, or had a way of disappearing out the back way—perhaps she had expected him to follow her out to the big road that led to the river, he didn't know. Anyhow, in the main, it always seemed to him that Elvira wanted her for this or that, and that Vickie wished to be at the older woman's beck and call, as if she was her own daughter.

Today, the salesman had come back to town a day or so before he was expected only to find, like Jethro, that nobody was "to home." Going up the stairs, two steps at a time, he had reached the second floor before anybody would have known he had come in the front door, despite the noise he made with the heavy grip he was carrying, and there the door to Vickie's bedroom was open wide, and she lay half-asleep over the coverlet, nothing on but her baby-blue panties. He had stopped like a man who has driven in the dark to a precipice and is too lightheaded to know whether to go forward or back. The thought, too, came to him, as if he had never shared the thought before with himself, that all the while he went selling soap over his route in towns in Ohio, Michigan, and Indiana, it was her face lying there before him on the bed which had seemed now always to have been with him, like a passenger on the seat beside him, and at other times, as he dozed by some roadside cafe he sometimes swore he heard her voice.

Then she had awakened and seen him looking at her, and had at once reached for the quilt and pulled it partly over her.

"Will you go away, and this minute!" she had only been able to whisper her command to him, but he no more heard her than had he been ten hundred miles away on his soap route.

His starved eyes went back and forth over her body like a man who must memorize a map carefully if he expects to make his way alive from out a shelterless desert. The sight of her coral nipples, the declivity between those small breasts which seemed like flowers just about to drink the dew, the delicate roll of her pubis, with its soft gold hairs, all deprived him of speech and motion, and finally her own fears for herself were changed to her wondering if he had not been perhaps injured and was about to fall senseless before her.

Then he found himself unaccountably in the bathroom, with the door locked, not having remembered how he had left her, or if indeed he had actually seen her at all. The unprepared-for unexpected sight of untouched blossoming flesh had literally made him sick at his stomach as if he had without stopping drunk an entire pint of whiskey, and he stood reeling, not knowing what his body would make him do, vomit, or pass out, or lie on the floor and groan and sob. Or whether he was going right back to the room where she lay, if she did lie there, and just take her, yes no matter what she said or did, or anybody said or did later, bring all the rose and white flesh into himself, and hold it there inside him forever. His erection, he told a spellbound auditor (Jethro), was so violent that it felt as if he had finally burst his guts, and he had then painfully undressed himself as a doctor might remove the clothing from a man who has been badly scalded. Naked, free of all cloth, he lay down on the bathroom floor, hearing himself from time to time let out a cry almost unrecognizable as coming from himself. He got up and bathed for what seemed hours in cold tub water, but as he pointed out to Jethro, where did the YMCA get the idea cold water is quieting to a stiff-on. Then when he saw he had no chance of controlling himself any longer without ending up in a strait jacket, and with just presence of mind left to put a towel about his middle before, he opened the door and walked out into the hall. There were some fleeting thoughts, like whispering from an invisible person, that after all Vickie was hardly a whore, she behaved, went to church, had a good job, dated only those fellows who like herself were churchgoers, and the very sight of her body had told him, as somebody who had slept with too many girls not to know from firsthand, she shone, bloomed, smelled virginity.

He opened her door without knocking.

"Vickie, give me—" and not finishing whatever he was going to say, threw himself at her feet on the bed where she was still stretched out.

"Be nice," he sobbed, as she stared at him, first incredulous, then converted to her worst apprehensions. At first she had thought he had been drinking whiskey, and then briefly she considered whether he had gone crazy. Part of her sleepy absent-minded expression came from the fact, which he learned only after all that happened had happened, she was having a hard menstrual period, and was wracked with pain and discomfort and distaste for herself. Vickie was and was not a virgin, furthermore, for she had been sleeping with boys since she was twelve, but she somehow had managed never to let herself be deflowered, and the boys with whom she had dallied had in the end found some substitute kind of relief, most of them shooting off at the mere proximity of her body; she did not want to part with her hymen, she said, for some country superstition mouthed about had it that a maiden-head kept intact would impart a lasting look of undiminished youthful beauty, and so she had kept hers until now when the look of unhinged desire on Garner's face made her fearful, dead certain she was to lose it. Yes, his face and body were handsome enough, she gazed at him with a sultry sick involuntary smile coming over her mouth, but as the towel he had wrapped about him came off, the throbbing battered piece of enormous flesh, veins and arteries like bleeding ribbons, its uncircumcised end drawn back in eloquent tumescence to its corona, made her mind swim, she did not know whether with loathing, or a kind of madness to be taken, forced, impaled on his shaft of flesh. But anger got the better of her now, perhaps because she had always wanted to be taken by somebody with just his endowment, instead of the country boys who had sued for her, and now she feared that in the condition she was in, flowing even as he lay on her, he would in a minute find her repulsive. He had spoiled everything, the future, that is, for she had decided in her long country walks, after watching him at table with rapt admiration, until she forgot to breathe—she thought once they might one day marry. Without knowing what she was doing, as she felt the pressure of his penis as struggling with a life of its own, reaching out for her sex, she hit him across the face such a blow it cut his lips badly. The swift jet of blood coming from himself added to his passion, and he drew her to him in a bone-crushing embrace. Vickie's hatred of force was even greater than her modesty about flowing menstrually. She sank her teeth now into his biceps. His hand had already, in forcing open her legs, pushed into her vulva, and came away stained with blood. Far from being sickened by her flow, his desire only mounted, he had never had a woman with the curse, and not even death could have stopped him now, and while the cut from his mouth bled over her face and breasts, he touched for a moment her clitoris which looked like some carelessly dropped ruby, then plunged himself into her crimson tight vulva. As he with all his accumulated force and enthusiasm burst through her hymen, Vickie to prevent herself from crying out and giving him any added pleasure at her being conquered, sank her teeth deep into his chest, so that the cry of defeat it would appear came from him. From then on it was one of those encounters which grace battlefields or bullfights rather than bed. Whatever ferocity the one acted out, the other strove to outdo the first perpetrator.

When it was over at last, they had been tearing one another's flesh and performing the act again and again for the space of three hours, and they at last had separated like two wild curs who must lamely concede no victory.

While Garner sat in his room too stunned to remember exactly what he had done or what had been done to him, Vickie, fearful of Elvira's wrath, had taken all the sheets and pillowcases down to the laundry room, but she despaired of doing much with the linens in the condition they were in.

At this worst of moments, Jethro had returned unannounced and unexpected.

"Go down and talk to that boy and keep him from coming up here until I tell you," Vickie had screamed from her room at Garner, for she was fearful even now he might return and force her again.

Vickie had sat a long time then, as evening passed into full night. She heard nothing, indeed saw nothing. Her past life seemed to be retreating from her like the green countryside will vanish from a slow-moving canoe, but with this difference, she would never again see this green grass and these gentle trees that were passing from her sight forever as she rowed herself over the water.

When she did look up finally she saw Jethro there standing at her threshold, just where Garner had stood so many hours before.

"Come in here, Jethro," she heard her own words as if they had come from the Victrola playing downstairs.

He came into the room.

"Close the door, darling."

He obeyed.

"Now take off all your clothes like a good boy," she ordered in a bitterness mixed with pity, as if she herself were commanded to say this by some absent supervisor.

Like someone tricked by a magician, he stripped.

"Come over here, little Jethro," she said.

She placed her hand securely on the curve of his penis.

"It's time for you, too," she told him, pulling him down on the bed. "You're ripe and you're ready. Besides, why should you go off scot-free when I've been taken by the hunters."

She drew him ferociously down into her still bleeding orifice.

"I'm going to pass the favor around now to everyone I may have missed before," and she took him now completely into her. "You've got more than enough, Jeth, you're no child, what are they talking about, and you'll make up for and soothe me for being torn by that prize bull downstairs.

Oh, Jeth, Jeth," she wept, as she slowly began to work him into her, his eyes rolling.

"I've lost all that I had," she cried on, "and I don't fairly know now where or when I will ever stop."

For some period of time after his encounter with Garner and Vickie, Jethro walked about in a kind of "sleep-by-day" expression on his face, in the alarmed phrase of Elvira, who watched him sharply, knowing something was amiss, but blaming his changed behavior entirely on his visit to his "harridan" aunt and "no-account philandering" father.

Jethro's new notebook remained untouched by pen, and never opened, but he thought all the time, paragraph after paragraph, with words legible in his head as if pen were held in hand, scratching over the ruled sheets of paper.

Because he had plunged into the same bloodstained hole which Garner had first forced his way into, Jethro would feel, he knew, Garner's presence with him in his own body, forever, along with Vickie's embrace. They had partaken of the same queer baptism of blood together, so he felt Garner almost closer to him than his own brothers.

Shortly after the strange awful Sunday in the deserted boarding house, Garner got himself transferred to another route, or territory, of his soap company, and was seen no more, until a later important day was to roll around.

Elvira always wondered why that "nice clean-cut young man" Garner went away.

"You act as if you knew something," his mother spoke up one day to her sullen brooding middle son.

But Jethro had promised both Vickie and Garner to keep the secret, and he did.

Love was supposed to smell April and May, but with

Jethro, for a long time afterwards, it gave off a slaughter-house stench.

Once, falling asleep, he had dreamed he had entered the entrails of his own mother, and was present at his own engendering by his father.

And then little by little the whole event of the butchery of love began to fade and grow imperceptible, like his father's late evening scrap amidst the cornfields and whip-poorwills.

And all the while the great divorce trial was getting closer and closer . . .

* * *

"Jeremy! Jeremy Cready!" I heard Uncle Matt's voice coming to me, as if from under miles of sea and tide. "Wake up, sit up. What am I playing out my dwindling inheritance for—to hear you snore?"

I jumped in my sleep, in my chair, and opening my eyes looked into Matt's. They resembled those of a burrowing owl which I had surprised in the woods a week before, and I couldn't help grinning widely, which put him into an even viler disposition.

Then I looked down at my writing hand, with the pen still held tight, for I had fallen asleep only for a moment, but my fingers, I realized, had stopped as if in unison and vibration with Jethro's pen, which had made no more entries in his notebooks after the time and place to which Matt had by now brought me.

Uncle Matt stirred in his chair, and then raising a large brandy snifter, drained it to the bottom, as if in that one swallow he was tasting again all the combined suns of the days he had just brought back from dim-lit memory.

"So we've traveled this far, dear Jeremy, and I've brought you up well to my own time, and into your own lifetime as well."

He stared into the night.

"And though it's late," he went on then, "well past your bedtime, almost past mine, I want to go on and finish this thing, do you hear. We must conclude the damned chronicle so I can get some rest. I need rest more than anything else in this brackish world.

"Drink some of this," he commanded, and I took a long swallow of his best brandy, resigned, I guess, at the age of fifteen to being a toper, though I loathed every drop. But it revived me, as it revived him, and I held pen to paper now, eyes wide, as if it were seven o'clock in the morning, and I had had breakfast and strong coffee.

"Declivity, declivity, it's all declivity," Matt would mutter, and then when he saw me staring at him so apprehensively, he would, by some extra human effort, come out of his cups, and go on with his narrative which he felt so compelled to finish owing to "time's running out" on him.

"There was a stir in the atmosphere of remote, crumbly old Boutflour, believe you me (at that period there were some trottoirs still fashioned of ordinary wood, and one of the main thoroughfares beside the old old post office, then used as a draft board, was yet unpaved), a stir not only in Boutflour proper but the surrounding towns and villages and crossroads, Gilliam, Mount Penworth, Blossom Creek, and Braithwaite. Summer had come to an end in a cloud of fierce heat, midges and droning cicadas, with only the blast of winter ahead as the next coming attraction, and there was, I don't need to emphasize to you, a hunger, in the fine fall weather we are blessed with, for news, and especially sensation.

"*A county court house divorce trial, with Elvira and her eldest son on the stand . . . You sit gape-mouthed, Jeremy, and that's good. I need to see such a face as I orate, prize of clodhoppers. Yes, I've brought you back to the time and place of my being not just young, but, do you hear, alive . . . So make it your time and place . . .*"

As he said these words his head fell over slightly, and a kind of paroxysm went through him, ending in his head twitching terribly. But he gave me a cautionary glance, and I dared do or say nothing, but held the pen tight to the page. He went on:

"*Rick practically lived with me those days before the trial. He was in a kind of dazed, even hypnotized state, for he knew of course what his duty to his mother was—he was to testify against his own father in court. (At the same time, the poor devil was about to sign a contract for a film, his dream come true, but on the wrong leaf of the calendar.)*

" '*Should I do it, Matt?' he kept imploring me.*

"*Thinking he meant go into the films, I kept nodding, saying again and again, 'By all means, yes, sweet Rick,' until he jumped up from his chair and shook me by the collar, shouting at me, with his spit, like hot embers, flying into my face, I mean testify against my father, can't you hear, you ever agreeable idiot!'*

"*Even I who had no remembered parents or loved ones, could find no look or word of encouragement for such a proposal. As he saw the expression of sick doubt gathering over my face, his hands relaxed from their hold on my collar, and then, with only the warning of the dread way his pupils had of dilating when in great passion, he cried: 'You timeserving cheap homeless bastard!'*

"*I was, I think, glad. It broke the tension, and it sent him to his knees before me begging my pardon, my forgiveness, swearing I was his only friend, and to guide and counsel him for Jesus Christ's sake.*

" 'It's murder, Rick, whatever decision you take,' I spoke loud and decisive. When he said nothing I went on with, 'It's treason, blasphemy, assassination to testify against your own dad.' That was everything of course, but I continued with, 'Wilders is, whether you acknowledge him or not, your dad, and he is putting up a fight, with hands tied behind his back, but still fighting to keep his family, and especially his eldest son. That's why he's contesting your mother's suit. Because he has an eldest son.'

"There was a silence like from some steep midnight valley.

"Then I don't know how, but I went on with, 'But Rick, you'll testify for Elvira, clear your mind on that score, you'll testify for her and you'll be on her side, but I don't need to tell you why you will, you, we, nobody knows why, all we know is you'll do it because you're her boy, and she's your greatest love . . .'

"He was weeping hard now, and he held on to my hand.

" 'But how can I face him, afterwards, Wilders, for there'll be, I suppose, an afterwards . . .'

"I tried to think of something, anything, to say, but I saw, to my relief, he was not listening in any case. I felt I had committed treason too, and all the rest, but I was weak, you see, Jeremy, you know me too well enough by now. I haven't the strength of a frog. And I was crazy in love with both Rick and Elvira . . ."

*　*　*

After Rick had left him to climb upstairs to his own sleeping room, Matt had sat on by himself in the moody silence of past midnight, but as overwrought and unalone as if he had taken a seat in the midst of a great orchestra of players of cymbals and bass drums. All the while in his mind he caught vivid glimpses of the motley crowd who would swarm the court house to gape and cup their ears and feast their orbs for the duration of the Fergus trial: farmers, loiterers from the reading room of the public library, a sprinkling from the old ranks of nouveaux riches and ruined millionaires, some retired whore from a peeling flat, and a truant here and there out of the junior high school.

The Ferguses were so vital, so larger than life for him, and yes, he thought, why not use the word, picturesque— in their own world and surroundings, but, and the thought gave him a sickening pause, exposed to the merciless hostile uncomprehending stare of the shoddy, seedy public, Matt feared that his Elvira and her brood, Wilders and his side of the house, would come off less than grand, that their glitter and charm which sparkled for him might fail to give off even a single flash of illumination to mean onlookers . . . But even if all his favorites, suddenly exposed to stony pitiless examination, were to turn before his eyes into rag dolls stuffed with sawdust, he would still cherish them for as long as he had memory. They were his only illusion, his passion, his life.

But if only he could spare them that public humiliation, that ride in the tumbril before jeering Boutflour!

* * *

"I won't say the scales fell from my eyes at last, Jeremy" Matt went on. "I had known what Elvira was for a long time, and I had known too what she had done to her sons . . . But as I listened outside of Rick's bedroom where she had stayed on with him alone, after dismissing her attorney (oh, I'm not above

listening behind closed doors, Jeremy, especially in my own house and where a matter close to my heart is concerned), as my ears drank in the pure meaning of her request, I saw complete and full the whole chronicle of Elvira and her boys, in all its horror and sorrow . . .

" 'You won't go back on me, will you, dearest Rick, in the name of all you hold dear' she was beside herself.

"I leant against the doorjamb, then, not to hear better but to keep, I think, from falling.

"I thought for a while I had missed his reply, it took so long in coming. Then I heard Rick's voice, changed beyond recognition.

" 'You can rest assured, Elvira, I will testify against your husband.'

"The decision, hardness, naked ferocious quality in his voice cut off any words in response from her.

"And then I heard Rick say, 'For once I've testified against your husband, I'll be free of you, so engrave it in your memory. I'll be free and go my own way, you tiger bitch, free of your damned plans, wiles and bondage. Yes, tell all the God-damned world I'll testify against your husband and then I'll break, in view of everybody, the fetters you've forged for me . . .'

"Elvira flung open the door, giving me a knock on the head that sent me spinning, but in her state, she was neither aware of my eavesdropping nor her having knocked me to the floor. A moment later I heard the front door slam behind her as if it had blown itself to smithereens."

Uncle Matt had made sudden personal intrusions into his own narrative before, and stopped my fingers from writing, but this time the violent change his appearance underwent during his "direct appeal" to me froze my hand to the page, for as he spoke of Elvira and Rick's quarrel, he too suddenly looked as if he had joined the ranks of the notable dead, and heavy shadows fell on his eyes and mouth which I couldn't help thinking looked like grave mold and casket lining.

But then with a convulsive start he was back in the living present, with me, and giving one of his imperious nods, he set my fingers scratching away again.

* * *

Rick Fergus was not to see his mother again after their violent, almost homicidal quarrel until the day of the trial itself. The eldest son waited outside the door of the court room, accompanied of course by Matthew Lacey (he had not slept a wink the night before, while Rick lying beside him had somehow gone into a sleep almost as profound as that of the tomb). Rick could not bear to go into the trial room itself, and so Matthew had had to inform the bailiff that "young Mr. Fergus" was not feeling up to par and would wait outside until he was called to the witness stand.

As Rick, then, approached his showdown, he was no more like his old jaunty self than had he been any country boy in a jam, brought for the first time into a hall of justice. He became almost a child again, he turned to Matt with wide-open eyes seeking, it seemed, not so much encouragement and stamina, as verification he was actually Rick Fergus. Sometimes he held the older man's hand openly as men will do when death or disaster has struck down the conventional inhibitions standing between them. One would have thought he was facing sentencing for the crime of murder, or was already in his last hours in death row. His face had gone the color of white cold ashes.

" 'Twill be over in a day or so at most, won't it, Matthew?"

Rick kept saying over and again, as the two sat waiting interminably.

"Over forever, Rick, and done with, and you'll be free to make your own way," Matt soothed him in bored lullaby tones, but his complete attention was taken up with the sounds of the court room; he heard the judge's gavel strike hard, followed by heavy silence, the judge's sepulchral voice issuing instructions to the court, and then a promiscuous wave of whispering and titters, and again the gavel and silence.

Whether it was the unpleasant odors reaching Matt's nostrils from the poorly aired corridors giving off a whiff like that of a mausoleum mixed with stench of urine from the comfort station nearby and spittoons filled to overflow, or whether it was Rick's sniveling and the appalling memory of Elvira's tyranny, or because he had had no sleep to speak of for over a week and was sick and tired it seemed now of the Fergus clan and their impossible demands on his energy and feelings, whatever it was, Matthew suddenly turned on Rick without warning:

"Do you know how damned weary you make me, watching you sit there feeling so sorry for yourself, Rick, when it's your mother and dad in any case who stand to be ruined today, not you. Besides, you've made your bed with her all these years, why can't you march in there then and tell the judge what you've got in your heart of hearts . . . Or turn against her, why don't you, and go over to your dad's side of the house. But act, for Christ's sake, and whichever side you choose, you'd best go in there now if you're going."

Rick got to his feet slowly, like a man who has forgotten his crutches, but showed no sign he would go into the court room, and indeed gave a move of his body as if he was about to dash from the building.

"You always have harped on how you wanted to be an actor, Rick," Matt went on, having risen also. "Always looking for your big part. Well today it's come, a choice one, if you ask me, for you're the star witness," he nodded in the direction of the trial room. "Yes, the role is big, but I guess the fellow selected is, now we see him at close range, more a frost than a find. At any rate, Rick, if you can't face a common pleas court room full of a few farm folk, loafers, and dowdy millionaires, you'll make some pithy showing before cameras or footlights . . ."

Perhaps it was more to Matt's own astonishment than to Elvira's eldest son that the older man suddenly slapped Rick smartly across the face with the flat of his hand.

"Get in there and testify, you crownless prick," Matt's voice rose loud enough almost to be heard in the trial room, "for you are a pukingly sorry sight to see . . ."

Rick's own fists rose now, and he stared relentlessly at Matthew, a deep flush replacing his pallor, the blow from his friend's hand making his mouth to come open in a kind of clown-like grin. Then letting his arms fall at his side, giving Matt a last look both of pugnacious menace and final open relief, he went bolting up to the heavy door of the common pleas court room, and walked through it and then over to the place reserved for witnesses . . . Matt followed him a few moments later, and sat down with the crowd of spectators.

At first all Matthew could make out in the vast gloomy chamber in which all sound reverberated with hollow doom-like tones was the wide shaft of motes of dust dancing in dark orange sunlight.

Catching his breath, he got a glimpse of Elvira, but just as he did so the shaft of light seemed to shift and move over to the bench, where he saw Judge Duggan presiding, a Scotsman of seventy, with ramrod posture, beetling red eyebrows, and turned-down white lips, obviously unsympathetic with both plaintiff and defendant, and, so word went through Boutflour, not overblessed with compassion for the entire erring human race in general.

Matthew's gaze came back perforce to Elvira. Accompanied by her mother, Melissa, seated at a massive oak table with lion-claw legs, she looked much as she had twenty years before when amidst the rest of the church choir singers she waited her turn to sing the anthem. Elvira Summerlad—nobody could believe looking at her expression of passionate self-will that she had ever been Mrs. Fergus, or had ever belonged to any man—was dressed in a sumptuous purple velvet dress which must have been made over from one of Annette's, her grandmother, and which gave her an impossible but convincing air of some crowned head of an obscure kingdom, remembered only in waxworks museums. Her eyes rested on Matthew only a second, and she flashed a tentative smile.

At the other end of the room sat Wilders Fergus, alone except for his attorney, for Winifred, who had directed his every move up till now, at the last moment had decided against being present, and informed him she would wait out the "ordeal" with her mother in Paul ding Meadows. Wilders, it seemed to Matt, looked ten years older at the very least since he had last laid eyes on him, and in the dim light of the court room his hair gave the appearance of being snow white, which together with his rich black, albeit frayed coat and high collar would have made him an impressive figure anywhere except perhaps in this mean tribunal, but unlike Elvira, who gave a kind of glint of bitter confidence, Rick's father resembled one who had already received a verdict of guilty, and is merely composing himself to listen to his sentence.

After studying Wilders, Matt indeed had to remind himself that this was a civil, not a criminal case, and nobody was in danger of being sent to the electric chair. After what had occurred in the corridor, Matthew could do no more than sneak a glimpse of Rick. The younger boys he saw with relief were not present.

Matthew realized then, to his shame, that his expectations of the day were hardly a whit different from those of the gawking onlookers and rubbernecks, for he too had come expecting sensation, even scandal.

For a time, at least, everybody must have been disappointed at what the morning had to offer, and the fools who came prepared for immediate entertainment or thrills were quickly disabused. The lawyers on each side addressed the bench in long interminable paragraphs, and the early "evidence" was largely sheaf after sheaf of figures, those presented on Wilders's side proving he had "supported" Elvira, while those on the plaintiff's proving he had not, and was guilty of all the counts presented to the court. One felt one was receiving a lesson in accounting or advanced arithmetic.

The only dramatic event of the first day came when Elvira's mother took the stand, and testified to the fact that she had lost over seventy-five thousand dollars to her son-in-law. There was a hush in the court room when such a denomination was mentioned in that bare-bones epoch, and the judge leaned over his bench to ask Melissa a few searching questions.

Melissa repeated her statement and verified again the exact amount of money she had lost through repeated loans to her son-in-law. As Melissa repeated her "charge" and with obvious reluctance enumerated again the large denominations of money "squandered," her eyes sought out Wilders, who looked straight at her for a moment, then fixed his eyes on the floor, but the expression he had seen in Melissa's face had comforted him faintly, for it was not one of condemnation or censure but rather of half-mended heartbreak and old sympathy for the once young promising banker whose hair now almost matched hers in whiteness.

By the second day of the trial, the curiosity-seekers had thinned, and only those who knew the Ferguses partially or well were in attendance. A few town loafers entered from time to time, but stayed only long enough to take a chew of tobacco and aim at one of the countless spittoons distributed about the court room. And then the second day too came to an end having been much like the first, with long drawn-out intricate wrangling over finances and transactions long ago nearly forgotten by everybody.

It was the third day that Rick was finally called to the stand.

He went up to the witness box in a jaunty arrogant spoiled and slightly effeminate manner, looking as if he had come direct from the hands of his dramatic coach.

According to Matthew, Rick had one of the most remarkable "vocal instruments" he had ever heard, but on this day he did not use it to advantage, and after a few fine tones and cadences, his voice lapsed into that of any small-town or country boy, slightly nasal and frequently drawling. He also showed an almost craven, obsequious manner toward the judge, which belied his ever having been trained for the theater.

The old Chesapeake and Ohio steam train rushed nonstop through Boutflour shortly after Elvira's attorney had begun to question Rick at length, and one could hear muted and distant—for those court house walls are enormously solid and thick—a kind of drawn-out scream repeated over and again, a sound which had its effect on all who sat in the oak-paneled marble-pillared room, and put a damper on any words being spoken at the moment.

But the locomotive's cry especially unnerved miserable Rick Fergus, for whatever calm and composure he had been able to maintain up to this point began to go, and his head, which he had held painfully erect, suddenly was bowed, as if some bundle of muscle had been severed.

But Elvira's attorney knew no respite, he asked on and on, more like the prosecutor than the defense, one probing question following after another. In Matt's opinion, Elvira had not suspected, and did not know what was coming. She had not rehearsed any such set of questions with her attorney, and they now came to her as disturbing and unanswerable as they did to Rick. All she had wanted her oldest boy to say was that Wilders had not been able to support them, or keep a roof over their head . . . Perhaps even the attorney, though a man of coarse fiber, did not know exactly how far he would go. And all he wanted to do in any event was win the case.

"Do you respect your father, then, since you say you feel he deserted you and your mother and brothers?" one question came, and when Rick was unable to answer with a definite yes or no, another similar question followed. "Do you feel your father deliberately neglected you?" which the boy faltered over, until this was followed by the question "And because of your father's neglect you had to quit school and support your mother?"

But something cataclysmic had happened to Rick Fergus, it was clear to all who had paid any attention at all. Up till now, after each of the lawyer's questions, Elvira's son had looked in the direction of his mother for guidance and hints as to how he should reply. And up until now he had found each reply he sought in some sign in her face and eyes understood only by him.

But now the unforeseen ultimate question came from the twisted insensitive lips of the attorney: "Tell us, Rick Fergus, do you love your father, love him enough to want him to come back at this time to be head of the household after you've borne the responsibility and the task of that for so long, or, in your opinion, should your mother be granted a divorce, and your father be forever separated from you and your home?"

Both the question and the terrible expression it brought forth on the boy's face sent a shiver of expectation and of alarm throughout the court room.

Rick no longer looked in the direction of his mother. Indeed his eyes seemed to be focused on nothing at all about him. He saw nobody, heard nothing more. Perhaps he had not even taken in all the import of the last dreadful question of a conniving and irresponsible lawyer.

Rising from the witness stand and beginning to move like a sleepwalker in the direction of where Wilders sat, heedless of the warnings of the judge, who asked him to resume his seat at once, or of the bailiff who attempted to take him by the arm, Rick walked on, resembling now more and more a man risen from the grave, toward his father. Wilders followed his son's progress toward him with a kind of stony gaze of incredulity, followed by blank horror.

"The court will, I feel sure, grant me now the right to speak," Rick began in clear, thrilling loud tones, "for it has permitted others to ask me the most endless string of pitiless and searching questions any human being can be required to reply to in public. And so, ladies, gentlemen, and spectators, why should not I, his eldest son, ask him, Wilders Fergus, my father, a question."

As Rick spoke, Matt realized for once and all that at last Elvira's son had gone far beyond the power and perfection of anything his dramatic coach ever could have hoped for, and Rick was also at last free of all affectation and self-consciousness.

"Let me ask Wilders Fergus," he continued before the hushed house which never took its eye from the young speaker, "let me ask him as his eldest son that he explain, if he can, what it is he has brought about over all these long years, and why we are all here today . . . You have all seen today how nothing has been spared me, as I sat there exposed to questions that can unhinge the mind. Why, then, shouldn't the fount and cause of all this trouble and shame, Wilders Fergus," and he pointed now at his father, as he stood directly facing him over the massive table at which Wilders was seated, "yes, why should we not come to the horse's mouth. Why break the son on the wheel when all the answers are here. Can't you still hear the sound of bones being crushed and see blood drawn from my veins, Wilders. Then let me be the prosecutor for a moment, though I will be more sparing and ask you only one question. Yes, enough of shyster lawyers and their tricks, enough of judges and spectators. Let me draw the truth direct from you, who know it, and then the trial can end, and all these people with all their time can go back to their mansions or hovels where they belong. For nobody belongs in this court but Wilders Fergus, my alleged father, and me."

The bailiff did not let go his grip on Rick all this while, but made no move to take him from the court room. And the judge, perhaps for reasons unknown even to himself, did not stir a hair.

"For if you are my father, Wilders, and I'm not some bastard got by a traveler who spent the night under our unprotected roof, why did you leave and desert me in the first place to the complete power and endless claims of Elvira Summerlad, allowing her to do with me anything her wishes dictated? If you can answer that, Wilders, the court can adjourn, and the case can come to rest . . . Give me, in other words, Wilders, the reason for my existence, since you were never here before to teach it to me, and I had only Elvira to crush out manhood with her lessons!"

Some spectators whispering said that Rick Fergus was drunk and was perhaps enacting a scene from some old play, perhaps a little-known one by Shakespeare, for they had never heard anybody speak in such uncompounded fury and rhetoric, in court room, house, or street.

But for Rick Fergus, it mattered not a whit where he was or indeed if anybody heard him but Wilders, for at length and at last all the accumulated pain, rage, humiliation, and shame of his young years had in one moment broken forth and come to the fore, and he had found himself as power-less to stop the torrent that came out from his mouth as he would have been to command his own heart to cease beating.

"Answer me, Wilders, and then be damned forever!" he shook his fist in his father's face, and a low murmur and moan echoed from the trial room. Turning to the entire court room, Rick shouted: "This man robbed me of my inheritance!"

Then the judge's gavel rang out, but without the force that perhaps should have been put behind it, and the bailiff took Rick out from the room.

"Rick's lost me my case!" Elvira spoke inaudibly amidst the loud babble of excited tongues, and without real care or concern for whatever the outcome of the trial might now be, she rose to leave. Her only wish was to go to Rick, for a sickening fear swept over her that he would die, was perhaps already dead.

They had taken him into the men's comfort station, but she walked unconcerned and contemptuous through its heavy curtained entrance, and went over to where Rick lay on a mohair sofa, his open eyes staring at the faded war murals of the ceiling.

She took him in her arms and pressed him to her. Looking up after a time, as she still embraced him, she beheld Wilders standing near them, staring uncomprehendingly. Elvira could say nothing and turned away, and Wilders himself, as stunned as they, sat down in a folding camp chair.

* * *

And so what the town and county seat of Boutflour had felt would be a thrilling, certainly a scandalous trial, full of spice, with a steady running revelation of long-locked-up secrets, had come to a jerkily abrupt end, without having been actually more than for the most part a dreary kind of lesson in accounting and arithmetic, save for the flourish of the coda, a "mad scene" in which an overwrought boy of twenty had tongue-lashed his beaten father with a strained queer rhetoric, disgraced himself, and made his mother lose what small reputation she so painfully had gained over the past few years.

And I saw to my astonishment again that Uncle Matt in re-enacting the trial for me had become almost as wrought up as on that first evening in winter when I had disturbed him from his talking reverie before his mantelpiece and he had rushed at me knife in hand; now again, speaking like a twenty-year-old boy instead of his sixty-year-old self, he came up to within an inch or so of my face, as if I was not plain Jeremy Cready but Wilders Fergus bowed and broken over that table by his eldest son's curses, and like Wilders I too lowered my head, whilst Matt in the voice of the long-dead Rick Fergus cursed false fathers, who turn their sons over to the tender mercies of whores and bad actors.

I sat on there, head down, hardly daring to look up, as Matthew roared out his "reading" of the dramatic" court house scene of long ago.

Then, as he always did, he subsided, and was Matt Lacey again, nursed his brandy, and stared into the fireplace.

The next day I took my wheel and rode over to the court house. Crawlers and creepers! but it was an ugly and imposing old thing, I observed all over again, and though I knew nothing then or now about architecture, it had a grand mammoth something, and they say its stone and marble are of the finest.

I began going up that endless succession of steps which lead from the sidewalk on Main Street to the big marble-colonnaded hall from off which all the trials take place. I asked a man, I suppose he was a bailiff perhaps, where the room was where they held the divorce trials. He looked at me suspiciously, contemptuously, and after taking his own sweet time he pointed at last to a room at the very end of the hall where we were standing. Going up to it I saw it was marked Common Pleas Court.

I stood there staring as best I could through its frosted glass apertures. The old court room was vacant now, and not lit, but the big stained-glass windows let in some illumination, and I could see the judge's bench, and fancied too the table nearby was the very same at which Wilders had sat when Rick condemned his father. Then looking past the judge's bench I saw the witness chair, and near it a silky faded American flag, with only forty-eight stars, the State seal, and some murals depicting battles of the Spanish-American and the First World Wars.

I had had to see with my own eyes the Common Pleas Court somehow, for the very reason that Matt had made it all so real to me, I had to step where they had all put their feet, and feel the wood and metal they had pressed -with their hands. And having gazed and gazed, I still somehow could not bring myself to leave, but went on pressing my nose against the glass until the light began to go from the stained-glass windows, and a bell in the corridor announced the building was closing.

*   *   *

Any other man than Wilders Fergus would have got drunk after such a trial. Those who had attended it said that the final effect was like that of having received a gunshot wound which first passed almost unnoticed or unfelt but later throbs unceasingly, threatening to engulf all the senses. Like many things which become finally memorable, the trial while in session had often seemed tedious or unconvincing. Rick's denunciation, despite its shocking overtones, appeared to many, irrespective of its "bad taste," almost silly, and certainly melodramatic. But his voice had carried in that cavernous room, with its thirty-foot ceiling, massive woodwork, dusty flags commemorating the carnage of past wars, and grim judicial gloom, and his words long afterwards went on making an abiding and ever-haunting impression. And later people talked and whispered about the fact, almost overlooked at the moment of occurrence, that in addition to Rick's wild and lyrical denunciation of his father, he had all but set hands on Wilders, and had Wilders so much as raised his head from the table, where he finally had let it rest as one dead, Rick had it in him to have drawn his penknife and stabbed him to death.

Coming out of the comfort station, without having said a word to his son or Elvira, Wilders had had no notion where he was going. There is no place for a nondrinking man to go after such an onslaught except the river, or for some few men, perhaps, church, but Wilders had never been a churchgoer, and who goes, he thought, to the Presbyterian church when in trouble or pain. He contemplated for some minutes going back to Paulding Meadows and getting the shotgun and then lulling himself in the woods. But thought of suicide if anything disgusted him, and did not tempt him. Once, he remembered back to his early career as a young, somewhat overbearing and rather successful bank examiner in the Yankee State, he had found, while going over the books of a small bank, a record of extreme misappropriation of funds, which could only be laid at the door of the youthful cashier, who had been uneasily watching Wilders from the moment of the latter's unanticipated arrival at the bank that morning, and out of the tail of his eye kept count of Wilders's least movement. When noon came, though the arrangement had been for Wilders and the young banker to have lunch together, the cashier did not make his appearance. After lunch, Wilders noted, he did not return to the bank. Two o'clock, three o'clock, and closing time, and still the cashier did not return. Wilders and the president of the bank, whom he had had to apprise of the missing funds, then walked over to the cashier's house. His white-faced trembling young wife said he had not been "to home." Then, on a hunch, Wilders had stepped out to the garage, which was double-locked. With the help of the bank president and a man next door, Wilders broke open the lock, and they walked inside to see the cashier seated in the front seat of his Studebaker, the doors of the car open, his brains spattered, from a double-barreled shotgun wound, everywhere, on the seat, on the walls of the freshly painted garage, and the dead man, eyes open, gazed at Wilders as if he saw his accuser and murderer . . .

Now, long years after that event, the eyes of the cashier seemed to follow Wilders today, as he too sat in his own car, bent double with his own sorrow, on the outskirts of town. He had parked absent-mindedly near some forest, his mind deeply absorbed in what perhaps would have seemed in his heyday a trivial, even contemptible pastime, that of trying to recall the name of the long-dead young cashier. On the tip of his tongue, it always just managed to elude him.

He began walking toward a stretch of woods in which serried ranks of pines excluded all light, and which filled acre after acre ahead and around him. Entering the thickest part of the woodland, he was soon walking on moist ground alive with ferns, moss and wild flowers. Suddenly as tired as when as a boy he had helped the threshers all day, he plumped down on a fallen log, and then removed his high shoes, and loosened his celluloid collar, and as he did so he caught a glint of something in the feeble light, and looking down saw his thirty-second degree Masonic pin as it sparkled feebly in his lapel. He touched it with his hand to see if it was secure, and as he did so his eye fell on an old gunshot wound in his palm, where his eldest brother Garret had mistakenly fired at him while rabbit-hunting. He looked another moment at the dark place deep within his flesh where part of the bullet still remained, and as he did so the name of the suicide cashier came to him, it was Bevis Striker.

What would he tell Winifred when he got home, he began to come out of his reverie and to think of one person at least who counted him among the living, how would he describe the trial to her . . . He grinned to himself as he thought of her coming indignation and wrath. He felt almost glad that there was a Winifred, and that he could expect of her a demonstration of a tongue-lashing for what she would consider his spineless performance in court, a tongue-lashing that would be worse than an old-fashioned hiding, but more welcome than pity or sympathy. Winifred alone of all the world held him accountable, responsible, and the rawhide of her tongue might make him perhaps quicken again to life.

But never until Rick's outburst had the word father struck home to him with such force, and a blow with a white-hot iron across the eyes would have seared scarcely deeper than Rick's scorching of the word across Wilders's brow, within the hearing, it had seemed, of all the world, and never until his son's denunciation had he felt himself say goodbye to all other appellations that may have existed previously for him, son, brother, husband, financier, failure, all vanished forever into air before his own boy's passionate calling him to account with *father*, and indeed until his death he would be able to think of himself only as Rick's father, perhaps for the very reason the boy had in effect spoken as one who would disinherit him and destroy their common bond—but no matter, he was forever henceforth, time immemorial, Rick's father.

And so he did not need to wait for the verdict from Judge Duggan, for he stood condemned in his own eyes, not by the charges brought against him by the plaintiff, but by the shortcomings and failure he now acknowledged were his touching his sons. His case was over, whatever decree the court would hand down. Wilders Fergus had been found guilty. Like thick maple sap in springtime his shame oozed thick over his brow, blinding him. He rolled from the log into a clump of trillium and dogtooth violet, and lay there, his full six-foot-four length stretched out in the cool spring mud and air.

Then there he was driving back home to Paulding Meadows. He had died inside himself, but he knew he would go on living. He would not raise his hand against a dead man. He would work and save. He would make this time not a fortune, but a tiny nest egg, and put it away so that when he died his sons would have a little something, and not think so badly of him, not think of him, that is, as a robber of a boy's inheritance. And at least Winifred and his mother waited for him. His news would be the worst he could bring, but hadn't he always brought home the worst news to them? Wasn't he bad news himself? Short convulsive groans came out from his rib cage, as unexpected, and seemingly as unconnected with him, as if some moving part of the auto had burst in two. His hand on the wheel became so unsteady that he nearly went into a deep ditch. He drew up to the side of the road until his pulse became normal again. But his temples throbbed furiously and looking down he saw that his high shoes, pants cuffs and the bottom of his mackintosh were covered with mud and the tiny petals of flowers.

With a final exertion of will power, his teeth set, he started the motor and drove home.

Though no word was forthcoming yet from the judge's chambers as to whether Elvira had been granted or denied a divorce from Wilders, a divorce of another kind had begun to make itself felt in the boarding house. Elvira found herself almost deserted by her two oldest sons, and even her own mother, Melissa, did not communicate with her regularly after the ordeal of the trial. Jethro was mum in his mother's presence, and remained away from home as much as possible. Rick had removed most of his belongings from the red parlor, and practically made his home with Matt. And the few times during the day Jethro was on the premises, he stared at his mother long and hard in a manner which confirmed her impression he must be, at times, mad. But she did not have the heart to correct anything he said or did from then on.

Rick's public denunciation of his father, far from vindicating Elvira, caused her to lose face wherever she was known, and she doubted now her own future course. Her coming "freedom" now meant little to her, though she had dreamed of nothing else for weeks, even years, and now she saw being free as unrelieved solitude and neglect, for she was convinced she had lost the love and respect of her sons, and the good name and honorable estate which she had finally with such difficulty upheld in Boutflour. The "prompting" for Rick's public outburst was all laid at Elvira's door. She felt this was unjust. She had never coached her eldest son in the exercise of such a vituperative, insensate, deranged diatribe against his own father. But the citizens of Boutflour censured her as if she had planned the whole thing. And whereas before the townspeople praised her for her gallant struggles to support her family unaided by a husband, they now were of the opinion that she had tried to be "too much" to her sons, and was overpossessive and blindly selfish.

During this "waiting" period, Elvira feared to see her lover George Gubell lest the judge, who was said to have got wind of her "adulterous behavior," might refuse to grant the divorce, and so she counted herself as the most shut-away member of the household, though actually each member now stood alone, and even Rick, who was never out of the sight or protective hand of Matt Lacey, saw himself during this time as little better than a castaway.

And so they waited, Elvira and her boys. But Judge Duggan took his time. The longer he took (one now remembered all the talk about his being stoutly opposed to any kind of divorce for even a good reason), the less hope there seemed to be. Days passed into weeks, and the summer was approaching again. But neither Rick nor his mother could make any plans to go away until they knew whether she was "free" or not.

One day when Jethro had been lingering about the

house more than was now customary for him, he had said a thing to Elvira which stung her to the ventricles of her heart.

"If you win the suit, Elvira, will you marry immediately?"

Her hand stopped in its task of turning a collar on one of Rick's old broadcloth shirts.

"Why, who in the world would I marry, Jethro?" she whispered her answer.

Jethro was silent, thinking of the many "husbands" whom she had slept with in the little summer cottage behind the boarding house, and as he thought of her wickedness with these common strangers, he remembered the pistol he had removed from Aunt Winifred's home, and he suddenly bent over convulsively and held his hand before his eyes.

"Tell me who I would marry, smarty," Elvira said, but looking up she saw his strange posture, and she held her breath in apprehension.

"I'm not going to marry anybody, you young scamp," Elvira rose from her task and stepped over to where Jethro was seated. His mother's voice was so unlike her own, so charged was it with feeling and its volume sending it far beyond the confines of the house that Jethro removed his hands from his eyes and looked up at her in astonishment.

"One husband was enough," she went on, "one man was enough! . . . What did I ever get out of being married, you tell me. Always holding the bag. With a man it's a different bargain altogether, for while he has his moment's fun, the woman gets saddled down, with the rest of her life to think it over, but he goes scot-free to the next fool's door . . . Don't mention the word marriage to me."

Pleased in a way by her speech, Jethro allowed a tiny

smile to cross his lips. Elvira noted his change of expression from his black scowl of minutes before and smiled faintly at him in return.

Then going closer to him, taking him in her arms, she pressed him delicately to her.

"Don't you ever comb your hair anymore, Jethro, darling," she looked down at the profusion of curls. "Your hair is as snarled as a little rat's nest . . ."

She went into the bathroom and took down from the cabinet one of Annette's elegant old imported ivory combs with the thick teeth, one or two of which were missing. "Now sit still, Jeth, and let me untangle all these snarls . . . I thought I taught you how to comb your hair better than this. But then see how mistaken I am about everything."

Halfway through her dressing of his hair, the comb stopped under her hand.

"Do go on, Elvira, for nobody smooths down my hair just like you," Jethro urged her.

"What have I done with my life, precious," Elvira cried, not having heard his adjuration, and the *precious* seemed to be directed to every kind heart in the world. "Oh, what have I done, that all's gone wrong," she continued, and he felt the hot current of her breath upon his head.

But even as Jethro allowed Elvira to comb his curls into some kind of manageable shock of hair, he was thinking of his pistol upstairs and saying to himself that as sure as sunup if she won the divorce, he would shoot her. The horror of it, for the thought seemed to come to him as if by destiny and decree, caused him to break out in a cold sweat, which Elvira observed.

"You'd best go outdoors now, Jeth, and get some air. You seem overwrought," she said, after giving his hair a few more touches. "You've had too much excitement these last days and weeks. We all have."

As Jeth went out the back door, she took the ivory comb and placed it in an old heavy silver washbasin, cleaning it and extricating each of the golden hairs, in hot suds and ammonia. As she did so, almost without realizing it, she hummed an old tune from her own girlhood, and then an even older one, from the days of Annette.

Elvira had lapsed into a brooding silence when

Smile a while ... Till we meet again

a strong baritone voice, a little tremulous from whiskey, broke in upon her, and she did not need to look up to know who it was. She had written Matt Lacey a note the day before to come over and talk about "something important."

"Do I have the right words for the melody you were singing, Elvira mine?" Matt kissed her full on the mouth, and when she did not answer, without warning lifted her up in his arms and carried her into the "music room," where so often in times past they had played duets on the piano.

Putting her down in a huge armchair, he kneeled in front of her, and between kissing of her hands, muttered, "And what does the only girl in the world want me to do for her?"

"Oh, forget what I wanted you to do," she chided. "You would have to come drunk, wouldn't you," she added bitterly, almost inaudibly.

"Tell me to do anything, including kill myself, and I'll oblige," he laid his head on her lap. "But, Elvira, haven't you worried enough in one lifetime over Rick!"

"This is about Jethro," her worry forced the words out, though she had resolved when she saw he had been drinking to say nothing about Jeth to him.

"Yes, what's eating him, anyhow," Matt looked up into her face, and seemed to sober up a bit as he turned his attention to the middle son. "He looked like a thundercloud as I passed him in the garden. Didn't even bother to speak to me . . ."

Elvira, despite a struggle on her part, could not stop the tears from filling her eyes for a second time that day, and Matt, ever watchful of each changing expression of her face, brushed them away with his finger, as they fell.

"I have such a terrible presentiment, Matt darling," she spoke near hysteria. "I feel, I don't know how, the boy is going to do something awful, if we can't anticipate him . . ."

Elvira's agitation, more than his own apprehension about Jeth's really being up to anything, made him sober up a bit more, but as he watched Elvira's care-worn face, he felt himself go pale, as if he too had a presentiment.

"Shall I talk to them, then, 'vira, my angel," Matt spoke in steady grim tones.

"Oh, if you think it will do any good," she buried her face now in his coat, and he held her then tightly clasped against him, his lips suddenly parted, kissing her again and again, but his eye kept straying about him, charmed by the rich light reflected from the adjoining room, Rick's "red parlor," where a masterpiece of furniture design, a bookcase, stretched its sumptuous height upward tin it nearly touched the twenty-foot ceiling, while the base of it, a shimmering construction of red glass, cast blood-red patterns upon the even more arresting red of the carpet.

"Yes, do go out and talk to Jeth, and try to reason with him, why don't you," Elvira gave Matt a last kiss. "The poor lad's eating his heart out about something, God knows what!" She disengaged herself then from his arms, and then rising, began to walk, head bent a little, so unlike her, toward the stairwell.

"You're cross that I've been drinking," he scolded after her, but she had already disappeared up the stairs. "And besides you don't love me," he added to himself, "You've got someone else."

"What have you said or done now to have upset Elvira so much, Jeth," Matt spoke out in reprimand as soon as he had located the boy, who was stretched out under a wild cherry tree. Nearby was a sloping uncultivated field rife with sow thistle, tiny wild asters, and meadow primrose. "You've hurt her terribly," the ex-sailor went on, as he flung himself down beside Jethro, who had just put a long blade of grass in his mouth. His corn-yellow hair was again snarled and wild, and falling in ringlets. On a sudden impulse, Matt bent over and touched Jethro lightly on the forehead with his lips.

"First you kiss the mother, then the son," Jethro said without pleasantness, but his blue eyes flashed less savagely than usual—perhaps, who knows, he was mollified even by unwanted attention.

"Why can't you be a little more human, Jeth?"

"Does that remark stem from Elvira now or from you, Matt? . . . Bet you never had an idea of your own, did you, without someone else cuing you beforehand."

As he finished saying this, Jeth raised himself up on one elbow and stared hard at the older man, and then went on: "You've been everybody's beau, and nobody's steady . . ."

"You have the most frightening pair of eyes I've ever seen, middle son," Matt mused, gazing into Jethro's pupils. "They're even more searing today than last time I looked into them. They look as if you'd seen everything, even if maybe you didn't understand what it was you saw."

"Maybe I have seen about everything," the boy looked away, grinning. "And on account of all I've seen I can imagine what the rest's like too, can't I?" and he laughed a tuneless strident laugh which made Matt's spine tingle.

"When you come to man's estate, Jeth, you won't be so hard on your mother or the rest of the world," Matt spoke confidingly.

"And will you be included in my future toleration, do you reckon, Matt," Jethro snapped.

"Oh, why are you so angry at all of us, Jeth?" Matt tousled the boy's hair, and tried to draw him to him, but Jeth pulled stubbornly away.

"Don't you want your mother to have her freedom?" Matt went on, holding his breath as he got out this last sentence. Then, going pale, he shouted, "Speak up!" and he shook the boy roughly.

"There's nothing I'm not angry about, for your information," Jeth riveted his eyes on Matt, and the older man dropped his hands.

"And why should Elvira be free or happy, when she's never made anybody else feel so? What's she ever done to deserve happiness more than anybody else of us all," the boy went on. "What about Wilders, and Aunt Winifred, and Grandma Fergus? Don't they deserve some freedom and happiness?"

"Yes, of course, for God's sake, they do, Jeth," Matt

replied lamely. "But you can't keep people living together who've grown so far apart . . ."

As Jethro scowled ferociously at him, Matt went on. "I came out here because I wanted to help you, Jeth, but you don't want anybody to help you. All you want is to go on being bitter, stay by yourself, and feel hate against your own loved ones . . ."

And Matt turned away, and began walking down the path that led to the river road, toward his house.

In a moment, however, to his considerable surprise, he heard light footfalls, and turning about saw Jethro again. Matt waited, keeping a poker face for the boy's next speech.

"Matt," Jethro spoke out of breath, the color coming and going in his cheeks, "do listen to me now for a moment . . . If someday, say, I was to do a terrible thing," and he stopped a moment, thinking then of the pistol, thinking of Elvira, "would you come then, do you suppose, after it was over and talk to me like you done today . . . I mean, would you still speak with me, visit me then, do you judge?"

Thunderstruck, Matt could only stammer pieces of words.

"You wouldn't then!" Jethro's earlier anger swept back.

"I didn't say that, did I!" Matt came to himself as if from slumber.

"You looked it, Matt!"

"You scare the daylights out of me, Jeth, and you always have . . ."

He put his arm on the boy's shoulder, and this time he did not get a rebuff. "I'd stick with you, Jethro, of course, no matter what you did," he finished hoarsely. Dimly Matt foresaw what might happen.

"But don't so much as think of it, Jeth, you hear," Matt cautioned, and he felt for a moment he had looked into the boy's heart. "Things are bound to work out, if we go calmly about, and not let ourselves think terrible things . . ."

"What about seeing terrible things?" the boy's mania seemed to return.

"Listen to me," Matt now sensed the full urgency of it all, "listen carefully, Jeth. Remember you have a father and a mother who love you, you're not a little wood's colt. You have parents, living parents. You have everything really to be thankful for," and here Matt's eyes fell, in spite of his attempt to forbid their straying, to the jagged scar on Jethro's neck. "Whilst I, Jeth, never had parents of my own, don't know who my own father is, or my proper name. Wood's colt is what the natives always called me, and the only family I ever had is yours . . . But whatever you're thinking," and here Matt's sudden first terror returned to him, "stop, Jeth, and prevent it. Collect yourself. But whatever you do . . . and if ever you need me, and this is a solemn promise, you come a-runnin' . . . Do you mind me?"

Jeth studied Matt's face for what seemed an interminable time by the clock, for the pupils of the blue eyes that looked at him contained depths dreadful enough to engulf anyone's steadiness of mind.

But for all Matt's words and embracing, something failed to happen, no bond was established between the two, for Jethro did not know he had everything, he only felt betrayed and shamed and greatly wanting to punish somebody. Matt might as well have talked to the prairie thistles, might just as well never have come searching out Jethro here in the calm meadow.

Silently following the older man for a piece as the latter took his detour on the crushed stone road back to his home, Jethro watched him till he passed out of eyeshot, then sauntered back to the place where Matt had discovered him, and then at a run went over into Elvira's garden where the summer seat was still in ghostly conspicuousness, and after bunking about him for a moment, he sat down.

"We'll see by and by," Jethro mumbled, his lips tightly drawn, and his eyes hard.

* * *

Some people in Boutflour said it was fear of what Jethro might do that set Uncle Matt off on his drinking bout, a bout which was never to come to an end, in one way of speaking, until his death. Others, however, said he had always had drink since he was a youngster, Jethro or no Jethro.

But the fact is Matt, as soon as he had left Elvira's middle son that day in the meadow, went to the nearest place where he could get illegal booze, which was Bert Meacum's, out past the stone quarry, and he sat there guzzling his liquor in Bert's back kitchen, with a few other "outlaws," but he didn't bother to speak to anybody. He listened, however, and no wonder. The drinkers were talking about Elvira and about Judge Duggan's coming decision. There was a scarcity of topics that year, and they stretched out the few facts they had picked up from the proceedings of the trial and changed them to fiction, and then to barefaced lies. They said all over again the usual things about Elvira's having had each of her boys by a different unknown father, and they went over again and again the gossip that the boys had used their mother's last name Summerlad in school and church more frequently than they had their father's surname, Fergus, until Matt, in order to avoid a fistfight, bought a whole fifth of rye, and started out the door . . . But as he was leaving he heard a man tell how Elvira could still win her case. He waited with his hand on the doorknob, like an agent trained to memorize each word, and when the man had said his say, Matt slammed the door behind him.

He found Rick in his parlor sitting in a big chair, staring at the grandfather clock, which had stopped.

"Do you know something, Percy Fergus," Matt purposefully used the boy's christened name now. "Your brother Jethro is going to kill your mother."

Rick's hand slipped from the chair arm, falling vertically, to resemble, as Matt had once before pointed out to Rick, the alabaster hand of Hamlet, painted by Delacroix.

"You drunken shitass," Rick replied, without heat or conviction. "Who told you?" he shouted with his back still to Matt, but already beginning to rise from the chair.

"He's crazy . . . Jethro . . . You're needed at home, I mean. Best pack and go."

"If you're tired of my company, why don't you say so? After all who invited me here?" and Rick had risen now and faced Matthew. "Gripes, are you stoned!"

"What if I do want you to go, Rick? . . . What if I want all the Ferguses to go? You're too heavy a load for me . . . I need rest from you all . . . But the part about Jethro is true . . . And there's more news," Matt wiped the sweat from his upper lip.

Rick ran upstairs to his room and began packing with methodical fury. Matt followed him after a discreet wait in front of the grandfather clock.

"Come to help me pack faster, Matt?" Rick quipped.

"Rick, listen good. I've been all over town hearing people talk about the trial," Matt began carefully.

"You always was a great listener, Lacey. Don't suppose you added any to the talk yourself, did you. 'Twould be unlike you, knowin' so little about the subject as you do . . ."

"The only way Elvira can win the case, Rick, is for you boys to write letters to the judge, begging him to give your mother the decision. It's gospel truth, Rick, don't look so ugly. The judge wants to do right by all young people, they tell me, it's his special care. If you boys swear to your mother's good character and how she's stood by you when nobody else would, he'll give her the divorce, he will. I'm telling you the truth, Rick . . ."

Rick dropped the pair of socks, which he had just folded, into the open valise, and then looked up to study Matt's face.

"And did you find out my brother Jethro was going to kill Elvira from the same party who told you we were to write these letters to the judge?" he sneered.

"No, Rick, Jethro's my own feeling. It's almost a psychic premonition, you might say."

"That makes it convincing, good and proper."

"All right make fun of me, but go home for these two good reasons, Jethro and the letters. I'm not driving you out, I'm pleading with you, I'm pleading for you, believe me. You want to be free of Elvira, or you've always said you wanted to be, so you could go to New York. Well, when she wins her case, Rick, you're free, you can go . . . But without the letters being written by you boys to the judge, she'll never be, and you'll stay in Boutflour forever . . ."

"You've got it all figured out and cut down fine," Rick

flared up for a moment, and then fumbling in his pocket for something, which turned out to be his pocket comb, he spoke more tractably, saying, "All right, then, Matt, if this isn't some of your clamjamfry, supposing you tell me what we're to say in these proposed letters of yours . . ." As he said this, he looked full into Matt's face, biliously studying him in the dim wine-colored light of the bedroom.

Matt spoke volubly, energetically, and at some length, his spit flying out in tiny spray from the corners of his mouth.

Rick listened, a kind of rapt and cunning expression in his eyes. "You'll tell the judge," the words went past like a flashing landscape in a picture show, "that your mother has always been your best friend, that it was Elvira and not Wilders who stood by you through thick and thin, kept a roof over your head . . ."

"That's enough!" Rick blew up, turning his face away from Matt's scrutiny.

"But you'll tell Elvira about the letters, say you will," Matt tried to take hold of Rick's free hand, the one not holding the valise, but Rick wheeled away from him. "You'll tell her how important those letters are, and you'll write Judge Duggan, won't you, Rick, say yes . . ."

"Yes, yes of course. I'll tell her, and I'll write the judge, and I'll keep Jethro from shooting her, and all the rest." Rick walked toward the front door. "But let *her* thank you for it all, why don't you . . ."

"It's your freedom that's at stake too, Rick!" Matt shouted from the door as Elvira's son went down the long front flight of wooden steps. "New York, Rick! New York . . ."

* * *

And so a "suggestion" made by a drinking man and over-heard by Matt Lacey in an illegal booze joint became the occasion of a council of war for Elvira and her boys, who assembled, shortly after Rick's return from his kindly eviction at the hands of the ex-sailor, around her kitchen table. Elvira had drawn the blinds, locked the door, and then as if some ponderous and illegal deed was about to be enacted, brought out ceremoniously from an old hatbox a sheaf of ancient, foxy letter-paper, with edges trimmed in gold, two well-worn pens (Rory was too young to write a letter to anybody), and then the mother giving Rick and Jethro carte blanche, she left them in peace to write the judge whatever their hearts prompted them to say. She was smart in this, for they were both good "writers," though perhaps not so good as she, and Elvira did not need to use any force or make any hints with regard to what they should put down. She trusted them, she knew they would do their "damndest," and help her now at least this last time. She spoke to them only with her eyes, and they acknowledged her appeal, and they set to work in earnest.

As Rick composed his letter, which was eloquent, which was long, he hardly remembered now the court room "scene" of some time past when he had denounced his mother almost as savagely as he had Wilders. He even believed now what he wrote, and a great part of it was true of course. Elvira had stood by him, she had kept the wolf from the door, she had loved him more than anybody else in the world, more than anybody else could, or ever would. Yes, she deserved her freedom . . . And then, he deserved his likewise . . . There was the reality of the motion picture contract, a small part in a film, waiting for him, as soon as he went east, and once Elvira received her divorce, he would be free of her, and as Matt had cried to him from the front door as he sent him back to Elvira and letter-writing, *New York, Rick, New York!*

But as his pen moved across the old-fashioned stationery, out of the tail of his eye he apprehensively studied wild Jethro as he too was writing his epistle. But if the boy was contemplating killing his mother, as Matt insisted, he showed no signs of it, his forehead and mouth were smooth as satin, and the look of animation in his eyes was explained easily enough in view of his writing a letter to a judge of the Common Pleas Court.

And then after an hour or so of silent labor, the letters were done, and the boys handed their "gift" to their mother. If the letters were from one limited point of view lies, or fabrications, as when Jethro wrote in one sentence that *I have never known my mother to do a dishonorable thing,* and when Rick wrote, *My mother is the first of all ladies,* in the very deepest sense what they had written was the truth, for whatever her faults and shortcomings, and they were legion, she was theirs, and she had, they dimly or perhaps even clearly saw, no other love in the world but her love for them.

Overcome by their letters, which surpassed her most sanguine hope, dry-eyed but shaken to the core, Elvira held all three sons to her in a kind of appeal on her own part to the God which she had refashioned out of her own interpretation of the doctrine of her church, a God that heard mothers, not fathers.

Then pleased as the young girl of long ago, Annette's darling, she sealed each letter with open mouth, and sent Rory off with the two appeals to the post office.

After Rory had deposited Rick and Jethro's letters in the big green mailbox on West Main Cross Street, the family had not long to wait for Judge Duggan's response.

The seventy-year-old judge of the Common Pleas Court, contrary to everybody's expectation or belief, including that of Elvira's, unconditionally granted the divorce to her, with custody of the children, and with even a tiny stipulation for alimony.

In Paulding Meadows, when Wilders learned how the judge had decided, he repeated his early foreknowledge and forecast to a grim-faced Winifred: "Didn't I tell you where a good-looking woman is concerned, the courts in this neck of the woods always let her carry off the palm—justice and the law be damned!"

* * *

Seemingly insensible to her victory, Elvira, having perused countless times the "decree," closeted herself in the music room, and so unlike her old self, neither wept nor smiled. She dismissed her lover, George, who had come with a bouquet and congratulations, as if he were a collector for an unpaid funeral.

A little later, she opened her door to Rick, and they sat together in their old corner like old times, though in more lengthy silence than usual. He noticed she still wore her wedding ring.

"What are they saying, sweetheart, now that I'm a free woman?" Elvira spoke up at last, the color beginning to come back by slow degrees to her cheeks.

"Oh, why care what they say, Elvira . . . You've won. You're vindicated."

"I asked you what they said, Rick!" she came close to scolding, "for that's a deal different from winning a Common Pleas Court decision in one's favor."

Rick gave a sigh, and rose, letting his eyes wander into the next room, and beyond it, into the next, where his sumptuous bookcase caught the eye like a dying sun in the gloaming.

"Oh, Boutflour says you wrote both our letters, Elvira!" he responded tardily. A feeling of surfeit and boredom had come over him, his thoughts were miles away, perhaps in New York.

"Well, in a way they would never comprehend," he heard Elvira's voice begin a kind of explanation of her own thought, "I've taught the Summerlad boys, as Boutflour calls you, everything you know. You've had, after all, only me to study and absorb. And whoever wrote the letters in God's eyes or the town's, my boys know what they put down was the truth, and for once the truth was given its due! They won me my suit, those letters, and let the damned stuckup snobs, vulgarians and millionaires say I rehearsed it all, and held my boys' fingers to the pen. For all the while old pious Judge Duggan, whose mouth wouldn't melt butter, dragged his feet, he listened to all kinds of talebearing and gossip against me, from the head of the W.C.T.U. and the little Methodist minister on up to the petroleum tycoons and their wives! And if you want to talk about ethics, his bending an ear to whispering and slander is a damned sight lower down on the scale than for a mother to ask her own sons to say a word in her behalf. Yes, Rick, dear heart, it was the letters which turned the trick, and if I'd been a moonshiner operating four stills or a whore as they try to make out, the judge would still have had to hand me over my freedom . . ."

"Now you sound like your old sweet self," Rick took her in his arms at last and pressed a kiss on her face.

"I did hear, too," he held on to her hand now, as he watched Elvira's eyes widen in anticipation of his next "news," "that when old Duggan got the letters, he was more than bowled over . . ."

Elvira nodded, smiling, waiting for more.

"He closeted himself for a whole day in his chambers, maybe he put his robes on, who knows. In any case, there he sat reading and rereading what your Rick and Jethro had composed. His stenographer says he shed real sea-brine tears . . ."

Rick paused for a moment, thinking of what Bout-flour gossip had said, that Judge Duggan had fallen all of a swoop into the grave dug for him by Elvira and her head-turned whelps.

"And then, Elvira, dearest, our old Scotsman set his ass down on the bench and signed your release!" and Rick kissed her again and again, until she pushed him gently away.

"Jethro's letter was in a way the best," Rick opined after a few moments of reflection, and speaking then in the manner he sometimes used, when alone, just to himself, he went on, "Mine was flamboyant and of course impressive, it glittered, in fact, for after all I've got the actor in me, you know. But Jethro's, though bone-plain, struck home." Elvira looked away, her eyes wet.

"We must watch that boy, and not let him out of our sight," Rick held her hand so tight she winced, but did not withdraw it.

"He's unsteady, Elvira, very unsteady."

She moved her head in anguished agreement.

* * *

All of a terrible *sudden, I found Uncle Matt shaking me hard, though I had not dozed off, which he accused me of, but my pen had stopped, true enough, though it was still held tight in my hand, but my eyes were focused nowhere in particular, and so, say I was asleep with them open.*

"Into the grave dug for him by her head-turned whelps!" I read in a loud voice from my notes and pushed my notebook into his hands.

"Upstairs," Uncle Matt began, "actually, in the garret, Jeremy, I've got those letters the Fergus boys wrote to Judge Duggan. They're covered with a sachet, probably lavender . . . Next to a good cemetery, Jeremy, I like old letters best . . . The past is all any of us has, young, old, dead, alive . . . Only the fetus in the uterus lives in the present . . . But back to Elvira, Jeremy . . . She was a free woman, you think. Like crumbling hell she was. Her freedom came twenty years too late, a lifetime behind schedule. Or, say, she'd had her freedom when she thought she was in shackles and irons . . . And what's more, the girl beside the lily pond in Annette's everlasting garden was, by her own hard standards, an old woman, with estranged sons, one mad, with no money in her purse, a lover who showed no more real promise than Wilders when ruined, except he was in Elvira's own phrase, 'good around the house,' whereas Wilders could hardly pound a nail straight . . . What was she free for? And as to future security, alimony, that would be like getting sap out of sawdust."

"You tell sad stories, Uncle Matt," I said, out of his earshot, and I got up, and put on my scarf and galoshes. It was two o'clock in the morning.

"I'm coming to the fairgrounds part!" he shouted, and blocked

my exit, and pulled at my scarf . . . "All right, sit down just five minutes . . ."

He paced about the room, while I felt sleep like some cold drug go through my arteries and my eyes stuck fast.

"The fairgrounds," his voice still reached me, "the best and worst part, call it the denouement, the all. There are only denouements, you might say, all the rest of any story rests in it . . .

"Jeremy, I have half a notion when you leave tonight, or more correctly, today, to go up to the garret and read those letters . . ."

Waking with a start, I stood up and held on to the mantelpiece, feeling scared somehow, this time I think for him.

"When I die," Matt turned and took my hand, as perhaps he had taken Elvira's, "listen well, goosebrain Jerry, I'm not being sentimental, there's no time for it. When I'm gone, get an Indian to help you and go upstairs and haul all that stuff out to the bonfire, yes, including the pictures, and burn every bit and piece and shred, you hear . . . I don't want the world to stare at what I loved."

"Can't I be the custodian?" I heard the words slip out of my mouth.

"What, you're that taken?" he dropped my hand. "Queer about people," he mumbled, "and queerer about time. For you've come, Jeremy, when the world's turned to frost, and yet I feel under your youthful skin and bones all the life that's left in the universe or me. Custodian, all right, I appoint you custodian. Go home now, for, Jehu, your eyelids are swelling shut from unwilling attention, or clodhopper politeness . . . Come tomorrow for the fairgrounds, and we'll write finis."

* * *

As Jethro looked down from his attic room upon the garden below, with its summer seat in large prominence, he saw or fancied he saw Elvira ever passing before his sight. She looked very young, as he imagined she might have looked before she had given him life, and before she had been Wilders's bride. And if she resembled a mother at all, she resembled one who had been recently delivered of a multiple birth, and Jethro recognized with bated breath, she was, in her careworn beauty, Elvira Summerlad again, now and forever.

Going back away from the window to his table, where he had written so many of the pages of his lost journal, he seated himself in slow ceremony, but instead of writing, he took up three dice he kept in a lacquered box, and shook them, demanding that they tell him if he would kill Elvira or not. He sobbed convulsively at times as he thought that he might have to kill someone whom he loved so dearly. Yet see how wicked she had been! See how she had taken everything away from him! Either Elvira must give up her lovers, now she was free, and love only her sons, correct that to love only Jethro, or she must be punished. He laid his head down on the mahogany table, where he had once played dominoes with Rory, a table which had been moved from the billiard room of Annette's old house in far-off Hittisleigh. In his right hand he held the pistol. He often fell asleep now while holding it, and somehow the pistol did not slip from his entwined fingers. Besides his sleep was shallow, interrupted by starts and convulsive twitchings, alarmed leaping from the chair or bed.

The throw of the three dice had been inconclusive, but the cold metal of the pistol was concrete and familiar—in fact he now carried it about with him, loaded, almost everywhere he went. He pressed it sometimes hard against his body, and fondled it, as he had fondled Rory when his brother had been a baby. He felt almost he should give the weapon a name. It had been in the family for many years, and had its history. It would have more.

Summoned peremptorily by Elvira from his reveries, Jethro came down to lunch, and his mother raised her voice in attempted cheerfulness: "See who's a visitor today, Jeth," and his eye rested then on Rick, seated tall at the head of the table. He had left Matt for good, Jeth supposed.

But Elvira had meant more by her remark, and she added, after a struggle with herself, "Rick has just received word he is to go to New York for a screen role," and she gave Jethro a searching look, for as if through the sudden opening of a door, by Rick's imminent departure, her middle son had become someone she must address with more formality and some dependence.

Not replying to her "news," Jethro walked off into the little lavatory by the kitchen, and here he soaped his hands thickly and then laboriously rinsed them.

Elvira had given her announcement of Rick's "luck" with neither joy nor enthusiasm, much in the manner that would have been hers had she told Jethro the doctor had found a dark spot on the lungs of her eldest boy.

Rory was reading the local newspaper, *The Courier,* and Jethro's eyes ran over a section of newsprint where, enclosed in a black-bordered box, "useful information" of the day met the eye: "The greatest depth of the ocean is situated off the Philippines and is called the Emden Deep, approximately 35,400 feet in depth."

"Well, Jeth, aren't you going to congratulate me on what's the turning point in my life?" Rick inquired, after a lordly pause, and in his most acid accentuation.

"Don't read at table, Jethro, dearest," Elvira cautioned when there was not a flicker of response from her second son. "We should face one another and pay attention to what's said when we're all together here today . . . It aids the digestion besides," she added in the ominous silence that now came from both her boys.

Jethro lifted his eyes at last, looking nowhere in particular, and then his gaze fell again on the newsprint, which always carried, along with its quotation of Useful Knowledge and One-Minute Pulpit, some additional quotations from the World's Great Poetry, which today had as its sample:

> *Lo, the young ravens, from their nest exil'd,*
> *On hunger's wing attempt the aerial wild.*
> *Who leads their wanderings and their feast supplies?*

But as he reached the end of the third verse, Jethro felt the paper snatched out of eyeshot by Rick's angry trembling hand.

"You heard your mother," his older brother roared. "You're not to read at the table she said, and now I say it too!"

Jethro leaped up, banged down his silver fork, and left the room cursing.

"Now see what you've done, Rick, on this first day we could all be together!" Elvira's tearful voice followed the retreating boy down the long hallway. "Jethro," she called, "come back now and finish your lunch. You can't go away on an empty stomach, you know you can't!"

Then suddenly to their surprise they could hear Jethro running all the way back to the kitchen, and with a leap over the threshold he snatched up the newspaper where Rick had let it drop wrenched from his fingers, and in

stentor tones read the fourth and last verse of Great
Poetry:

To God ascend their importuning cries!

and followed this with a war whoop and an imp's burst
of laughter.

"Mad as a hornet!" Rick shrugged his shoulders, but he
spoke with a grudging kind of good humor and affection.

After she had washed the last of the luncheon dishes,
Elvira stepped into the long narrow, soundproof buttery,
where no one was liable to come at that hour. As on those
days when her "time of the month" came unexpectedly
after an emotional upset, Elvira now kept close to the confines of the isolated room, but depressed this time with the
fear that the very apex of her heart was about to burst.
Then came a tempest of tears harsher and more full of gall
than any flow of blood from heart or womb. She stood in the
buttery, her rings coming loose from her fingers from
the soapsuds on her hands, weeping. The divorce, which
once granted, was to have ushered in freedom was now, she
saw, only a herald of a kind of nothingness which she had
never before experienced or dreamed was in store for any
human heart, least of all her own. And she had promised
herself that once she was free she would "celebrate" in an
outing and picnic supper in the fairgrounds! She had
thought, she now looked backward, that once the decree
was granted in her favor, she and her boys would live on
together in an ever-deepening happiness and content. She
had never considered squarely until now that boys changed
into men and are in due time gone forever, and her boys

appeared more eager to leave her than any young ones she had ever met: Rick could barely wait until he was out of her sight, and safe in New York; Jethro would soon follow, she supposed, and even Rory, whom she thought of still as the baby, she now saw would be one morning not too far distant just like his brothers. The wonderful and terrible years she had had with her three boys, her real, her overwhelming life—all, all was coming to an end, and with it, their daily "banquets" over which they had laughed and talked, quarreled, insulted one another, confided what joy and sorrow they could claim, this would be over, the big house empty of all voices except perhaps those of strangers, who, in the gloom of her coming childlessness, would in quick time desert her also.

Quailing under this almost apocalyptical vision of her life-to-be, she broke into an empty tirade against thrice-beaten Wilders. Why hadn't he stayed away forever! Why had he come home to make claim on her real freedom, and drive her to a court's public and devastating justice, for the trial was what had destroyed all of them! Why hadn't Wilders—yes, why shouldn't she say it?—why hadn't he died in Virginia, for then her boys would still be hers. For she was their mother, she was their all, and he was only a stranger who had come out of the backwoods and got her in the family way. She thought finally of Annette and she thought of Hittisleigh, and then suddenly at the acme of her madness she saw Jethro's scared face gazing at her, wide-orbed, puzzled, even sympathetic and loving.

"Is Mama sick?" his voice came from the extreme length of the buttery.

"Yes, Jeth, with something the doctor don't have any medicine for," she answered.

He waited for her to say more, but when no more was forthcoming, he turned slowly like a very old person who must mind each step, and went out.

"Oh, Jeth," she called, but her voice did not carry in a throat so full of grief, and then he was out of earshot.

She dried her face on a worn Irish linen napkin which she had been mending, and stepped out on the back porch. A hermit thrush rose twittering indifferently before her coming. Elvira placed a clean newspaper on the top step, and sat down.

* * *

On Elvira's wedding day the bride had run into the groom early in the morning contrary to popular superstition she should meet him only at the church; she forgot to place a piece of silver in her shoe; the sun did not shine; and though she did wear "something old, something new," she had neglected or ignored too many other rituals and precautions, and in the eyes of Melissa and Annette, the very fact Wilders had appeared, however briefly, at their home before they were dressed to go to church spelled heavy misfortune.

On the other hand, on the day of Elvira's elaborate and elegant celebration of her having been granted a divorce, the sun shone bright, and the air was soft as April or May, although it was August, It was pretenaturally balmy and soft, with a sighing breeze, and speckled sunlight everywhere. And the only ritual that faced Elvira this time was a leisurely banquet at the fairgrounds, and no preacher with book and scowl to demand of her oath of fealty.

Although Elvira wore a rather elaborate dress which

had taken her some lengthy time to put on, she was ready and eager to leave the house long before her three sons, who today were unusually "pokey" and dilatory.

Elvira had laid out Jethro's Sunday best summer suit on his bed the night before, but he took forever to put it on. He carried his gun in a small leather pouch, which she mistook for a game of dice.

Rick was got up in an outlandish mauve jacket and slacks which Elvira showed she disapproved of by her never gazing at the cloth, but only at his face.

Rory was perfect in a sailor suit.

Elvira's lover, George, held her by the arm.

Matt was at everybody's beck and call, but the first surprise of the day came when Garner, the soap salesman and former lodger, blew in, as out of nowhere, just as they were about to leave for the fairgrounds. He looked handsomer, trimmer and more prosperous, Elvira opined, and she hugged and kissed him, exchanging a few remarks about "old times," and insisted he go with them to the celebration.

Avoiding Vickie's astonished but not hostile stare, Garner sidled up to Jethro, who struggled between joy at seeing his "old friend" and embarrassment at the memory of the circumstances of their last meeting together in Vickie's bedroom.

"And your mother's really been divorced?" the young salesman kept repeating to Jethro, who seemed too lost in admiration and hero worship of Garner's vibrant and forceful presence to hear anything he said.

"Let me drive Jeth to the fairgrounds," Garner begged Elvira's permission. She gave a questioning, indecisive sad glance at Jeth, but seeing the look of broad pleasure on the boy's face at being with Garner, she gave her consent.

*   *   *

*As Uncle Matt began the "fairgrounds" or "denouement section"
of his story at our next, our last meeting, he became even more
agitated, if possible, than he had been in times gone by, and as
was often his custom when bringing back long-past happen-
ings, he came abruptly to his feet to speak like one of the characters in the narrative, for of course he was one of them, but I
could not help reflecting that in that long-ago day Matt had
been a handsome young man, only briefly out of the navy, and
now his voice and appearance, at least tonight, was as ghost-
like and raddled as if he too moldered under the sod with the
Ferguses.*

*And the flesh of my scalp always crawled when he would step
out of the pages of his own book.*

*"I suppose," Matt whispered, "I exaggerate the 'feasts' of
Elvira as much as she may have exaggerated the grandeur of the
goings-on in her grandmother's mansion. By 'feasts' of course,
you blinking little fool," he looked quickly in my direction, "I
mean the great American ones, Thanksgiving, Christmas,
Easter, Decoration Day . . . All these, and more, were to Elvira,
I'm precious certain, perfect occasions for her to extend her sway
over youth and grown men, and her favorite benefactors and
patrons of those days, Jesus and Mary, had no faintest resemblance to any Jesus or Mary countenanced by organized religion, certainly not her own First Presbyterian Church . . .
Elvira reached dizzy heights especially at Christmas and out
and down from the mammoth garret came decorations, primi-
tive American handicraft, yards of tinsel and ribbon and
sparkles of silver and gold ornaments that stoned the eye that
focused on them for long (I believe she was unaware of the
worth in dollars and cents of her 'trinkets'). It must have taken*

her a good month to get ready for any of her 'occasions' (The
fairgrounds outing was to be the most elaborate of all.) Of
course Rick was always at her side, and he was most like
Annette in the skillfulness of his hands . . . But merely looking at
Elvira, no matter what the date or season, I saw Christmas,
and spruce trees loaded down with ancient handmade beautiful animals, stars, toy harps, well, my memory can't quite
bring back everything. Boutftour says if I weren't so fond of
drink, I'd recall more, Jeremy, at least my brain would be
clearer, but the truth is, without a little something to wet my
whistle now and again, you and I wouldn't be here together
these long winter nights, and you'd have gone to your own
grave without knowing the meaning of 'amanuensis' . . . But
we've no time for thought of Christmas when we're about to
look at what happened that August afternoon at River-glades
Park, as fall was withering summer . . .

*   *   *

Elvira was one of those blessed women who need not touch a
drop to be intoxicated most of the time. She was drunk, say, on
her own mirrored reflection, but she also made all others drunk
who came within her circle and her presence . . . But though the
celebration at the fairgrounds was intended to be every whit as
sumptuous, dazzling, and unforgettable as her Yuletide or
Easter orgies, for she was now and forever a 'free woman,' there
was from the first something ominous in the air, a wicked hint
that all would not go well at her 'feast' at Riverglades Park.
She had done nothing but prepare for over a week, and again
down from the attic came those strange, excessive decorations,
ribbons and whirligigs. A queen freed from bondage must give
a royal celebration and gala . . . The fly in the ointment was

Rick . . . Unlike his unstinting assistance at past Christmases and Easters, he now held back. He had sunk into a paralysis of melancholy and brooding, spoke to nobody, and stared out of those widening sky-blue eyes with their malevolent bulging pupils. I could not face him when he was like that, and neither could Elvira.

"It was little Jethro's vehement 'letter' to his mother that turned this tide, that is rallied for the last time some kind of token support from Rick for Elvira. Jeth had written a long 'declaration' addressed to Elvira, and the 'world,' a day or so before the fairgrounds catastrophe. The letter is up in my garret" and Matt stopped, swallowing, "and one day we must go up there together, Jeremy, for I'll need your strength to do so, for Elvira's garret of course is now mine . . ."

Here Matthew stopped, whether overcome by strong emotion, brandy, or both, who can say, or just the continuous tenor of his life which swept over him now with even larger vividness, an incessant echo repeating forever: Elvira had been the greatest thing in his life, and next to her, Rick.

"This letter," Matt went on after a bit, "for I can usually always recite it by heart, was probably the most awful thing a son has ever written to a mother in recorded history. Elvira cried out on reading it as if she had fallen on her butcher knife and it had dug through to her heart. The letter enumerated her 'crimes' and reminded her that the entire world knew she was a whore, and that Judge Duggan had given her a divorce not because she deserved to be free but because marriage, being a sacrament, had to be severed in her case, by reason of God's wishes as well as man's, and so on . . .

"Rick stepped around to Jethro's room, cried, 'I wonder at you!' and cuffed him a few times, without force or conviction.

" 'Let the child alone,' Elvira called out dispiritedly to her

eldest son. 'It's none of your business, Rick, what he writes to me and me alone . . .'

"*Elvira kept the letter in a special little box, wrapped in a gold embroidered cloth, where I found it after her death. I see now she knew what it was, and I see now what it is. Not all love letters, Jeremy, are soft-spoken and tender, full of praise and adoration, the deepest are sometimes those which cut and wound, and the fathomless love is disappointed love—it has all the rest of its life to bleed.*"

Matt, like an old silent film director, then "shot" again the scene of their departure:

* * *

"You should take that well-licked whelp and send him packing to his father without another moment's delay," Elvira's lover spoke to her of Jethro, as they were all assembled in the driveway, waiting for the boy to come down to join them.

Elvira had been fretting both about Jeth's keeping them from going to the fairgrounds on time, and also of course over the letter which he had written to her.

But George could not have said a worse thing than offer a word of criticism of Jethro to her face, and turned spitfire, Elvira flared up at him, giving him a tongue-lashing of a kind he had never had before, or indeed imagined. He shriveled like tissue paper in a bonfire before her wrath.

Then going back into the house, Elvira hallooed up to Jethro, crouched in the middle of the back staircase, alone, begging him not to dally any longer.

"Come down, Jethro, precious, I've laid out your best pongee suit on the sofa in my room, and do grant me this one favor, put it on, dear lad, and come with us to the fair-grounds. Mother can't go without you, you know that . . ."

To everybody's disbelief, consternation, certainly amazement, Jeth did come down, he put on the summer suit, and joined the party. He still carried the strange little leather pouch with him, which Garner studied unquietly as he put his arm around Jeth's shoulder, and then looking down on the boy, he realized that for all that might be wrong with Jethro, he had a good figure and carried his "broken head" like a prince, and indeed looked as handsome as many another boy who had never seen a sorrow.

Elvira even for herself was extraordinary. Wearing a dress of soft white tulle at least twenty years out of fashion, made over on her Singer sewing machine, of a cut which only a young woman would have dared choose, despite a bit of stoutness, from a distance she gave the appearance of an eighteen-year-old. She had spent a great deal of time on her hair, and it had profited from it, for its natural gold was gleaming in the fierce morning sun, but when one looked at her full in the face one could hardly hope to find a sadder expression.

The August day, though perfect, was spoiled for her, she said, because the cicadas had begun to sing, and Elvira hated the sound they made, and invariably shivered when they began their drone.

"Mrs. Fergus!" Matt Lacey's voice boomed, just as Jethro had joined the procession. He always said *Mrs. Fergus* when George was present, but another reason perhaps may be given, he was beside himself.

"I've got to have a minute with you alone," he took her arm.

"Matthew, dear, we're already an hour late as it is!" she

cried. But Matt was already leading her back toward the house.

"Please don't begin on Jethro now," she whispered.

"Don't marry him," Matthew went suddenly nearly to pieces. "Now you're Miss Summerlad, you must remain her . . ."

"Is that all?" she burst into laughter.

"He, *he*," Matthew looked in the direction of George, "is dirt beneath your feet."

She hesitated, won over at least for now by his eloquence, in spite of herself.

"Trust entirely to me in the future, why don't you . . . I'll make money, I'll work. But don't ever marry again, Miss Summerlad."

Something in his words, his expression, and again a premonition of some sort made her pale.

"Stand back there, a pace or more so," Matthew went on, forgetting again there were other persons present. "There, by the peony bush, Elvira . . . See, you're not eighteen! You're sixteen!"

And now as if they had been alone together in the music room, Matthew Lacey pressed her to him.

Then they strolled back together in the deepening silence of all those who stared at them, and the procession started at last.

* * *

Matthew Lacey had "sensed something" of course for weeks past, but instead of following through on his hunch, and keeping close watch on the middle son, he had almost ostentatiously entrusted Jethro to Garner, for there had always been something between those two, Matt was sure, some "secret," and they seemed to feel a kind of strange content, born of deep confidence, when in one another's company, and indeed Garner acted more like an older brother to Jeth than Rick, for Rick would ever be too passionately jealous of Jeth, whom he saw only as one who had tried to dislodge him from Elvira's undivided affection.

His arm still on the boy's shoulder, Garner walked off with Jeth, while the banquet preparations went ahead, toward the amusement park section, chattering away about "old times," telling Jeth again and again that Elvira and her boarding house had been the "realest" thing in his life, and confiding his homesickness for Bourflour, and his joy and relief at coming back. Jethro, who barely listened, clutched ever more tightly his little leather pouch in his right hand.

"Jeth, has Vickie forgiven me?" Garner spoke, not without halting effort, between clenched teeth.

Jethro looked up into the former lumberjack's flushed face, and grinned. "Well," the boy said, laughing, as he remembered that weird and hectic late summer encounter in the deserted boarding house, "well, she's been making calf's eyes at you ever since you blew in . . ."

"Jeth," Garner smiled, "you know you're getting on to being a young man now, and you carry yourself so well . . . I'm proud of you!" Garner suddenly blurted out. Garner took a sudden busy look about him. "The old boom town," he said aloud, but not loud enough for Jethro to hear, who, in any case, was more and more absorbed within himself, and a thin deposit of globes of sweat began to appear on the highest part of his forehead.

"You know it's a fact," the former Michigan lumberjack went on, "that Boutflour had the biggest Circus parades in this part of the country, and along with circuses and oil scandals, this amusement park was about the grandest thing of its sort in the whole Yankee State. Farmers and townsfolk alike came from miles around to visit here . . . Pretty-seedy and down at the heels now, if you ask me, though, ain't that right, Jeth."

They looked all about them. The great Dutch elms were already losing their leaves, partly because of drought. Trees of heaven were springing up everywhere, interspersed with wild asters and pearly everlastings. In the distance one heard the blare of a band-organ, and when it stopped, the merry-go-round's monotonous sleepy sad duets played over and over again.

They reached now the "zoo" of the amusement park, a long-ago endowment by a forgotten millionaire, small isolated cages containing forlorn beasts, some Rhesus monkeys, a coyote, a timber wolf, a few baboons, a giraffe, and a moth-eaten king of the beasts. On the bank of the river, which they were fast approaching, rose the green wood structure of the dance hall, where Jeth had worked occasionally.

"Why do you look so sober, Jeth?" Garner inquired, after studying the boy's features for a second, and for the second time he looked questioningly at the little leather pouch the boy carried with him. "You know," he went on looking out toward the river which they were approaching, "I've always agreed with Elvira maybe, that you know more or too much than other boys your age . . . But there's one thing you don't know and can't at your time of life, Jeth, when you're still at home with your loved ones and have all their protection and care. It's the happiest time of your life, Jeth.

There'll never be anything else like it ... Out in the world, you know, like where I am, nobody cares a tarnished damn about you. A fellow can vanish and die, and he's not missed or wanted back. But where you're at home, like you, everybody cares about you and your least want or concern ..."

Jethro stopped walking, and turning slightly from the path they had been following leaned his head back against the bark of a huge tree. His face flushed, and his breath came in labored short gasps.

Unconscious of the turmoil going on in the boy, Garner talked on.

"I really would have liked to marry me, and settle down with Vickie," and he looked back now to where the "banquet" was being prepared. "But she wouldn't have me, as you know." He grinned sheepishly. "That's why I took her, and I don't think I'm sorry.

"But things have changed since I left you," Garner sighed and took Jethro's free hand in his. "I can sense all that's gone on, though I'm not the most observant cuss in the nation, Jeth ... I know your mother and you boys have been through a lot. And I guess your old runaway dad too ... I'm sorry your parents busted up ..."

They had reached the river by now, and they stared down briefly into its muddy surface, which though it might pass for serene to some, as in the case of the early settlers who had christened it Sunshine, it had a sullen, ominous look for those who like Jethro and Garner could remember when it had gone on rampages, drowning, wrecking, and ruining.

"Look, Jeth, the swings are still up!" Garner ran toward the biggest of the playground contraptions, and put steadying hands on the thick ropes.

"Sit down, middle son, and I'll give you the push of your life."

Too tempted to hesitate long, Jeth released his iron hold on the little leather pouch, placing it in a clump of grass, and planked himself down in the big swing. Garner gave him a push of such force it seemed he was soon as high as the tree tops.

Then it was Garner's turn, and Jeth pushed him, if not so high, high enough, as the soap salesman gave out one shriek of satisfaction after another as he moved skyward.

They sat then, squatting in the grass, sometimes rolling about in thick clumps of vegetation, laughing aimlessly, as Garner would recall one "funny" thing after another from old times, or one good time and then a better one which they had in common, until presently an inexplicable something seemed to come over them, as if each one remembered some nagging gnawing sorrow that would not leave off its molesting hold, even for such innocent sport.

Presently they found themselves sauntering along in silence again, and then they detoured back to the picnic grounds.

Everybody was seated at the long table when they arrived, impatiently waiting to begin the meal which had been so long in preparation. Garner stopped in his tracks when he caught sight of Elvira, hardly noticing Vickie, seated beside her. Elvira had put on a glittering gold lavaliere, which she had not worn while she performed all the offices of a housewife, and seeing her now one would never have known she had ever lifted a finger to do anything in all her life. She looked, he saw, like his come-awake dream of all women.

"I've brought your young man home, Elvira," Garner said, his eyes glued to her eyes.

"Brought him where he belongs," the soap salesman was somewhat astounded to hear himself add this afterthought.

"Sit down, then," Elvira was still a bit distant and sharp. She asked grace briefly ending with words about, "Be present at our table . . ." She was still vividly annoyed they had kept her waiting so long, for the one unforgivable sin with her was for anyone to be late to one of her banquets. Garner had watched her pray, his eyes starting from the sockets, and she had felt his eyes on her, and when she finished grace, she winked at him.

As knives and forks began to make sharp little sounds against the hand-painted china plates, from the far distance of the fairgrounds, in the band shell, one could hear the voices of the young men's glee club, the Liederkranz Singing Society, so-called in the old days, but loathing of things German had officially changed the name today to the Boutflour Young Men's Singing Society, but everybody still stuck to the old name before the war.

Then the terrible, long premeditated, unbelievable thing threatened at last to occur in the midst of this sad festooned commemoration banquet, and he who held the gun, Jethro, was, when it was all thought over so much later, the one who least wished it to happen, his hand directed less by himself than by a blind and irresistible concatenation of events from before his birth.

Both Matt and Garner had caught sight of the raised nozzle of the gun at the same moment, as it was held naked in Jethro's fingers, freed of the covering of the leather pouch. Both men cried out, eliciting responsive cries from the other guests, shattering and ending the banquet as one earsplitting cry of unbelief and shocked horror echoed another.

Although Jethro was looking at Elvira, perhaps he had never meant to shoot in her direction.

"No, Jethro, Jesus, God, no!" Garner attempted to seize the boy's hand.

"Elvira," Matt had only time to cry and then threw himself bodily between Elvira and the cocked pistol. Garner had already seized the boy's hand, and then there came the sickening report as it was fired, just once, very loud, and Matthew doubled up in pain, and bright crimson blood spurted up and came sizzling down streaking the Irish linen tablecloth, a casserole rose in the air almost noiselessly, and the whole picnic table followed, rising upwards, with all the dishes and silverware tossed up also as if drawn into the air by tiny strings.

Everybody had risen, except Jethro, who remained sitting, and Matthew, who lay in his own blood on the tablecloth stretched under him on the grass.

Jethro still held on to his pistol, but with the nozzle pointing down at his own heart.

Elvira's cries now seemed to fill the entire fairgrounds. "Listen all," Matthew's voice came strong, "I'm not hurt bad . . . It passed through my arm . . ."

His jacket and shirt and underwear had all been stripped off him, but so much blood had flowed onto his bare chest and arms, it appeared, as he suddenly rose from the ground, that he was wearing some ornate highly decorated shirt, suitable to his temperament.

He walked steadily over to Jethro, who seemed to have gone into a trance, white as those angels who preside over crypts, and simply took the pistol from him, and handed it to Garner.

"Get Jethro away, for God in heaven's sake," Matthew spoke to a thunderstruck Garner, "take him in your car as soon as you can get out of here, to his father's . . . Do you hear . . ."

"I'm not hurt, Elvira, it's a bad graze at most," Garner heard Matt's words vaguely as retreating he took Jethro with him, and they had soon disappeared out of eyeshot into thick trees, when suddenly they could hear Elvira calling Jethro to come back, without anger, or reproach in the wavering treble of the brokenhearted.

"Come, come, don't look back," and the lumberjack seized the boy roughly now, and pulled him with him.

Jethro and Garner walked on in dogged silence, stopping from time to time until, in Garner's words, Jethro began to "get his bearings." They paused a few moments again when they reached the dam of the river, its waters sounding like dull unenthusiastic applause coming from a half-filled auditorium, say at the Grand Opera House. They passed by the band shell where the Liederkranz singers were still pouring out their lungs, and then there they were, sure enough, in front of La Primadora Arcade, with its pool hall tables, peep shows, and the main concession, the shooting gallery with the baby doll prizes.

Garner marched up and bought Jethro a ticket, the old man attendant, inattentive, half-dozing, handed Garner a rifle, but Garner put down this fake weapon, and took up the pistol Jethro had shot and wounded Matt Lacey with, pressed it hard into Jeth's right hand, held the hand and put it into aim.

Both Jeth and Garner gasped as they saw what was

coming by on the moving trestle as the target to fire at, a bearded lady.

"Shoot her or shoot me, Jethro," Garner said, "it don't matter much which, but fire . . ."

His face frozen, looking maniacally at the moving target, the boy shot.

Hearing real gunfire, the old attendant came to with a start and roared, "Do you want me to fetch the sheriff, damn your dirty hides . . ."

"Go on, empty the cartridge, Jeth," Garner commanded, "and this time shoot the damned thing empty . . ."

Hardly had the sound of the last shot died away when Garner pulled the pistol from the tight but trembling fingers which held it, and wrapping the gun in its little leather pouch, closed it with its leather thong. Then the soap salesman, with a beautiful high pitch of his arm, threw pistol and pouch far into the swiftest part of the river.

They moved off immediately into a part of the fairgrounds protected by maple trees, where there was a solitary bench or two, usually a favored site for lovers, and they sat down there, in a seeming easy-going manner, hardly acting like "fugitives," and in no mind to follow Matthew Lacey's advice to get going fast and not take time even to look behind them.

Leaving Jethro plunged in thought, Garner sauntered over to a hot dog stand, and brought back sandwiches and coffee.

Jethro left his food untasted, whilst Garner, grumbling, munched dispiritedly explaining he did so to keep up his strength.

The sun was setting and a chill breeze came over the

landscape from the river, and Jethro staring into the heavy green foliage before him thought that not too long ago when all this had been thick forest, one might have spied an Indian passing by as silent as these moving evening shadows.

"Are you ready now for me to take you over the county line and deposit you with your dad?" Garner spoke, after wiping his fingers on a blue pocket handkerchief.

Jeth nodded.

"Don't need no extra clothes or socks or toilet articles for your trip?" Garner winked at the boy.

"No," Jeth replied, and then coming a bit out of the thick haze which seemed to envelop him, he added, "I guess my aunt will have everything I'm needing this summer weather . . ."

Garner looked at his wrist watch, one of those cheap glinting things he had won perhaps in some other shooting arcade.

"Shall we push on then, middle son?" Garner rose, his voice breaking with the force of other words which battled to come out of him.

Suddenly he took Jethro's hand in his, pushed the palm up, and spat into it.

"That's for luck," the soap salesman grinned.

The hand and the boy looked pitiful, white, and small, and yet Garner knew he had been capable of having killed, and plunged a whole household into unending sorrow and heartbreak.

"Now, Jeth Fergus, mind me," Garner said, when they had driven within a few miles of the big iron bridge which marked the county line, "what kind of a damned tomfool do you judge Matt Lacey took me for, letting me act as your kidnapper . . . And what if Matthew dies, by Christ!"

Garner stopped his coupé with a shriek of rusty brakes by the side of a ditch. "Maybe I've got to think this one out, Jeth, before I take you another crazy mile . . . Jeth, forgive me . . . I'm shaking like some damned old woman."

It was true, the calm collection of the past hours had collapsed, and his huge hulk and heavy arms trembled.

"Crossing a county line is some kind of felony, crime, whatnot, I judge, with you in the seat, old kid . . ."

Then, all of the anxiety and confusion of the day came upon him, and pulling Jeth toward him, as if they both had shot the gun together and both stood under condemnation, he wailed, "Oh, Jeth, what happened back there . . . How you could raise your hand against the one person you love, and who gave you your life . . ."

Jethro had gone all to the consistency of jello. When Garner, in fright, shook him, there was barely a movement of eyes or body.

"All right, Jeth," he patted the boy, "don't take on so . . . I'll stick with you, come hell or high water, hear? And if that shitepoke of a sheriff gets me, let him . . . And so, as per promise, I'll take you to your dad," he started the motor.

"Maybe he will know what to do about you this time, even if he never done so in all the years past and gone by . . ."

They were too far from any town or even village crossroad by now to go hunting rooms, and it was getting very late, and in addition to the fact Garner had very little gas left in his tank to go on hunting about in the dark for a place to sleep, he had not enough money in his pants pockets besides to pay for a room for two.

"We could spend the night in this cracker box, Jeth, but

we'd both come out of it cripples for life . . . Tell you what, we'll hunt us a haymow or a nice grassy slope of a bank somewhere . . . Then when we're stretched out you can tell me what's wrong with the world and everybody in it, including you . . ."

"One thing though," Garner went on, as he led Jethro now through a lane, which in turn led to a stretch of open land. "I've never been able to stomach that Matt Lacey . . . In a way I'm glad he got shot, so what the hell . . . He's a busybody . . . Just the same I hope, for us, the bastard recovers his health . . ."

Garner held a dying flashlight before them. They came to a stile, and the soap salesman jumped it, and then as if coming out of a long reverie, Jethro raised his legs and jumped high over it also.

Near a creek a dilapidated barn loomed up before them, and Garner lost no time in entering the building in order to investigate its fitness for spending the night within. In a few moments, Jethro heard the salesman's voice speaking through a window-like aperture some distance from the place where he had entered.

"It don't look too bad, to tell the truth, Jeth—at least for an old road man like me. But come on in and nose around a bit, and see how it suits you. Just don't be expectin' clean sheets and towels, though, like at your ma's . . ."

Too sleepy and burdened to care much how fine the barn was, just so long as Garner kept with him, Jeth hastened through the big entrance way.

"'Twill do, won't it, Jeth?" Garner poked with his foot around in the straw. "It's got to."

Jethro nodded enthusiastically.

"Then at sunup we'll be off, and away," he studied the

boy's face in the weak ray of light cast by the flashlight.

They found a spot which Garner considered the "best they could do" in the farthest corner of the barn, and they lay down in some straw not overly clean, as it turned out, and which was alive with some kind of crawling things.

It was so quiet outside Garner said he could hear the grass growing, and perhaps because of the stillness, which seemed to weigh on him, he talked a blue streak about a lot of things, and his stream of words eased Jethro's heartache somewhat as the soap salesman went back to his own boyhood in some little town in Michigan, then to his days as a lumberjack, and finally to the time when, as a salesman, he had first set eyes on Elvira as she opened the big frosted plate-glass front door on him, and looking at her he knew that he was in the place where he wanted to room.

Then there came a long silence, during which Jethro felt sure Garner was reviewing the dire events of that day in the fairgrounds, and it seemed to the boy the salesman had quit breathing.

When the quiet became intolerable, Jethro raised himself up on his elbow, and looking at the whites of Garner's eyes, all he could distinguish with any clearness in the barn, he announced, "You blame me in your heart."

"Did I say that," Garner cried, violently stirring in the straw. "I did not, and I never would," he contradicted the boy.

"Maybe you're afraid of me too," the boy lay down again, dispirited.

"Scared shitless," Garner quipped, but with an edge of bitterness.

"Do you *blame* me?" Jeth raised his voice.

"Shh, pipe down, middle son," Garner put his hand over

the boy's mouth. "Listen, I don't blame nobody for nothing," he told him, whispering. "Get that straight. Else why would I have took you with me in the first place, if I thought I was your judge? So shut those big blue eyes, and take your sleep . . ."

They lay there for some time in the fetid straw, rigid, hardly breathing, and then mustering all his strength and will, Garner hugged Jethro briefly, with force, and the two counterfeited sleep for an hour or so, when Garner began to snore heavily, while Jethro lay, wide-awake, and stiff as someone dead and unclaimed in a crossroads accident.

* * *

In the morning they found they had slept in the vicinity of an orchard which had been almost entirely destroyed by the big cyclone of the year before. The barn appeared to have been the only building spared. Measly skeletons of the house and some outbuildings appeared on a hilltop before the rising sun.

A few apples hung on the boughs of some of the trees, and Garner picked up one that had fallen on the ground, wiped it off with the back of his hand and tasted it.

"Not too bad, though ain't much juice in it," he pronounced and he picked up another then and handed it to Jethro, who munched dispiritedly on it, all the while gazing searchingly at Garner.

"I know what you're asking me with that look, Jeth, but don't open your mouth to say it, and don't you *beg* me . . . I can't take you with me, though maybe I'd like to, and maybe I need company more than anybody, and if I could choose yours, perhaps I'd do so . . ."

They walked on down then to the car. It was always a hard one to start, as Jethro remembered from the time Garner had been a roomer at Elvira's boarding house, and with an almost empty tank, today was to be no exception.

Once they were spinning along on the road, they did not speak till they came to a White Rose Gasoline Station, and while the attendant filled it all the way full, Garner went inside to help himself to a toothpick, and then, so it seemed to Jethro, just to have something to say, the soap salesman leaned his head in the window, and inquired:

"I hear Rick is leaving your mother's too, is that right?"

Somehow Jethro was so tied in knots by the events of the past day or so, that though he had wanted to answer, nod his head, or raise a hand, he could do nothing at all, and after studying the boy for a moment, Garner left him to talk with the station attendant, and after a few questions about what route to take, he paid him and they were on their way again.

When they began to see the signs of Welcome to Paulding Meadows, and Visit Shawnee Indian Battlefield, Jeth came out of his trance, and clenching Garner's shoulder hard, he begged him not to take him "home."

"Don't let me have to go to them," he intoned again and again.

"They're your own blood relation," Garner said, his lips compressed white.

"Let me go on with you, why don't you," Jethro begged. "See, I'll drive for you, and I'll behave, Garner, I'll be perfect for you . . ."

"And get the both of us sent to jail?" Garner smiled. "Still, the idea did come to me," he went on, looking blankly at a small sign that said: Daniel Boone Hunted Partridges Here. "It's ghostly lonesome on the road, if you only knew, and I've thought of you as company, I already told you so. But these are your own blood relatives who I'm taking you to, and you can't go back to your ma, after what you done, not for a cold long day, Jethro Fergus, and you know it . . ."

Garner had already drawn up in front of the big pillared white house, and Aunt Winifred, alerted by telegram of what had occurred, came out of the door, as if she had heard a cannon go off, and stood on the mammoth front porch with folded arms, waiting. She looked worried and grim and happy and mean and welcoming all at the same time. The many lines on her face made this perhaps possible, or perhaps Jethro imagined it and she was as poker-faced as usual.

"So long, Jeth, keep a stiff upper, and so forth," Garner held out his hand, and Jeth held on until the soap salesman pulled away from the boy's tenacious hold, and slammed the door of the coupe, stepped on the gas pedal, and was gone.

*　*　*

A long prison term began then for Jethro, and Aunt Winifred indeed may have fulfilled her long-standing desire to be, in the words of Elvira Summerlad, a matron of a penitentiary for young men. Jethro was kept under lock and key, and allowed to wander about only in the evening, in the large, back yard and the grape arbor, and stumble through the ruins of the gardener's cottage, where now only discarded tools, sheep shears, broken lawn mowers, rakes, and snow shovels were kept.

One evening, as he sat in utter detection by the summer cottage (he could never return to his home town, it was implied, even for a visit, despite the fact Matthew Lacey was mending from his gunshot wound, and no charge had ever been placed against the boy, and the whole thing was put down to an accident, by reason that the people of Boutflour were convinced he was a potential murderer), someone approached the high iron fence, whistled to him softly, and when Jeth, eager for any change in the deadly routine, approached the locked entrance, a young man threw him a crumpled envelope.

Jethro would never have been able to read it had the moon not slowly and majestically risen, nearly full, at that moment over the chimney of the cottage. Breaking the envelope, he smelled at once the special lavender perfume that could only come from something touched by Elvira, and he thought of her then as a garden of flowers whose petals never closed, while Winifred reminded him of an unopened attic where nothing fresh-growing was ever admitted.

The message, which he held so tight in his hand its delicate paper tore slightly, read:

> My dearest Jethro,
> I will come past tomorrow night, and hope to say a few words to you. Worry about nothing—your Uncle Matt is coming round, and bears you no grudge. Do not doubt me. I have had you on my heart and mind every minute we were parted, precious boy, and do not think I hold anything against you. You have always been my particular treasure.
> Ever, Your Mother

The harsh weeks with his aunt and his desolate father (it was now close to October), his having thought that Elvira had given him up forever, and that she was convinced he had never loved her, his own ineffaceable memory of his rash and premeditated act of last summer, the inebriating attar of flowers, all this gave him such a rush of feeling that he toppled off the chair on which he had seated himself and fell into a bed of late-blooming marigolds.

So Elvira had not given him up, he thought, content to lie merely in the flower bed without making any effort to rise. Perhaps it was his mother's intention to rescue him! And perhaps she would be waiting in a touring car, and they would go off to some wonderful city far off, where nobody knew them, and they would spend the rest of their days together, never to part . . .

A harsh cry from Aunt Winifred startled him from his musing. It was most fortunate the shadows prevented her from seeing him lying amid her marigolds, but even so she was cross and suspicious.

"Till tomorrow night, then, Elvira!" he cried, as if she or her messenger were waiting outside the iron fence. "I can live somehow till then," he whispered to himself.

Marched in by his aunt, he was sent immediately to his room, a look from her pursuing him with the meaning that he should thank his lucky stars he was here with loved ones rather than behind the bars of a reformatory where he might easily now be, had not everybody concerned closed his eyes and kept tight his mouth. For all—his father, grandmother, and aunt—had focused accusing eyes on him all these weeks, and there was nobody who did not believe that he had planned to kill his mother, and per- haps his brother. Yet the very one who had the most cause to hate and mistrust him, and tear out his memory from her heart forever, she was coming to see him! He wrote all his "impressions" down in a new notebook which his father had reluctantly purchased for him at a notion store, and this time Jethro hid his jottings under a giant feather bed in a room seldom entered by anybody.

Circumstances, however, did not shape up at all favorable for Jethro's reaching the gardener's cottage the night of the promised meeting between Elvira and himself. The main thing was Aunt Winifred's suspicions had been aroused, and as a result she kept a closer watch than usual over her nephew tonight. Acutely sensitive to his every change of mood, least nervous gesture, or change of color, the aunt studied him closely as the two played a long-drawn-out game of chess in the parlor, which she had lit tonight with gas lamps in order to please him.

"What has come over you, Jeth," she suddenly could not contain herself, as he slowly studied his last-remaining bishop.

Winifred's voice reached into the living room where Grandmother Fergus and Wilders stirred from their dozing over their reading material.

"Has some *wicked* person been in touch with you?" she lowered her voice to a whisper.

Her having hit on the very truth of the matter made him all but betray his secret, but at that moment he was able to put her queen in check, and her eyes went back to the chessboard.

Having conceded the game to him, after a few vain attempts to place her queen in safety, she told him he did not look well, and must go to bed, but first she made him accompany her to the kitchen, where she took down a high bottle of red medicine from the cabinet, and insisted he drink it. He flinched as she waited for him to down it, for he knew this bitter-tasting stuff made him always very sleepy. And whatever happened tonight, he must not go to sleep ... But even if he kept his eyes glued open, would he be able to get out to the gardener's cottage without being discovered?

Off he was packed to his room. Once he had slammed the door behind him, he hurried into the lavatory and sticking his finger down his throat, soon brought up both the medicine and his dinner.

Then he leisurely sauntered into the untenanted room which contained the feather bed and, hidden under it, his new notebook, and waited for the court house clock to strike the hour. Taking off his shoes, he climbed out on the back roof, and easily slid down the eavespipe, to fall into the plot where all the choice flowers of his grandmother's were sleeping till spring.

Dizzy with expectation he hurried over to the gardener's cottage. He had put on his darkest suit of clothes so that Aunt Winifred would be less apt to spy him, and thank the gods, he thought, the moon was later in rising than the night before, and the sky, too, where she would come up, was full of threatening clouds besides. At that very moment, indeed, a fine rain began to come down. He crouched under the protection of the old snowball bush, and pulled out his grandfather's heavy pocket watch. Elvira was late! Perhaps she would never come, and he would be soaked to the skin for his pains.

But just then he heard the rubber wheels on the slick pavement, and he ran in his stocking soles to the iron grating, where Elvira had suddenly appeared under a beautiful fragile purple parasol. She kissed him avidly again and again through the dripping iron rails of the fence.

"You hold no grudge against me, Elvira, dear?" Jethro beseeched her, and she could not control her tears.

"None whatsoever, all's done, and forgotten, Jeth, as if it had never been," she comforted him.

She hesitated then, perhaps to postpone what it was she had to communicate to him, and whispered, "Isn't it a wretched dirty shame it would have to pour!"

Jethro looked up into the ink-black eastern sky. "You can't stand here, Jethro, darling, with no hat to your head, and no covering other than your jacket." She reached through to button down his collar. "Tell me you've completely forgiven me everything," he was insistent.

"Oh, Jeth," she said distractedly, and then looked back briefly into the car waiting for her. "I forgave you everything before you were born . . . Long ago, Jeth, you were forgiven . . . Nothing is your poor dear fault, and don't mention it again," and her hand, having buttoned his collar, rested feather-gentle on his neck and throat.

"But listen closely, Jeth, and then I'm afraid you must go back into your aunt's house, for this is a terrible storm that's brewing now . . ."

"I can never go back into that house, Elvira, dear, now that you've come here tonight to see me, and now you've forgiven me . . . For all the time I have loved only you, Elvira . . ."

She pressed against the iron grating for support, and then, after a long wait, managed to say, "But you have your father, inside, Jeth . . ."

"That's unlike you, Elvira," his voice came as from very far away, "to mention Wilders as anybody . . ."

Caught in her own contradiction, she could only let her hands wander through his tangled sopping hair.

"Listen close, dearest, and then I must insist you go into the house," and she held her umbrella as best she could to shield him from some of the rain.

"I've lost everything, Jeth . . . The boarding house is up for sale to pay all my debts, and your older brother has gone to New York to try to make a name for himself, and has left for good . . ."

This catalogue of disasters strengthened her and she dried her tears for the present.

"Mother has no choice, I'm afraid, but to marry again . . . I'm too old and weary ever to work so hard again as when I raised you three boys," she spoke as if to herself.

"I'm penniless, Jeth, do you hear," she pressed him to her.

He heard her words with dizzying unbelief. She did not even need to add, "So there is no place now for you with me," for Jethro said it for her, and the rain washed his open mouth as he spoke, so that it looked like that of a corpse at high tide.

A single sob escaped her, but she warned then again of the rain and his injuring his health, and they gave one another goodbye in which the storm and their tears were so mingled they could not distinguish one from the other.

When he heard the rubber of the tires of the car departing, he had not experienced any loss of consciousness at all, as Wilders had thought when he found his son some twenty minutes later, but he had laid himself down with all the calm and collection he would have exercised had he been preparing for bed, putting himself down on the wet flower bed, and waiting for what he hoped would be death.

In his hand he clutched an ornament which he had torn from Elvira's brocade coat, a tiny jeweled lily.

He heard his father's voice from as great a distance as the eclipsed moon itself.

"Let me help you up, Jethro, this is no place for you in all this downpour."

* * *

"Wake up, Jeremy! Jeremy Cready, do you hear me? . . . It's half past twelve o'clock, in the P.M."

I could see sister Della's features, but they seemed a long way further off than they actually were, partly because I had stayed at Uncle Matt's until almost four o'clock in the morning, and had helped him finish a whole bottle of imported brandy.

"When you come downstairs for breakfast, Jeremy, I have something mighty sad to tell you, but I'm going to insist you take a good hot bath first, and when you've had your breakfast, I'll tell you all about what has come to pass . . ."

I think it took me another hour to get downstairs, and break-fast had almost turned into early supper, and I had forgotten all about Della's preparing me for sad news, maybe because she gave me such fare every livelong day.

When I had finished my dish of fried mush and bacon, she sat down close beside me, and folded her arms. I put down my toothpick. She had placed around her waist a fine new cotton apron, with pretty little embroidered hummingbirds flying around trumpet creeper, and when I studied the lines around her mouth, I felt myself swallowing hard. Then she burst into tears.

"Jeremy, he's gone," I heard her say.

So clouded was my brain from all the sessions and the drinking with Matthew, that I blurted out, "Did Jethro kill him then?"

She looked at me with a dark glower of disapproval, and then remembering the importance of her news, she looked sorrowful and sympathetic again, and expanded her statement to "Uncle Matt's been called home, Jeremy, my boy . . ."

I sensed she must mean what I was afraid she meant, but I always hated indirectness in moments of crisis, then and now, and so I shouted:

"Can't you be explicit, Sis, for once in your life?"

"Uncle Matt Lacey passed away this morning at the Home and Hospital here in Boutflour . . . Never regained consciousness after he suffered a cerebral hemorrhage about six or seven o'clock this morning.

"Jeremy! Do you hear me . . . Where in the name of reason are you off to?"

I didn't know, and found myself a while later on my wheel, riding around town.

It was a Sunday morning, or seemed to be, and nobody was about, on South Main Street. I felt then that not only Uncle Matt had died, but everybody in town too had been laid away, and that I too was dead, but there was nobody left to prepare me for my burial service and my unmarked grave.

I kept holding my hand out, for I was sure it was raining, but the street pavement only looked rained on because the town sprinklers had been past a few minutes before . . . Just the same I felt dripping wet.

Then I turned my wheel around and headed back north, and as if I had intended to go there in the first place, I saw coming into view the old Opera House, as I reached the top of Fairoak Crest.

The gold green front door was wide open, for they had had some shindig in there the night before, an "entertainment" by the Knights of Pythias, and some other lodge.

I pulled my bicycle in with me, and left it standing against the ticket window, and walked right down the center aisle on the thick worn carpet, and then stopped to stare at the big crimson stage. The curtain was up, and the spotlights on the stage itself were on, showing some painted backdrop of forest and glade.

Before I knew it I was standing there in the middle of the stage, gazing down into all those empty black mohair seats, once occupied by the quality who had come to see Sarah Bernhardt and Ellen Terry and Joseph Jefferson.

I think I began to talk, or maybe I imagined it, I began to tell, it seems to me now, something about Matthew Lacey and the Ferguses, and to tell the story as I felt he would want it told, and then feeling lightheaded and nauseous, I sat down with my legs dangling over the footlights, and my bare legs, without garters, showing, and I think I said in a loud voice, "I can't, I won't ever believe there will not be more!"

"Now, Jeremy," Sister Della motioned for me to sit down on the high stool in the kitchen, the next afternoon, after we had finished a late luncheon, "I hate to have the kind of talk I am going to have with you now, when you've just come back from the funeral home to pay your respects to Matthew, and maybe folks will say I have not loved you as much as a real mother would have, but I done my best, Jeremy . . . I see by the expression on your face you don't consider that enough . . . But sad as the loss you've suffered, you and I are going to have it out now, for it won't do to postpone things, now that you're out of your job, and you can't go back to your school, and so on . . . You cannot go on the way you are going, and you must know it. Here you are, get-

ting on to be a young man and she twisted a wire hairpin and looked sheepishly at the hooked rug under her feet, "and though you don't have some of the badder habits your companions have got, I'll just speak my piece now and have done with it, for in many ways, Jeremy, you have turned out a lot worse than some of our real bad boys . . . Uncle Matt turned you into a kind of ear, but since you was paid for it, I said nothing at the time, though perhaps I should have . . . He made you over into a kind of chronicler, and vital statistician for a family that is best forgot, if you ask my opinion. For if Uncle Matt, Jeremy, to quote him and you, for these words was repeated often enough by you to make them your own, if he, then, fell in love with a whole family, you have followed right along in his footsteps. I won't moralize, and I won't scold, so quit your deep sighing, but I'll tell you this, I didn't have no choice but to go to the expense of calling Cousin Garth long-distance, and he's agreed to take you off my hands, if you'll be willing to go and accept his hospitality . . . Go there to live, I mean, Jeremy." She wiped her mouth with a worn doily. "You'll be better off, I'll be better off, and I think, as a matter of fact, you'll take a shine to Cousin Garth. He's not an old man, mind you, and he maybe can teach you some of the things somebody ought to have been teaching you up till now, but which a woman can't do even if she tries . . ."

"When does the bus leave, Della," I stood up, and pretended to yawn.

"Well, for pity's sake, brother, you don't have to be in that big a hurry. I'm not driving you off the premises after all . . . But since you ask, I've marked the bus schedule right here . . . Bus goes in a little over an hour, Jeremy, unless you want to wait to the midnight one, which I don't reckon you do . . ."

"I'll be on the early one," I told her, and I went off to pack up my few things.

As I put an extra corduroy pair of pants, a shirt, and two pairs of B.V.D.'s in my valise, I felt more like Jethro Fergus than ever before, and there his poor form had turned to dust long ago in Oak Bend Cemetery. Like Jethro, I carried under my arm a long fat dimestore notebook that contained everything Uncle Matt Lacey had ever told me.

For a while I was the only passenger on the Maple Valley bus line, until three country women with heavy luggage and packages, and an old Indian from the county home got on, but somehow above the sing of the bus tires, all the time I kept hearing the kind of refrain Della had repeated all these weeks I had been amanuensis to Matthew, "Think of it, will you, a mere child as town chronicler . . ."

Then there I was at my stop, the old quarry road, down which I would have to walk for about sixteen miles till I reached Prince's Crossing, where Cousin Garth had his house.

As I walked down the gravel-stone road, all upon a sudden, in addition to her chorus about me being town chronicler, I could remember now Della's last speech to me, while I was closing my valise, and which somehow I don't think I paid heed to while she spoke, but for some reason it came to me now, as if I had written it down and was reading my own scribble in my notebook.

"Once, Jeremy," she had said, "there was four fine railways run through this town, and you would be going on one of them today to visit your Cousin Garth. There was the Big Four of course, the Nickel Plate, the old New York Central, and of course best of all to my mind, the Chesapeake and Ohio, and come to think of it, the Baltimore road too, which brings it all told to five . . . There was interurbans, and three good bus lines, also . . . Today there ain't nothin' to speak of, and that's a

shameful fact . . . I'm glad you got strong arches, Jeremy, you'll need them today . . ."

It was heaven to leave the old thing behind, I thought, and her running of me down all the time, with her harping always on the fact that I had nothing in my head now but them, *meaning the Ferguses, and Matt Crowder Lacey, and that I had no biography of memories of my own . . .*

Della's only interest in life was her canaries, parrot, and goldfinches, and her house wasn't so much like an aviary (though she called it so, graduate crapehanger), as a prison farm for winged creatures.

My wings didn't thrill her, and I was, after all, only her half brother and another mouth to feed.

I had flown the cage, in any case, and was free, but with nothing to feel good over having done so, and like Elvira Summerlad, stuck with the word freedom *itself.*

Still, I was relieved of the change, and a stay with Cousin Garth, whom I had never set eyes on, couldn't be a whole lot worse than Boutflour. Anyhow he was a man, at least he wore pants, and if he wasn't too ancient (I believe she said he was crowding forty), it might turn out to be a half-bearable life with him, in Prince's Crossing.

About the Author

James Purdy was born in Ohio, and educated in Ohio, Illinois and Mexico. He taught school in Mexico, and spent time in Spain. He has received wide critical acclaim and a growing popular following with his eight previous works, including *Color of Darkness*, a short story collection, and the novels *Malcolm*, *The Nephew*, *Eustace Chisholm and the Works* and *Cabot Wright Begins*; the latter has been purchased for film production. *Jeremy's Version* is the first of three independent works, collectively titled *Sleepers in Moon-Crowned Valleys*, about towns in America's Middle West and the people who live in them. Mr. Purdy is now at work on the second volume, in his home in Brooklyn Heights.